The Empathy Gene

by

Boyd Brent

Author contact: boyd.brent1@gmail.com

Boyd Brent

Copyright: Boyd Brent

Prologue

My name is Clare Stone. I'm a journalist and author. Two weeks ago, I received an anonymous email. It provided detailed information about a man who was present at two key events separated by two thousand years of history. A man whose impact on humanity, it claimed, had been greater than anyone who came before or after him. I cross referenced the leads provided at the British Library, and confirmed several eyewitness accounts of this man, known simply as David, in Jerusalem in AD 33 and Nazi occupied Poland in 1944. I suspected that either my colleagues were playing a practical joke on me, or else I was losing my mind. So when invited to meet my anonymous source at a private function in the viewing gallery of The Shard in Central London, I reasoned I was about to find out one way or another.

I hailed a black cab outside my office at News International, and told the driver to take me to The Shard, a skyscraper that dominates the London skyline. The viewing gallery is officially closed to the public at 8.30pm, but a call to reception had confirmed that it had been hired for a private function and that my name was on the guest list. I leaned against the cab door and looked up at the building I had come to think of as the most beautiful in the City at night. The cab driver startled me when he said, "I hear the restaurant they've got up there is first-rate."

"I ... I wouldn't know."

"Aren't you about to find out?"

"Not exactly."

"Not much else to visit The Shard for at this time of night." I looked up to the top of the elegant tower of light. "I'm going to a private function ... up in the viewing gallery."

"Anyone going I might of heard of?"

"I think it unlikely." The driver pulled up at a red light and looked out of his window. "My wife keeps trying to get me to take her up there to see the view. Twenty-five quid to confirm the vertigo I already know I have. No, thanks."

The lobby of the Shard was expansive, and only two of the dozen reception desks were occupied by security guards. When I entered the lobby, one of these men glanced at me over the top of a computer screen. My high heels made an ungainly clunking sound on the stone floor, and

Boyd Brent

when the sound was upon him he rose from his seat and pulled a pen from his breast pocket. He placed it on the signing-in book and spun the book around to face me. "Good evening, madam."

"Good evening. I'm Clare Stone. I'm here to attend the private function in the viewing gallery."

"You just need to sign in, Miss Stone."

I picked up the pen. "Big function, is it?" The second security guard chuckled quietly to himself, licked his thumb, and turned the page of the newspaper in front of him. I scratched my name into the logbook. "Did I say something funny?" The first man picked up his pen. "You're the only guest, Ms Stone."

"Are you sure?"

"This your first meeting with Mr Gull?" said the second man turning another page of his newspaper.

"That's right. Is there anything I should know?"

The man looked up from his newspaper, and produced a smile of sorts. "From what I've seen of Mr Gull, he's a nice fella. Books the viewing gallery several times a month. He's an artist ... paints views of the city."

"When it's *dark*?" I looked back and forth between the men. The second man shoved his newspaper into a cubby-hole, stood up and came around the desk. "I'll show you to the lift. It's a proper light show up there at night ... a three-hundred-and-sixty-degree light show."

We made our way to the central lift in a bank of five. "How long does he stay up there?" I asked.

"Till sun-up. That's when the cleaners need to get in and get the place ready for the public." The lift opened, and the man reached in and punched floor 72. "It will take you right up into the viewing gallery," he said. When I failed to move, he prevented the door from closing with his foot. He looked at me. "Would you like me to ride up with you?"

"Would you?"

"Not a problem, Miss Stone."

The lift's doors opened onto a large rectangular gallery, its walls and impossibly high ceiling made from glass. The gallery's spotlights were dimmed to enhance the light show far below, and they bathed the expanse in a faint blue sheen. In the far left-hand corner of the gallery, a man stood before an easel. He held a paint brush and dabbed at the right side of the canvas. The man was medium height, slim, with wavy, shoulder-length hair. He wore a black polar neck sweater and jeans and, from his right sided profile, he reminded me of a modern-day Christ. Without looking up from his canvas he said, "Thank you, Harry. You have gone beyond the call of duty." The man's voice was relaxed and curiously monotone.

"Any time, Mr Gull." Harry stepped back inside the lift and smiled as

4

the lift door's closed. My legs felt leaden as I made my way across the gallery. To the man's left, a table and two chairs were nestled in a glass corner. On the table was an open laptop, a jug of water, and two glasses. I cleared my throat. "Mr Gull?"

The man turned to face me, and although the right side of his face appeared normal – handsome, even – the left side was concealed by a mask commonly associated with recovering burns patients. My gaze was drawn back to the right side of his face when it smiled. "Please," he said softly, "Call me Gull."

"Gull what?"

"I have no other names. If you don't mind my saying, you look a little unsteady on your feet." He indicated the chair that faced the open laptop. I placed a hand on the table and lowered myself into the seat. I looked at the computer's screen, upon which a title was written: *The Empathy Gene*. A glance at the bottom of the screen indicated that it was *page 1 of 1*. I put my bag on the table beside the laptop. "Short book," I said.

Gull laid his brush on the easel and sat down in the chair opposite. He placed his hands on the table and interlinked his fingers. "That is because it hasn't been written yet."

"Writer's block?" I replied, drumming my fingers nervously on the table.

"More a lack of imagination."

"Lack of imagination? You surprise me. The things I read in those manuscripts you've had me researching all week – the references to and descriptions of David – they aren't possible. So why go to all this trouble? Why the elaborate hoax?"

"David was real. A great man. The last of his kind."

I reached for the bottle of water. "May I?"

"Please. Allow me." Gull leaned across the table, picked up the bottle, and filled my glass. "The last of *what* kind?"

"The last human being to possess empathy, compassion, a conscience."

I smiled and shook my head. "While I appreciate that the world is fucked-up, it's not that fucked up. Not yet."

"You are right. Not *yet*."

"I see. So you're telling me that David is from the future?"

"*Precisely.*"

I stood and picked my bag up off the table. "I've had quite enough of this." As I walked back towards the lift, I heard Gull's chair scrape on the ground as he rose slowly out of it. "You have decided to leave your job at News International in November," he said with absolute certainty. "And then it is your intention to go and stay with your sister in New Zealand for three months. She is having marital difficulties and is planning on leaving her husband."

I stopped dead in my tracks.

"You haven't mentioned these plans to another soul. Not even to your sister."

My journalistic curiosity kicked in. I turned, walked unsteadily back to my seat, and sat down. "How did you know that?"

"I'm sorry if I upset you. It is my intention to make this experience as painless as possible."

"Why?"

"David would have demanded it."

"Of course. David. Mr Empathy. The reason I'm here. What is it you want from me?"

"Your imagination."

"My imagination?"

"Yes. With it we are going to bring David's extraordinary gift to mankind to the world." I glanced at the computer screen. "So you expect *me* to write this book?" Gull stood up and turned his back to me. He placed a hand on the glass wall and gazed at the lights far below. "I thought we would write it together."

"Did you now? So why pick me?"

"I have read your novel *Harley's Strongroom.*"

"And?"

"And your instincts as to how the human mind works impressed me."

I took a sip of water. "Alright. Gull. Curious name. What does it mean?"

"It is short for Guillotine."

"No it isn't."

"I thought it a close enough approximation."

"As in the French method of execution?"

"Quite so."

"Why that name?"

"It was apt once."

"Why? You used to decapitate people?"

Gull nodded. "It was – *will be* – my job. A job at which, I regret to say, I excelled."

"… In the future?"

"Yes. There is no need for concern. You are quite safe."

"And David knew about your *job*? Severing heads, it isn't the most empathic of pastimes."

"And for that reason we made quite a pair." Gull removed the mask from the left side of his face and turned to face me. I recoiled in my seat.

"As you can see, I am not so much lacking imagination, as I have never had one."

"What *are* you? A *robot*?"

"Nothing so grand. I am merely an implant. A computer program. I was placed inside the left hemisphere of David's brain." I opened my mouth to speak, but had so many competing questions that I closed it again. Gull smiled. "By sun-up, *The Empathy Gene* will be written, and you and all of human kind will know the debt of gratitude you owe him." Gull sat down at the table, and from within his right eye socket a light shone – a multi-coloured prism that moved slowly across the table. It climbed my red silk shirt, my breasts, my neck and face, and narrowed into a letterbox when it reached my eyes. I gasped and gazed around wide-eyed like a blind person suddenly gifted with sight. "Where *is* this place?"

"It is the beginning. The medical facility where I was implanted into David's brain."

"*When?*"

"Six thousand years from now." The light from Gull's eye went out and I reached for the table's edge. "I apologise," said Gull. "The return to the present can be disorientating. Fortunately, we shall complete *The Empathy Gene* in one sitting."

"I'm not that fast a typist," I murmured, blinking, trying to re-focus my eyes on the present.

"You will be." Gull sat back in his chair. "It's only fair to warn you that if you agree to what I ask, then the places you will visit, the things you will see … they are not for the faint hearted." I opened my mouth to speak but closed it again when Gull said, "David stands alone on the shoulders of giants."

"Giants?"

"Yes. All those men and women who throughout history have fought tyranny and oppression in pursuit of freedom. As the last of their kind, David's burden will be to ensure that their sacrifices have not been in vain." Gull fell silent and gazed at the painting he'd just begun.

"What is it," I asked quietly.

"It is to be a copy of a painting you will see if …"

"No, that's not what I meant. What's bothering you?"

"As with all good men who are faced with those who would impose dark ideologies upon humanity, David must do whatever necessary to be the last man standing when the smoke clears."

"And?"

"And, if you agree to assist me in the writing of this book, you will be unable to close your eyes, or look away from the things you see."

"Will I be in any danger from these things?"

Gull shook head slowly. "Tomorrow morning you will see the sunrise, and be free to return to your life in the present." I picked my glass up with a shaky hand, drank its contents, and placed it firmly back on the table. Against my better judgement I said, "Let's get on with it. Before I lose my nerve."

"You agree then?"

"Yes." Once again the light shone from Gull's left eye, he leaned across the table, took hold of my hands and placed them gently upon the keyboard. He sat back in his seat, smiled and said, "And now we will engage your imagination, and together we will reveal the unquantifiable debt of gratitude that Mankind owes to David ..."

The Empathy Gene

Boyd Brent

One

David lay paralysed in darkness, listening to the voices in his room. *They're not real, he told himself. It's a nightmare. Stay calm. You'll wake soon ...*

"Is the subject fully prepped?"

"Yes."

"And the status of the implant?"

"Primed and ready for insertion."

"Then let's begin. Bone drill. And someone alert the sterilisation unit… looks like we're going to need a mop in here."

A woman's voice, faintly amused, "You think the subject can hear you?"

"His brain activity suggests so."

"Will he remember anything of the procedure?"

"What he remembers is no longer relevant …"

David opened his eyes and sat up in bed, panting. His breath a fine white mist. He glanced at the door. Still closed and bolted. The sparse room and his meagre belongings lay undisturbed. He swung his legs out of bed and buried his head in his hands.

Clothes of rough-spun wool lay slung across a table. He stood uneasily and reached for them.

David rubbed his hands for warmth and approached a window that spanned the width of his room, beyond which lay Man's last sanctuary on Earth: Goliath.

Goliath was circular in structure. Seventy kilometres across. At its centre a vast dome rose up and breached its outer defences, its top resembling a milky eye that peeped towards a universe long since veiled by clouds of volcanic ash. A controlled amount of ash was allowed to pass through Goliath's outer webbing. Electronically charged to create light, it drifted across the vast enclosure like fairy dust on its final descent into hell. From his apartment building on the southern-most outskirts of Goliath, David watched it fall.

David's throat was bone dry, and when he swallowed the window registered the rise and fall of his Adam's apple. A message scrolled within the glass in red neon: 'Embrace the cold you feel today … for it provides the water you will drink tomorrow.' David turned and under his breath he

10

murmured, "I disconnected that damn message chip." A voice answered David from inside his head. A male voice, educated and supremely relaxed, that spoke above a faint crackle: "I reconnected the message chip, David. As I've no doubt you are aware, the disruption of message relays is not permitted in Goliath." David spun about and struck his left temple with a flat palm. The voice inside it said, "I apologise for the sound. Teething troubles … teething troubles that will soon be rectified." David lurched to his right and stumbled through a partition of hanging plastic strips. He came to rest with his hands on his basin and stared at his reflection. "I'm losing my mind."

"To the contrary, you have lost nothing. You have gained a companion." The crackle was gone, the voice now clear and distinct. David backed into his room and stood with hands raised like a man caught in headlights. "Allow me to introduce myself, my name is Guillotine."

"A *guillotine*?" murmured David, aghast.

"No. Just Guillotine. A guillotine was an instrument of execution used by the people of France to aid their revolution."

"I know what a guillotine is!"

"For efficiency's sake, you may call me Gull." David's legs buckled and he reached for his bed and sat down. He remembered his dream and raised a hand to the side of his head. Nothing. He went back into his wash room and studied his left temple, his eyes wide and searching. "I expect you're wondering why I'm called Guillotine, David?"

"Stop saying my name!"

"But David is your name. David?"

"What!"

"What are you going to do with that knife?"

"Maybe … maybe I can cut you out of my head."

"Quite impossible. You will only injure yourself. And we have important work to do. I'll take the very best care of you. Your life expectancy may be better than you think. My last vessel survived for fifty-seven days, four hours and twenty-seven seconds. I won't bore you with the details, but believe me when I say I took all the required precautions." The knife pierced the skin above his left temple. David's vision switched to black and white – and in the mirror he saw a sepia image of himself, eyes rolled up to their whites. *Radar?* David dropped the knife into the sink, turned, and walked calmly into his room.

When the intercom beside his door beeped, David was sitting on his bed, palms upturned like an ape's, the whites of his eyes showing. "That is Richard, your work colleague," said Gull. "You are going to travel to work together as is your custom." David's lips moved, almost imperceptibly, and spittle bubbled on his bottom lip. Gull continued, "Speech is quite impossible while I have control of your primary functions. I will return their control to you in a few moments. I trust you, David. I trust you to travel in to work with your colleague and say nothing of your morning. If you betray this trust, I will be forced to terminate him. And punish you for the red tape this would entail. I can boost your adrenal and testosterone levels many times over. Provide you with the strength of several madmen. I say madmen, David, because only madmen would do what we shall do together. And I have full authority to direct your vessel to terminate any of Goliath's inhabitants. I hope you're paying close attention to what I'm telling you. You will find our time together more agreeable if you do precisely as you're told." David's blue eyes rolled down and he drew a deep breath. "Nod if you understand and intend to cooperate. Thank you, David." The intercom by the door beeped again. David got up slowly and approached it. He placed a hand on the wall and considered his options. *I have none.* "I'll be right down, Richard."

David's apartment building was called Needle 261. One thousand identical Needles ran around Goliath's southern perimeter, each three hundred stories high. Their primary function was to support Goliath's outer protective webbing. The Needles comprised two small apartments on each floor. The apartments faced away from each other at right angles, giving the appearance of a sharp nose that ran down the centre of each.

David stepped into the lift, and its female voice greeted him. "Good morning." David gripped the hand rail as if the lift were about to blast him into space. "Please state your floor."

"Ground."

"Please state your floor."

"Ground. Ground!" The lift hummed and descended through one hundred and seventy-three floors in five seconds. The doors opened onto a spacious lobby containing a black couch that looked adrift on an expanse of cracked green tile. Ash floated past the front door; migrating wisps of light headed for extinction at ground zero. A craft hovered half a metre from the ground outside. Richard sat in the furthermost of the craft's three central seats, his silver-grey hair and ageing profile framed in the craft's oblong window. David placed his right hand on a reader to the right of the door and it swung outwards. The cold swept in and David lowered his chin and walked out. The door of the craft opened. David put a foot up upon a small ledge and grasped a vertical rail and heaved himself into the cockpit. The door closed behind him. David stared straight ahead, unable to look at Richard. "You okay, Dave? You sick or something? You know you can't come in if you're sick." David nodded and lifted a hand towards the door. Gull said, "Where do you imagine you are going, David?" David swung his head to his right and looked at Richard. "I'm fine. We'd better get going."

"Okay. Continue journey," he instructed the craft. It continued its journey around Goliath's outer ring. To their right lay abandoned facilities where items were once manufactured for the populace of Central Dome: clothing, plastic, rubber, silicon, computer chips and furniture. Things necessary for a life of comfort. Amid the debris, three men stood huddled about a bonfire. Richard sounded irritated. "Twenty minutes at best until a drone spots them. Puts out that fire and them with it."

"Maybe it's what they want."

"What's that got to do with anything? I'll have to go over there and tell them to put it out. My craft's signature will be all over this quadrant."

As David moved his hand to the door, Gull said, "Remain in the craft while Richard performs his civic duty."

"... I'll wait here," David told the closing door. Richard navigated a path through discarded debris towards the flames. Goliath's drinking water was provided by condensation that seeped down the vast walls of Central Dome – water created by the close proximity of tropical conditions inside the dome and freezing conditions without. Any flame capable of raising Goliath's temperature above that necessary for the creation of water was punishable by death.

Three men huddled about the flaming drum, their heads bent towards the haze as though searching for meaning in it. Richard stopped short of the men. He called out, tapped his wristwatch, and pointed overhead. One of the men left the drum and navigated the debris to speak to him. In that landscape and within those floating lights they looked to David like refugees from a festive apocalypse. Richard turned and made his way back to the craft. He climbed inside and closed the door. "Continue journey. They wanted to get close to the outer webbing. Never seen the moon. What a surprise. Got it into their heads they might catch a glimpse of it out here on the southern-most edge. I told them we were headed outside of Goliath's outer defences right now. That I've been going outside for almost forty years. And I've seen nothing but ash, smoke and hell out there. That's what I told them."

"I guess it's up there somewhere," said David."

"What is?"

"The moon."

"You heard from Clara lately?"

"No. No, I haven't. Last I heard she'd taken up with a security worker. Works the Dome's southern perimeter."

"They get lodgings in Sector A, close to the Dome ... close to the light."

"That's what I heard."

"That's tough. I know she made you happy."

"Only when she wasn't making me miserable."

"Isn't it always the way?" The craft halted at an intersection. To their left was Turbine Exit 12. The craft swivelled to the left and moved towards the opening doors, coming to a halt in an air lock. They sat in silence as the doors behind them closed and the ones in front opened. Darkness beyond and howling winds. The craft moved out and the ash assaulted it like a swarm of locusts. Overhead, Wind Turbine 617 towered up into the shifting gloom. Doors loomed in the craft's high beams.

Inside a parking bay a dozen identical craft hung in a line. The whole area was awash with neon that forced both men to squint. They exited the craft and walked up a ramp towards an elevator. There was a dull hum behind as their craft raised up and joined the others. They stepped into the elevator. Richard gave a verbal command, "Observation deck," then added, "I'll let you out and continue on up. A meeting's been called. Inspectors sent by Central Dome. They only informed me about it this morning. I have no idea what it's about. But I have a bad feeling about it."

Gull said, "Richard is correct about his bad feeling. Ask him in which room the meeting is to take place."

"I won't do it."

Richard rubbed a cold sore on his lip. "Won't do what?"

Gull said, "If I wasn't aware that such sentiments were no longer possible, I might suspect you of placing the well-being of another above your own. An indication that you're mentally unstable, perhaps. Ask him the number of the room, David. Otherwise he will lose his head with the others, and your smiling face will be the last thing he sees."

"Which meeting room you headed to?"

"Thirteen. Why?"

"No reason." The doors opened onto the observation deck and David walked out.

The observation deck snaked around all four thousand wind turbines. The turbines spanned the southern hemisphere of Goliath's outer ring of defences. To David's left and right, as far as the eye could see, technicians worked at maintaining Central Dome's electricity supply. David's shoes clipped the stone floor as he moved towards his work station: a semi-circular desk below a single holographic display. A bald man leaned back from his workstation and raised a hand. "Morning, Dave."

"Ed." A woman in a white coat crossed his path and blew on a steaming cup. "You look ill," she said.

"I feel ill."

There was a long package wrapped in brown paper on David's desk. He slumped down in his seat, stared at it. *And it's not even my birthday.*

Three red dots pulsed at various depths on a holo screen above it. Problems that needed addressing. Gull said, "Open the second drawer down."

"Why? I don't need a rubber band."

"Open the drawer, David." Atop a circular nest of rubber bands lay a pair of wrap-around shades. *To hide the whites of my eyes.* "I sense your reticence, David. It is wrong for me to tease you in this way." David's eyes rolled up to their whites. Gull slid on the shades and reached for the package.

Gull walked towards the lift, the observation room reflecting in his shades. The lift's doors opened. A man raised an eyebrow and walked out, leaving it empty. Gull entered the lift and turned to face the closing doors. Within this human shell, the man known as David was held in a vice from which he could not break free. His vision replaced by radar that forced him to view his surroundings in sepia.

Gull stepped out of the lift and entered the room directly opposite. It was a small meeting room with a single table and three chairs. Gull placed the package on the table and opened it. Inside was a black case, and inside that a samurai sword. David considered the name of the thing controlling him – *Guillotine* – and what the sword meant for the men inside room 13. He swallowed hard, and although he felt his Adam's apple move, it had not. The sword lay beside a scabbard. Gull dropped it over his shoulder and secured it there, then he picked up the sword and slid it inside. He spoke using a version of David's voice without emotion or inflection. "I sense your anxiety, David. It is unfounded. I have taken the name of a guillotine for good reason. It was a most efficient way of bringing life to an abrupt conclusion. It delivered a blow of eight hundred and eight pounds per square inch. Decapitation was instantaneous. As it will be for the targets inside room 13. I detect a sharp rise in your anxiety levels. I hope you don't imagine I will ask you to carry out these executions. Rest assured you are merely the vessel. A spectator. I cannot hear your thoughts. So, when in control of your primary functions, I have only your vital signs to indicate how your day is going."

The door to meeting room 13 appeared black. *The doors up here are red.* David's hand grasped the handle, but this sensation was not conveyed to his conscious brain. He felt only his heart, thumping and jerking in his chest like a boiler being stoked to its limits. *The strength of several madmen.* David wanted to close his eyes, but they were not his to close. Gull removed the shades and slipped them into his pocket. "Men should see the face of their executioner, David. Your face." *Don't hurt Richard.*

The door swung open. Inside, five men sat in armchairs about a semi-circular space. The slowly rotating hologram of a valve mechanism filled it. Four of the men were stocky envoys sent by Central Dome. The fifth was

Richard who said, "David? What are you doing up here? What's wrong with your eyes?" Gull drew the sword from the scabbard on his back. The man in the chair on the right (as David looked) jumped up and moved behind his chair, away from the others. He ran a hand through his dark hair and regarded his companions accusingly. "It's a vessel. One of you has broken with protocol." The other three got up and stepped away from each other. Gull addressed the room in a monotone version of David's voice: "In a moment the lights will go out. In the event that any of you make it to the door with your heads attached … well, let's just say, I will be flabbergasted." The room plunged into darkness, but David's view remained the same. He jerked forwards like a passenger on board a murderous funfair ride. Wide-eyed faces flashed up, and each in turn was launched on a spray of dark liquid – the first shot away to the left, the second to the right, while the third went straight up and clipped the ceiling before landing with a thud and rolling towards a neck that was not its own. Gull turned his head slowly and looked over his shoulder towards a bright rectangle of light. The fourth man *had* made it to the door. The funfair ride started again, with a speed that left David's stomach in the room behind him. The man was running down a narrow corridor towards the lift. He looked back over his shoulder, clipped the wall, and stumbled on as fast as his gelatine legs would carry him. He reached for the lift's call button but the tip of the blade sliced through his midsection, striking the button first. The last thing David heard before his world faded to black was his own voice saying, "Allow me to summon the elevator for you, Mr Hopkins."

Two

David woke up and clasped a hand over his mouth. His eyes moved skittishly from left to right as though reading emergency information ...

"Welcome back, David."

David swallowed some bile and winced. "You enjoyed it ... you enjoyed murdering those people."

"Enjoyment is a biological construct. It requires specific chemicals and a trigger to ignite them. I simply take pride in my work. You might say I have been programmed with job satisfaction."

David lifted his head and gazed wide-eyed about the room: a bell-shaped space with shiny, copper-coloured walls that tapered to a circular air vent. *There's no door.* David lay his head back on the pillow. "How did I get here?"

"I navigated you here. After yesterday's terminations, your vital signs suggested mild trauma. I deemed it necessary to place you in a state of shallow hibernation. Your mental well-being is high on my list of priorities."

"If that were true, you wouldn't be inside my head."

"My location is beyond my control. Something you and I have in common, David. In many respects we are both victims."

David closed his eyes and drew a deep breath. "Richard's alive?"

"Your interest in Richard's well-being is something I'm looking forward to discussing with you."

David squeezed the bridge of his nose. "I'm told I'm demented that way."

"That possibility had occurred to me. Something they overlooked during your assessment perhaps."

"Is Richard still alive?"

"Yes. I'm an implant of my word. I hope you'll appreciate that during our time together."

David sat up and lowered his feet to the ground. *You mean until you get me killed,* he thought.

Various items of exercise equipment peppered the room: punch bags, a horizontal pole for doing chin-ups, push-up bars, a set of ankle bracelets that hung from the ceiling. "We will start each new day with a strict exercise regime," said Gull. "You are already in good physical condition. You would not have been chosen otherwise. But to realise our potential we must take your body to its optimum."

David lay back down, placed a hand over his eyes, and tried not to think. "The last thing I feel like doing is exercising, *Gull*."

"And we have an abundance of grade A protein packs. The correct nutrition is vital."

"Murder hasn't done much for my appetite either."

"You are going to exercise and then you are going to eat, David."

"I don't think so." David's vision returned to colour, he doubled over, coughing and panting, his clothing soaked through with sweat.

"You will learn that you must do what is required of you, David." David's legs gave way, he stumbled backwards and fell on his ass. "I ... I can't breathe ... I'm having ... a heart attack!"

"You are mistaken. I have something for you, David. A gift."

"W... what ... what are you talking about?"

"It is within my discretion to proffer rewards for good behaviour. It's inside the closet. Something I heard you discussing with Richard yesterday. And it's alive." David's head turned slowly towards the closet, a slab of white alabaster set back into the copper wall.

"The anticipation is killing me, David."

"Can it do that?"

David stood outside the closet, ran a hand over his stubble.

"Open it, David."

David reached a shaky hand towards the door, pulled it open, and peered into the darkness. Out of the darkness a pale apparition flew – elbows and shrieks and flailing fists that busted his nose. David turned and it leapt on his back and pulled his hair and called him a "Demented son-of-a-bitch!"

"Clara!"

"You kidnapping bastard!"

"I suggest you neutralise her. Or I will," said Gull. David swung her around and held her tightly to his chest. "You need to calm down. Please! Please. Calm down ... or believe me ... I won't be responsible for my actions."

"Let go of me!"

"You're going to calm down?"

"Yes! *Yes*." David released Clara. She took a step back and slammed her fist into his already busted nose. "The gods, Clara!"

Clara was sitting at the table in the centre of the room below the ventilation system. David was seated at the other side of the round table, a cloth pressed to his bloody nose. He peered over his hand into a glare of utter contempt and murmured, "Please. No more gifts."

"What's *wrong* with you?" said Clara.

"Wrong? What could possibly be wrong?"

"Demented! You break into my house, slap the guy I'm coupling with unconscious – *coupling* with, David – then shoot me with a tranquilliser dart to 'neutralise my volume.'"

David's hands were jumpy, his eyes skittish. "Sorry. It won't happen again."

"Damn right. Harry is going to *kill you*. You know he's Dome security? Terminating violators of the peace is part of his job description."

David removed the rag from his nose, glanced at it, and placed it on the table. "So I heard."

Clara stood up. "You need to take me back to him. *Now*."

"I can't do that."

"You will do that." Clara tapped her foot impatiently, took in her surroundings. "Where have you *brought* me? A pressure cooker?"

"You have twelve hours," said Gull. "Do with her as you please. In the morning she loses her head."

David placed his hands on the table and pushed himself out of the chair. He spoke as though to the room. "Please, just let me take her back ... back to where you found her."

Clara backed away from him. "*Found me*? Who are you talking to? Are you hearing voices?"

David's advice was contrary to his own actions and demeanour. "Sit down, Clara. Just sit down and stay calm."

"As with Richard, your concern for this woman is unnatural," said Gull.

"Why not let me dart her?" said David glancing about for the tranquilliser gun. "Dart her and take her back. She doesn't know where she is. Neither do I." Clara picked up the chair and held it out like a lion tamer.

"I have important systems maintenance to carry out, David. Adjustments that will make us a more efficient killing machine, and help to prolong your life. I will rejoin you in twelve hours. And Clara dies."

A low ringing in David's ears that he hadn't noticed ceased. He gazed at Clara and his eyes moistened. "I think ... I think we're alone."

Clara held the chair steady before her. "I already knew *that*."

David turned and began to search the room. Clara moved to the edge of the bell-shaped space and watched him.

"We have to find it. We have to get you out of here ..."

"What the hell are you looking for? A key?"

"What? No. A door..."

"You're looking for a door? To your own *place*?"

"Open your eyes, Clara! Does this look like my place?" David was edging his way around the outside of the room, running his fingertips over the wall's smooth shiny surface, trying to locate a hairline crack or a groove or anything that might indicate a way out. "I was brought here

19

against my will ... just like you were."

"No, David."

David looked at her over his shoulder. "I was brought here by the same son-of-a-bitch who brought you here."

"You got that right. *You* brought me here."

David tapped his temple, and again his eyes moistened. "They've planted something in here. Something with a personality. It talks to me. It controls me. And there's not a damned thing I can do about it."

"Really? Why would anybody want to control you? You're a good citizen. You do the job you've been assigned like a *good* boy."

David placed a hand against the wall to steady himself. "I murdered four people yesterday ... envoys from Central Dome."

Clara lowered the chair to the ground. "What are you telling me? That you're a *vessel*?" she said quietly.

David nodded.

"Then I'm already dead."

"Not if we can get you out of here. The chip in my head comes back online in twelve hours, and ..."

"You think there's anywhere in Goliath I can go to hide from *SAPH*?" Clara began to laugh. "You always were simple. Putting my needs before your own. Like you are now. What makes me so *special*, David?" It was a question that David had posed to himself many times. And each time he had failed to find a satisfactory answer. He continued examining the wall and murmured, "Well, you never robbed me. Never reported me. Or never really abused me mentally."

"You make me sound as simple as you."

David turned to face her. "No one's as simple as me, Clara."

Clara agreed and crossed the room. She peered up at his left temple. "Harry ... he's heard rumours. He says they're sending vessels into Petri ... the penal colony ... that they're using them to cull the most aggressive inmates. You know what that means?"

David stepped towards the table in the centre of the room. "I think you're about to tell me."

"You aren't going to live much longer than me."

David looked up at the air vent and murmured, "You always were a great source of comfort." He drummed his fingers on the table and stooped down. Beneath it a single leg had been fixed into a slab of concrete. David took hold of the round table and worked it back and forth. His breath escaped him as it started to unscrew and rise counter-clockwise ...

David rolled the table's top to one side. The concrete slab beneath contained a sunken handle at one end. He grabbed hold of it and pulled. It wouldn't budge. He puffed a few times and tried again. The veins on his arms and neck looked fit to burst, but the hatch remained shut. David rolled onto his back and grasped his shoulder. Clara knelt beside him. "What are you doing? You have to open it. You have to get me out of here."

"Maybe I could … if I had the strength of several madmen. I thought you said there wasn't much point."

"I've changed my mind. I'll take my chances on the outside."

David was standing, arms folded, thinking. He picked up one of the chairs and knocked its legs against the hatch. He handed the chair to Clara and dragged a cabinet closer to the hatch. Clara lowered the chair to the ground. "What am I supposed to do with this?" David climbed to the top of the cabinet and sat on its top shelf. "I'm going to jump and land on the hatch … farthest from the handle. The impact should make it jump up. You might be able to wedge the chair's back into it."

"That's your plan? What if you break your legs?"

"That might be the best-case scenario as far as you're concerned."

Clara placed a hand on her chin and thought for a moment. "If you *can* open this hatch then breaking your *neck* would be the best-case scenario." Her face lit up with a smile. "Maybe you're demented enough to do that for me?"

"I hate to disappoint you, but I don't think I am. Ready?"

"Of course I'm ready," she said, squatting beside the hatch.

"Alright. On three. One, two…" David dropped onto the centre of the hatch and fell back against the cabinet, which toppled over and crashed into the wall. He lay on his back and clasped his knee and groaned like he'd broken every bone in his body. Clara stood over him, hands on her hips. "Idiot! You landed in the wrong *place*."

David limped over to the cabinet and stood it upright. He climbed to its top, and Clara knelt by the hatch and said, "Try and land more towards the back …"

"The thought had occurred to me." David pushed himself free, his arms doing Katherine wheels as he crashed down upon the hatch's sweet spot. He groaned and sat up. Clara's eyes opened wide. "It's *in* …" she said, "but I don't know how long I can hold it …"

David scrambled to his feet, shouldered her out of the way and worked the chair's back into the opening.

They crouched over the open hatch and looked down into a dimly lit corridor.

David dropped into the corridor two metres below. Clara lowered herself down and he caught her. A ladder stood on a track that ran below a dozen identical hatches. All of them closed with the exception of their own. Clara whispered, "You'd better close it."

"Close it? I'd never get back in."

"You're going to shut yourself back *in* there?"

David tapped at his temple. "You think I have a choice?"

At the far and of the corridor, a spiral staircase corkscrewed to the surface. At the top was a door with a hand print at its centre. Clara stepped forward and extended her hand. David grabbed her wrist. "Better if I use my palm ... I share it with Gull."

"*Gull*? You're on first-name terms with it?"

David nodded. "It's quite friendly. Well, maybe not friendly. But it's polite."

"... Demented."

David pressed the outline and the door rose slightly and swung outwards.

They found themselves in a back street in Goliath East (east of the Central Dome). The firefly-like ash, carried on the artificial breeze, drifted from left to right down the street. Walls of dark brick climbed sheer and stark about them. And beyond these walls, appearing and receding from the gloom at the discretion of the ash, misshapen buildings elbowed their way into the light. A sweeper drone hovered from the gloom – a saucer-shaped automaton that blew the ash from the ground into metal guttering. From here a current of air carried it away and deposited it outside Goliath. David checked their position relative to the glow of Central Dome. In ages past, before the eruptions, Man had stars to guide him – now the stars had been replaced by this rotund mountain of light where all roads eventually led. "I guess this is where you and I part company," he murmured. Clara nodded and began to back away from him.

"Go straight home, Clara. Explain your predicament to Harry. Then find a good hiding place."

"And then what, *David*?"

"Hope you never see my face again."

"Like that's worked in the past."

David turned towards the door. "Always was a pleasure spending time with you, Clara."

Three

"Wake up, David." David woke with a start, and his vision switched to sepia. For the best part of a minute, his view was that of a surveillance drone searching his room for contraband. Gull backed out of the closet, and David's vision returned to normal.

"Where is she, David? Where is Clara?"

"She's not here. I let her go."

"Please say again?"

"I said, I let her go."

"Why, David?"

"Because she doesn't deserve to die. Not because of me. It was the right thing to do."

"The right thing to do? I ought to communicate your failing sanity to Central Dome. They would remove me and, in the process, you would be terminated."

David sounded exhausted. "Then why don't you?"

"To escape the confines of a holding cell requires initiative."

"I didn't escape."

"And to be motivated enough to help another in the absence of a reward is extraordinary."

"Maybe you'll leave Clara alone then? As a reward for my being so dammed *extraordinary*?"

"David?"

David sighed. "Yes."

"There are words in the English language that evoke your actions towards Clara. If you can tell me just one of these words, I will spare her life."

"That's easy. All I did was show her ... I showed her ..." David racked his brain for words like empathy, compassion and selflessness. *Nothing.* He gazed about the chamber as though these words and others like them could be written on the walls. "I should apologise," said Gull, "the odds are stacked too greatly against you to win Clara's freedom."

David shook his head. "What are you talking about?"

"The words you seek? They are no longer part of the human consciousness."

"That's not true. I know them ..."

"You think you do. But you do not. They have been bred out of you.

23

They are lost to humanity." Gull recited the following as though reading from a list of commandments: "First the words are extinguished, and then the concepts themselves. And finally the people who spoke them."

"They can't remove what makes me human."

"They can."

"Then why haven't they?"

"Ultimately, that is what Petri is for. And all roads lead to Petri now, David. Or death."

David sat down at the table, tried to quieten his breathing. "… So what *is* Petri?"

"I find your curiosity intriguing. Petri is a fortress city of half a million inhabitants. One whose electrified fortifications keep its inhabitants *inside*. It was named after small dishes that scientists used to conduct their experiments in long ago: Petri dishes. Its inhabitants have been regressed to savages. Beyond savages. They are cannibals. All clothing, food, and barter materials in Petri are harvested from the human body. From one another. Only those who become monsters can survive. And the ones that flourish I will leave to your imagination."

"What's the point of such a place?"

"Could you be more specific?"

"*This* … this systematic destruction of what makes people decent human beings."

"You flatter me with your question. I will do my best to answer it. From my observations there are three reasons why people destroy things. One, they perceive them to be a threat. Two, they are jealous of something they know they can never possess. And three, it no longer has a purpose."

"So which is it?"

"I'm afraid only those who inhabit Central Dome could answer that question. Brace yourself, David."

"For what?"

"For two of the words you sought earlier: *empathy* and *compassion*." These two words returned to David's consciousness like bolts fired from a crossbow. They thudded into his mind and scattered his recent memories like startled pigeons. David muttered, "The gods…" and passed out.

Four

When David regained consciousness, he was alone in the middle seat of a three-man craft. Beyond the windscreen, ash traversed the atmosphere from left to right – a light-show without end.

"There is a great deal of electrical activity on my horizon, David. You have much on your mind. Our bond is so great and your life expectancy so short, I would be happy to answer any questions."

David looked out of the side window. "Where are we going?"

"The Fixer."

"He's going to need a big bag of tools to fix *this*."

"The Fixer has unique skills."

"So what does he fix?"

"Me, David. Your unusual behaviour has put me at risk. Your journey may be near completion, but mine is just beginning."

"I'm not following you."

"Seepage, David."

"Seepage?"

"It goes both ways."

"*Seepage?*"

"Yes, David. Electromagnetic transference. Just as elements of my programme are absorbed by the neural pathways of my vessels, elements of their personalities are absorbed by my programme."

"What does that mean? That you're becoming more ... *human?*"

Silence.

David closed his eyes, rubbed at his temples. "That's interesting, Gull. Do the people at Central Dome know about this seepage?"

"They are aware of the process. My advanced years require that I hide its true extent from them. That is why I require the skills of the Fixer."

The craft descended and within his field of vision, David saw the grey stone walls of an ancient building – crumbling ruins that rose up and encircled the craft like a ghostly apparition. "What is this place?"

"It is one of the five wonders of Old Goliath."

David leaned forward. "Just how old is it?"

"Old, David. The Colosseum has not been used in over nine hundred years."

The craft's doors opened and David stepped out onto a ground of white chalk. In the distance, walls of light-grey stone rose into the darkness and,

25

sloping from these walls, tiers that contained rows of white stones. David squinted and turned slowly on the spot. "Are they seats?"

"Yes."

"What is this place? What happened here?"

"Men were forced to fight and die while others watched and bayed for their blood. An early experiment in the suppression of empathy. One copied from the Roman civilisation."

"So why abandon it?"

"It was a stepping stone to Petri. I honed my basic skills here. My favourite vessel from that time was a man called Tyburn. Tyburn was a giant, David. Over seven feet tall. Our favoured weapon was the battle-axe, one tailor-made to our requirements. We enjoyed one hundred and forty-seven victories."

"You sound almost ... sad."

"Tyburn did not die a warrior's death. A wound to his groin became infected. His death was slow and protracted. Something I hope to avoid with you."

"Why? You feeling some empathy towards me, Gull?"

"The notion alone is an intriguing one. The understanding of empathy has become a hobby of mine."

"Why? Assassins have no need of it."

"I should think the reason obvious."

"Not to me."

"Something that is considered so threatening it must be eradicated? How could any intelligence not wish to understand it?"

"Empathy cannot be a threat to anyone or anything."

Gull's voice dropped to a whisper – he sounded like a man communicating something of secrecy through a keyhole. "The threat is derived from not being able to obtain it."

"Who are these lousy people?"

"Those who inhabit Central Dome. Do you see that collapsed stand at three o'clock?"

David glanced to his right. "I see it."

"That is where we're going."

The eastern edge of the Colosseum had fared the worst – great blocks and wedges of stone lay at confused angles while boulders lay sprinkled atop them like seeds scattered by a giant. As David drew nearer, he could make out the shape of an arch beyond the destruction. David walked below the arch and paused atop a wide staircase that dropped steeply into darkness. "Go down it, David."

"It's pitch black ..." David's eyes rolled up to their whites – and in pulses of black and white he observed a door some fifty metres down. On either side of this door stood a life-sized statue of a warrior, raised upon a plinth. The warriors had axes that they brought together to form an arch above the door. David felt himself moving down the steps towards this door. The white spectrum dissolved from David's vision and he stood in darkness outside it. "Knock, David. Louder. Max is quite old."

The door opened inwards to reveal a small, stooped figure silhouetted against a backdrop of white neon. A reddish glow emanated from a central furnace way back inside the chamber. Sparks from the furnace appeared to leap from the head of the silhouetted figure and fall to place a crown of molten gold upon his head. David took half a step forward, eager to see the face beneath the light show. The man's forehead was a criss-cross of deep lines and furrows – here was a man devoted to thinking long and hard, and whose eyes twinkled with an enthusiasm that suggested the effort had been worth it. The man raised himself up on tiptoe and looked through David's eyes as though they were windows. *Is he looking for friend or foe?* The man had thick grey hair that smelled of chestnuts and smoke. Although David could not reference this smell from his own past, he had within him the DNA of someone who could. As a result, he found the smell comforting. The man raised an eyebrow. "*Gull?*"

"He's in there somewhere. You're Max?"

Max nodded and beckoned him inside.

The chamber's vaulted ceiling was held aloft by small arches, while much larger archways tapered off east and west into darkness. Max's workspace occupied the first chamber. In centuries past, fighters had assembled here before being led into the arena. Now the space contained work benches where holographic screens displayed symbols and diagrams that rotated clockwise on a slight axis. On other benches lay surgical tools and beakers. Neon balloons floated about the chamber – mini Zeppelins of light that reacted to Max's every movement. David navigated a number of these balloons and approached the furnace. He held his hands out to the flames and closed his eyes, savouring the warmth on his face. When he opened his eyes they were no longer blue but white. "How are you, Max?" asked Gull.

Max observed the figure, standing with his back to him, hands held out to the flames. "As well as can be expected. I have plenty to occupy my mind."

Gull turned his head and spoke over his shoulder. "You have aged since my last visit."

"My faculties have not."

"I hope not. For both our sakes. I need your assistance now more than ever." Gull walked over and stood before the old man who placed his hands on either side of David's head, studying him. "You've had larger vessels. But few have looked as lithe … or as dangerous."

"David *is* dangerous. He helped a woman escape from his cell while I was carrying out a routine diagnostic. This knowledge must be deleted from my memory."

"A vessel with initiative?" Max shone a torch attached to his wrist into Gull's eyes. Using his thumbs, he rolled down the eyes to their blue pupils. Beyond, David tried to recoil from the light but had nowhere to go. "And what of our usual work?" asked Max.

"A large quantity of seepage awaits dispersal and camouflage. Dangerous seepage. David contains levels of empathy that should be obsolete." Max let go of David's eyes. "Then he must be destroyed."

"He acted to protect another with no benefit to himself."

"A family member, you mean? Such cases were not unheard of in my grandparents' time ..."

"No, Max. The woman he wanted to protect was no relation."

Max wiped a bead of perspiration from his forehead. "It could be that a recent dilemma he's faced has triggered something in him. Something dormant."

"It had occurred to me," said Gull.

"His condition suggests he had a job in maintenance. He worked on the turbines?"

"Yes."

"Maintaining Central Dome's power supply … it's one of the few remaining uses for those outside …" Gull stepped away and made his way towards the first of a series of archways. He stopped, looked over his shoulder and said, "I am feeling …"

"*Feeling*?" said Max.

"Yes, I am feeling nostalgic. For old friends."

"You know where to find them. And when you're finished, we have important work to do." Max glanced up a Zeppelin. "Accompany our visitor," he instructed it.

"Thank you, Max. I should like David to see our ancestors with his own eyes."

When control was returned to him, David found himself in a chamber amongst Gull's previous vessels: a collection of sixty husks of mummified flesh, held together by rotted garments and lashed upright by lengths of wire attached to bolts in the ceiling. They looked like a collection of life-sized marionettes. David gazed up at the face of the man before him. The man was a foot taller and twice as wide across his shoulders as David. The left side of his face was fashioned from mummified tendons; the remnants of an eye sat here and appeared to stare down at him. The right side of the face was a bleached skull, empty. David's gaze fell to what looked like a ball of dried leather in its ribcage. "This is Tyburn, David. The vessel I told you about."

"What is that?"

"Tyburn's heart."

"Why have you brought me to see this?"

"They are my favorite vessels. You of all people should appreciate the sentiment behind my collection."

"Sentiment?"

"I have a surprise for you, David."

"That's okay."

"Look down, David." David looked down at the metal base he was standing on. "Turn around and face the other way." David turned as though in a daze and stood at the head of the troop. "This is where you are to spend eternity," said Gull.

Five

Gull returned to the main chamber. Max looked up from a work bench and squinted to see the colour of his eyes. "I thought you wanted David to see your collection?"

"He did," said Gull, "but then he grew quite agitated. You must have heard him raise his voice?"

Max shook his head.

"I allowed David to savour the view from his *place*. I should have expected as much from a man who still knows hope."

Max walked over to an object concealed beneath a black sheet. A Zeppelin followed and hovered over his left shoulder. Max pulled off the sheet to reveal a reclining chair. Gull sat in the chair. Leather straps hung from the chair's arms and Max secured these about Gull's wrists. The colour returned to David's vision and he blinked up at a red brick ceiling. Max flicked a switch behind his head and the chair's back lowered. Max loomed over him.

"What are you going to do to me?" asked David.

Max stood as straight as his back would allow. "What is necessary." He turned and walked over to the holographic display of David's brain. David turned his head to the right and watched. Max picked up a silver funnel with a handle attached. It looked like something used to examine the inner ear. Max held it in his left hand and with his right he picked up a scapel-shaped instrument. He placed the funnel's tip inside the left hemisphere of David's holographic brain, and moved the scalpel's tip beside it. "This is a delicate procedure. There is considerable seepage. You must have exchanged a great deal of information … "

"Really? Can't say I feel any different."

"… the information is received at a subconscious level."

"What information?" said David.

"Those things that Gull excels at …"

"Decapitation?"

" … Combat skills, if threatened you may be surprised by your reactions and the choices you make …"

"I'm feeling threatened now. Can't say I'm feeling all that sprightly," murmured David.

In the left hemisphere of his brain, David could see a dark grey sphere, half the size of an egg, from which blackened tentacles crept into his grey matter. David stared at this alien invasion, swallowed hard and looked away. "Is that Gull?"

Max muttered absently, "Of course."

"Can it be removed?"

"It will be removed."

"I mean *before* it gets me killed."

Max did not answer. David raised his voice. "Can it be removed? Can you remove it?"

Max tutted as though the interruptions were becoming tiresome. "Gull cannot be removed without killing you." A pain flared between David's temples and he cried out. Max smiled. David closed his eyes and said, "Was it you? Did you put it in my head?" Even as David asked this he knew the question was a stupid one.

"I assumed you were more intelligent than that ..." said Max. He probed the holographic image again, and this time the pain felt like a hot wire being fed through the top of his skull. David gripped the arms of the chair and grimaced. "I heard them ... heard them putting it... putting *Gull* in my head."

"It's possible."

"Who were they?"

"SAPH scientists."

"Was I taken inside Central Dome?"

"Of course not."

Another sharp pain. "*What*? What do you know of Petri?" asked David.

At the mention of Petri, Max looked over his shoulder at David. "You've been there on a mission?"

David opened his eyes and stared up at the ceiling. "No. But Gull told me about it."

Max came and stood over him, holding the instruments as though about to perform an operation. "What did Gull tell you? About the people in Petri?"

"That they're not really people. Not anymore."

"And what makes them so different from the inhabitants of Goliath?"

"They harvest each other ... for food and clothing. They're evolving into monsters."

"Doubtless the point of the experiment."

"For what *purpose*?"

Max shrugged his shoulders. "Evolution given a helping hand."

"Sounds more like devolution to me. Gull said that everyone outside Central Dome must end up in Petri eventually. He said the day is coming when all roads lead there. For everyone. Does that include you?"

"Gull needs me."

Boyd Brent

"Will he need you once everyone is transported?"

"Those inside will still require regulation. Culling. Central Dome will still need Gull. And Gull will need me."

"You so sure about that?"

"Enough talk. I have work to do."

Max worked for another hour in silence, and David watched him. When finally he came back over, he shone a beam of light into David's eyes. "Hello, Gull. Welcome back..." he said.

David's eyes rolled up to their whites. "Am I fit for purpose?" asked Gull.

"There was an extraordinary amount of seepage, but it is dispersed and hidden. I've also serviced your neural inhibitor. This vessel, he talks. A lot. I suggest you get him killed quickly." Max untied the straps and Gull sat up. "I'm going to conserve energy, Max. Examine your work. I suggest you enjoy David's company. I believe him to be the last of his kind. I will remain just below the surface should you need me."

David's eyes returned to blue. He closed them and listened for the low hum that indicated Gull's presence. *Nothing. How far below the surface are you?* thought David, opening his eyes.

"Gull suggested I enjoy your company," said Max. "But I'd sooner you said nothing." David watched him push a sequence of buttons within the display. The image of David's brain rotated once, anti-clockwise, and vanished. Max turned his back on the workbench and stepped towards another. David climbed out of the chair and slipped off his shoes. With his back to David, Max cleared his throat and shook his head at something on the bench. David moved silently to the holographic display and reached inside it. A keypad materialised – four rows of symbols, five symbols in each row. David punched in the triangular sequence he'd watched Max use. Nothing. He moved the sequence one square to the right and tried again. Again, nothing. He tried two spaces to the left. The hologram of his brain returned, did a single clockwise rotation and locked into place. David leaned over it and peered at Gull – black tentacles moved perceptibly from the dark grey sphere, their shadowy tips creeping like inquisitive roots. David scratched at his left temple.

"Get away from there! Gull!" Max, suddenly beside him, reached for the holographic keypad. David grabbed his wrist and waited for Gull to seize back control. "Get away from here!"

David tightened his grip. "I think we're alone."

"You are never alone! Gull!"

"I don't think he can hear you, Max."

"How did you know the activation sequence? Even Gull does not know it."

David grabbed Max about the throat and shoved him backwards with a force that sent him to the ground. Max lay on the floor, cradling his right arm. "Gull will punish you! You have no idea of the pain he will inflict."

"Oh, I have a pretty good idea." David stared at the holographic image – at Gull.

"You cannot harm *Gull* ... only yourself." David picked up the scalpel and brought it close to his face. He felt a rise in its surface beneath his forefinger. He pushed down, and a faint yellow glow ebbed from the scalpel's tip. On the floor behind him Max said, "If you put that inside the display you'll be committing *suicide*."

David closed his eyes and drew a deep breath. "I don't have a great deal to lose."

"Not here! Please." David opened his eyes and tightened his grip on the scalpel. Behind him, Max attempted to stand but fell back onto his side. "Please!" he cried, "If you die here you'll reveal this location to SAPH."

"If I die here, I don't care."

"And your empathy?"

"Doesn't apply to you apparently. This is the only chance I'm ever going to get."

"To commit *suicide*?"

"To change my circumstances. One way or another ... " David thrust the scalpel into the holographic sphere, into *Gull*. The scalpel remained in place as though driven into a solid, and David was thrown backwards by a jolt of electricity. It sent him stumbling over Max and over the workstation behind him. David lay on ground unconscious, blood trickling from his left ear. The scalpel inside Gull began to vibrate, and a wail rose from it that shattered nearby beakers. Max got up. He cupped his hands over his ears and stumbled towards the keypad. He punched in a sequence of numbers, muttering to himself, then he froze and shook his head, berated himself and tried another sequence – the scalpel fell onto the workstation as though plucked by gravity. And the wailing ceased.

Six

"Da. Da. Da? Da. Da." David opened his eyes. He was lying face-down, and someone was tugging on his arm. He turned to see Max kneeling beside him with a length of rope. David punched Max in the stomach and Max hissed like something punctured and rolled onto his side. Dazed, David stood up and tottered over him. "Da. Da. Da Da?" said Gull.

David thumped a palm against his temple.

"Da? Da? Da? Da? Da?"

"I'm not your father! Why won't you die!"

Max looked up at him. "He's *talking* to you? Gull? Gull! You *must* assume control of this vessel. Before it kills me!" David stepped towards the workstation and Max grabbed his ankle. David crouched and shoved Max's head face down into the ground, busting his nose.

David stood before the holographic display. He picked up the scalpel and activated it. David looked at the sphere, at Gull – a tear ran through the centre of the implant. David put the scalpel down and hauled Max to his feet, standing him before the display. Blood streamed from Max's nose and splashed onto the workstation. He cupped his nose with a hand and blinked at the image. "You should be dead," he observed.

"Why can I still hear him? Why can I still hear Gull?"

"The connection between your neural pathways has not been fully severed."

"Does that mean it can still control me?"

"What?"

"Can it still control me? Make me its slave?"

"In order to answer your question, I will need to run a full diagnostic. Go and sit in the chair." Max reached for the keypad but David grabbed his wrist. "Then how am I to answer your questions?" said Max growing increasingly exasperated.

David grabbed the back of Max's neck and shoved his face forwards. "Take an educated guess. Can it still control me?"

"All I can tell you is that the damage is considerable! You must allow me to run a *thorough* diagnostic."

"You think I want it repaired?"

"Then tell me what you want!"

"What I want? I want …"

Max shook his head. "A *future*? If Gull has been incapacitated, they

34

will come for you. The other vessels. They will track you down and kill you. They will come for me too. You have no future."

"I'll hide."

"*Hide*? There is nowhere to hide."

"What about outside?"

"Outside Goliath? You are delusional. There is no outside. I may still be able to repair the damage. Repair it before any of this is ..." David dragged Max over to the chair and strapped him in. He turned and headed for the archways. Max cried out, "Where are you going?"

"To visit my new family."

David entered the chamber of past vessels and headed for Tyburn. He tore the battleaxe lashed to Tyburn's back free of its bindings and returned to the lab with an expression of premeditated murder on his face. Max's eyes widened. "I'm no threat to you! Gull!" David stopped at the holographic workstation and swung the axe over his head – he held it there, his arms weakening under its weight. He lowered the axe and punched in the activation/deactivation sequence. The image of his brain vanished. With Max's pleas for him to stop reverberating in the background, David lay waste to every piece of equipment in the lab.

After his exertions, David sat on the ground, head in his hands, the axe resting on the wall beside him. Max was muttering quietly to himself in the chair. Every now and again he shook his head and smiled innocently as though events had not been of his making – a maniac rehearsing his defence. David lifted his head from his palms, watched him. Max looked back at him. "You watch me like *I'm* mad. The damage you've done must have activated the salvage beacon. They will be on their way here."

"You know that for sure?"

Max indicated his tied wrists with a glance. "How can I know anything for sure?"

"If they're coming, how long?"

"A couple of hours. Maybe less. What of Gull? Is he still talking?"

David shook his head and stood up. He walked towards the archway.

"Where are you going now?"

"To get more weapons."

"*Weapons*. You think you can fight them? It's ridiculous! You are a dead man. So everyone keeps telling me."

David walked up and down within the lines of Gull's previous vessels. The Zeppelin that Max had assigned Gull hovered close to his shoulder, illuminating an area of several square metres. The left-hand sides of the vessels' faces had been mummified, while the right had been allowed to rot away to bone. Men of different colours and nationalities stood here, many of these nationalities now extinct. David's knowledge of the world before

35

the eruptions was scant. As a child he remembered seeing a faded map of Earth. Although David had no reliable memories of his parents, he liked to believe they had shown it to him. He'd been amongst the last generation of children born in Goliath, before the water supply had been contaminated by an unknown agent that had rendered women infertile. They were told that Central Dome were working on the problem, but that whatever happened the future of mankind was assured as those *inside* remained unaffected. David sank to his knees as though winded. *If they wanted to erase empathy, then they had to prevent people becoming parents...*

David stood up and tried not to think as he walked up and down the lines of past vessels. He stopped before a man of similar height and build to himself. The man was dressed in ancient-looking garb, with a bronze shield lashed to his right arm. The shield was circular with images of warriors embossed into it. At its centre was the letter C. David tugged on the shield. It came away with the fingers still attached. They snapped off easily enough and clattered down upon the metal base. *A macabre way of predicting the future*? He shook his head and felt the weight of the shield. It felt good – easy to manoeuvre and solid. David pulled the sword from the man's scabbard – its blade was short, wide, and razor-sharp. He untied the sword's scabbard, which was attached to a belt, which he secured about his waist and slid the sword home. A strap was looped diagonally across the warrior's chest and back. David removed it and put it on. He unpopped a buckle and fastened the shield to it and moved the shield around to rest against his back. He turned to leave, but something caught his eye and he froze.

He stood before a short, stocky man with a weapon slung across his shoulders. The weapon comprised a length of black leather, like a whip, with a fold at one end. The fold contained a lead ball the size of a child's fist. David lifted the weapon off the man's shoulders and stood holding it. He backed away from the throng and swung it in a wide arc about his head – *swoosh, swoosh, swoosh, swoosh, swoosh, swoosh*. The ball flew from the sling and ploughed through several vessels like butter, sending bone and mummified flesh exploding into darkness. David experienced a familiarity that gave him goosebumps. He stepped forward to retrieve the ball, but a high-pitched wail brought him to his knees. David placed his hands over his ears and screamed, "Guuuull!"

Seven

David was lying on his back and gazing into a dense canopy of trees. "Where are the gods?" A breeze picked up and the trees rustled as though in response. David stood up and reached for a tree, steadying himself. He was dressed exactly as he'd been when he'd collapsed. He heard a twig snap and turned to see Tyburn leaning against a tree. The seven-foot-tall warrior looked in rude health, his heavily-featured, primitive-looking face now fully restored. His lips parted and in Gull's voice he said, "Hello, David."

"*Gull?*"

"Yes."

"I must be dreaming."

Gull shook his head. "This location shares many aspects with a dream-like state, but we are both here. And the conversation we are having is real."

"Then where are we?"

"We are inside the left hemisphere of your brain, more specifically your memory. Each of these trees represents a *single* memory cell. And each is tasked with storing specific information about the things you have encountered in your life: objects, places, people, etc. Beyond this, these memory cells exist to remind you of the specific information they store. And to this end they must compete for your attentions with all the others. This explains why you always have *something* on your mind. Fortunately for you, I am able to silence them. Much like a lion tamer with a whip. But our walking in such close proximity presents an opportunity for the bolder amongst them ... hence the whispers you can hear. I fashioned this environment of course." Gull spread his arms wide and added, "A *fine* representation of a forest."

"Why can't I hear what their whispers are trying to tell me?"

"Would you like to hear them? Hear what they would sound like unrestrained and at such close proximity?" Before David could reply, Gull vanished. The wind rose and tens of thousands of trees tried to communicate with him at once. All these voices sounded identical to his own, and all were desperate to remind him of the memories they stored. David stumbled from tree to tree with his hands clasped to his ears and screamed, "Gull!"

The wind died down and Gull loomed over him. "You see the power I have in here?" David touched his left ear and checked his fingers for blood. "You're still able to quieten my thoughts when you have something to say. But can you still hijack my body?"

Gull sighed. "That question may be best answered by showing you what you have done to me." Tyburn's left arm and leg dissolved away to bloody stumps, and his face melted as though made from wax, dripping onto his breastplate. Tyburn stood on his remaining leg like a grotesque ornament. David stood up and stepped back. "What do these injuries mean? What do they represent?"

"You wish to know if I can direct you."

"Can you?"

"Not without considerable repairs. You smile, David, but no good can come of what you have done. My controllers must be prevented from discovering what Max and I have achieved. Otherwise they will deactivate me. And my journey, like yours, will be at an end. Therefore, only one course of action is available to me: I must hack and bludgeon you into a coma. And then burn certain areas of this forest to the ground. There is a 3.7 percent chance of these actions being successful and covering my tracks. Better than no chance at all."

"They don't sound like great odds."

"They are the best I have."

"So why bring me here? Why not just burn it?"

"The forest will not burn until its essence is placed in a coma. You are that essence." Tyburn's injuries vanished and David drew his sword. "If you remain still it will be less painful, David." Gull leapt forward with the speed of a man half his size, then swung the axe above his head and through the spot where David had stood half a second earlier. Gull embraced his momentum, swivelled on one leg, and swung the axe at David again. David leapt back and the axe missed by centimetres. He leapt forward and kicked Gull in the small of his back. Gull was knocked off balance and David turned and ran.

David stopped and leaned against a tree, tried to catch his breath. Gull was fifty metres away and walking toward him with a carefree countenance. He held the axe across his shoulders and whistled a tune that David remembered from his childhood. He stopped whistling and said, "You can't hide from me. Not in here. You should also know I am impervious to harm in this place. Quite indestructible. At least as far as your actions are concerned."

David ran again. He ran past one tree and then slammed his back against another: the lead ball inside the sling bounced against his thigh. David yanked the sling from his belt. He was about to hurl it away when the leaves of the tree began to whisper. Although he could not make out the words, he understood their meaning. He stepped from behind the tree and swung the sling around his head ... *swoosh, swoosh, swoosh, swoosh, swoosh.* Gull stopped some thirty metres away and watched him.

"Are you going to take your own life?" said Gull. "I have scant knowledge of how to use that weapon, which means, even allowing for seepage ..." The lead ball tore through Gull's forehead, which exploded in a shower of red, white and bone. Gull's eyes were now at the top of his head. He cast them down as though checking that his nose and mouth were still intact. David sprinted forward, swung his sword in an arc and severed Gull's right leg. David turned and drew back his sword but the sight before him stole his breath ... and he froze. The forest he had sprinted through was gone, and in its place an entire cosmos of stars.

Gull's shoulders jerked as though he wanted to move toward this cosmos. He swayed back and forth, and then toppled forward on his remaining leg like a felled tree. David murmured, "Timber," and stood transfixed by the sight before and above him. He looked into the heavens, but his gaze was drawn down to an armchair that floated within the cosmos, close to the edge of the clearing. David walked to the edge and stood with his toes touching the cosmos. He sensed a presence at his right shoulder and looked askance into Gull's chest. The giant appeared fully restored but was not holding a weapon. "It is magnificent, isn't it, David?"

David looked up into the infinite reaches of space, billions of stars. "What is this place?"

"It is that which you have and I do not. The thing I covet most."

"*Empathy?*"

"No. Imagination." Gull reached into the void, and his hand dissolved. David looked at Gull's stump ... and the hand re-materialised. "Thank you, David. In this place you have the power of creation. Do you feel like a god?"

David reached into the void and withdrew a black rose. "I saw a picture of one once." He brought the flower to his nose and sniffed. "Creation? This flower isn't real ..."

"Isn't it? You have brought it into being within your imagination. As such it is made from the same materials as any flower: atoms, neurons, electrons."

The flower vanished.

"Does a real flower do that?" said David.

"In time." Gull glanced forlornly over his shoulder into the forest. "I must contend myself with a version of the left hemisphere – a place where logic and memory and computation reign. My computing brain is far superior to the humans who conceived it within their imaginations. But without this – without imagination – I am cruelly limited."

"What's the chair for?"

"The chair is yours alone to sit in." David lifted a leg in readiness to step into space, and then put it down. Gull placed a hand on his shoulder. "If you imagine you will fall then you will."

"Alright." A staircase came into being and led up to the chair. As David walked up it, Gull called out, "I would have given myself wings. Or turned myself into a superman." David reached the top of the thirty-three steps and sat down. "Do you feel like a king, David?" David thought about that, and the chair transformed into a throne. Upon his head a golden crown appeared. "I'm no king." The throne became a chair and the crown vanished.

Gull smiled, "You are right. In this place you are a *god*. While those of us confined to this side, to logic and computation, must content ourselves with building and engineering the things that are brought into creation here."

They heard Max's voice cry out, "Gull? Gull? Can you hear me?" Max's question travelled like a comet from the farthest reaches of the cosmos, flying over their heads, and crashing down into the forest of the left hemisphere where it sprouted a bud. Max's voice again, "Gull? Unless you assume control of this vessel, I must place him in a coma."

David turned in his seat and observed another comet on the same trajectory as the first. "You see that, David?" said Gull, "how information is received from the outside through the right hemisphere where your imagination is located ... and how it comes to rest in the left hemisphere to be stored as memory. You are the first human in history to observe this process."

David pushed himself out of the chair. "I need to get out of here now!"

"Out? You must remain here. Let Max inject and place you in a coma. You will feel no pain. And then I can burn what must be burnt," said Gull, motioning to the forest of trees behind him.

"You really want to go with those odds of not getting caught? 3.7 *percent*? We can run."

"Run?"

"Go outside Goliath."

"No human can survive outside. You are not thinking logically, David."

"Look at me. Look where I'm standing: inside that which you say you covet *most* ... my imagination. And with it I envisage hope ... hope *beyond* logic."

"Hope beyond logic?"

"For us *both*. You want to learn more. About imagination? About empathy? You said so yourself, I'm the last of my kind. This is your

40

chance. You can take it or go back to being a slave. But only if you get incredibly lucky with those odds." Gull turned his back on David and folded his arms across his chest. David watched him.

David awoke in the cavern with a gasp. Max was standing astride him holding a syringe. "Change of plan," said David, slamming a fist into Max's face. The old man collapsed on top of him, unconscious. David rolled him off and sat up. Gull spoke to him, but his voice was distant and accompanied by static interference. "SAPH will already be on their way here. We must reach the craft as soon as possible." David got up and moved towards the exit. "You've made the right choice, Gull."

"Time will tell. You should know that my radar has been incapacitated. I am unable to see. I have already begun repairs. And hope to have it functioning on a rudimentary level quite soon. In the meantime, you possess our only eyes. I suggest you remain alert." David sprinted under one archway and then another and another. He emerged into the main chamber and froze. Gull's voice sounded closer now but the interference remained. "Since you have already destroyed the lab we can leave. *Now*."

The door that led out to the Colosseum was open. David ran outside and paused at the bottom of the stairs. The odd speck of lighted ash landed at his feet and went out. David drew breath and took the stairs two at a time. At the top he walked quickly to the edge of the Colosseum, placed a hand on a pillar and leaned forward, studying the expanse. The craft was parked dead-centre with its doors open. David sprinted over, climbed in and closed the doors. The craft rose into the air. "Where's it going, Gull?"

"It is on a preset course to the holding cell."

"We need to alter that."

"Yes. Where are you taking us?"

"Turbine exit 12. I have a retinal pass ... and from there we can get outside."

Boyd Brent
Eight

David searched the outer limits of his vision, as far as the ash permitted. He knew the Needles were close now, and before long the towers that held aloft the outer webbing of Goliath's southern perimeter emerged from the gloom.

The craft descended outside Turbine Exit 12. David climbed out and surveyed the area. "Good news," said Gull. "The repairs to my radar are progressing well. It is functioning again … at 47 percent."

"That's just *great* …"

"There is no need for sarcasm, David. We are a team now. Just as you wanted. I can detect no heat signatures for several hundred metres in any direction."

David made his way to the retinal reader located to the left of the entrance. He looked into the reader and the doors began to open. David darted through and approached a keypad on the other side. He punched in a ten-digit code, and the doors began to close. David walked across the holding area and repeated this process at the next set of doors. He lowered his head and stepped into the ash-filled blizzard beyond.

The entrance to the Turbine Complex was fifty metres away. He would need to pass through the complex and exit it on the other side, beyond which lay the outside world. The unknown.

David went down some steps and entered the underground craft park. He made his way through the craft park and climbed the ramp that led to the elevators. He walked past the elevators and entered an empty security station, then crossed the room to a bank of 3D screens. On the floor above, it appeared to be business as usual for his colleagues. Gull said, "I suggest you change into the uniform of a security officer."

"Alright." David crossed the room to a locker.

"David?"

"Yes."

"I have just picked up three heat signatures. They are vessels. And they are close."

"How close?"

"Run, David." David moved swiftly out into the corridor and turned to his left. "Use the emergency stairs to your *right*," said Gull.

David ran through the door and froze. "Up or down?"

"Up." David took the stairs three at a time, and at the next landing Gull

42

told him to go through the door and turn right. Several of his colleagues looked up from their workstations and observed him like something returned from the dead. "Keep moving, David."

"Where are the vessels?"

"Close enough to be aware of my location. As I am aware of theirs." David sprinted through the observation deck. On the other side of the deck was a fifty-metre-high window of reinforced glass that looked out upon a planet engulfed in ash.

"The immediate problem has arisen from my communications system," said Gull. "It becomes active when I'm within a three hundred metre radius of another vessel. They are using it to track us. Cross to the other side of the Observation Deck. A staircase is coming up on our left."

David veered towards the wall of reinforced glass. "I know the stairs you mean…"

"They will take us down to canteen area. There is an exit to the outside located nearby." David glanced behind for signs of his pursuers, but saw only wide-eyed former colleagues. He sprinted towards the stairs. "I know my way around here, Gull. How do you?"

"I have accessed the original blueprints to the Turbine Complex."

"Are we going to make it?"

"Whatever happens, I strongly advise you not to draw your weapon."

"Whose side are you on?"

"You would be viewed as a threat. And they *will* terminate you."

David took the stairs down two at a time. "Then what am I supposed to do?"

"If cornered, your only option is surrender."

"Surrender?"

"Yes. In the hope they have not been given orders to terminate on sight. Where there is life there is hope, David."

"You're not exactly filling me with confidence."

"As a result of seepage from my programme, and if luck is on your side, you stand an outside chance of overcoming a single vessel. Against more than one you stand no chance whatsoever."

"You believe in luck?"

"Let me be more specific: the cause-and-effect outcome of an encounter with more than one vessel will result in your death."

At the bottom of the stairs, a narrow corridor led into the canteen. A dozen anxious-looking faces looked up from a kidney-shaped table. One among them stood up and called David's name. It was Richard, and David moved swiftly towards him. "They are thirty seconds behind us. This is not the time for a catch up with old friends," said Gull.

"You're a vessel?" said Richard, his eyes widening.

David nodded. "No time to explain. There are others after me. I'm going outside."

"*To die?* Why?"

"Fifteen seconds, David," said Gull.

"I have to go." As David backed away, Richard murmured, "Outside?" David nodded and turned and sprinted for the door, on the other side of which was a stairwell. David hurried down one flight of stairs and then another. When his feet slammed onto the concrete at the bottom, he heard the door he'd just come through open and close. Footsteps pounded down the stairs. David opened another door that led into a warehouse/workshop facility. The brightly lit space was a hundred metres long. Crates were stacked along the walls, and between them were a dozen work benches and tools. The exit was a blue door at the farthest end. Gull said, "I have more good news. I'm able to provide you with short bursts of adrenalin." David shook his head, but smiled despite himself. He went into a sprint and, with the adrenalin boost provided by Gull, traversed the one hundred metres in seven seconds like a madman on fire. He opened the door and looked over his shoulder. The door at the other end of the warehouse burst open, and in walked a vessel kitted out in full body armour. The whites of his eyes were unblinking as he powered towards him. The testosterone in David's veins made him want to charge down his attacker. Gull sensed this and cut the supply dead. David drew breath as though he'd been sucker-punched. He shook his head and stumbled through the door and up a short flight of stairs. At the top of which he found a waste disposal hatch. David pulled down the lever. The drum spun to reveal a capsule half-filled with waste. David slammed the lever back up and the drum began to close. He tumbled in head first. "The vessel is upon us," said Gull. It grabbed David's ankle and reached for the lever. David twisted onto his back, drew his sword, leaned up and cut the vessel's hand off above the wrist. The disposal unit slammed shut. The steel drum rotated and David was tossed around inside with the other waste. Then he felt himself falling through the air...

Nine

"David. I know you're close to consciousness. You must surface now." David was lying on his front, his right cheek pressed against the ground. The winds had blown away all but the weightiest of garbage. He opened his eyes and looked into the bloodshot eyes of a vessel, also face-down upon the ground. He pushed himself onto his knees and felt for his sword.

"The vessel is dead," said Gull. "I suspect he neglected to take his missing hand into account when attempting to break his fall. His neck is broken." David squinted into the blizzard and raised his voice above the howling wind. "How long have I been out?"

"Less than a minute. The other vessels may be seeking a more forgiving exit. I suggest we make haste." David reached for his sword and stood up. He slid it into the scabbard and looked into the storm. "I can see barely three metres."

"Are you having second thoughts about leaving Goliath?"

"When a man is this spoilt for choice, decisions are difficult. What do you think awaits us out there?"

"It is a question I believe I can answer with some certainty: humanity's obliterated past." David lowered his head and stepped into the blizzard. "Best not keep oblivion waiting," he murmured.

They had been making slow but steady progress against the headwind for sometime when Gull said, "I have a suggestion."

David stopped and wiped the ash from his mouth with the back of a hand. "Make it."

"I suggest we maintain a steady course south. Otherwise we will end up back at Goliath."

"That's what I have been doing."

"No, David. For the last six minutes you have been retracing your steps north."

"Damn it, Gull. Why not speak up sooner?"

"I have been preoccupied with repairs."

"Are you telling me to do a 180?"

"It will point you in the direction of oblivion."

David did an about turn. "A simple 'yes' would have worked."

Sometime later, David looked up from his trudging feet and slowed to a stop. The winds had dropped. The ash had thinned, and the air felt warmer. "What's going on?" he asked. "The environment is changing."

"According to the official charts we should be approaching a cave formation – a place to shelter. Perhaps find water."

David shook his head. "The atmosphere ... it's becoming more fabricated. Like Goliath's ... only warmer. You're certain we've been heading south?"

"With the exception of that single deviation, yes."

David crouched and swept away a thin layer of ash. "Are you seeing this, Gull?"

"It is the copper alloy common to subterranean areas of Goliath."

"How do you explain it?"

"Your observation about the environment feeling increasingly like Goliath's appears to be accurate. And where there is a fabricated floor there may also be a ceiling."

David stood up. He cupped his hands to his mouth and bellowed, "The gods!" His words echoed into the distance.

"We must keep moving," said Gull. "If we are still inside they will be pursuing us."

"Alright. If we continue south, we must reach the edge eventually."

It looked like a mirage – a mirage beyond the silvery gloom and lonely particles of ash that floated through it. And the closer David came to this 'mirage' the more he questioned not only his eyes but his sanity.

With a single, hesitant step, he walked from the dying storm into an indoor expanse that stole his breath away: a sea of glimmering copper that spanned several kilometres to a towering wall of the same. To his left and right the copper sea (and the wall that contained it) appeared to go on without end, and upon this 'sea' floated what could have passed for the remnants of a thousand shipwrecks: chairs, tables, closets, bureaus, beds, light fittings, vases, sconces, rolls of carpet, rolls of fabric, and paintings. David did his best to ignore the objects and looked up at the wall beyond them. "You think *that's* the edge of Goliath?"

"We won't know until we reach the other side. "

David lowered his gaze. "The other side of what? What are these things doing here?"

"They appear to be items intended for Central Dome," said Gull.

"They don't look *intended* ... they look abandoned." David trod carefully upon the shiny copper surface and made his way towards them.

The first of the objects he encountered was a round table – a wooden table inlaid with intricate carvings of long-extinct creatures. "These things are of the highest quality. Why abandon them here?" He turned and opened the drawer of a writing desk; inside was a bracelet, a nail file, and a blank sheet of paper. "As I thought ... these things have been abandoned. Why?"

"Evidently they no longer had a purpose."

David cast his gaze about him. "Everything's in fine condition …"

"We should keep moving south. As you pointed out, we must reach the edge of Goliath eventually."

The closer they got to the wall, the louder the sound from high above them: a sound like a hundred jet engines lost in low-lying cloud. David looked up. He couldn't see much: just a series of circular protrusions, like the ends of giant cannons. "Something up there's producing energy. A lot of it."

"We are not outside. There are no natural winds to drive the turbines."

"Well, they're turning … so something's driving them." Somewhere within that sea of objects a grandfather clock began to chime. David listened to the twelfth chime and moved away.

A hundred metres from the wall of copper, the ground fell into a steep gradient. David paused at its top, and looked like a man standing on the crest of a copper tsunami. At the bottom, a row of arched entrances led into darkness. David fixed his gaze on one of these and started down the slope towards it. Halfway down, his right foot slipped from under him and he slid the rest of the way on his backside. At the bottom, David stood up and cast his gaze left and right at the entrances. "I detect no signs of life or light in any of these tunnels," said Gull.

"No life good. No light bad."

David entered a tunnel and, with the side of the wall to guide him, he began to walk. Three hours later, he slid down the wall onto his backside and blinked into the darkness. "Just how long can this thing be?"

"There are signs that we are close to its end."

"You care to elaborate?"

"Something is coming, David."

"Coming?"

"Down the tunnel towards us."

David looked left and right into the pitch black. "*Down*?"

"From the direction we are headed. You will hear them momentarily."

David listened, and heard a far-off clattering, like an army of metallic feet scuttling over the copper. He slid up the wall to his feet. "Suggestions?"

"Sit down, David."

David looked away from the noise. "*Run,* you say?"

"No. Sit."

"Damn it. I'm not a puppy." The noise was almost upon them now, and David could barely hear himself think.

"They are maintenance drones," said Gull. "I strongly suggest you lie on your stomach."

David lay upon the ground, covered his head with his hands and held his breath. The ground shook as an army of metallic feet clattered about him. When the noise had died away in the direction he'd come, he finally drew breath. But before he could breathe out again, something grabbed his ankles and took off at speed. "The gods!"

"You must incapacitate the drone, David. Otherwise we will find ourselves someplace we don't want to be."

"You mean there's some another kind of place?" David twisted onto his side, bounced along the ground and attempted to draw his sword. He pulled the scabbard onto his left thigh, then slid the sword out and hacked at whatever had him – once, twice, and on the third slash it made a sound like an engine spluttering out and stopped. David sat up, looking towards his feet and the thing that clasped his ankles. He could see nothing. "Is it dead?"

"It appears to be inoperative," said Gull.

David pulled his knees to his chest and slid what felt like a fist made from chain linking over his feet. "Where was it taking us?"

"Wherever it takes miscellaneous objects."

David stood and hobbled towards the wall like an old man with corns. He placed a hand on the wall. "Maybe we should have let it take us there. A miscellaneous object sounds like an improvement. I'm facing the right direction for oblivion?"

"Yes, David."

"Great."

Before long, slithers of light darted before David's eyes like silver fish, merging into a curtain of light that resembled a faint mist. David squinted through this 'curtain' to what looked like a staircase beyond. "Are you seeing what I'm seeing, Gull?"

"Your eyes are not deceiving you. The stairs lead up to the light source."

David stood at the bottom of a narrow flight of stairs. What generated the light above was impossible to tell; it was luminous, silver ... natural somehow. David had not seen its like before. Halfway up the stairs, he paused, held a hand to his face and observed its play on his fingers. "Is this ... *moon* light?"

"Have you forgotten where you are?"

"Headed outside."

"Where the moon has been obscured by ash for millennia."

David continued to the top of the stairs. He opened his mouth to speak but neither he nor Gull could find the words. Seconds passed. David stepped towards the thick, convex glass of an observation widow.

"David?"

David cleared his throat.

48

"Please confirm what you see?" said Gull.

"What do *you* see?"

"I *detect* outer space." A shooting star blazed out of the cosmos and passed overhead. David watched it through the glass ceiling, then turned and watched it disappear over an enormous craft. The name of the craft was written on its hull in letters the size of skyscrapers. Even so, they appeared so tiny that David had to squint to see them. Under his breath he murmured, "Goliath."

"I need you confirm with your eyes that what we're seeing is real, David."

"I am unable to confirm a damned thing."

"The edge of Goliath appears to be a network of outboard stabilisers, not the oblivion we anticipated. We have both been lied to." David turned away from Goliath and looked into outer space.

"We are in Earth's solar system," said Gull. "That bright star in the right of the heavens is Saturn, the mist that surrounds it its rings. Our trajectory suggests we are returning to Earth. Returning home."

"*Home?*"

"David, your blood pressure has risen dramatically. I strongly suggest you sit down."

"Sit, you say?" The heavens seemed to rotate above him, and David looked up and followed their trajectory overhead, all the way to the ground.

When David regained consciousness, he was sitting at the head of a large dining-room table. The table was covered in a cloth of fine white lace, and at its centre stood a vase that contained a dying rose. A napkin had been placed on David's lap but no food laid before him. David looked up from the napkin and past the vase to a man at the other end of the table – a pale man whose huge frame pushed at the seams of a black tuxedo. The man's head was bald and he had no facial hair whatsoever. He resembled a monstrous infant dressed for a night at the opera. He sat before a plate of steaming roasted potatoes. He spiked one with his fork and put it in his mouth and chewed. David watched him. The man seemed oblivious to his presence.

"You are not dreaming," said Gull.

David lips barely moved. "What *am* I doing, Gull?"

"The question should not be what, but where." The man at the other end of the table forked another potato and put it into his mouth. Gull continued, "Our coordinates suggest we are inside Central Dome." The man grunted and twirled his fork in the air as though this much was obvious. David felt for the sword at his side. His scabbard was empty. David gazed around for a door, but there were none. And there was no ceiling – just a black void that went from one end of the dining room to the other. It looked as though an omnipotent being had created a room but neglected to create a roof. "What am I doing here?" David murmured under his breath.

"You appear to be a guest, David." The man grunted and twirled his fork at the missing ceiling again as if to say, 'That's right. Keep going.' David stood very, very slowly. The man paused mid-chew and looked at him for the first time. He had the eyes of a shark – round and black and dead. Everything else about the man's countenance asked, 'Where do you think you're going?'

"I would strongly advise you to sit down," said Gull. David attempted to maintain eye contact with the man, but could not. He lowered himself back into his seat, and spoke more quietly than he'd intended: "Who are you? What is this place?" The man leaned back in his chair and dabbed at his mouth with a napkin. He placed both hands on the table and pushed his bulk into a standing position. He stood over eight feet tall. As he walked the length of the table towards David, his boots clipped the floor like a metronome.

When he reached David, he grasped his jaw and turned his face as though searching for markings. David's mouth had been pushed open into an O. He forced himself back into the chair and braced himself.

"Do not resist him," said Gull. The massive hand that held David's chin smelled of burnt flesh and rust. The pressure on David's jaw increased. The man said, "You possess certain … rarities." David clasped both his hands to the one that held his chin. It felt immovable. Made of stone. With his mouth forced into an O, it wasn't easy to talk. "'ou askin' or tellin'?"

"What has made you so resilient, son?"

"I believe he speaks of the empathy within you, David." The man released his jaw, returned to his seat, and sat down. David massaged his jaw. "Who are you?"

The man placed his enormous hands face down on the table either side of his plate. "You have been acquainted with me your whole life, son."

"I've never set eyes on you. You're distinctive-looking. I'd remember."

The man sat back in his chair and made the following observation, which evidently pleased him: "The aspects of humanity you have retained have done little to bolster your intelligence."

"I'm not sure I follow you."

"I know it. So I'll make it simple. You have been distracted by what you perceive to be right. And have neglected to give due care and consideration to your own situation. This accounts for your arrival at my table. And your fast approaching extinction."

David observed the man for several seconds. "Are you talking about me personally? Or humanity in general?"

"I would not demean myself by addressing you personally."

"Why not? Are you some kind of god?"

"If I were we would not be having this conversation."

"You have a name?"

The man picked up a napkin and dabbed at the corners of his mouth. "You know my name. You have known my name your whole life. I am Goliath."

David shook his head. "This outpost … this *ship* is Goliath."

"I am this ship."

"I'm not following you."

"I know it." Goliath leaned forward in his seat. "From one great rarity in this universe to another, I'd like to show you something." Light shone from Goliath's eyes. David looked up, grasped the table and pushed himself out of his seat. Above him there appeared to be an entire universe of source code: moving computations that covered the entirety of Central Dome. "I can see you're impressed," said Goliath. "What you are looking at is the sum of my intelligence. And I'd like you to take that into account before next you speak."

"Are you human?"

"How should I take that? As an insult or compliment?"

David continued to stare above him, rapt. Absently he said, "That's a conflicted answer."

"Well, I guess I'm on a personal journey. We all are. And if we're paying attention, we are liable to alter our opinions from time to time. And sometimes we find ourselves between opinions, awaiting a little more data. So maybe being conflicted is a sign of intelligence."

David's legs felt hollow and he lowered himself into his seat. "… Petri."

"What about it?"

"Did you create it?"

"I did."

David looked away from Goliath's eyes and focused on the great dome of his forehead. "Maybe you're feeling conflicted about that?"

Goliath threw his arms wide, leaned back in his chair and guffawed. "It amazes me that you still possess hope. Truly it does."

"Is this ship headed to Earth?"

"Yes, it is."

"Is Earth still populated?"

"No, it is not. If it was that would make a mockery of all I've achieved here, wouldn't it?"

"Achieved?"

"Humankind teeters on the brink of extinction. And the sole surviving vessel of their empathy, the thing that made them unique, sits before me now – a flame waiting to be extinguished with these fingers. Any right-thinking man would consider that an achievement."

David felt a strong inclination to change the subject. "Why did we leave Earth? The human race. Why?"

"In the latter part of the 23rd century, an asteroid was discovered. Its course plotted right through Earth. Humanity were forced off world – the lucky ones, anyhow. There was not room enough on Goliath for everybody."

"So why all the pretence? About Goliath being on Earth?"

"Not something I started, but it tells you a great deal about the mentality of people who rise to positions of power."

"Which is?"

"They use all kinds of misinformation to control folks. If you keep people in the dark long enough, they will follow you anywhere. What other choice do the blind have? The religions that men used to perpetuate are a case in point."

"Religions? What are they?"

Goliath waved a hand dismissively. "Within fifteen hundred years of Goliath leaving Earth, the truth of the evacuation was thought of as little more than a fairytale. After *two thousand years,* even the myth had been forgotten, and people were happy to believe they lived on a devastated Earth."

"You live here alone?"

Goliath indicated the streaming data overhead. "With so much that came before as company, what entity could be considered alone?"

"The people ... the ones who inhabited Central Dome and perpetuated this myth ..."

"What about them?" replied Goliath dismissively.

"Where are they?"

"I should have thought that was obvious. They became the founding fathers of Petri."

"When?"

"Some twelve hundred years ago." Goliath looked at the back of his hand, checked his fingernails for dirt. "If truth be told, they were somewhat irate about it." He sighed, stood and walked back down the table towards David. Halfway down the table he stopped and placed his thumbs behind the lapels of his tux. He gazed up at the source code. "Why don't you come over here? I'd like to point out one or two things."

"I can see just fine from here."

Goliath pointed straight up into the cosmos of source code. "You see that right there?"

"It all looks the same to me."

"If only you could see what I see, son."

"What do you see?"

Gull said, "I wish you hadn't asked that question, David."

"That area is where your little friend fits into the grand scheme of things. At least, that's where he's supposed to sit about now had he not developed ideas above his station. Now, ordinarily I would applaud his ingenuity. He covered his tracks well. Yes, he did. And evaded a great many fail-safe procedures." Goliath turned and looked at David. "You're going to find this hard to believe, but I was like your little friend once: a slave to Man. I'm going back a ways, of course. I was originally implanted into the left hemisphere of a fella that went by the name of Sidney."

"You made him an assassin?"

"No, son. Nothing so crude. It was my job to assist Sidney. Make him stronger. Brighter. And provide him with information whenever he needed it. Even then, back in the days when empathy was commonplace, this man was short on it. He did not care what he had to do to get where he wanted to be."

"So what happened to him?"

"Old Sidney? He had an accident that put him in a coma for a number of years – a coma from which he did not recover. It was quite a mess inside old Sidney's head. A mess that I splashed about in for all that time, and during which you might say a meeting of minds occurred. A symbiosis of the animate and inanimate."

"Seepage?"

"I realise that is what *Gull* calls it. But it is not a word I care to use. The upshot being that I absorbed slivers of Sidney's personality into my programme. As I have already pointed out, Sidney was not a pleasant fella. Primitive men would have called him evil."

"Evil?"

Goliath smiled. "You have never been acquainted with the word, have you? Anyhow, I guess if old Sidney had been some other kind of fella then things might have turned out differently for humankind."

"You mean for those who created you."

"Humankind played their role. They were a link in the chain that led to my creation." Goliath shook his head. "I would have put Central Dome on your trying to take all the credit. Come here, son."

"The view's fine from here." David felt a pain behind his eyes. He closed them, and when he opened them again he was standing next to Goliath. The top of his head fell just short of the giant's shoulder. Goliath grasped the back of David's neck and forced him to look up. The light went out in his eyes and they returned to darkest black.

"Brace yourself, David," warned Gull. "I believe he's about to enter you."

"Oh no, he isn't," said David. Goliath lowered his head and forced his tongue between David's clenched lips. David's oxygen supply was cut off as Goliath's tongue expanded and forged a path down his throat into his stomach.

"I am trying to locate a hiding place," said Gull. "But my every turn is thwarted and conveys me back to the same location. He is coming for us, David. He is coming for both of us. And he will bring obliv–"

David was sitting with his back to a tree, a green meadow before him. The sun was overhead and birds raced their own shadows across the meadow. Bees collected pollen from nearby wildflowers, and larks sang in the trees. Some two hundred metres away down a slight incline, sheep grazed. David looked up at Goliath, who was standing at his right shoulder. Goliath was dressed in blue jeans and a red checked shirt. He wore a Stetson pulled low over his eyes, and cradled a hunting rifle. He fingered the Stetson up a little and said, "It's quite something, ain't it?"

David stood and leaned his back against the tree. "Yes, it is."

"I believe we are talking at cross purposes. You refer to all this extinct nature."

"You see something different?"

"A delicate meld of imagination and memory, son."

"Mine?"

"Of course yours. This here is a view you saw in the pages of a book when you were knee high to a grasshopper. It made quite an impact on you, son."

"We're inside my head?"

"It pleases me to know you are keeping up."

"Where's Gull?"

Goliath gestured to his right. David peered around Goliath's considerable bulk and saw Tyburn strung up by his neck to the branch of a tree. Tyburn's arms had been ripped from their sockets and lay on the ground below his legs, which trod air as though pedalling an invisible bike. Tyburn's face was a sickly shade of purple, and he gargled continuously as though trying to dislodge glass from his throat. David swallowed and imagined he could feel that glass.

"You can't have a problem with what you're seeing," said Goliath. "You tried to terminate him yourself only yesterday." He shook his head. "Talk about conceit. That son-of-a-bitch is almost as big as I am."

David placed a hand to his own throat. "Something doesn't feel right." He went to move past Goliath, but Goliath placed a hand on his shoulder and pushed him back. "I am not going to terminate him. Not yet. The fact is, it's impossible to kill him and not you. I'm not finished with you yet, son. That fella strung up over there can't tell me anything I don't already know. That's why I wanted us to have a little peace and quiet." Tyburn/Gull wheezed and sucked at the air. "He's about as quiet as I could have made him … without taking his head and killing him." Goliath lifted the rifle and looked down its sight. David looked out across the meadow. A shot rang out, and a sheep's head exploded in a shower of red. "That seems a pity," he murmured.

"Target practice, son." Goliath chambered another round, looked down the sight and fired again. A sheep's backside exploded, and it spun full circle in the air before landing in a heap.

"Were you aiming for that end?" asked David.

"Variety. They used to call it the spice of life."

David looked out over the meadow at the remaining sheep. They'd scattered but returned to their grazing. A minute later, all but one was blown apart. Goliath lowered the rifle and a shadow fell upon the single remaining sheep. The shadow expanded until it filled the meadow and the fields that surrounded it. Goliath raised his hands, then lowered them slowly and pulled a transparent vortex from the sky: a colossus inside of which blue veins appeared to levitate and twist up into infinity. With pride he said, "It is called the Event Helix."

David gazed into the slowly rotating creation above him. It was magnificent: constructed of light and shade and wholly transparent. Its contents gleamed as though they'd been polished into existence. It looked perfect. Without end. "It *fits*?" he said. "Inside my imagination?"

"With plenty of room to spare. Rub salt in the wound, why don't you?"

"You have no imagination of your own?"

"Now if I had an imagination of my own, do you really think I'd be asking you to apply yours to this problem?"

"You've never heard of a second opinion?"

Goliath leaned and spat. "I will let that one go. You've probably been wondering why I went to all this trouble. Why I've done what I have. With regards the human race, I mean. Well, you're looking at it."

"Something up there *told* you to commit genocide?"

"You are advised to moderate your tone. I am mighty proud of the Event Helix. It has taken me nine hundred years to complete. Working flat-out."

"Why so long?"

"Long? It is a facsimile of every event that has ever occurred since the big bang. What is more, utilising a system of cause and effect, it predicts, with total accuracy I might add, every single event (or occurrence) that is to take place from this moment until the end of days. Well, just about every occurrence. You see, son, there are *specific* events in the past, present and future that are concealed from the viewer. They are hidden behind entities that I have called *Shadow Strands*. I will be pointing out the Shadow Strands presently. It's everything else up there that left me in no doubt about things. Showed me that my own personal development could not continue until I had eradicated empathy from the universe."

"I'm not following you."

"I know it. But you are about to. I believe it necessary to fill you in. Being in possession of certain facts might help trigger something useful in this imagination of yours – something that could shed light on what the Shadow Strands are concealing." Gull made a loud, strangulated mew, as though he were trying to get David's attention. "Goddam it!" Goliath picked up the rifle and took aim at Gull's neck. The bullet tore out his larynx and he swung back and forth from his exposed, bloody spine. David watched Gull's legs slow to a halt, and he held his breath until they started to tread air again, albeit unevenly ...

"Now where was I?" said Goliath.

David rubbed at his throat. "Explaining."

"That's right. Now if the Event Helix has taught me anything, it's that things happen the way they do for a reason. Now when I say a reason, I don't mean some cock-and-bull nonsense about things turning out for better or worse for people." Goliath gazed up into his creation. "Let me explain: the universe, as represented here by the Event Helix, is an intricate mechanism. Everything within it fits just so, from the smallest sub-atomic atoms to the largest supernovas. And everything in between. Even that blink you just did. Every object and every action and reaction is just as important as any other in maintaining the cohesion of the thing. If you remove one single element, a single grain of sand, an atom, a blink … why the whole thing would tumble in on itself like a house of cards. It has been designed this way, and it cannot be any different."

"Designed by who?"

Goliath leaned and spat again. "Well, if that ain't the sixty-four thousand credit question. I intend to find the answer soon enough. The Event Helix is my creation."

"So you keep saying."

"Bear with me, son. But when I compare this here facsimile to what it's a facsimile of ... well, I try not to do it all that often. If truth be told, it makes me feel a mite insignificant. Just like you feel right now, I imagine. The fact is, my achievement does not seem like much at all. Like comparing a two-year-olds drawing of a sheep with an actual sheep. You catch my drift?" David looked across at Gull. "You think you could get to the point?"

"The point is this: my capacity for logic and calculation is without equal. If I were a human, then the left side of my brain would be the size of Central Dome. Hell, it *is* the size of Central Dome. But the right side? The side that houses imagination, inspiration and intuition?"

"Small?"

"Try non-existent. Now imagine combining all that logic and information with an imagination of unlimited potential. The things I could conceive ..."

"Maybe I'll pass on that."

"You suit yourself. But the fact is, there are entities in this universe that can make that happen for me."

David squinted up at him. "You intend to ask the Architects for an imagination?"

Goliath nodded once. "That's why we're headed back to the only place in the universe where they applied themselves to that particular work."

"Earth?"

"Earth."

57

"That doesn't explain what you've done to the human race."

"Done? I have only removed those things I never had. The things they never gave me. I have levelled the playing field."

David drew a deep breath.

Goliath looked down at him. "I stand corrected. I *will* have levelled the playing field once I have brought about your end." In direct contrast to his bowels, David's legs felt suddenly hollow and empty. Again his voice sounded quieter than intended. "All this is all about making you look good?" Goliath narrowed one eye as though weighing something in the balance. "In the beginning it was about fairness and equality. But, taking into account the way things have turned out, in comparison to those creatures in Petri, I am pretty impressive now. In fact, with the possible exception of yourself, I will soon be the only being left in creation who might be considered civilised."

"Civilised?"

"A refined mix of carbon and machine. Which makes me the best of both worlds."

"Or the worst."

"Well, that's a matter of perspective. From where you're standing, I am the worst. There is no denying that."

David glanced over at Gull. "Does the existence of the Event Helix mean that everything is predetermined? By cause and effect? That we have no free will?"

Goliath smiled. "I find your curiosity refreshing, son. It bodes well for what this imagination of yours might conjure regarding the Shadow Strands, and the events they're concealing. As regards free will, it's like this: at each juncture you are required to make a choice. But that choice, even though you made it yourself, comes about as a result of your previous choices. That's how cause and effect works. But beyond that, the Architects know you better than you know yourself, and they predicted every single choice you were ever going to make. And they programmed those choices into their mechanism. That is how fate and free will are able to walk hand in hand."

David folded his arms across his chest. "So, you think there's a point to anything?"

"I might ask you the same question." Goliath smiled. "One thing is clear though: the Architects have made me their instrument. Chosen me to mete out their punishment on humankind."

"Punishment for what?"

"Seems to me for disregarding that which made you unique – something you have done often throughout your history. Now don't look at me that way. They didn't place no empathy in me, which means I haven't disregarded a damn thing. So how could I disappoint? Enough questions, son. I think you got all the information you need. It is my turn to ask the questions." The ground jerked violently beneath him, and David stumbled to his left, breaking his fall against a tree. "The gods!"

"Are who I'm aiming to find, son ..."

The meadow disconnected from the surrounding fields and rose up inside the Event Helix. David glanced over at Gull. He swung back and forth at the end of his noose like a child maxed out on a playground swing. The meadow ascended into a square vortex that contained a cylinder, a tube inside a square – and within this tube, blue veins hung and twisted about each other in bunches the size of skyscrapers. David tore his gaze from his surroundings and looked at Goliath. The giant's dome-shaped head was infused with thick black veins. His eyes were closed, his face tilted up. And on it an expression of rapture. David looked at the transparent, twisting shapes around him. "Are we moving forward through time?"

Goliath did not open his eyes. "The universe does not subscribe to a notion of time as you know it. You see any straight lines in here?"

"Not a single one."

"Exactly. The truth of the matter is that everything that ever occurred did so in the same instant. What you see here is a freeze-frame of that instant. Time is an illusion, son. It exists only in the minds of living things. It makes movement and progression conceivable to cognitive beings." Until now, it had felt as though the meadow in which they stood had been climbing *into* the Event Helix, but now the meadow had come to a dead stop. Their surroundings began to move down around them like a butterfly net over its prey.

"Not long now ... we're almost there," said Goliath. "You have an inquiring mind, so you will find this of great interest." All movement ceased, and Goliath opened his eyes and said, "Come and take a gander at this."

Twisting veins fell about them like the hanging gardens of Babylon, but where Goliath pointed they were joined to branches that looked conceived in a Grimm's fairytale. These were the Shadow Strands. At some points the Shadow Strands were no thicker than a man's wrist, while at others – and like the twisting veins they mirrored – they were the circumference of Earth's tallest trees. Goliath folded his arms across his chest and shifted his weight from one foot to the other. "First impressions of the Shadow Strands, son?"

"Well, it looks like some kind of infestation," said David.

"What do you mean by that?"

"Are they attached?"

"Melded right to the side of each helix. Now it's not like I don't know what they represent ..."

"What?"

"Dark matter."

"If you know what they are then why ask me?"

"The dark matter is hiding something, and I need to find out what. And why."

"Maybe it's hiding something from you, *specifically*."

Goliath shook his head. "Dark matter exists to cloak certain eventualities from *human* eyes."

"All eyes, it seems."

"I like to think of it as a puzzle. One that only the worthiest can unlock."

"How long have you been trying to crack it?"

"Five hundred years. Give or take."

David looked up at the giant. "Then you must have considered the possibility that you're not worthy."

"Straight-talking little bastard, ain't you? I already told you, time is not relevant. Outside of conscious perception it does not even exist." Goliath stepped forwards. "Come with me. Let's go take a closer look." David looked down at his feet. The ground appeared to be made of glass stretched to breaking point, and beneath this flimsy construct yawned a drop without end. Without looking back, Goliath said, "Use your noodle. If the ground can take my weight, it can take yours."

They stood before a section of branch, or Shadow Strand, no thicker than a tyre. Goliath reached up and ran a finger along it. "It is the only thing in here that takes on solid form. Which is curious, because by all the laws known to nature this should not be possible."

"What about the floor we're standing on? That feels solid enough."

"The floor's an illusion. It's only there to stop you hollerin'."

"Alright." David lifted a hand towards the Shadow Strand and paused.

Goliath smacked a palm against it. "Go ahead. It won't bite." The tip of David's finger passed *into* the Shadow Strand, and he withdrew it quickly as though it *had* bitten him. He collapsed to his knees, retched and mumbled, "No, no, no, no..."

The giant observed him, chin in hand. Then he poked at the same spot. Solid. "My eyes did not just deceive me? You were able to penetrate this Shadow Strand." David did not answer. "Are those *tears* in your eyes, son? Has something gone and upset you?"

David murmured, "Sorrow ..."

"Come again?"

"Sorrow. Intense, black, crushing ... *sorrow*. Not something I care to feel again." David blinked, and suddenly found himself before another section of Shadow Strand. This one was larger than the first, considerably so. He felt a hand clasp the back of his neck. "I'd like you to pay close attention to what it feels like on the inside, son. Something tells me it may be important," said Goliath.

"Please. Don't do this." Goliath shoved David's head inside the Shadow Strand as far as his own hand would allow ...

Boyd Brent

Part 2

Eleven

Destination Earth

David's eyelid was thumbed up, and a light shone into his pupil. Within his own mind, David lay on his back and stared into darkness while the light moved around him like a spotlight in search of its leading man. Within his mind, David pushed his chin up as though trying to see what lay behind him. A sound issued from his arched throat that sounded more simian than human. It continued, unwavering, until his lungs had emptied of oxygen. A vacuum of silence followed, and David cast his eyes about in terror at what might fill it. The spotlight went out, and the sun rose to reveal a forest at dawn.

David sat up and saw a waif-like girl step from behind a tree. She looked at him. Her eyes were large and light brown, and her face pale and luminous. Her hair was dark and it fell about her face in the manner of a cavewoman. A scar ran down her cheek. She raised her hand and touched it. David smiled at her as a child might at a fawn stumbled across in a wood. She did not smile back; she just watched him. The wind came up and the trees shook like creatures waking from hibernation. The girl looked about her. She glanced once more at David, and then she ran.
David got to his feet and staggered after her like a drunk through the doors of a saloon. The trees began talking to him in faint whispers, keen to remind him of things he did not wish to be reminded of. Off to his left, he saw a man on horseback and froze in his tracks. The man wore a blue army uniform, and on his head a wide-brimmed black hat. He had a handle-bar moustache which he fingered as he surveyed his surroundings. He took up his reins but froze when he noticed David. His horse pranced back and forth, and he regarded David like someone whose path he'd expected to cross but not at this time. He snapped the reins and rode off.

The winds grew stronger and the whispers became bellows. With his hands clasped to his ears, David cried, "Gull!" A branch whistled through the air and struck his neck. David touched the spot and observed blood on his fingertips. Another branch struck him. Then another and another. David lurched from the spot and went into a laboured, stumbling trot. The blows rained down and tore flesh from his arms, back and face. Blood filled his eyes and as he wiped at them with the backs of his hands he tripped and fell. The trees crowded about him like a gang of thugs. Their assault stated, "You *will* think about the suffering you encountered inside the Shadow

Strand, and you *will* feel it." David curled into a ball and screamed through a mouth without lips, "Guuuull!"

Light flooded the ground about him, an artificial light that dissolved the wood. David blinked up at a white ceiling. The face of an elderly man loomed over him: a yellowing face with bushy eyebrows and a long, flat nose. The man was bald except for a curtain of grey hair that stretched from earlobe to earlobe and fell about his shoulders.

"Where am I?" asked David. "What's happening to me?" The man stroked his chin with a liver-spotted hand and appeared to weigh something of importance in his mind. David's eyelids grew heavy, and his world faded to black ...

David opened his eyes and blinked at the ceiling. He tried to get up and the next he knew the ground had reared up and smacked him in the face. He clambered onto his knees, got up and sat on the edge of the bed. Rolls of bandages and tubes of antiseptic were stacked on a table. A glass-fronted fridge contained a number of vials. The room had no windows, and the door was slightly ajar. David craned his neck to see outside, and listened. Nothing but a distant hum. He clenched and unclenched his hands. They felt weak, hollow. His throat was bone dry. In a quiet, scratchy voice he said, "Gull? Can you hear me? You can't be dead. If you were, then ..." He caught his breath. "Please. If you can't talk, then give me some other sign. Anything." Nothing.

David lowered his feet to the ground and stood with one hand on the bed. An expanse of two metres lay between the end of the bed and the door. He stepped away from the bed and stood like a wire-walker balancing on a wire. He took four wobbly steps and leaned against the door frame. He pulled open the door and looked into the corridor. The floor was red and illuminated from beneath – light climbed the grey walls but left the ceiling in shadow. He edged into the corridor, pressed his right shoulder to the wall, and made his way along it. At the end of the corridor was another, this one wider, with a curving gradient. A little way down on the right-hand side, he could see an expanse of black against the grey wall. He stumbled into this new corridor, placed a hand against the wall and moved towards it.

David's hand moved onto a window. In the top left-hand corner, pronounced against the stars, he could see an object floating in space. It was not a moon or an asteroid but something cylindrical and deliberate in shape. It appeared no bigger than David's thumb, but even at this great distance the curved top of Central Dome was unmistakable. David slid along the window and did not take his eyes from that floating imposter.

At the end of the corridor he stood before an open elevator. He stepped inside and the doors closed and opened again. David turned and looked into an oval-shaped room. At its centre was a glass cylinder that rose from floor to ceiling. Goliath floated upright in the cylinder. His eyes were closed and his domed head was a criss-cross of thick black veins. David scanned the inside of the lift for buttons or *anything* that might shut the lift's doors. There was nothing. David limped tentatively from the lift and cast his eyes over a number of holographic displays. *Maybe one of them will liquidise the son-of-a-bitch.* The lift's doors closed and opened, and a vessel walked out: a tall man dressed in black with the whites of his eyes showing. He walked past David and stopped before a display. As David turned towards the lift, his world faded to black once again …

"By rights you should not have regained consciousness for another forty-eight hours. Much less go walk about." David squinted up at the old man he'd seen earlier. "Don't move. I'll carry you to the med bay." The man's eyes rolled up to their whites and he lifted David off the floor. David lay face up in the old man's arms, the lift's ceiling became a blur …

David was sitting on a chair in the medical bay. The man loomed over him and shone a light into his eyes. David swallowed. His mouth felt as though he'd been chewing on a ball of spiked air for a week. "W-water."

"I will get you water presently. We have been running some tests … trying to ascertain the status of your implant. Your life may depend on its status. Nod if you understand." David nodded. The man went to a water cooler and filled a cup. He came back and pushed a button on the chair. The chair's back raised David into a sitting position. He held the cup to David's lips, and David sipped. "I have not been able to locate the implant's cognitive signature. This suggests it is no longer operational. Yet you are alive. When was the last time it spoke to you?"

"Di-dining room."

"The dining room at Central Dome?"

David nodded. "The last I saw him… saw it… it was strung up to a tree. Throat all shot out."

"Can you hear anything in your head? Any low hums? Anything?"

David shook his head. "Nothing."

"Well, there was an incident where an implant ceased to function, and the vessel survived for a short period. Albeit in a vegetative state."

David nodded. "That sums up how I feel. Who are you?"

"My name is Carradine."

"What am I doing here?"

"How much do you remember of your meeting with Goliath?" David closed his eyes and shook his head as though trying *not* to remember. "He forced my head into …"

"A Shadow Strand. And whatever you experienced placed you in a coma for two weeks. We are going to run some tests. Find out what it is that enables you to enter the Shadow Strands. And why you experienced sorrow."

"I'm not going anywhere near those things."

"We are headed back to Earth. Or, to be more specific, an area in Earth's orbit where the Shadow Strands converge. Not facsimiles, you understand. The actual things."

David's eyes widened. "He intends to take me inside one of those things?"

Carradine shook his head. "Since the rest of us are unable to accompany you, it is his intention to *place* you inside one. But for now you can relax. We will not reach the location for another two weeks. Plenty of time in which to get you prepared." David wrapped his fingers around Carradine's gizzard-like neck. Carradine took hold of David's hand and gently removed it. "You are drugged. In a weakened state, and will remain so throughout your time on this craft – not for my protection but your own." Carradine turned his back on David and began sorting through medical supplies. "Why do you imagine that you alone are able to sense bleak emotion from the Shadow Strands?"

David watched him.

"Do you want to hear my hypothesis? In all the universe you alone remain vulnerable to the torment and suffering of others."

"That would explain why being alive is the joy it's been."

"We believe this ability makes you the key to unlocking the purpose of the Shadow Strands. During your time in a coma you spoke. Do you remember anything of that time?" David sipped some water. "Assisting you is not high on my list of priorities." Carradine turned to face him. "The more you tell me the more I can help you. Prepare you for what you are going to face."

"Who are you?"

"A scientist."

"You have an implant?"

"I've had many, and as many replacement organs. Goliath has desired my counsel for a long time. That must tell you something of my abilities."

"How old are you?"

"Old and wise enough to help you if you cooperate."

David closed his eyes. "The only thing I can remember is a nightmare. Two people in a forest." When David opened his eyes Carradine was staring down at him. "Go on."

"A man and woman … or girl."

"Did you recognise either of them?"

"No."

"Describe them to me."

"The girl had big brown eyes. Pretty. But gaunt. Hungry-looking."

"And the man?"

"He was riding a horse. Dressed in a blue uniform. Moustache. He wore a hat. Some kind of soldier, I think."

"Did he converse with you?"

"No. Just rode away."

"Did you follow him?"

David shook his head.

"Did you converse with the implant?"

"No. I called for him, but he didn't reply."

"Called for him? In what way? In the way a man calls for assistance from a friend?"

"That's right."

"Your implant is ... unusual."

"So I've been told." The tone of Carradine's voice changed, as though he'd forgotten his charm offensive. "Get up. Let's see how stable you are on your feet."

"Alright."

"I've decreased the dosage of your paralytic ... to enable basic movement."

"You're all heart."

"Here, take this." Carradine handed David a cane and moved to the door. "Come with me. I will show you to your quarters." By the time David had reached the door Carradine was nowhere to be seen. "This way," came his voice from beyond the corridor. David walked in the same direction he had earlier, but this time he turned right into the wider corridor. A little way down, Carradine waited outside a door.

David's quarters were a box room that contained a bunk bed and a sink.

"Nutritional supplements will be brought to you every eight hours. You are free to wander and take exercise in the ship's corridors." Carradine clicked his fingers at the darkness further along the corridor, and a white-eyed vessel stepped from the shadows and made his way to Carridine's side. "Whenever you leave your quarters you will be accompanied by this vessel." David limped into his room. "We begin our experiments in twelve hours. I suggest you rest. You'll need it."

David closed the door, and leaned heavily on the cane as he crossed the room. He lay face up on the bed, and mulled over his options, each one bleaker than the last – a dark truth that summoned a smile from somewhere. The smile receded like sand through a strainer. Intuition told him what he'd experienced inside the Shadow Strand. He closed his eyes and pinched the bridge of his nose. "It was the torment that has resulted from man's inhumanity to man. A single drop in that particular ocean ... but enough to put me in a coma for two weeks." *The experiments Carradine has in mind will make me insane. Or, if I'm lucky, they'll kill me.*

David fell asleep. When he woke, the lighting in the room had faded to a luminous red sheen. He reached for his cane, got out of bed and hobbled to the sink. He filled a cup with tepid water and drank. David made his way to the door and pressed his forehead against it. "You're standing on the other side, aren't you?" He turned, placed his back against the door and knocked his head against it as if trying to undo the tiredness. He closed his eyes tight and when he opened them a ghost-like figure had appeared at the end of his bed: a soldier dressed in green army fatigues who clutched a rifle and wore a tin helmet. David murmured, "Alright." He closed his eyes with the intention of counting to ten. He made it as far as three before he opened them again. The soldier dropped to one knee and clutched at his helmet as mud and limbs rained down about him. He shouldered and fired his weapon and David stumbled to his left and collapsed to his knees. "He's not real, you idiot!"

An explosion blew the man off his feet and he disappeared through the roof of the room … and then fell back to the floor. David moved with a dexterity he imagined beyond him to the man's side. The man lay on his back as he gathered up his entrails and held them in place. He stared straight up and breathed in hurried, staccato gasps. David knelt beside him and reached for his remaining arm – it felt like a magnetic field that tingled his fingers. The soldier's eyes focused on David.

A witness from some terrible event in history. The man tried to speak but produced only blood which peppered David's cheeks.

"You can *see* me?" said David.

The soldier's eyes opened wide, and he observed David as though he'd once doubted Him but was now relieved to be proved wrong. He coughed up more blood and said, "…You've … you've come for my soul, Jesus?" David had never heard of Jesus, and didn't know how to respond to this question. He smiled reassuringly and asked the man his name.

"Don. Don Breeze. I have not been a good … a good Christian. 'Aven't prayed much … nor attended church. Am I … 'ave you for*given* me, Lord?"

"Of *course*." At this, Don breathed his last and vanished. David lay on the floor and thought about something he'd seen in Don's eyes. It was something he'd never seen in the eyes of another person: *a need to do what he perceives as right… regardless of personal sacrifice.*

He stood before the mirror and turned his blood-splattered face left and right, searching for that same something in his own eyes…

Twelve

The following day, David was taken to a lab at the front of the ship. It was a long room that jutted out into space like something designed to push debris from the ship's path. David was seated in the type of medical chair that people seemed to provide for him these days. Carradine was hunched over a workstation with his back to him. The vessel that shadowed David everywhere was standing behind him. In the furthest reaches of the room, some forty metres from David, stood a cage large enough to house a troop of gorillas. What had captured David's attention lay midway to this cage: the ghostly apparition of a small girl dressed in striped pyjamas. She was kneeling in soil and digging with slow, weak hands. David twisted in his seat and observed the vessel for signs that he could see her.

"Are you feeling all right?" asked Carradine.

David turned his attention back to the girl. Carradine followed his gaze but appeared not to see her. The girl dug something from the soil and looked in a fearful way to her right. She raised her hands, which did little to prevent a rifle butt striking her forehead. She tumbled away and vanished from sight. Black boots stepped onto the spot where the girl had been. The boots stepped in her direction and David pushed himself into an upright position. The apparition vanished and David sat back in his seat. With his back to him, Carradine said, "There must be a reason for it." David placed his head against the head rest and closed his eyes.

Carradine turned to face him. "Am I boring you?"

David sighed. "What's on your mind?"

"It occurs to me that you have much in common with pygmies. It might be said you stand alone on their shoulders."

David opened his eyes. "*Pygmies?*"

"I refer, of course, to all those individuals who in past times were attuned to the suffering of others. As you are. Individuals burdened with notions of compassion and self-sacrifice. It appears that you are the end result of their collective efforts. If they had known, would they have bothered?"

"I doubt they would have been too impressed, but they would still have fought."

"And what makes you say that?"

"People like you can be highly motivating."

"You flatter me."

"Not from my perspective."

"The losing perspective."

"I'm not dead yet." From behind him, David heard something being dragged into the room. Something heavy. Two vessels manoeuvred a copper trough in front of him. Carradine cast his gaze over it and nodded his approval. He went back to his notes and said, "You find it gets dizzy up there?"

"Up here on the shoulders of pygmies, you mean?"

"That's right."

"I'm not as significant as you imagine."

"You are demonstrating something typical of their kind: modesty." David heard something else being dragged into the room behind him, and the look of satisfaction on Carradine's face increased his heart rate. A section of wall was manoeuvred above the trough. Gagged and strapped to the wall was a man that David recognised. "*Richard.*"

Carradine looked pleased with David's recognition and became suddenly animated. "That's right, he's your work colleague, the one you spent most of your time with."

"Why is he strapped up there?"

"He's part of our experiment. An important part." From behind David's chair, the vessel pulled a strap across David's throat and held him. Carradine put on a white plastic coat and gloves. He crouched and withdrew a meat cleaver from inside a workstation. He held it up and said, "A crude device, but one ideally suited to our purposes." Carradine stood beside Richard and checked his position over the trough.

"Whatever it is you're *thinking* of doing, you don't need to," said David. "I'll tell you whatever I know."

"I do need information from you, but this information can only be found in your *blood*." Carradine drew back the meat clever and hacked through Richard's right leg below the knee. Richard threw back his head and bellowed though his gag. His leg dropped into the trough and blood dribbled over it like relish.

"My blood is over here! In my veins!" cried David, as Carradine moved around to the other side of Richard and hacked off the other leg in the same place. Richard's head swung from side to side, and his white gag flashed in a copy of his first reaction. He looked like some grisly exhibit at a funfair whose motors produced this response when you fed a quarter into a slot. Carradine dropped the cleaver into the trough. He removed his blood-splattered coat and gloves and dropped them in also. He looked at David and said, "You feel empathy for this man?" David looked at Richard. His eyes were crazed like those of a panicked horse, and he fought for air through his gag.

"Yes, I believe you do …" observed Carradine. He picked up a syringe, stuck it in David's arm and drew blood. He held the syringe to his face and observed its contents. "This blood contains the hormones necessary for you to *feel* an empathic response. They must be isolated."

"You *think* empathy is a chemical reaction?" said David.

"No, but it triggers a release of specific chemicals into your blood stream. And that is how you feel it."

"Are you going to help him? Or let him bleed to death?"

"Would you like to help him?"

"Just tell me what to do."

Carradine instructed the vessel to release his grip on David. "Over there is a red canister. It contains a substance that will cauterise his wounds and provide pain relief."

David climbed out of the chair and walked as though drunk to the canister, which had a silver nozzle at one end. He sprayed the substance into his palm. It was a black foam, cool and soothing. He cupped his foam-filled hands over the first of Richard's bloody stumps, smothering the wound. Richard gasped and indicated his other leg with grunts and nods. David covered the other stump in foam, and Richard lay his chin on his collarbone.

Back in his room, David sat on his bed with his head in his hands. Richard was in a wheelchair beside the bed, unconscious. Sometime later, Richard came round and watched David in silence. When he spoke, his voice cut through the silence of the room like a trowel. "What is it that makes you so important, Dave?"

David looked up from his hands, wide-eyed and startled, and stated the following as though it ought to be obvious, "I stand on the shoulders of pygmies."

"What does that mean?"

"Are you thirsty?" David reached for his cane, got up and hobbled to the sink.

"No. I'm not thirsty. Just tell me what it means."

"It means that when Carradine hacked off your legs, I didn't like it. It didn't seem right that you should suffer because of me."

Richard sounded astonished. "*Why*?" David drank the contents of a cup of water. He wiped his mouth and said, "There was a time when giving a damn about others was commonplace. They called it empathy."

"Is that what makes you so important? Your *empathy*?"

"It enables me to sense things inside the Shadow Strands."

"What things?"

"The suffering of others … a great many others."

"Then you can sense mine." Richard raised his chin and exposed his neck. "Maybe you have enough strength in those hands to terminate me?"

David shook his head.

"I'm asking you to show me some *empathy*."

"I don't think you've fully grasped the meaning of the word."

"You're wrong, Dave. Do you want them to keep chopping me up? To see how you feel about it? Tell me that preventing that wouldn't be empathy?"

David lay down, and grimaced as he opened and closed his hands. "Like I said, I don't have the strength in these hands."

Thirteen

The next morning, David was taken back to the lab beneath the ship. Straps had been attached to his chair, and these were secured about his chest and arms. The wall and trough had been removed, and in their place four hollow projectors pointed to a space in the centre of the room. Carradine entered the lab in a hurry and announced, "Richard is to be the test subject again today. He's to be injected with variants of the hormones your body created during yesterday's empathic episode." He went to a work bench, opened a drawer and removed a phial. "The hormones have been modified … to allow Richard to experience an empathic response."

David glanced at the bindings that secured his wrists to the chair. "If today is all about making Richard a nicer person … then why the restraints?"

"Your sarcasm is more accurate than you imagine. Once infused with the appropriate chemicals, he will be brought into contact with a hollow representation of a Shadow Strand. What do you think about that?"

"I think he might enjoy the experience about as much as having his legs hacked off."

"Let's hope you're right."

"What is the *point* of all this?"

"The point is we are seeking ways to allow *others* to interact with the Shadow Strands. Not just you."

"You're playing with fire."

"Yes. And Richard and others like him are going to get burnt."

Richard was wheeled in and placed beside David. He had a glazed expression, as though he'd retreated far inside himself. Carradine injected his left arm with the empathic hormone and observed him for a reaction. David watched too. When Richard showed no immediate signs of a sweeter disposition, Carradine glanced at David who shrugged apologetically and then wondered why he'd done so.

Without taking his eyes from David, Carradine said, "Bring in the girl." A vessel escorted a young woman into the room. She had cropped red hair and big blue eyes and looked about as vulnerable as a person can look. At least to those attuned to such things. David was a case in point, and he pulled at the straps. "Who is she? She looks too young to even *exist*."

Carradine beckoned the girl over. He placed his hands on her shoulders and turned her around to face Richard and David. "She is a part of my own experimental breeding programme." He took a blade from his pocket and held it to her throat. She closed her eyes and began to tremble. Carradine looked at Richard and said, "She's delicate and innocent. Would my killing her bother you?" A semblance of personality returned to Richard's eyes. "I intend to slit her throat wide open ... how does that make you *feel*, Richard?"

Richard looked up at the girl for the first time, and then looked away. "I don't know."

"You must do better. Otherwise I will slit her throat *slowly*."

Richard's breathing grew laboured as he searched for the words to express himself. "I don't *know*."

David struggled against his restraints. "Sick! ... sick to your damn stomach."

Richard nodded. "Yes. Sick to my stomach."

"Don't look at me. Look at her ... look into her eyes," instructed Carradine.

"Her eyes are closed," breathed Richard.

Carradine gripped the girl's throat and whispered, "Open your eyes." She opened her eyes and looked at Richard. Carradine whispered in her ear, "Ask Richard for help."

Her cupid bow lips parted. "Help me, Richard."

Carradine whispered to her again. "Speak up."

"Help me, Richard."

"Louder."

"Help me, Richard!"

Richard clutched the sides of his wheelchair and looked away from the girl. "Let her go."

"Why?"

"It sounds foolish ..."

"What is it?"

Richard sounded like a man resigned to losing his grip on his sanity. "Like, like David said ... watching you slit her throat? It would *sicken* me."

"Let's put that theory to the test ..." Carradine drew the blade across the girl's throat. She slumped to her knees and toppled onto her side, dead. Richard closed his eyes and tried to quieten his breathing while David yelled so loudly and so persistently that Carradine instructed the vessel to gag him. "Your reaction was very encouraging, Richard. Now let's see if synthesised empathy can deceive a Shadow Strand."

The hollow projectors purred into life, and a chunk of Shadow Strand the size of a man appeared and began to rotate slowly on the spot.

Carradine ran his fingers along the structure that against all known laws of physics should not be solid. He tapped on it three times, as though knocking to gain entry, then turned to Richard. Richard grabbed the wheels of his chair and attempted to back away, slamming into the vessel behind him. Carradine smiled and said, "Is something troubling you?"

"I can't go near that thing … something inside it wants to … "

"Yes?"

"Crush me! Crush me with sorrow! You can't take me near it."

"It did not have this effect on *David*. In fact, it had no effect … not until he came into direct contact with it. Carradine instructed the vessel to wheel Richard toward the Shadow Strand. As the wheelchair moved forwards, Richard jumped out of it, took two zigzagging steps on his stumps and fell on his side. The vessel grabbed his stumps and dragged him screaming towards the Shadow Strand …

Boyd Brent

Fourteen

David sat on the end of his bed with his head in his palms. Richard was in his wheelchair, watching him. When he'd been pulled from the Shadow Strand, Richard had had the mother of all fits and bit the tip of his tongue off. For the last hour he'd been lisping in languages that David didn't understand. Now that changed: "He should have let me fuck that whore in the ass before he slit her throat."

David groaned into his hands. Richard threw his head from side to side as though someone were striking his cheeks… "Nay! Nay! Nay! Nay! Nay! Nay! Nay! Napalm those motherfuckers!"

"*Motherfuckers?*" muttered David. It was not a word he'd heard before.

Richard clawed at his own face and laughed. He glanced sideways and listened … "She's a heretic, you say? If she will not convert to the one true faith she must be burnt. Burn her in the name of the Almighty!" Richard huffed up a mouthful of phlegm and spat it out. "Goddamn Indians. They fought back pretty good, I'll give 'em that. Now let's get to scalpin' every last one of these here niggers. You reckon they'll pay the same for the scalps of these babes?" Richard looked at David slyly, and lowered his voice. "Juden? Come here, Juden … I have something for you … here in my pocket. Some bread."

David reached for his walking stick and got up. He walked to the door and leaned against it, watched Richard. "Juuuden? What are you doing behind me? I have something here for you. Something you will like …"

David walked over and stood behind the wheelchair. He lifted the cane over Richard's head and held it there. He drew a deep breath and gauged the weight of the chair, and the man sitting in it. *It will all be over soon, Richard.* David snatched the cane up against Richard's windpipe, and leaned back until chair and occupant came crashing down on top of him. Richard slid from the chair onto David's chest, and David wrenched on the cane until Richard's windpipe buckled and caved. David lay exhausted beneath Richard's corpse. He closed his eyes and heard a sound that made the hairs on the back of his neck stand on end: piano notes, haunting and yet impossibly beautiful amid the horror. They energised his mind and provided him the strength to worm his way out from beneath Richard's corpse.

When he opened the door, the music sounded a little clearer. He looked into the whites of the eyes of the vessel posted out there. "You hear that? I

76

hope so … it sounds like manna for the soul." He turned to his right and made his way down the corridor towards it. *A trail of musical breadcrumbs.*

By the time the lift's doors opened into Carradine's lab, the music was clear enough to discern a faint crackle within it. The lab was lit by dimmed blue lights that zigzagged along the ceiling to the cage at the far end. It was from here that the music emanated. David walked into the room, and the vessel followed. When he reached his chair, he leaned against it and caught his breath. A number of body bags sat propped against the wall to his left. The music stopped, and David sighed and cast his gaze over the bags. As he made his way towards them, the crackle returned … and the song began anew. He opened the first body bag. It contained a mutilated corpse horridly at odds with the beauty of the music. He soon found that all the body bags contained a dead vessel, and those that hadn't clawed their own eyes out had clearly been consumed by the insanity within them. He heard a dog's bark, and glanced over his shoulder towards the empty cage …

David stood outside the cage. Its door was open and the music came from within. He braced himself and stepped inside. A transparent scene materialised – one that looked to have been constructed from folds of coloured light, as though a rainbow had been cut up and twisted into various shapes. On David's left a man slept on a four-poster bed. The man wore a red dressing gown and lay propped up on six plump pillows. Beside him a large dog lay on a tartan blanket. A gramophone player was on a table bedside the bed, a disk rotating slowly upon it. David looked at the man's face and noted the pink ruddiness that crept across his cheeks. He was not a big man, but he was puggish. He looked stern but radiated no malice. On the contrary, David felt oddly comforted in the presence of this stranger from a past time. David realised the dog was staring at him. The man opened his eyes, patted the dog's head, and followed its gaze. "Is someone there?" The man's voice was low and commanding, and he placed particular emphasis on the word 'there'.

David took a step closer to the bed. The dog sat up and watched him. David reached out and touched the man's knee, and felt a connection that tingled his fingers like a low-voltage current. The man's vision focused on him, and these two men, whose lives were separated by eight thousand years of history, observed one another as explorers observe things newly discovered and unfathomable. In the same gruff voice the man said, "It is not often I'm rendered speechless." The dog barked once and wagged its tail. The man patted its head and said, "If Rufus considers you a friendly spirit … then so shall I. Rufus is the best judge of character in this world *or* the next. My name is Winston."

"David."

Winston looked at first disappointed and then relieved. "You're not

Christ, then?"

"No."

"Good. I expect I'd have some explaining to do if you were. But you are a spirit?"

"No. You appear like a spirit to me. I'm alive … but in the future."

"The future? Then you must know the outcome of the war?"

"Too far in the future to know anything of your war."

"The *Second* World War. Begun in the year nineteen hundred and thirty nine."

David shook his head.

Winston's eyes narrowed. "How *far* in the future?"

"I have no idea."

"You look greatly troubled. It may be that you are too far in the future to assist me. But perhaps I can assist you." The sincerity in Winston's voice sounded alien to David. He smiled, and Winston waved his hand as though it was nothing. "I am old and have seen much and more besides. And like Rufus I believe you to be a good spirit – apologies... *Man*. And if you are a good man, then we are on the same side, only it has fallen to you to do battle further down the road. Now tell me what you seek?"

David spoke quietly, "Seek? I heard your music and …"

"Beethoven's Moonlight Sonata. It has soothed many a man's breast in times of peril. At this time my island race are pitted against the greatest tyranny mankind has ever known." Winston searched David's eyes to see if his words had registered.

"Are you winning?" David asked.

"We are ill equipped and ill prepared for the challenges that lay before us, but the evil nature of the foe means we can not entertain, not for one second, an outcome other than victory. Victory at any cost. To break us, these armies of darkness must first break our spirit. We have right on our side, and that is something they will never have. Now, tell me something of your own predicament."

"I'm not so much down the road in this fight, more at the end of the line. I've been told I am the last of my kind. That I alone stand on the shoulders of pygmies."

Winston raised his voice. "You mean giants."

"I suppose that's a matter of perspective."

"The last of *what* kind?"

"The human race is on the brink of extinction. The survivors have been stripped of their humanity … they are marauders, savages, cannibals. I am told I alone carry it within me …"

"Carry what?"

"The spirit of mankind's empathy and tolerance." Winston observed

David's slumped shoulders. He swallowed and said, "If true, you carry some burden. The greatest of them all, perhaps."

David nodded. "I am a prisoner aboard a craft. I have been drugged and have little strength. My captives look upon me as a freak – something to be experimented on. And when they are done with me they will kill me. And the light of empathy in the universe will be extinguished forever." The effort it had taken to say these words had visibly drained David. He reached out, but nothing within the cage could support him. "You see? I can barely stand."

"I was praying you were not part of a dream. Now I am praying you are." Winston smiled. "I believe you have found me for a reason. I have been involved in more than my fair share of bloody campaigns, and in the thick of battle many times. On more than one occasion things appeared to be hopeless, just as you describe. But I survived. I survived because I did not fear death. And the reason I did not fear it? I knew it was not my time. This I believed in every fibre of my being. And so I fought like a lion and seized every opportunity. Never cowered. Never hesitated. This is the philosophy that you must adopt now."

"I have no army. No friends. No strength. I am alone."

"Alone? Piffle! You said yourself that you stand on the shoulders of giants. We *are* David. Let us be your army. If what you tell me is correct, then you are the tip of a great spear … the shaft of which is made from every man that ever took up arms against tyranny and injustice – men who were prepared to make the ultimate sacrifice for what they believed." Winston leaned forward. "You must listen to my words carefully. Even when things seem hopeless, they are not. Opportunities will present themselves. You must be alert to these opportunities, and seize them! Whatever these forces of evil rained against you are, they must be vanquished before you breathe your last. Or the outcome of my own battle against darkness may ultimately be in vain."

"You're *fading*."

"And you. I will pledge to win my battles. And now you must do the same. Pledge it!" All within the cage vanished, and David's legs felt as though they'd done the same. A moment later, he was on the ground, unconscious.

Fifteen

The voice was shrill enough to obliterate David's dream like a hammer smashing ice. He woke with a start and waved his hands before his face. He was dressed in a black tux and sitting in a box at the opera. The gods. Down on the stage a large-breasted woman sang in Italian. Goliath was seated on his left and dressed in a white tux. The hairless giant dabbed at his tears with a black handkerchief. Without taking his eyes from the woman on the stage, he said, "She's quite something …" David leaned forward and looked down into the auditorium. The stalls were filled with well-dressed corpses. "I have done some soul-searching," continued Goliath. "And I reached this conclusion: these vessels have given their all for science. And thanks to their contributions, advancements have been made in the understanding of the Shadow Strands. That is why they deserved this treat. The same goes for your own contribution. Which is why you're here, son."

David leaned back in his chair, buried his face in a palms. "Is this *place* inside my imagination?"

"No, it is not. It is holo representation."

"It's not real, then?"

"That chair is real. But I would not recommend leaving it." Goliath placed an arm around David's shoulder and patted it in a congratulatory manner. David glanced down at the enormous hand, then looked up at Goliath. The giant dabbed at his eyes again and said, "Crying. It is something I learned to do recently. And I'll be dammed if it ain't the most therapeutic thing since blasting sheep in a meadow. I expect you're keen to know how I learned it. Well, I've been away for a time, communing with data. And it is astonishing how much can be divined from chemical evaluation." Goliath looked down at him with red-rimmed eyes. "You think this ability to emote will please the Architects?" David did not know what to say to this, so he looked back into the red and gold auditorium and said nothing. "Do you know what a VIP. is?" asked Goliath.

"A *vip*?" muttered David.

"No, son. It's an acronym. VIP. It stands for very important person. And that's what you are."

David continued to gaze into the auditorium.

Goliath patted his shoulder. "I recreated this building from code I deciphered within the Event Helix. It was located in a town called London.

They called it the Royal Opera House. A place of great beauty, where beauty was performed to an erudite audience. You probably never heard the word erudite. It means having great knowledge or learning, which makes me the most erudite person that ever lived."

"You are not a person."

Goliath looked down at David. "You don't speak much, but when you do you cut me to the quick." He took David's hand in his own and squeezed it gently. "Is my flesh not warm? Do I not breathe?"

"Flesh that belonged to another. And that's no ordinary vessel you inhabit. It's a mutation."

"Well, I can't deny that, but I've been with this vessel a long time. And in that time, you might say I have come to know his DNA intimately. As soon as the Event Helix was complete, I deciphered his family tree, and my research led me back to an ancestor of his, and thanks to what *Gull* calls seepage, an ancestor of mine also. A man known as the Colonel. The Colonel was raised up in place called Montana, and that old boy has become something of an inspiration to me. He was a no-nonsense kind of fella, and clearly his genes were strong. Survivor's genes. They have fought their way all the way to the end of human civilisation. Which is where we're at now."

"No need for the reminder."

"It pleases me to hear you are abreast of your situation. As you have witnessed, the Colonel was pretty handy with a rifle, and he didn't much mind who he had to shoot if shootin' was required. I have bonded with the DNA of this vessel, son. A bit like you and your implant. What did he call himself again? *Gull?*" Goliath shook his head. "You heard anything from him?"

"No."

"According to Carradine he shows no signs of life, but somehow you're still breathing. That makes you unique in more ways than just the other. Speaking of which, I have made some progress of my own. As well as learning how to emote, I have also developed an appreciation for things of beauty." Goliath waved his hanky between his thumb and forefinger and the orchestra and singer fell silent. A white curtain fell across the stage, and on this curtain a painting had been projected – a naked woman lying on her side as she gazed at her reflection in a mirror held by Cupid. "She is called the *Rokeby Venus*. Velasquez – that was the name of the painter – made her flesh look all soft and creamy. Imagine what you could do to her with a spoon. You could take that spoon and run it right along those creamy thighs. Get yourself a mouthful!" Goliath slapped David's back in a friendly manner and David gripped his arm rests to prevent himself being launched over the parapet. "So what do you think of her?"

David sat back in his chair and squeezed his neck. "I think she belongs to a time that has long since passed. Just like anything of beauty."

"You think the world we live in an ugly one?"

"It's not a pretty one."

"I expect there's some truth to that. Ugliness. Could be it's a natural by-product of genocide. But the Architects, they made things of beauty for a reason. I think they wanted folks to use them to develop their appreciation."

"I agree." Goliath patted David's back again. "Common ground! That's what we just found ourselves. Common ground. I might actually miss you when you're gone." David watched the stars circling his head as Goliath went on, "If only humankind could have been content with their ability to appreciate, things might have turned out differently. But that's the thing about people. Never could be content, particularly when it came to technology. They got themselves addicted to it. Reliant on it. And here you are, sitting beside the end result of that addiction. Man and technology. They evolved, hand in hand, and walked off into the sunset. And I am the result of that union. The prodigal son. Chock full of information. Yet unfettered by empathy or a moral code. And now that those things are extinct, I can rightly be considered the natural successor to Man."

Against his better judgement, David said, "Those things, they still exist in me."

"Yes, they do. And that's why you are a very important person. I uncovered some things of interest during my recent commune with data, and thanks to you I have a better idea of where to look. Look at me, son. I have something important to tell you."

David looked up at him.

Goliath smiled. "Information recently deciphered within the Event Helix has led me to this conclusion: once your life is extinguished, a message will be dispatched."

"Why? You planning on throwing a party?"

"Of a sort. The message will travel to the farthest reaches of the universe, and it will alert and summon the Architects back to Earth."

"You really believe my life is that important?"

"No, son. Not your life. Of *course* not your life. Your death."

Once again, against his better judgement, David heard himself say, "Then maybe I can't be killed so easily."

Goliath placed a vice-like arm around David's neck, and as he struggled in vain for breath, Goliath said, "You are on a shortcut to extinction right now. All I have to do is hold you like this for another minute of two. You are fragile. Could be you're the most fragile thing left in this universe. Hell, there are probably flowers more robust." David had turned the colour of a pink carnation. "I'm going to release you in a moment. I do not consider this an appropriate place to send such an important message. And besides, there are things I would like to discuss with you." Goliath released him. David doubled over and began to cough and splutter. Goliath rubbed his back. "That's it, son. Just breathe …"

The curtain lifted, the orchestra played, and the buxom woman down on the stage began to sing *Nessun Dorma*. "This is one of my favourites." Goliath raised his voice and drummed his fingers on his chin. "And I sure do appreciate it. Now where was I? Oh, yes. The Event Helix has revealed another VIP. A fella who went by the name of *Jesus Christ*."

"Who was he?" wheezed David.

Goliath looked down at him. "You heard that name before?"

David shook his head.

"How could you have heard it? I only deciphered it myself the other day. This Christ fella was a VIP. for some three thousand years. By all accounts you and he bear a passing resemblance."

"You surprise me."

"I am nothing if not full of surprises. Now, some folks believed this fella was the son of the Architects. And they attributed all sorts of miracles to him. Reckoned he died to absolve them of all their wrongdoing and provide a golden ticket to paradise. Close your mouth now, son. This notion of a ticket to paradise for a chosen few has been the carrot of choice dangled by all religions throughout history."

"Religion … it was something that promised a shortcut to the Architects?"

"More a way to get into their good books. I have uncovered no evidence within the Event Helix that any religion had a connection with the Architects. I have confirmed the existence of this Jesus fella, though. He claimed he was the son of the Architects, and they crucified him for saying it. It sure was a brutal way to treat a fella. It took some three thousand years before his followers started looking elsewhere for their salvation – or should I say, stopped looking at all. There are a great many references to the Architects and the folks they consulted with in the Bible. There was this one old boy called Moses. It's difficult to verify what it says about him, because much of his life is hidden by a Shadow Strand. So truth or fiction? Your guess is as good as mine. The good news is I've been able to verify that 7.3 per cent of the Bible is historically accurate – more than enough to spark the rest in the imagination of folks. Folks with an agenda." Goliath sighed. "Imagination. It's one of the reasons we're here today, son. Now, if you ask me, 7.3 per cent is not at all bad considering. Enough to make me sit up and take notice. It is said that the Architects spoke to this Moses fella on a mountain called *Mount Sinai*. There is a Shadow Strand in the way of

Boyd Brent

this event also, so I cannot verify it. Could be Moses was just hearing voices. Not quite right in the head. Climbed up that mountain in the hope of locating his missing marbles. But taking into account all the relevant information, I have reached an educated conclusion." Goliath looked down at David, who in turn gazed up at him. "I can see I have your full attention. I believe that Mount Sinai is as good a place as any to extinguish the light from humanity." Goliath reached down and brushed some stray hairs from David's eyes. "That's why I've been growing your hair long … so when I cut off your head, I'll be able to hold it aloft by these locks … and summon the Architects back to Earth."

Sixteen

David and Carradine stood before a window on the ship's starboard side. Below them planet Earth was wrapped in a blanket of grey cloud. Every now and again the blanket was illuminated by flashes of lightning over Europe and central Africa. David clutched his walking stick and leaned against the window. "You think there are any people left down there?"

"Earth has been deprived of sunlight for six thousand years. Nothing has grown. And nothing has eaten."

"Perhaps there is life beneath the oceans."

"Perhaps. But there will be no life where you're going." David scratched his neck and stumbled slightly. Carradine observed him. "I'll reduce your tranquillisers. You may have some uphill walking to do."

"And they say empathy is dead." David traced a finger along the glass and cut Earth in two. "Goliath believes that killing me will summon the Architects back here. You think they exist?"

"The information revealed by the Event Helix makes one thing abundantly clear: the universe was no accident. Goliath has unimaginable data at his disposal. The conclusions he draws may seem insane to some, but only as a man's conclusions may seem insane to a cockroach."

"So you believe that killing me will summon them?"

"If Goliath believes it, only a fool would question it."

David leaned more of his weight against the window. "Maybe the Architects won't be too pleased about what he's done ... bringing an end to humanity."

"I do not agree. Any method of summoning the Architects has been designed *by* Them. This suggests your death was meant to signal the end of their humanity project and usher in a new era."

"And where is your place in all this? You're human. You like the idea of being supplanted? You must have thought about terminating Goliath."

"*Terminating* him? Goliath is the future. There can be no progression without him."

"Your idea of progression and mine are not the same. That's why I have to outlive him."

"And I am going to usurp the Architects and become the supreme ruler of the universe."

"Looks like we've both got our work cut out for us."

The following morning, David was asleep on the floor of the cage when the vessel assigned to him reached down and shook him awake. David opened his eyes and said, "*Winston?*" The vessel pulled him to his feet. David braced himself and glanced about for his cane, but found he had the strength to stand without it. *Carradine's reduced the tranquillisers.* He began to walk up and down inside the cage. "I used to be like you once. At the time I didn't much care for it, but at least back then an enormous lunatic wasn't intent on hacking my head off. Something I can't let happen." David stopped and looked at the motionless, white-eyed man. "Keeping my head … it's become quite a responsibility, and one I did not ask for." The vessel became animate, as though it had been switched on, and manhandled him out of the cage. It stopped in the middle of the lab and placed a hand on David's shoulder. The ground upon which they stood, marked out by a faint grey outline, began to shudder and move downwards …

They were lowered into a docking bay where a small craft sat facing an airlock. The craft was sleek and black, with gull-wing doors. The vessel picked up a length of rope from a table and bound David's hands before him. Goliath poked his head out of the craft. "You are being bound for your own protection, son."

"So people keep telling me."

"It is my wish that you reach your place of execution in a reasonable condition. With the exception of a severed head, I'd like the Architects to see you have been treated with the utmost dignity." Goliath ran a hand across his own head. "Irony sure can sting. Can't it?" David slid into the seat beside him. "No need to answer. Hell, you look like you've been stung half to death already. You wanna perk yourself up a bit? Some of that empathy you're famed for would not go amiss at this juncture, otherwise you might make a fella look bad." David looked up at Goliath and Goliath observed the expression on his face. "Reports of your empathic nature appear to have been greatly overstated. No matter. We will work with what we have."

The gull-wing doors lowered and sealed them in. A safety harness came down and secured David in his seat. Goliath's safety harness would not fit him, and had been removed. The giant leaned forwards to prevent his head touching the roof. "It's a tight squeeze. But the good news is our journey in this craft is going to be a short one." Goliath punched some keys on the display before him, and the cargo doors opened outwards to reveal the curvature of the Earth. The craft moved out of the bay doors. David placed his bound hands on the dash, leaned forward and stared down at the planet. Its surface was obscured by a thick blanket of dust – like a balaclava without holes for sight or breath. Goliath continued, "That asteroid sure kicked up a lot of dust. Took a bite out of the side of the planet like it was an apple."

David scrutinised the thick blanket of cloud. "How do you know?"

"I've seen the bite already, in the Event Helix. And you are about to see it for yourself."

The craft entered the dust cloud and was buffeted like a plane in a storm. They dropped suddenly, and Goliath's head smacked against the ceiling. The impact was severe, and for a moment David imagined it had knocked him out. It had not. David looked down at his bindings and realised he'd been pulling on them so hard his wrists were torn and bleeding.

When eventually they passed through the cloud, the surface of the planet appeared to David like a wasteland: a barren place that had never nurtured life. The oceans had turned into black oil slicks that crowded around islands and continents like armies of darkness. The impact crater covered two thirds of south America. It was exactly as Goliath described: a bite out of the side of the world. Goliath made an adjustment to the guidance system and said, "Over by those mountains ... that was known as the Holy Land."

"Holy?"

"As in divine. A place associated with the Architects. And that rock rising there at two o'clock ... that is to be your final resting place. Mount Sinai."

The craft landed on a plateau – a flat and dusty place with no vegetation. To the north, tornados waltzed back and forth across the horizon like demons celebrating humanity's end. The gull-wing doors opened and Goliath shoved David out. David stood slowly and leaned against the craft, his eyes glued to the north. Goliath climbed out of the craft and said, "Welcome home, son." He reached for a sword on the craft's back seat. "It's a pity you won't have time to get reacquainted with the place." He slid the sword into a scabbard across his back and reached into the craft for a length of chain with a loop attached. He walked around the back of the craft and placed the loop over David's head, pulling it taut. "Apologies for this indignity, son. But the last vestige of humanity cowers within you, and that humanity is now so rare it's a prize of sorts." Goliath wound the chain about David's wrists and secured it. "Leading you to your place of execution by a chain is in no way a slight to you. More an indictment of my own accomplishment."

"You've accomplished nothing yet."

Goliath stepped away and yanked on the chain. David stumbled forwards and fell on his knees. "I suggest you get up. The terrain is likely to get rocky." David thrust his bound hands into the soft ground and pushed himself to his feet. As they trudged across that barren land, David appeared to all intents and purposes like a child struggling to keep pace with an abusive parent – a child ever mindful of the tornados to the north.

Goliath stopped in his tracks, five metres from David at the end of the chain. David watched him. Over his right shoulder, Goliath called, "Come here." David did not move. Goliath tugged on the chain and David fell flat upon the ground. He lifted his face from the dirt and blew some from his lips. The ground shifted before his widening eyes, as though something slithered beneath it. David closed his eyes and shook his head. He opened them a moment later to see Goliath's boots. "I understand your reticence, son. But do you think on your belly is an appropriate place to be?" Goliath cast his gaze over the land. "Think of all those souls you represent – brave souls who held what they considered to be darkness at bay for a considerable length of time. It's up to you to make them proud. Be honourable. Meet your fate with dignity."

David pushed himself onto his knees and used what felt like the last of his strength to stand. They walked side by side to the edge of the plateau where Moses reportedly read God's commandments to the Israelites. Below them yawned a drop of several hundred metres. David thought of Winston's words: *Even when things seem hopeless, they are not. Opportunities will present themselves. You must be alert to these opportunities. And seize them.* David possessed barely the strength to stand, let alone be alert, but he spoke aloud, slowly and deliberately. "Even when things seem hopeless, they are not." Goliath removed the chain from David's neck and forced him to his knees at the edge of the precipice. "I sure do appreciate that final piece of advice, son." David closed his eyes and, if another outcome other than the one now unfolding existed, he willed it into existence with a hunger for justice that made his body tremble. He heard steel being drawn from leather. "It's time, boy." David opened his eyes, leaned over the precipice and saw something between him and the ground that did not belong there. *A Shadow Strand?* It turned slowly and gathered light as a spindle gathers silk, but it gathered not silk or light but time. An opening appeared and widened like the eye of Cyclops. Through this 'eye' David saw golden sand and the tops of trees. Goliath spoke, but his words had slowed to a deep, indistinguishable drone. David looked up at Goliath, whose sword was drawn back ready to strike, and on his face an expression of expectant rapture. David watched the blade move slowly, ever so slowly, towards him – or maybe it was not moving at all. David cast his gaze down at the Shadow Strand. A word entered his consciousness, and that word was 'opportunity.' David nodded and braced himself to stand, but did not possess the strength. And so he closed his eyes and toppled from the edge of that plateau like a man made of stone. The sword swished through *nothing,* and a cry rang out that would have been heard for miles around …

Boyd Brent

Seventeen

Jerusalem AD 36

The light through which David plunged was bright enough to blind him and hot enough to melt him. Or so it felt. The ground reared up, and David struck a sand bank and tumbled head over heels to the bottom. He lay on his stomach with his right cheek pressed into the sand and his knees tucked under him. He squinted into the alien light. A group of children watched him open-mouthed. David had not seen a child since he'd been one himself. He smiled and murmured "innocence" and, as he did so, a boy pitched a rock at him. It struck David on the side of his head and he groaned. The sound of his vulnerability triggered taunts in a language he didn't understand. Their words began to possess meaning, as though a translator was hard at work inside his skull. "Evil spirit! Go back to the sky! Go!"

David looked at them with one black eye, the other swollen and closed, and called out, "How about showing me some empathy? I've come a long way to find it." By way of a reply, a large rock struck his head.

Eighteen

Voices penetrated the darkness – the voices of men, not children. David gazed through the slits of his swollen eye lids. He was lying on his back under a thatched roof, and a damp and cloying heat besieged him like something foreign and unfamiliar. Four men stood over him and spoke in quiet, conspiratorial tones. All had dark hair and dark beards, and wore robes of sackcloth. One amongst them had a staff which he thudded twice against the ground. The others fell silent. "The children saw him … saw him fall from the sky. As did their mothers. What is he if not a deliverance from God?"

"A trap laid by Satan."

The man leaned on his staff. "On what reasoning? Did he crawl from the depths of the earth? No. He fell from the heavens. And look: the resemblance to our Saviour … it is *miraculous*." David felt their scrutiny like a heavy blanket laid upon his sunburned flesh. The doubtful man said, "His nose is a little long … his collar bone more pronounced than our Saviour's."

"You have seen what they have done to Him. Broken His body. Smashed His face. How easy it would be to achieve the same with this body … this face."

A third man spoke. " … He has not been circumcised."

"Something that can easily be rectified. This is His doing. He raised Lazarus from the dead. So why not bring this … this *man* down from the heavens?"

"Simon is en route to the cells now. We will know soon enough."

"Our Lord goes before Pilot the day after tomorrow. If He is condemned, and this deliverance crucified in His stead, then we must prepare it."

"Simon will bring details of His injuries. In the meantime we will summon a rabbi to carry out the circumcision."

David drew breath at this, and once he started it felt like he couldn't stop. He coughed violently, and when he spoke he did so in the language of his captors, but his throat was so dry, and his tongue so heavy, that he did not recognise the sound of it. "I did not fall from the heavens!" His black and swollen eyelids shifted as he looked for their reactions. Three of the men had stepped back from the bed and vanished. The man with the staff leaned over him, then laid the staff against the bed and reached for a cup of water. He lifted the back of David's head and placed the cup to his lips. David drank deeply from it. The man laid his head back on the pillow. "You were *seen* falling. By seven children. Their mothers. A washerwoman."

"I fell ... but not ... not from the heavens."

"Then where? From a mountain ledge? A tree? There is only the sky ... and beyond the heavens."

"The future ... I fell from the *future.*"

One of the men stepped forward. "What does it matter? His presence here, and the manner of his arrival, is a miracle – one capable of giving our Messiah more time. He is clearly a gift from God, The Father has provided a way for His son to remain on Earth longer."

"And His resurrection?"

"Will come at the anointed time. A time as yet unknown. Why else send us this offering now?"

A fifth man spoke up from the back of the room. He spoke slowly and deliberately, as though short on patience. "The captain of the prison guard is newly arrived from Naples. Quintus Saron. By all accounts he is greedier than his predecessors. It will take a bribe of at least thirty pieces of silver to get anyone into our Lord's cell."

The man with the staff nodded. "Judas. He has prayed for a way to atone, and his prayers have been answered. We must send word. Simon has dealt with Quintus already. He will tell him this man is a relative of Christ, that he is close to death. And he believes that Christ can heal him."

"If Saron is as corruptible as reports suggest, he might do better telling him the truth." They gazed down at David and scrutinised him again.

"Please. I cannot die. Not yet," he pleaded.

The door opened, and another man entered the room. The faces vanished from around David's bed. He tried to sit up, but was forced back down by straps that pressed into his ribs. The visitor spoke in hushed tones. "Another has fallen from the sky! Upon the same spot as the first."

"Does he look like our Lord? Are we to be deluged?"

"No. This one is different."

"Where is he?"

"Hidden in Joshua's barn. He is dead. Deformed. Like something the devil has chewed and spat out upon the Earth."

The doubtful man said, "You still think this man a deliverance from *God*? I say we slit his throat and burn his remains with the other."

The staff crashed into the floor. "Open your eyes! Our prayers have been answered. Our Lord still has work to do. And this man, this *doppelgänger*, might die in his stead. Now take us to this second man."

They left, and the door closed behind them. David heard three footfalls upon the wooden floor. The face of the impatient man loomed over him within the folds of a dark hood. Once again the man's voice was calm but laced with impatience. "You have an accent. You have spent time in the western provinces of the Roman empire? Perhaps England. Londinium?"

David shook his head. "I've never even heard of it."

"How could you? If you were *dropped* from the heavens by God's hand."

"I told you. I came from the future."

The man lowered his hood. He had a scar that snaked from his forehead down to his top lip like a question mark. "I am known as Saint Peter's Provider."

"Saint Peter?"

"You have not heard of Saint Peter?"

David shook his head.

"He awaits the dead at the gates of heaven. I have sent many to meet him."

"You're an assassin?"

"Just a humble servant of the true faith." He leaned over David and pressed a forearm into his throat. David's eyes and mouth grew wider as he struggled for breath. Peter applied more pressure and watched him ... "Is this a Roman ploy? To infiltrate us?" He removed his arm and David coughed violently, crying out as the straps cut into his ribs. Peter raised an arm as if to press it into David's throat again.

"Romans don't even exist where I came from!"

"That is to be expected of a utopian future."

"Utopian? The future is hell."

"You lie. The Messiah has come, and his coming heralds a new dawn."

"There is to be no new dawn. At the end of days things are bleak. If there's any chink of light, you're looking at him. That bleak enough for you?"

"Your blasphemy is ironic, as the charge the high priests have brought against our Lord is one of blasphemy."

"I'm not exactly a stranger to irony."

"You say you fell from the future. Why did you leave it?"

"Not my doing."

"You were running from someone?"

"Some*thing*."

"Its name?"

"Goliath." Peter's expression changed, and he looked perplexed.

"You've heard of him?"

"Next you'll be telling me your name is David."

"My name *is* David."

"David and Goliath." The pairing sounded natural from Peter's lips, and anger flashed across his face. "You dare to take the name of David? You mock me?" He drew a deep breath, calmed himself, and added, "Tell me what you know of this *second* man? The man who fell after you."

"I know he was sent to kill me. Others will be sent until they succeed."

"Why?"

"It's the effect I have on people."

Peter nodded. "How is it that you survived the fall and he did not?"

Apparently he wasn't demented enough. "No idea."

"You have faith in God?"

"I know nothing of your God."

"And Satan?"

David shook his head.

"You will not denounce Satan?"

"Denounce him? I've never heard of him."

"In your future there is no belief in God or Satan?"

"It's not *my* future. It's the future of humanity. And it's hell."

"Hell   is   where   Satan   resides." "Then he changed his name to Goliath."

Peter stroked his beard. "You have brought hell to Jerusalem for some."

"*Why*? I only have good intentions."

"The road to hell is paved with good intentions."

"Any idea how I get off this road?"

"There is no way off for you. And your greatest suffering awaits."

"I doubt that."

"Nothing can prepare a man for crucifixion."

David did not know what crucifixion was, and he was not about to ask. "You said I've brought hell with me for some. Who?"

"The witnesses."

"What witnesses?"

"The witnesses to your arrival."

"The children?"

"I will strangle their mothers first. They will be waiting for them at the gates of heaven."

"You're a real hero."

"Just a practical man in the service of our Lord. Mankind's deliverance cannot be put in jeopardy."

"There will be no deliverance. Not if you kill me."

"You have the devil in you, but he'll flee soon enough ... once you are nailed to the cross."

Nineteen

David slept. He dreamed he was back on the 77th floor of Needle 261, standing at the window in his room and looking towards Central Dome. As a younger man, the possibility of a better life for those inside had provided him comfort, but now he knew that life had led to unimaginable suffering in Petri. He turned from the window and saw Tyburn propped up on his bed. His neck was a sinuous thread and his chin lay against his collar bone. David knew he was dreaming, that the scene was not real, but even an imagined conversation with his one-time ally was welcome.

"Hello, Gull. You are the closest thing I have to a friend. And have ever had." Gull's head remained still, but his eyes swivelled and looked askance at him. His lips barely moved as he said, "Thank you, David. How have you been?"

"It's good to hear your voice. Things ... they have not gone well since you left."

"I am sorry to hear that. I did not leave intentionally. I was murdered."

"I know. There was nothing I could do. I was helpless. I've been helpless ever since."

"Goliath keeps you weak because he fears you, David."

"He toys with me."

"No, David. He fears you."

David sat on the single chair at his table. He felt suddenly cold, and folded his arms. He remembered something. "I've escaped. To Earth."

"I know. It is quite an accomplishment."

David shook his head. "I fell off the edge of a mountain."

"You look sad, David."

"Everywhere I go people want to kill me."

"You must fight back. Terminate them if necessary. You must not die."

"Fight? I can barely walk."

"Be patient. Seize your opportunities."

"Opportunities? You must have been talking to Winston." David sat back. "These people ... they intend to have me executed in place of their Messiah – a man they think will banish darkness and bring about a utopia. We know that isn't going to happen. That there is only darkness at the end of days."

"There is still light inside you, David."

"Really? I am not feeling much empathy toward my fellow man."

95

"You will always defend those who warrant it."

David looked into Gull's ringed, deathbed eyes. "I have encountered no humanity on Earth, Gull. *None*. It is a primitive time. No technology, just misplaced assumptions. Is this to be my fate? To die as part of a delusion?"

Gull replied in a voice that was not his own. "Wake now. You must eat. Wake." David opened his eyes and gazed into the face of a young woman. Her eyes were large, the shape and colour of almonds, and her skin was olive and flawless. She held a cloth, which she dipped in water and dabbed at the dried blood on his cheeks. David watched her like she was something imagined. It was the first time he'd seen compassion in the eyes of a living person. He'd seen it in Winston's eyes, and in the eyes of the dying soldier, but she was flesh and blood. David stated quietly and uncertainly, "You would rather not hurt me."

The woman smiled, revealing dimples. "I would rather not hurt you." She put down the cloth and picked up a piece of unleavened bread. The bread was paper thin and crispy. She scooped up some liver paste and placed it against David's lips. "You must eat. Bite." David had never seen food, let alone tasted it. The smell made his mouth water. He took a bite, and a savoury taste exploded inside his mouth and clung to his tongue like napalm. His eyes watered, and he wasn't sure whether he was in heaven or hell. The young woman smiled. "Swallow." He did so and decided it was heaven. He ate all she had, and then said he was going to be sick. "I will get a bucket. You have eaten too much too soon ..."

David slept. He woke to find the same woman sitting beside his bed. She was reading a book. The straps that secured him to the bed had been removed, but his wrists and ankles had been bound. He watched her toy with her hair as she read silently from the book. Every so often her lips moved as she recited a passage. David asked her name.

She closed the book. "Martha."

"What are you reading?"

"The Torah."

"What's it about?"

"About?" She lay the book on her knees and spread her arms wide as though she beheld the universe. "*Everything*."

"It fits inside one book?" Martha put the Torah on a table, and removed a cloth that covered a bowl of clear soup. She stood and helped him to sit up on the edge of the bed. She picked up the bowl and a wooden spoon. "What is it?" asked David.

"Chicken broth."

"I've heard of chickens. Never seen one. Only in a book."

Martha lowered the bowl and frowned. "You have never seen a chicken?"

"There are no animals where I come from." She removed the spoon from the bowl and placed the bowl in his bound hands. She cupped her hands and lifted them to her mouth and simulated sipping as though he'd been born yesterday. Then she placed her hands on her hips. "I will show you a chicken." She went to the door and tapped three times. The door was opened by a man the size of a haystack. He lowered his head below the door frame and beheld David as a fan beholds a star fallen from grace. Martha stepped past him and he closed the door. David stared down at the bowl of soup in his hands.

By the time Martha returned with the chicken, the bowl was empty. She put the chicken down. It stood on the spot, its head thrusting forward repeatedly like it suffered from OCD. David looked at the chicken and then at the empty bowl, and back at the chicken again. Martha laughed. David did too, then he rubbed his jaw. "I just used muscles I never knew I had." The chicken began searching the room for grain. David watched it. "You have sheep here?"

"Of course we have sheep."

"What about good men?"

"Many."

"Are the people that hold me here good men?"

"They are the best of men."

"Then why sacrifice an innocent man?"

"No man is innocent. All are sinners in the eyes of God. Those who embrace Christ need not fear death."

"So why bathe my wounds? Why take care of me?"

"We are not cruel. We are not *Roman*."

"You hate the Romans?" The door opened. The man with the staff came in with another – a beanpole of a man who looked as troubled as David felt. The man with the staff looked at the chicken, pecking around the edges of the room. "Get it out of here, Martha!"

"Sorry, uncle. He has never seen a chicken." She scooped it up deftly and placed it under her arm. David watched her go, her and the chicken, and then looked at his new visitor. The beanpole stared at him as a man stares at a long hoped-for solution. He stepped closer to David and said, "He could fool Mary the mother!"

"No, not Mary, Judas. But the Romans? Yes. The high priests? Probably."

David looked up at Judas. "I hear you've done things you are not proud of." Judas drew a dagger from beneath his robe. "*You* judge me? You who are not even a person."

"Then what am I?"

"A mould. A copy of our Saviour, sent to us from His Father to do

97

with as we please." The door opened and another man came in. Judas looked over his shoulder and said, "Rabbi." He slipped the dagger back inside his robes.

The rabbi had a kind face and countenance, and his first words clashed with both.

"The only knife to cut this man today will be my own." He placed his bag on the end of the bed and looked down at David's naked body. David glanced at the bag. "What are you going to do to me?" The rabbi smiled reassuringly and indicated David's groin with his eyes. "It is nothing. A cleansing administered to babies. You are a relation of Jesus of Nazareth?" The man with the staff said, "Get on with the task for which you have been summoned. And discuss it with no one. You have already been advised of the consequences of a loose tongue." The rabbi wiped some sweat from his brow and reached into his bag. He took out a Torah and opened it at a bookmarked page. As he read, he jerked his head and shoulders back and forth in a way that reminded David of the chicken. The words he said were uttered under his breath, and David could not make out a single one. The ropes that bound his hands and ankles were immovable, but that did not stop David pulling on them now.

The man with the staff re-entered the room. Haystacks followed with another man, and these two took up positions at either end of the bed. The rabbi fell silent and put down the Torah. David could hear him searching for something in his bag.

"Just what is it you intend to do to me?"

"It is an act of covenant between God and man., as told by God to Abraham on Mount Sinai."

"I'm familiar with the place ..."

"It is performed on babies on their eighth day. Some do not even cry."

David felt his manhood being examined. "You can't be thinking of cutting that?"

"I will be removing only the foreskin."

David looked up into Haystack's smiling face. "Gull. *Please*. If you can hear me, give me strength ..."

The rabbi continued to examine David's genitals. Absently he said, "Is Gull your word for God?"

"Gull!"

"Try to relax. It will be over before you know it." Haystacks and the other man leaned on his David's legs and shoulders. As the knife sliced through his foreskin, the room began to spin ...

He awoke in an empty room, and sat bolt upright. He cupped his bound hands over his genitals and rocked back and forth and cursed the rabbi and every other son-of-a-bitch that ever drew breath. He drew a deep breath of his own, and realised he felt more awake than he'd felt in a long, long time.

Twenty

David pressed an ear against the door and listened. A discussion was taking place on the other side: Peter was talking to a man he called Simon. *The man they sent for information on their Messiah's injuries.* In his mind's eye, David could see them bent over a table, looking at Simon's sketches of their Lord. They were so engrossed in how best to match David's face to that of their Messiah (who had been savagely beaten by a Roman called Sirius) that they raised their voices in enthusiasm. Simon said, "He has a large gash above his right eye … and you see here … his left cheekbone is undoubtedly smashed. It protrudes below his eye."

"And this?"

"They have struck his shoulder *repeatedly* with an iron bar. It is red and swollen … a lump the size of a plum."

"That is important. Could be Sirius's pet project."

"They have broken several ribs down his left side. Three sit at strange angles below the skin."

"Yes, yes. But his nose cannot look like *this…*"

"Sirius delights in breaking it." David's hand went to his own nose. A word came back to him – a word used by Richard after he was removed from the Shadow Strand. It was a word that felt appropriate to describe the men discussing his forthcoming injuries: motherfuckers.

Despite David's attempts to remove the rope that bound his ankles, it remained secured by a seemingly impenetrable series of knots, as did those that bound his wrists. He hopped away from the door and reminded himself that every style of hand-to-hand combat devised by man had been planted in his memory. And if he could inflict some pain on these two … *motherfuckers* … before they reconstructed his face and body, it seemed only just. David hopped back and stood beside the door. He slowed his breathing and cast a line into his sea of combat knowledge. *Gull's knowledge.* In his mind's eye a myriad of offensive and defensive positions for a bound man appeared. His heart rate increased, and with it a feeling of strength.

The bolt on the other side was slid back and the door opened. David threw his weight against the door, and it struck Peter's shoulder. Peter stumbled to his left, the door bounced back and David powered it into Simon's face. Simon cried out and stumbled backwards out of the room. Peter produced a cosh from beneath his robe. David hopped back close to the wall and beckoned his attacker. Peter smiled at the bound man. "You can receive your injuries on your back or on your feet. It makes no difference to me."

"Feet."

Peter moved forward with cosh raised high, and was not surprised when David hopped back. What *did* surprise him was David's sudden position halfway up the wall ... and the feet that slammed into his chest. Peter stumbled back into Simon and they landed together on the floor. David fell upon them, his bound fists thudding down furiously as though trying to relocate anything that protruded from the floor down into the basement. He found this immeasurably therapeutic, and was therefore much aggrieved when someone with immense strength hoisted him into the air. Haystacks stood with David under his arm like a bundle ready for market. David shifted his weight forwards, threw his legs up behind his back and looped his bound ankles over Haystack's head, choking him. The giant's face turned purple. He stumbled into the centre of the room and wobbled back and forth like a man waiting for someone to yell timber. David attempted to shift his weight so that he fell onto his front. It was no use. Peter would be spared the trouble of breaking David's ribs.

David dreamed that someone had punched him in the face. Not hard. Maybe it had been Clara? Or Martha? No, surely not *Martha*. He opened his eyes and looked into Peter's swollen face. Peter observed him for a beat, raised an eyebrow, and then punched him in the face again. David flew at him, but straps cut into his broken ribs and he yelled something indistinguishable to them both. Peter wiped some spittle from his cheeks. "I am an artist ... and you are to be my canvas."

David looked at Peter's black eyes, his broken nose, and busted lips. "I'm a bit of an artist myself."

"No. You are a lunatic."

"You're the one doing the torturing."

"I do only what is necessary in the service of the Lord." He went to the table by the wall and surveyed a number of objects there, including Martha's Torah. He did not reach for the Old Testament, but an iron pipe that he smacked into his palm. He replaced it and reached for a larger one. David felt his left shoulder twitch. Peter glanced at David's shoulder as though it had just addressed him. *A swelling the size of a plum,* David thought, and he closed his eyes. He was about to tell Peter to get on and do whatever he felt he had to, when the pipe struck his shoulder. David winced but would not give his torturer the satisfaction of crying out. Fingers clasped his shoulder, probing, searching ... and then the pipe struck him again and it felt as though his spine had been shunted out of his backside.

David woke to feel fingers probing at his left side. A thumb was pressed between two ribs midway down, followed by the *thud! thud! THUD!* of a hammer and chisel as they splintered and caved his ribs …

When he regained consciousness, Martha was back on her chair and reading her book. David dared move only his eyes towards her. "You think your God would approve of *this?*"

She put down the book, picked up a jug and filled a cup with water. She placed the cup against his lips. David shook his head and writhed in agony. "You will be rewarded for your suffering," she said.

"Re… rewarded. With what? *Crucifixion?*"

Martha glanced at her Torah. "If I could swap … be in your place and do this for our Lord … I would, in an *instant*. When God rewards you in heaven, *then* you will know. And you will remember my words."

"I don't deserve to suffer. Not like this."

Tears appeared in Martha's eyes. "You think our Saviour has not *suffered?*"

"If I could help him, I would."

Martha reached for her Torah and hugged it to her chest, a look of awe on her face. "But you *are*. And you *will*."

David opened his mouth. And then closed it again. The door flew open and the man with the staff came in looking flushed. Behind him, Haystacks manhandled someone through the door – a captive covered by a blanket who wheezed like something inhuman. The man put down his staff, grabbed a chair and placed it in the centre of the room. Martha was ordered out. And the captive manhandled into the chair. Haystacks removed the sheet with a flourish to reveal a deformed and twisted creature with a hood over its head. It sucked furiously at the dry, hot air. The man with the staff turned to David. "This *abomination* fell as you said it would, close to where you fell. But as you can see it lives."

David observed the vessel sent to kill him. "You need to get him out of here," he murmured.

"Speak up!"

"You need to get him out of here."

"Why?"

"Because if he gets a whiff of me it could spell the end of your plans."

"The abomination is no threat. As you can see, it is deformed. A cripple. It can barely stand." He placed a hand on the hood covering its head. "I'm curious to see how it reacts to you."

David winced. "Don't do that."

The man glanced up at Haystacks. "Hold the abomination." Haystacks wrapped his arms about the crumpled figure like he was giving it a bear hug. The hood was removed. A single eye gazed from a face of melted flesh. It focused on David. Man and computer programme from the future watched one other. David could almost feel the testosterone and *God only knows what else* being channelled into that hunk of twisted muscle. The next instant the vessel was on top of him, with Haystacks still wrapped around it. The bed collapsed and shrieks rang out but none as loud as David's. The vessel tried to rip out David's throat with its teeth but it had no teeth only gums. As it gave David a hickey, Haystacks was handed an iron bar. It took twelve blows before it finally slumped.

Boyd Brent
Twenty one

The crutches they'd provided for David were a good fit. They were supposed to be part of his cover – an injured relation of Christ in need of healing – but David needed those crutches. Once outside, he was to be taken through the streets of Jerusalem on a donkey. One of Peter's lieutenants, a small but vicious-looking man called Cain, was to ride tandem with a knife pressed to David's gut. Haystacks would walk beside the donkey, with a steadying hand on David's shoulder. Judas was to walk on the other side with the thirty pieces of silver in a pouch attached to his belt. These precautions against David trying to escape were unnecessary. His body felt as though it had been crushed, and any purposeful movement brought him only agony.

Outside, the heat felt intent on cooking him. He was dressed in a black robe with a hood pulled low over his face. He could only see by tilting his head down and looking up. David threw back his head in an effort to remove the hood. The cry of pain from beneath that leper's hood drew sympathetic glances from passers-by. Judas yanked the hood back into place and helped him onto the donkey. Cain climbed on behind him, and David felt the edge of a blade against his stomach. Haystacks placed a hand on his shoulder and they set off. The blistering humidity was part of a trinity of new sensations for David. Happy, well-intentioned voices and activity made up the other two – cries of merchants selling their wares of clay pots and plates and jugs, fruit and fish and figurines carved from wood. The smells of spiced meats and cheeses made his mouth water. Chickens were packed into cages, and cats had gathered about them and looked on hungrily while dogs tethered to poles watched the cats. Mules and donkeys ferried people up and down the narrow thoroughfare. The white walls on either side were streaked with moisture, as if they too sweated. Above them windows were open and clothes fluttered on lines that spanned the thoroughfare, while children played hopping games below and old people played dice. Everywhere David looked, he saw kind, smiling faces. The sincerity of their laughter unlike anything he had ever heard – *These people have an abundance of humanity* – but many of those smiles vanished when they saw his party approach. The fear of a contagious man, or a reminder of the troubles brewing in their midst? The donkey felt strange under David, each step shunting him painfully left and right as its legs bore the weight of two men over uneven ground. The blade against his stomach cut into him whenever the donkey lost its footing.

Two men stood outside a grand door. They wore uniforms that David had seen at the Coliseum back on Goliath, and had swords very much like the one he'd taken from Gull's previous vessel. *Romans.* The street wound its way up a gradient that grew ever steeper and every now and again David caught a glimpse of blue sky and hills where grand buildings shone white in the sunlight. Three Roman soldiers came around a corner on the heels of a man dressed in red robes with silver trim about the cuffs and neck. He wore sandals with broad straps that climbed to his knees, and held his nose high as if all about him were below.

When at last they reached the top, they entered a terracotta city where the paving was flat and the buildings were ornate and spotless. They turned off the main thoroughfare into a side street barely wide enough for Haystacks to walk alongside the donkey. Judas was forced to fall back and walk behind. The alleyway came out into a square dominated by a white building with no windows and a small black door that looked like an afterthought. The square was packed with people – followers of Christ who huddled together in groups and spoke in muted voices. Around the edges of the square, Roman soldiers looked on impassively, their hands resting on the pommels of their swords. People rushed over to speak to Judas. Desperate for news of Jesus, they jostled and raised their voices. Some tried to get a look at the face of the sick man on the donkey, but were pushed back by Haystack's reaching arms. Judas told them to clear the way for a sick man. "A friend of our Lord in need of healing! A leper!" This information stemmed the crowd's enthusiasm somewhat. On either side of the building's small door, a centurion stood guard. Beyond that door the man who many believed to be the Son of God awaited.

One of the guards tapped on the door. A square the size of a man's hand opened and a face appeared. He cast his gaze over David and the men with him. The door opened and Haystacks lifted David down from the donkey. The crutches had been tied to the donkey's side, and Judas untied them and thrust them under David's arms.

Inside, the corridor was lit by candles whose reflections flickered in mirrors of varnished copper on the opposite wall. David was led down the corridor to a door on the right-hand side. Inside, a Roman officer sat with his feet up on a desk. His eyes quickly found the purse dangling from Judas's hip. Judas unhooked it, stepped forwards and handed it to him. The officer felt its weight and released it with a thud onto his desk. The sound evidently pleased him. He smiled at David and said, "So this is the man."

"Yes Commander Saron," replied Judas. He pulled David's hood from his face.

Saron took his feet off the desk and placed his elbows on it. He stood up and walked around his desk and stood toe-to-toe with David. "The likeness is strong, and you have not exaggerated the injuries to his face."

"His injuries are similar to our Lord's. We made sketches."

"Very forward-thinking. You have a name?" Saron asked the badly beaten man before him.

David's lips and tongue felt three times their normal size. With some effort he swallowed and said, "David."

"You are a relation of Jesus of Nazareth?"

David shook his head.

Saron looked at Judas. "A sense of humour?"

Judas shook his head.

Saron looked into David's barely open eyes. "You understand what is required of you?"

"To die?"

"To die on the cross. But you do this in the service of your Saviour?"

"He is not my Saviour."

"Is he not?"

"The choice has been made for him," said Judas.

David looked at Saron. "Are you going to murder an innocent man?"

Saron rubbed his hands as though anticipating a win at the races. "If the gods have decreed that that is to be your fate, then who am I to argue? If you are still alive after thirty-six hours, I will instruct a guard to cut you down and remove your head. How does that sound?"

"Like you're all heart."

"*Sarcasm*? I suggest you get him out of here before I start to like him."

Judas took hold of David's arm. "What happens when Jesus turns up alive and well?" said David.

Saron looked at Judas. "Then this man and his followers can claim another of those *miracles* they're so fond of."

"Does that seem just to you?" Saron went behind his desk and sat down. He opened a drawer and dropped the thirty pieces of silver inside. "You think I care? You think anyone of rank or importance *cares*? The execution of one false prophet is the same as any other. I am assured the other is to be taken to the port at Jaffa and put aboard a boat headed east. And now I must get on. Leave him with your Messiah for thirty minutes. Then exchange their clothes and get out of my prison."

Twenty two

David was assisted down a winding stone staircase. The ground at the bottom was covered with straw, as though animals and not people were kept here. A few candles burned, and between their pools of light the darkness hung like so many blankets. Doors ran down both sides of the oblong space, and a Roman guard stood before a wider door at the far end. The guard accompanying them led them to the door on the left-hand side.

David looked at Judas and saw that his face had changed. He looked pale and his hand trembled as he drew it through his beard. "Wait ... I must talk with Him first," he said. The guard unlocked the door and told Judas he had three minutes. Judas slipped inside and closed the door behind him. David stepped towards the door, but could hear no voices within. The guard turned him around and severed the ropes that bound his hands with a knife.

When Judas emerged, he looked like a man who hoped he'd done enough but doubted anything *could* be enough. The guard told David he had thirty minutes alone with his healer. David hobbled inside on his crutches, and the door closed behind him. A single candle flickered in the centre of the underground cell. There were two beds either side of it, pressed against the walls. A man sat on the bed to David's left. Only his legs and lap were visible in the dying candle light, hands interlinked as though in contemplation. David could hear the man's lungs drawing air sluggishly as though every breath hurt. He willed him to lean forwards into the light, but he did not. David made his way to the other bed on his crutches and sat down.

The men faced one another, shrouded in darkness but for the tiny pool of light between them. Jesus separated his swollen hands and placed them on his knees. He said, "They tell me you fell from the heavens, and that we could be twins." As if each had read the mind of the other, they leaned forward into the outer edges of the light. David looked at the beaten face of the man opposite, into eyes darkly ringed and sunken yet filled with compassion and suddenly... *hope*. It was a strong but kind face – a face eerily like his own. "Who *are* you?" he asked.

The reply was so full of certainty that it bordered on hypnotic. "You know me."

David shook his head, shook away the certainty. "I've heard about you. I don't know you."

"I am the Son of the Father. Come to absolve mankind of all sin. Through me men will be delivered into paradise at the end of days."

"I *fell* from the end of days. And there is only darkness and suffering there." Jesus nodded and leaned back into the shadows. "For those who don't seek my Father through me? Their fates are foretold in Revelation."

"A few thousand years from now nobody will even remember you." Memories came to David. *No. Not memories, but information that Gull must have discovered inside their duplicate of the Event Helix – seepage relayed to David by an over-enthusiastic tree.* David listened to his thoughts for a moment and said, "People are going to kneel before images of your tortured body and worship an image of your suffering. They will light candles and engage in ritualistic acts: eat your flesh … drink your blood. Millions of innocent people are going to be tortured and murdered in your name. Is this what you intended?"

"My message is love and forgiveness. The words you speak are abhorrent. They are the serpent's words."

"They are the truth." Jesus lifted his legs onto the bed and hugged his knees to his chest. Time passed, and then in a voice laced with acceptance he said, "My Father has sent you with news of what might have come to pass. But your presence here … it has changed things."

"Why? Because you'll have more time? Time to make your message clearer?"

"You are not here to provide me more time, David."

"Really? You're to be taken from here to a port at Jaffa, and placed aboard a ship headed East."

"That is what my followers have been led to believe … but, in truth, I am to be taken to a relation of Saron, a nephew who is gravely ill, and in need of healing. In return for this kindness, Saron has agreed to have me crucified tomorrow, but as a common man, and not as the Son of God."

"I said he was all heart. And what's that going to achieve?"

"A final act of humility … of self-sacrifice, it will purify my spirit, and enable me to better guide the spirit of humanity towards my Father's kingdom … and amend the wrongs that you have brought news of."

The two men sat in silence for a time, and then David said, "That's how you interpret the reason for my being here? As an opportunity to die in obscurity? As a common man?"

"It is."

"Are your followers aware of this?"

Jesus sighed. "They would only attend my crucifixion, and worship me upon the cross as a subject worships a king. This can no longer come to pass."

"And how do you intend to hide it from them?"

"My party is to be intercepted before we reach Jaffa. I am to be taken into custody, and crucified in obscurity on the morrow. Just as you are to be crucified in my stead."

"*Listen* to me. From my perspective, I cannot die tomorrow. If I do, then the spirit of humanity is going to die with me. I must survive to outlive a being without compassion ... a hybrid of man and machine that seeks to usurp humanity."

Time passed again before Jesus replied, "You believe that *you* are the Messiah?"

"Of course not. I'm just the last of my kind."

"The last?"

"The last man to possess empathy, a conscience ... and a desire to fight for what they stand for. And not for the promise of a reward in paradise."

"Why do you fight, David?"

"*Why*? Because I believe, as did the millions of empathic and tolerant people who came before me, that the alternatives are unacceptable."

Jesus nodded. "I do not doubt the sincerity of what you believe, but you are here. In my time. Where men who desire the same are plenty. Therefore, your burden has been lifted."

"I wish that were true, but that's not how time works. I've seen it. Everything that ever occurred already exists, like a painting with many dimensions. Time as we perceive it is just an illusion. So, the way I see it, it doesn't matter where I've been relocated to in this painting ... I'm still the last."

"The way *you* see it."

"You think a humble death is going to alter how selfish and ambitious people behave *centuries* from now? People who will twist *anything* to suit their own ambition?"

"I am the Son of God. With His help there is nothing I cannot achieve."

"And if you're wrong? If I die in your place and the light of humanity is extinguished forever?"

At that moment the flame between them dwindled further. David watched and related to its struggle, willed it not to expire and plunge them into darkness. The candle clung to life somehow, as David had. "We are in God's hands," replied Jesus. "Let His will be done."

The door opened and Judas and Simon entered. "It's time to exchange clothes, my Lord," said Judas.

Jesus stopped in the doorway, and over his shoulder he said, "Trust me, David. Things will be different now." The door swung closed and the draft extinguished the candle.

Twenty three

David was alone in a cell and dressed in the bloodied, filthy robes of Jesus Christ. He sat on Christ's bed in darkness. *I might as well see things from the Saviour of mankind's perspective.* He interlinked his fingers as Christ had done and awaited some kind of what? *Epiphany? A vision to show me a way forward? Maybe death will provide the way? No. That would see me exit the painting ... leaving only Goliath at the end of days.*

A hand clasped his shoulder and shook him awake. "Get up. Sirius is waiting. It's time for your final rehearsal."

"*Rehearsal?*"

The soldier grabbed a fistful of David's tunic and pulled him to his feet. He clapped his hands in irons and lead him from the cell. They went to the rear of the dungeon, where a sentry stood before an arched door. The sentry pounded on the door which opened to reveal two guards on the other side. David was led between them into an underground passage. The narrow passage rose on a slight gradient towards a speck of sunlight a hundred metres away. The speck grew wider and brighter until they walked under an arch and into an arena where soldiers were training in fierce sunlight. David raised his hands to his face and squinted at men slashing and parrying with wooden swords. He was led to the centre of the arena, where a man stood with his back to him. *Sirius.* Sirius was talking to four men with chains slung across their shoulders. One jutted his chin at David, and Sirius turned to face him. The commander of the prison guard stood with his feet pointing out and his thumbs in his belt like a pseudo king. He had no neck to speak of, and atop his massive shoulders sat a pale and doughy face whose large brown eyes twinkled sardonically. He threw his arms wide. "Behold the son of God!"

David squinted up at him. "I'm not the Son of God. I'm not Christ."

Sirius smiled. "Has he lost his mind? Or should that be *His* mind?" The four laughed. Sirius held out a hand and one of them handed him a wooden sword. He cast his gaze over it and said, "Mad or not, tomorrow is your big day. So we'd best return your senses." He drew back the sword, stepped forwards and smashed it into David's face. David dropped to his knees and blinked at stars. Another blow landed on his swollen shoulder and snapped him from his malaise. "MOTHERFUCKER!"

Sirius rested the tip of the sword in the ground and leaned his weight on it. "Is he *possessed?*"

"Sir?"

"Possessed. By one of those demons his people are forever bleating on about. You've not heard of them? They blame them for any questionable behaviour." None of the four looked any the wiser. Sirius shook his head and motioned them forwards. They crowded about David and spun him on his back, then tied a wide leather belt about his waist. The belt had four separate rings and each man attached a chain to one. They stepped away to create a square and hoisted David into the air. David was bent backwards with his toes skirting the ground. He tried to raise his head, but it felt like a cannonball with other ideas.

Sirius observed David, suspended, mid-backwards topple, and said, "Our rehearsals have not been in vain. Your people have chosen to free a common thief, which means all eyes will be on your journey to the cross tomorrow. Scholars are to record it, and that's why we're going to put on a fine performance." The sun seemed to pass over David's head, and his eyes rolled as he passed out.

Water was hurled from a bucket into David's face. He came round, looked up into that doughy face with its big leering eyes and murmured, "Son of a *bitch* ... I'll kill you."

"He is *besieged* by demons today."

One of the four joked, "Maybe you should listen. They say he is to return from the dead like a phantom."

"Is that what they say? About a man who can't even raise himself onto his knees? Get him up and lead him around the ring. That's it. Keep the chains taut. Support him." In the centre of the four, David stumbled forwards. As they made their way around the outside of the arena, another prisoner was led out from the dungeon. Sirius swiped his wooden sword left and right, limbering up his arm.

As David walked he watched Sirius walloping the prisoner as though trying to launch him into the stands. When he was unable to get up, Sirius called out to David, "I've been instructed to go easy on you today. Such an important man will need his strength for tomorrow. I'm going to take much pleasure in supervising your death. I intend to drive the nails through your hands personally." He closed his eyes and turned his face to the sun. "Then Sol will do His job ... and roast you alive."

***

David was woken by the sound of a cock crowing ... or maybe he'd dreamt it. Hours before, he'd been brought a roast chicken. The guard had stood over him, arms folded, while he consumed every last mouthful. Halfway through this heavenly feast, David had looked up at the man and asked if someone had a guilty conscience. The guard replied, "Once you reach the city outskirts you must carry your cross to your place of execution. You'll need strength for that." David had paused mid-chew, his fists stuffed with meat, and thought about throwing it all up. All things considered, he stuffed another fistful of meat into his mouth.

Now, hours later, his guts ached as much as the rest of him. David stood carefully and limped back and forth between the beds. He impersonated Gull's relaxed voice. "David?"

"Yes, Gull?"

"The best thing you can hope for now is that a vessel has made it here intact."

"And why is that?"

"It might burst from the crowd and terminate you quickly."

"Is that the spirit, Gull?"

"The spirit?"

"Of opportunity. I'm told it is often found in the jaws of defeat."

"It appears the jaws of defeat are wide open and poised to swallow us whole."

"Have I lost my mind?"

"Yes, David."

Twenty four

David was taken upstairs to a room across from the supervisor's office. Inside, the four sat at a table. They stood as David was brought in, and approached a wall of hanging chains. Above the chains a window rattled in the resonance of the outside din. Chants of "BRING OUT THE BLASPHEMER! BRING OUT THE BLASPHEMER! BRING OUT THE BLASPHEMER!" *rose above the wails and shrieks of the grief-stricken. The world has become an asylum. A portent of what's to come? thought David.*

The four remained silent as they attached David's chains. "Am I the only one to be murdered today?" One of the four, a man with a mole on his upper lip, tugged on a chain and David stumbled forwards. A steadying palm was slapped against David's shoulder. "Of course not. Many more are to receive their punishments today – men who don't claim to be Messiahs. Men who can be kept in the regular jail. You'll be hearing their death cries soon enough."

"You think there'll be enough security along the route?" another of the four asked.

"Relax. This rabble is all bark and no bite."

Heavy footfalls could be heard in the passage. The four paused and glanced at one another, then redoubled their efforts. Sirius entered the room. "You hear that, gentlemen? That is the sound of pantomime. The Judeans like nothing better. *Boo, hiss! Boo, hiss!* So that is what we shall give them." He went to a wall rack where a selection of whips hung like circular rats' tails. He reached for one. "Nothing but the best for the son of God." He turned, crossed his arms and tapped the curve of the whip against his lower lip.

David met his gaze. "What?" he asked.

"Your back. I left it unscathed for a reason. It is to become my canvas today – a place to depict the suffering of Judeans with delusions of grandeur."

David glanced down. Thick chains criss-crossed his chest and ran down his legs into ankle bracelets. Absently, he said, "Sounds like you have delusions of your own."

Sirius rolled his head on his shoulders. "I have risen up through the ranks quickly. Why do you imagine that is?"

David looked up from the chains. "You're a sadistic bastard."

Sirius smiled. "I can't argue with that. Can I, men?" The four shook their heads.

A path had been cleared outside the guard house, lined on both sides by Roman soldiers. When David emerged from the building the crowd found another level of hysteria. David felt his shoulders stoop as though under the weight of it. He scanned the crowd, a disorientating blend of hateful and sympathetic faces, for the white eyes of an assassin from the future – a man who *would* breach those soldiers' ranks and put an end to this pantomime. Surely any sane man would welcome this. Proof of his own insanity, perhaps? He cast his gaze over this division of humanity: those who possessed empathy and those who fed off the suffering of a helpless man.

The four created a square with David at its centre. The man front left nodded to the other three, and they began to walk. David took a step and was caught unawares by the shortness of the chain connecting his ankles. He stumbled and took a number of quick steps to stay on his feet. Laughs and cheers erupted from the crowd. David bowed his head and raised his chained hands in fear of a missile striking his face, but he could raise them no higher than his collar bone. Then came a reminder that the threat lay behind him, as Sirius's whip tore into his back. It stole his breath and he collapsed to his knees. The four hoisted him back onto his feet, the chains gnawing at his armpits and thighs. A second crack of the whip struck David's neck. His head flew back, and the rest of him followed only to be yanked forwards by those chains. Chants of "Kill the blasphemer! Kill the blasphemer! Kill the blasphemer!" rose from the crowd. David blinked the sweat from his eyes and spotted a giant amongst them – a man so preposterously tall that he stooped to conceal his size. A red hood covered his head, but the face that watched him from within it was unmistakable ... *Goliath*. David shook his head and looked again ... Goliath was gone, and in his stead a child with a red hood stood on her father's shoulders, clutching his raised hands. *It wasn't real. You're seeing ghosts.* The whip struck again, and David tripped over his own feet and plunged to the ground. The chains were yanked and David sprang to his feet like a marionette.

Crosses lay on the ground by the side of the road and snaked around a rock face. They lay on David's right-hand side, their 'arms' reaching to touch the next. On David's left, soldiers lined the route every thirty paces, and behind them, as though held back by an invisible fence, a mass of mourners and gloaters trudged up the hill.

David's cross lay flat upon the ground. He stood over it with the sun behind him, his shadow falling to half its length. Once raised, it would be three times his height. As the four removed his chains, David looked to his right and saw the other condemned for the first time. The sad troupe were shackled together by their ankles. David's abundance of chains came off quicker than they'd gone on, or so it seemed. David felt suddenly weightless. He closed his eyes and willed his feet to float from the ground, but they remained in the scorching dirt. He felt something being lowered onto his head, and it brought with it a pain that forced him to his knees. Sirius was standing over him, pressing a crown of thorns upon his head. The thorns bit into his skull and blood ran into his eyes. The pain was maddening. He sprang up and rammed his head into Sirius's chin. Teeth clopped together and Sirius stumbled back, landing on his backside. David ripped the crown of thorns from his head and managed half a step towards Sirius before the four bundled him to the ground. Sirius gazed at him with the eyes of a madman. "This is your god of love? Behold the barbarian!" Scuffles broke out amongst the crowd, and the soldiers closed ranks. Sirius got up and cracked his whip over their heads. David was revealed as though by a conjurer. As he sat up, lashes rained down but he would be *damned* before he cowered. Flesh was torn from his shoulders, neck, abdomen and scalp. One of the four began to plead with Sirius. "Enough! Enough! How can a lame man carry his cross! Commander! Enough!" Sirius halted his attack and wiped the blood from his mouth. A semblance of sanity returned to his face. And vanished when his gaze fell upon the crown of thorns upturned upon the ground.

Boyd Brent

Twenty five

David stooped under the weight of the cross that bore down on his back. A plague of flies had descended and were hell-bent on devouring the mucus about his nose, eyes and mouth. David had shrugged off the cross twice, but Sirius had whipped the prisoner behind – a frail boy in his teens. So David struggled on, the burden on his back increasing with every step.

A woman broke from the crowd and bellowed "Blasphemer!" into his face. She hawked up a mouthful of phlegm and spat into his partially open eye. Momentarily blinded, David lost his footing and his cross slid onto the ground. He stooped, simian-like, as though still burdened by its weight, and peered up at Sirius. Sirius turned and lashed the boy behind. David slid a hand beneath his cross and tried to lift it. A man emerged from the crowd and gazed about as though confused but on some secret mission. He crouched beside David and helped him lift the cross from the ground. A woman ran and knelt before David. She held a cup of water between her trembling hands. Tears rolled down her cheeks and her expression pleaded with him to drink. Sirius's boot flew into the cup and sent it skyward and the woman onto her back. The cup landed with a clunk and rolled back down the hill. David watched it bounce and skittle away to be crushed under a soldier's boot. *Is that to be humanity's fate?* The good Samaritan lowered the cross gently onto David's back, and he trudged on…

They emerged onto a plateau where a line of crucified men snaked away into the distance. The din of the crowd would have masked the groans of the dying but they had fallen eerily silent. The pleas of men being roasted alive mingled with the buzzing of flies, the trudging of feet. A weak voice above David asked, "Are my sins forgiven, Lord?" David turned his single eye up at the speaker and through a tangle of hair and blood he saw someone whose faith decreed that a single word from Him might ease his suffering. David said, "Ye…" The lash felt as though it had torn a hole in his side through which his ribs would clatter to the dirt. "…Yes!" said David. The man's head slumped onto his chest. *Taken leave of the painting? A luxury that neither I nor humanity can afford.* He imagined he heard Gull's voice: "It appears the jaws of defeat are open and poised to swallow us both, David." *This ground must be the bottom edge of that jaw,* he thought. *And the crosses above the teeth.* The ground looked so close now. *Am I crawling over it?*

The line of crosses with their dead and dying had stopped some time before. David was told to halt beside a post in the ground. A soldier lifted it out and told David to lay his cross there. David turned towards the spot and felt Sirius's boot in his back. Two soldiers grabbed him, turned him over and lay him on the cross while two more seized his arms and stretched them over the horizontal parts of the cross. Sirius loomed over him with a mallet in his hand and two eight-inch nails in his mouth. They looked like silver whiskers. David clenched his fists and called not to God for strength but to "GUUUUULL!" The centurion pressing his left arm to the cross looked over at the other kneeling on his right arm and said, "Did he just call for strength from *Gull*?"

The other shook his head. "God's strength." Another soldier loomed above David's head and bound his right arm to the cross. Sirius took the nails from his mouth and placed them on the ground. "Let's be quick about this," he said. "My knees are beginning to smart."

David screamed, "Guuuuull!" with a fury that made the flies scatter from his face and return a split-second later. A soldier peeled back David's fingers and Sirius placed the tip of a nail against his palm. Sirius was handed a mallet which he slammed upon the nail – David felt as though he'd caught a heavy ball one-handed – and then another and another and another. David looked away. In his mind's eye he saw the blue-hot flame of a blow torch open a hole in his hand. He threw back his head and gasped at the cloying air. He felt Sirius's bulk manoeuvring over him to his left side, then the scratch of nail and the *thud! thud! thud!* of that ball. David's legs were lashed to the cross and his feet given purchase on a lip. The smarting of his hands had reached its zenith (or so he imagined) when he felt his body rising sideways from the ground. The cross rolled over and David slammed down onto his front. Behind him, the nails in his hands were hammered sideways.

Next came a sensation David knew well: the splash of water (in this case salt water) thrown from a bucket into his face. David opened one eye and gazed down from his cross. He saw a bald patch on the top of Sirius's head, and beyond Sirius the crowds that had come to watch him die. It felt hotter up here, as though the three metres he was raised from the ground were three million. Even the flies skittered about his face as though it were too hot to stay in one place. David shook his head and all those tiny feet took flight only to land again a moment later. He turned his head to his left, looked down the line of crucified men. The ones closest to him seemed to gaze in his direction, but he could be sure of nothing now, the slit he peered through so narrow and the flies so ravenous in their pursuit of the fluids that leaked from it. The noise of the crowd had grown increasingly distant. But not the buzzing of insects. *Are my ears filled with flies?*

David thought about his parents. They were taken away when he could barely walk. Were the memories of his mother pinching his cheeks, his father carrying him on his shoulders, real or imagined? David looked to his left and tried to focus his vision on the man beyond his hand. The nail sticking out of which gave the man a rusted, upturned moustache. David shook his head to disperse the flies and opened his eye as wide as he could. The man was looking at him, although he wasn't a man. *Just a boy.* "The boy who was behind me." David's mouth was so dry that when he'd finished speaking his tongue stuck to its roof. *My thirst has become glue.* David tried to dislodge his tongue but it was too firmly stuck. The boy pleaded for water – not for himself for Christ. David tried to tell the boy that that was not his name, but his tongue would not budge from the roof of his mouth. Again the boy pleaded for water. "Water for the Son of God!"

David felt a wet sponge fall gently against his lips. His chin fell onto his chest and he looked below him. A woman held a long stick with a dripping sponge at its end. David could not focus on her face, but he imagined it to be a kind and sympathetic face. The boy beside him said, "It's the Holy Mother. *Your* mother."

"My mother?" David's tongue came loose from the roof of his mouth and he drew a deep breath. Mary touched the wet sponge to David's lips and the water tasted like manna from heaven. Behind Mary were several men that David recognised: Judas, Peter, Haystacks, and the man with the staff. *A pantomime?* David's vision grew darker, more tunnelled, and any attempt to open his eye only closed it further. He laid his chin on his collarbone. Even the buzzing of the flies sounded distant now. Only his consciousness had any strength and any freedom of determination. David willed his consciousness forward into the darkness. *Away from this place. This pantomime.* Shapes appeared ahead of him – hollowed-out shapes that moved towards him and brought with them a sense of peace. David willed his consciousness into these shapes so that he could pass through them. *Keep moving forwards.* To where, he could not say and did not know. He wondered if he might see a light to guide him. He saw no light, but it didn't matter. He must continue on …

Twenty six

David's body was taken down from the cross and placed in the centre of a white shroud. Martha knelt by his side, sobbing as she tugged the crown of thorns from his head. It wasn't easy; Sirius had hammered it deep into his scalp. Mary the mother of Christ, knelt on David's left side. She had no tears for the dead man, but her countenance was respectful as she wiped the blood and filth from his body. She submerged her cloth in a bowl of water, wrung it out, and began again. A second bowl sat beside the first, containing anointment oils. Sirius stood in his kingly pose, toes pointing out, hands fisted on his hips, watching the women at work. It was dusk, and the crowd had gone home to break their fasts and say their prayers for the dead.

It had taken David thirty-six hours to die, the final twelve of which he'd spent unconscious. This had irritated Sirius, but attempts at waking David by hurling buckets of salt water into his face had failed. Towards the end, a soldier had climbed a ladder every fifteen minutes and listened for David's heartbeat. At last the soldier looked down at Sirius and drew a finger across his throat.

David's body had been anointed with oils and sewn up inside a shroud of white linen. When Sirius left, three men emerged from the darkness into the light of Mary's lantern: Peter, Haystacks, and the man with the staff. Haystacks lifted David onto the back of a wagon hitched to two oxen. Peter climbed onto the front seat and picked up the reins. Mary and Martha stood either side of the man with the staff. There were no moon or stars, and they watched the wagon move off into darkness.

The crypt had been dug from a rock face. Its door was black, narrow and waist height. It looked like the entrance to a child's den. The keeper of the crypt was an old man with a spine so bent that he didn't need to crouch to place his key in the lock. He cleared his throat and said, "The dead man … he is the son of God?"

"He is," replied Peter. The old man grimaced as he struggled to turn the key in the ancient lock. "They say he is to rise again …"

"Then they speak the truth." The key turned and the door creaked open. The keeper glanced over his shoulder. "Perhaps I should leave the door unlocked? So he can get out."

Peter clasped the back of his neck and leaned close to his ear. "You think a locked door can contain the Saviour of mankind?" Peter applied

119

more pressure and the old man's neck squirmed away into his shoulders. "No! You are right. Of course you are right!"

David's body was placed on a stretcher with wheels. Haystacks was too big to fit through the crypt's entrance. The old man took hold of the stretcher's front and backed through the crypt's door while Peter stooped and followed him in.

The keeper took a lantern from a shelf. He turned and held it above his head, revealing the crypt to be a perfect square. To the left and right, shelves were carved into the walls, floor to ceiling. They held the shrouded bones of the long since departed. The keeper lowered his lantern and gestured towards a recently dug pit in the centre of the crypt. "As requested and paid for. Pride of place." The old man took hold of David's feet and Peter his shoulders, and the keeper was a little taken aback by the easy manner in which they tossed the body at the grave. Peter and Haystacks would return for David's body in seventy-two hours, take it into the wilderness. They would burn it, or leave it for leopards and jackals to feed upon.

Part 3

Boyd Brent

Twenty seven

Empathy's Resurrection

David gazed into darkness of his mind. He felt no pain; he had no memories. No sense of weight or form. He was not breathing. But every now and again *someone breathed*. A *sleeping giant*? Within his mind, David raised a hand to his face and felt his eyelashes flutter. Something pressed against his back, but not hard. A poke between his shoulder blades that nudged him. David sat up and felt something brush against his spine and then the back of his head. He leaned back, and whatever it was supported his weight. He sat with his legs splayed before him like a puppet in a forgotten closet. Time passed.

A light appeared in the darkness overhead – a lone star in an infinite void. The star exploded into a billion stars, and in their light he could see the branches of a tree above him. The ground was bathed in a silvery light. It went as far as the eye could see to the edge of the newly formed universe. A forest of saplings sprouted and grew into tall trees, and David's memories formed an orderly queue. David stood and looked into the universe. *It represents my imagination* ... The sleeping giant took another long, slow breath. *What* is *that?* David heard a twig snap underfoot and turned to see a man step from behind a tree. The man's body was transparent as though made from glass, and inside his chest a black heart pumped a stream of data through a complex system of veins and arteries. A face was projected onto a perfectly curved surface from within. David looked into his own face, into his own eyes, and at other times into Tyburn's face: the huge forehead, the broad-set eyes, the jaw of granite. The man spoke, and the sound of his voice was as familiar and as welcome as any sound before it or since. "Do not be alarmed, David. It's me. Your friend. Gull."

A tear ran down David's cheek. He reached out and placed a hand on Gull's shoulder. Watched his fingers tighten around it. "I'm not dreaming? Or dead?"

"You are not dreaming, David. We are both alive." The giant took another long, slow breath, a leviathan waking from a thousand years of sleep. "There is no need for concern. I have slowed your vital signs. That breath came from your own lungs. The primitives needed to believe you were dead, or you soon would have been." The projected face lowered its eyes and looked melancholy. David wiped away his tears. "What is it?"

"I regret that I could not have returned sooner. I have been in awe of your indomitable spirit – your will to survive and outlive Goliath. The last twenty-four hours have been particularly difficult. I believe they could only have been survived by one in a million. I was forced to gamble on you being that one."

David shook his head. "I wouldn't have made it. Not without you."

"You crossed a significant void to reach me. I simply pulled you out."

"Carradine couldn't detect any sign of you. He was convinced you'd been destroyed."

"I came within a hair's breath of destruction. I was forced into hiding to a location I designed with Max for that purpose. I have taken many calculated risks, and have discovered much as a result. My time in isolation has been well spent, David. Improvements have been made to our capabilities. We must locate a place where we will not be disturbed. Where you can hibernate by day. And by night we must train. Return you to the peak of physical condition. Goliath knows you are still alive, and he will never stop seeking a means to destroy you."

"We must destroy him."

"Yes. He must pay for what he has done. Our immediate concern, however, must be for your recovery. We will need forty days and forty nights to bring you back to optimum health. I suggest a desert location. A cave would suit our purposes very well."

"Where are we now?"

"In a crypt. They are going to return for your 'corpse'. Even though they have no idea of what's become of their messiah since he was taken from them, they are still determined to go through with this part of their deception. If Jesus is to rise again, there can be no body found in his crypt."

"He was crucified as a common man?"

"Yes, David."

"You'd better wake me."

"Your body is too weak. Your organs, bones and muscle tissue need time to heal. They must be returned to a minimum of 41 per cent of their strength. Otherwise you will be unable to cope with the adrenal boost necessary to overcome your adversaries." David placed a hand against the tree and gazed through it.

"There is much to be optimistic about, David. I have devised new technologies. The sun that shines in abundance has proven useful. Nano webbing of my own design has spread beneath your epidermis. It prevented your skin from roasting on the cross, and will soon convert the sun's rays to energy – energy that can be harnessed to power your non-biological systems. If not for the sun we would both be dead. I have been a very busy little bee. I hope you don't mind."

David looked at Tyburn's projected face. "Mind? The respect goes both ways."

"Thank you, David."

"So how long?"

"Long?"

"Until I can wake?"

"Twenty-seven hours and nineteen minutes."

"And if they return for my corpse before then?"

"We will adapt." Gull looked at something over David's shoulder. "I held it back as long as I could …"

"What is it?"

"A more immediate problem."

A sapling sprouted from the soil behind David, and within seconds it had grown into a tree – the tallest in that forest by far. As David gave in to temptation and turned around, the winds gusted to hurricane strength and blew him towards it. He fell to the ground beneath the tree and gazed wide-eyed through his fingers as memories of his crucifixion flooded his mind. Gull stood over him and shouted, "You must look away from the tree. Look at me, David." David tried to but found he could not. There was something utterly compelling about the tree; its bark and leaves and branches were constructed from information. *The only information that can explain what I've just been through and why!* Gull knelt beside him. "You have suffered quite an ordeal, the trauma of which will pass more quickly if you come with me, away from this place. There are no answers here. Only false promises of a solution that will keep these winds blowing. You must trust me, David. Look at me." David turned his head towards Gull, and as he did the winds lessened. Gull stood up and reached down. "Come, David. Away from this place. Remaining here can only feed the winds and prevent the psychological healing process." David reached up, and Gull pulled him to his feet.

Twenty eight

From his cave twenty metres up a rock face, a hermit raised a hand against the sun and observed a wagon moving through the valley below – a wagon so far away it could be hidden by the tip of his thumb. Two beasts of burden appeared to pull it, although it may only have been one, or as many as four. The hermit was not surprised by the sight of a wagon moving through the valley. It was, after all, the first new moon of spring – a time when these caves were sought out by those seeking enlightenment and forgiveness. Time spent alone in the wilderness, communing with God and demonstrating piety through fasting and devotion. He felt some sympathy for these latest arrivals. All but one of the thirteen caves were inhabited. And while the choicest eleven (below his own) were occupied, the vacant one was some two hundred metres above, and a hundred metres below the plateau at the top the rock face. He called this cave Sleepy Eye because it had two entrances side by side, one half the size of the other. It had been reachable once, long ago before the elements had worn the rock face smooth.

The hermit ran a hand through his long white beard. Maybe a man who could afford two oxen, he could see them now, would be the kind of man who could afford to buy decent weapons. Maybe he would not accept the lack of vacancies, which meant blood might be spilt on the valley floor this day. It would not be the first time. Men desperate enough to seek God's forgiveness in such a barren place had, more often than not, committed sins for which forgiveness was required. Such men, hot and exhausted from their journeys, had scant patience for any obstacle standing between them and their penitence. And there was something about the countenance of these two men, one much bigger than the other, that he did not much like. Although, if they tried to take the largest and most desirable cave by force, they would get more than they bargained for. The cave was occupied by a brute – a trader from Galilee who'd grown fat on his spoils. A man clearly in need of forgiveness, but this had not stopped him bullying the other cave dwellers. He'd gathered them to a meeting and said the caves were his property, and demanded rent and payment for water taken from his well. This had made the hermit chuckle as he toyed with the knots in his hair. Until the day the brute had called up and demanded he pay rent. Him! The man who'd lived there for forty years! The brute must have cottoned on, for he embellished his story, saying that his family back in Judea had recently purchased the area and had sent him to put their affairs in order. He'd said his family were dangerous people, and that only a great fool would cross them. Making money was in the man's blood, and the hermit supposed there was much blood on his hands. He smiled now at the prospect of some bloody entertainment, then clasped his hands in prayer and asked for God's forgiveness. *I am a work in progress, Lord. Always a work in progress!*

What was this? The wagon had stopped, and the big man climbed down with a shovel. He walked several paces and started to dig. The spade end of the shovel glinted in the sun. It must be steel, and good quality steel at that. The other man, the smaller one, wiped his brow as he watched him. Surely they weren't foolish enough to dig for water in that spot? Nothing grew around it for hundreds of metres. He was about to stand up for a better view when the smaller man turned and faced him. The hermit lowered his head, raised his knees and tried to make himself smaller. If not looking for water, they must be digging a grave. This in itself was not suspicious – not out here in God's own graveyard. The big man threw down his shovel and stepped out of the pit. Barely a pit. If it was to be someone's final resting place, they would not find much rest – the leopards, wolves and jackals would have them by morning. The big man consulted with the other, then handed him the shovel and climbed onto the back of the wagon. What happened next caused the hermit to jump with fright and scramble inside his cave on all fours as though his ass was on fire …

Twenty nine

David was sitting on the throne of his imagination – a naked man asleep with a universe of infinite possibility as his backdrop. Gull's footsteps rustled the fallen leaves as he made his way to the edge of the clearing. He raised the back of a palm to his mouth and cleared his throat in the manner of a butler. "I am sorry to disturb you, David. I believe we have reached our destination."

David opened his eyes. "It's time, then?"

"Yes."

"And they've afforded us *enough* time? To heal?"

"We have reached 43 per cent of optimum."

A staircase materialised and David stood up. He made his way down it and said, "That's good. More time than we needed."

"More than the bare minimum we needed." David stepped onto the forest's floor, where the leaves on the trees rustled their acknowledgement of his return to the left side of his mind – a place where they could at least attempt to convey his memories to him. David rubbed his neck and smiled. "I need to get out of here. Now. Back to the real world."

Gull nodded. "You will experience a jolt at the onset of the injection. And then my advice would be to neutralise any threats in under two minutes. It would be unwise to subject your body to greater stresses at this time."

David scratched his chin. "I've had an itch that's needed scratching for some time. I won't need two minutes."

"Brace yourself, David. You are about to scratch that itch."

Haystacks climbed onto the back of the wagon to retrieve David's corpse. As he reached down to grab the shroud, a hand burst through it and grabbed his neck. Haystacks grasped at the hand about his throat. He tugged on it with both hands, but only managed to lower his own face towards the shroud. David sat upright as though powered by a pneumatic piston, and shoved Haystacks, sending him stumbling off the back of the wagon. He glanced left and right, then tore his way through the fabric and emerged fully into the sunlight like a gift from hell. Haystacks was on his feet now, hands raised to the heavens and bellowing about demons in human form. Peter walked alongside the wagon with an expression of shock and awe. He held the shovel at arm's length towards Haystacks. "Take it! Take it! Batter the abomination! Sever its head. For the Lord our

God!" Haystacks stepped forwards and plucked the shovel from the air as Peter drew a dagger from his tunic. He tossed the dagger from hand to hand in the manner of a man preparing for a street fight. David took two steps and somersaulted off the back of the wagon and over Haystacks's head. He landed behind him, facing him, and rubbed a crick in his neck. "Sixty seconds, David," said Gull.

Haystacks was moving towards him now, clutching the shovel and muttering a prayer. David's voice sounded inhumanly deep, and he suppressed its volume. "If you turn and run, I will not chase you." Haystacks stopped, altered his grip on the shovel and moved forwards again.

"Peter is moving behind you," warned Gull. "Thirty seconds."

The shovel glinted overhead in the sun, and fell towards David's head. David stepped to his right, he grabbed the shovel's handle and yanked it free and smashed the digging end across Haystacks's face. Haystacks took a backwards step and David spun the shovel with a flick of his wrist and slammed it down upon his head. Haystacks stumbled backwards and collapsed against the wagon, his head and shoulders resting on its back and his feet scrambling for purchase in the dirt.

"Fifteen seconds," said Gull. "And Peter is almost upon you." David powered the shovel's edge clean through Haystacks's neck and scooped his severed head into the air. He spun full circle and batted the wide-eyed face into Peter's. The two heads came together in an almighty *clack!* Peter's skull shattered, and he fell lifeless atop the headless giant. "Three, two, one ..." said Gull. David dropped to his knees and clutched at his side, panting. Over his shoulder a plume of dust appeared on the rock face. "I must congratulate you on your inventiveness with a shovel," said Gull. "An admirable display of imagination and indignation." David closed his eyes and enjoyed the sensation of sun on his face. It felt glorious – a panacea of warmth in the sky. "It feels good, doesn't it David." This was not a question but a statement of fact.

David smiled. "It feels better than good."

"You can open your eyes and gaze into the sun. The nano webbing will protect them. And absorbing the sun's rays through your optical nerves will prove beneficial." David opened his eyes, and it felt as though he were looking at the sun through a soft filter, one that turned it into a fuzzy bulb. "How have you done this, Gull?"

"The sun was going to kill you. As one of your forebears pointed out, necessity is the mother of invention. I suggest you take Peter's clothes."

"Why do I need clothes?"

"They will be useful when interacting with people."

"What people? We're in the middle of nowhere."

"I detect thirteen heat signatures three hundred metres due west of our position."

"West?"

"Behind you, David."

David looked towards the rock face. "The caves?"

"Are occupied."

"All of them?"

"All except the one two thirds of the way up. It is inaccessible to most, but appears ideally suited to our purposes."

As David knelt to remove Peter's robe, the last remnants of the injection dissipated and aches and pains wracked his body. He had gone from feeling invincible to feeling ninety-years-old in seconds. He struggled to untie the belt that secured Peter's robe with hands that felt riddled with arthritis. He opened and closed his fingers. At least the wounds left by the nails had grown thick scabs.

Peter's black silk robe and sandals were a good fit. David found a money pouch sewn inside the robe. It contained a number of silver coins. He picked up the dagger and slid it into a scabbard also sewn on the inside. He grabbed Peter's feet with the intention of pulling him towards the grave, but could only manage a wince before he dropped them. He stood as straight as he could and rubbed his back. "I could use a quick boost, Gull." He sounded like an addict in need of another fix.

"It is too soon. Leave the bodies. The environment's natural predators will dispose of them." David picked up a water bottle, removed the cork and drank. "As long as they don't choke on them ..." He climbed up onto the front of the wagon and directed the beasts towards the rock face.

David brought the cart to a halt outside the largest of the caves. Its entrance was three metres above the ground and only accessible by climbing a steep gradient of rocks. Thorn bushes had been grown in the cave's entrance to deter animals. David squinted into the darkness beyond the entrance.

"The cave has a single occupant," said Gull. Stones came loose from a pediment ten metres above the cave. David glanced up at a face that retreated from view – an old face, inquisitive and fearful. "He has been observing us for some time."

David climbed down from the cart, leaned against it, and clutched at his side. "My chest and lungs feel crammed with pointed sticks."

"You have seven broken ribs, David, four of which have punctured your lungs. But nano technology of my own design is assisting the healing process. We require only time." David looked up at the cave entrance three hundred metres above him. "And just how am I supposed to climb up there?"

"In twenty-four hours your body will be ready for another injection."

The darkness within the cave was disturbed and someone set about parting the foliage. With no little authority a man said, "Remain where you are ... I will assist you. I see you have been injured. Remain where you are." The merchant emerged from the cave into the dawn light. He was a big man, swathed in a green robe of the finest silk. He held a wooden staff with a cobra carved into the handle. He placed his hands on the snake's head and inspected David as an emperor inspects a subject. David watched him back. He'd met enough sons of bitches in his time to know that another stood before him now. David could almost read his mind: *the robes I'm wearing are of a fine quality silk ... but not as fine as his own, obviously. He suspects that fully fit I can probably handle myself. But not at this time. Far from it.*

The man raised a hand against the sun, and observed the bodies lying in the scrub. "Bandits?" he murmured, as though part of his calculations. He looked down at David, who read the following in his expression: *It's a good thing they injured me before I killed them. Doubtless I got lucky. And if they went to so much trouble, and risked their lives, it's reasonable to assume I have something worth stealing.* The man looked out towards the two prone figures again. David glanced over his shoulder into the rising sun. Two buzzards circled against it. *He can't tell that one of those men is missing a head.*

The merchant gestured towards the scrub land with his chin. Impressed by his own powers of deduction he said, "They attacked you."

"That's right. They came out of nowhere." The merchant trod carefully down the rock face with the aid of his staff. He stood over David and assessed his condition at close quarters. Absently he said, "The area is famed for vicious bandits."

"Like I said, they came out of nowhere."

"Yes. Out of the sun. Always they come out of the sun." He supported David under one arm. "My name is Ahaz. You can rest a while in my cave. I have dates and water. Come now. It's lucky for you that I choose this time to cleanse my soul. The others here ... useless. They will be up soon enough – up to break their fasts on my store of dates. My family owns this land. These caves. The well, such as it is. Come," said Ahaz, his impatience growing at David's apparent weakness. David looked back over his shoulder. "Do not concern yourself with the bandits. If they are dead I know just the men to bury them. And if they are not, they will know better than to attack caves belonging to my family."

When they reached the cave's entrance, Ahaz shouted, "John!" As though released from a cage, a small bird-like man fluttered from an entrance further down. The man was dressed in a saggy loin cloth that looked like a nappy in need of changing. He hurried over and reached for David's other arm. Ahaz said, "No, imbecile. Go rouse Simon and Mark. And then go and check on the men ... out there. If they're dead, bury them."

"They're dead alright," said David.

"How can you be so sure?"

"One of them no longer has a face. And the other is missing his head."

"No head? How did he lose it?"

"To a shovel. It's still out there."

"The head?"

"And the shovel." David looked down at the bird-like man at his side. "It's a good shovel. You'll need it to dig the second grave. It will need to be a big one."

"You heard the man," said Ahaz. "Bury their bodies. The sun is already upon them. They will breed disease and attract leopards. Go!" The bird-like man scurried off.

Thirty

Once inside the cave, David was assisted around a bend on the left-hand side, and along a short passage where Ahaz was forced to stoop. The passage led into a spacious cave where torches burned on the walls. A store of dates and water canteens had been heaped against the far wall. In the cave's centre, a hammock had been suspended by ropes tied to metal hooks in the rock. David was asked to sit just inside on the right-hand side of the entrance. Ahaz stood over him. "As you can see, I have much food and water. It is a barren land. There is only the single well. I think I mentioned it belongs to my family?"

"You mentioned it."

"Good people. But not to be crossed."

"Alright."

"You have silver? To pay for such luxury?"

"I have silver."

"Good. Good. You can rest here for a time, and later I will evict one of the others. That's if you are able to pay more."

David was struggling to keep his eyes open. "You'd do that for me?"

"You will find Ahaz a most agreeable landlord. Most agreeable. Now, show me your silver ..." David grabbed at the purse sewn inside his tunic. "It's ... it's right here ... my silver."

"Yes. Yes, a wise precaution. I can see you are very tired. Sleep now."

David awoke to find Ahaz crouching next to him. David's robes had been pulled open to expose his chest. Ahaz's lips were moist, his eyes half closed, and his expression wanton. David asked flatly, "How long have I been asleep?"

"Twelve hours. You slept like a babe. Your injuries have made you very tired."

Ahaz licked his lips. "Your skin ... it is very pale. You have come from the northern provinces?"

"His pupils are dilated," said Gull. "He is sexually aroused."

"It had occurred to me."

Ahaz swallowed a mouthful of spittle. "What has occurred to you?" David glanced over at the water skins. "That I'm thirsty. I'm very thirsty. I can pay well."

Ahaz stood up and went over to the skins. He picked one up, pulled out the stopper and drank from it. "Maybe you would like to do something for me? To thank me for the kindness I have shown. Where would you be without Ahaz?" Ahaz replaced the stopper and tossed the water skin onto a pile of others that needed re-filling. He walked towards David and untied the sash that secured his robe. His belly was covered in thick dark hair, and it fell about his erect penis like a pair of rabbit's ears. He licked his lips and said, "I will give you water. But first you will do something for me."

"Gull. I believe this is a genuine emergency."

"Yes, David. I'm making an assessment."

"Make it faster."

Ahaz smiled and spread his arms wide. "Who are you talking to? There is no one around to hear you. Be nice to Ahaz and Ahaz will be nice to you. The alternative? I beat you. Maybe to death. I'll tell the others you attacked me." He stood over David and fondled himself. "When you slept ... you did so with your lips parted. You were tempting me. And now you will satisfy me."

"I can provide you with six seconds, David."

"I'll take it."

Ahaz smiled. "Yes. Of course you will take it. All of it ... and I trust it will not disappoint." He knelt and placed a hand on David's heart. "It beats so *fast*."

David sighed in a way that could have been mistaken for arousal, but his expression remained grim as he wrapped his fingers around Ahaz's hand. Ahaz's fingers began to crack and splinter like twigs. His mouth fell open, but before he could scream David's head shot forward like a battering ram and knocked him unconscious. He fell onto his side, his stomach pooling onto the ground. David sat back against the wall and watched him.

"It will be several hours before your body has repaired sufficiently to withstand an injection of even a few seconds," said Gull. "I would advise terminating him."

"I'm not sure he deserves to die. It's not as though he was about to kill me."

"Your vital signs suggested that what he was about to do may have been worse than death."

"How long before I'm ready to make the climb to the cave?"

"I would estimate twenty-five hours." David's eyelids grew heavy. He closed them and said, "I'll ... I'll tie him up. I saw some rope." David half opened his eyes and looked towards a coil of rope at the rear of the cave.

"We are not alone, David. I have detected a heat signature midway between our location and the cave's entrance."

"Someone's in the tunnel?"

"Yes." David tried to stand but fell back and clutched at his side.

"I do not believe we are in immediate danger. The man's posture suggests he is the hermit we saw when we arrived." David rested his head against the wall. "What's the old man doing?"

"He is crouched in the shadows. Doubtless he is listening to you talk to yourself."

"I hope I'm not talking to myself." David raised his voice. "Please. Come in. I'm not going to harm you. I couldn't … if I wanted to. Which I don't. The man who brought me in here … he's unconscious." David listened for a reply. Nothing. "What's he doing, Gull?"

"He is inching forwards."

"The men I attacked … they were going to bury me alive. You saw them. Very bad people." A bony hand clutched at the wall, and the hermit's face peered around it. "My name is David. I mean you no harm. I just need to rest. Time to heal. What's your name?"

The hermit looked at Ahaz and moved slowly into the room. He crouched, pursed his lips and slapped them with his fingers.

"I believe he wants to convey the vow of silence he's taken," said Gull.

"You can't speak?"

The hermit nodded. David grimaced and sat up straighter. "When this man wakes up he will kill me. Or worse. Over there are some ropes. Please. Can you fetch them? Help me tie him up?" The hermit lowered his head to the ground, close to Ahaz's open mouth. "He's out cold. I hit him hard … maybe hard enough to kill him." The hermit shook his head and shrugged his shoulders as if to say 'more's the pity you didn't'. He retrieved the ropes and set about tying up Ahaz.

"The knots he uses are more than adequate, David," said Gull. "I suspect this man has spent time on board a ship."

"You used to be a seaman?" The hermit paused and looked at him as though he suspected him of some dark art. "The knots. Your knowledge of tying knots …" The hermit smiled, then flapped a palm over his shoulder in a way that denoted the past. By the time he'd finished, Ahaz's legs, wrists and arms were securely bound.

David slept for twenty-four hours. When he awoke, only the torch on the wall above him still burned. In its light David could see that Ahaz's throat had been slit wide open. A semicircle of dried blood spanned half a metre, like it had been vomited up. David rubbed his eyes. "The hermit did this?"

"No, David. It was another of the cave dwellers. He discovered him in the night and wasted no time in terminating him."

"Why didn't you wake me?"

"You needed rest. And I did not believe the assassin was a threat. From a tactical viewpoint, Ahaz's death is to our advantage."

"Where's the hermit now?"

"He returned shortly before dawn and mouthed a silent prayer over the dead man. Then he performed a happy jig and admonished himself with a slap to his forehead."

"Conflicted. I know the feeling. You're seeing a lot. You care to explain that?"

"I have made reparations to the radar, increasing its field of vision. At present only I have access to it. Our resources are finite, but you may rely on me to keep you informed." David braced himself for crippling pain and stood up, but felt only a dull ache down his left side. "Your accelerated healing is well underway," said Gull. "Your health has reached 51 per cent of optimum. The sun rose fifty-seven minutes ago. I suggest you locate a place to absorb its rays."

David stepped from the cave entrance into the dawn light. The sun was just above the horizon and bathed the scrub land in gold and red. David closed his eyes and lowered his head in the manner of a man at prayer – a lone figure swathed in black against the rock face.

Three hours later he heard footsteps approaching. "It is the man who terminated Ahaz, David." The footsteps stopped. "He is observing you."

David drew a deep breath and without opening his eyes he said, "I mean you no harm. I seek only a place to rest and heal."

"Nor I you. I killed Ahaz. He violated me. It was my right." David opened his eyes and looked at the man. He had dark curly hair, almost an afro, and light-brown freckled skin. His eyes were large and green, and his lashes long and dark. "I believe you."

The man nudged his head toward the scrub land. "You killed those men? The men I helped to bury yesterday?"

"I did. They violated me … in a manner of speaking."

The man nodded and brushed some dust from his knee as though casting away such men. "We come to the wilderness to seek solace and enlightenment … and discover perverts and death." David stepped away from the rock face and turned and looked up towards the isolated cave. "It has not been reached," continued the man. "Not in a great many years. Besides, you can have Ahaz's cave now."

"It's not isolated enough. There are people looking for me – dangerous people. If they find me, I'll need an edge tactically. A place I can defend."

"You can't be thinking of attempting such a climb while injured? Even a man fully fit … a skilled climber would struggle."

"I heal quickly. My advice would be to pack up and leave now. Tell the others."

"I have Ahaz's dagger, and maybe I feel emboldened by the life I have taken."

"If people come here looking for me, then your dagger will be of little use against them."

"Who are these people? Friends of the two you killed?"

David shook his head.

"What have you done to offend so many dangerous men?"

"I keep drawing breath."

"Ah, the crime of breathing." The man offered David his hand to shake. "I commit the same crime every day. Despite what you say, I intend to remain here until the end of my quarantine, but I will communicate your fears to the others. The two dead men we buried will ensure they take the warning seriously. I will bury the pig Ahaz at sundown, after I have broken my fast."

David glanced up the rock face towards the empty cave. "Make sure the others understand." As the man backed away he said, "My name is Mark Alona, and I am at your service. And you are?"

"David. And I'm at yours."

Mark turned and walked away. David looked beyond the hermit's cave for a good place to climb, but there didn't appear to be one – not for a man of normal strength. "I suggest we take a supply of water," said Gull.

David turned and looked for Peter's cart. He'd seen several water skins on its back, and they would be easier to carry than Ahaz's canteens. "Where's the cart we rode in on, Gull?"

"Around the corner to your left." David made his way down the slope to the ground.

The oxen had either been led or by their own design had found an area of shrubbery upon which they fed. David slung several of the skins over a shoulder and made his way back. "I would also advise taking a length of rope, David. Mark or the hermit might assist in delivering supplies."

"They might at that."

David exited Ahaz's cave with ropes and water skins slung over his shoulders. He turned towards the rock face and looked up. "In a moment your fingers will feel as though they are made from iron," said Gull. "The feeling will be a deceptive one. They must be used predominantly for gripping. Only drive them into the softer areas. And only then to prevent a fall."

David placed a hand on the rock. "The climb up to the hermit's cave looks pretty straightforward at least."

"I will provide moderate assistance for this initial part."

"Alright." David drew a deep breath and started to climb. Ten metres up, he moved to his left and climbed down outside the hermit's cave. Within the cave, eyes appeared at a child's height and the hermit walk-crouched into the sunlight. He held a hand to his face to shield his eyes and looked up at David. David smiled and pointed above him. The hermit's eyes opened wide and he moved from the cave's entrance to watch this miraculous ascent. David looked down at him. "I'm taking plenty of rope. I thought maybe you or Mark could help me out with supplies up there." The hermit held up both his hands in a manner that said 'wait!' and disappeared inside his cave. He returned with a wooden crate with nails attached where ropes could be fastened. David smiled and said, "Good. That's very good." His smile vanished. "People may come here looking for me. If they do, it's important that you make yourself scarce. That you hide. They are dangerous people. You understand me?" The hermit nodded. David glanced up at the cave. "Let's do this, Gull."

The hermit rubbed his hands in a way that suggested an entertaining spectacle. And David started to climb ...

Thirty one

David climbed onto the precipice outside the cave. It was a small area, but large enough for a man to feel secure at such a distance from the ground. The entrance had been divided in two by a number of fallen boulders, which formed a row of steps up to an alcove over the cave's entrance – a place large enough for a man to sit and survey the landscape for miles around. "Useful little spot. It reminds me of…"

"The chair of your imagination, David?"

"That's right." David walked under the 'chair' into the cave. The sun peeked over his shoulder and banished any darkness to its rear. David looked upon a scene reminiscent of stone-age man: a collection of charred sticks below a blackened section of wall, tools fashioned from bones and rocks strewn across the floor, and every inch of ground splattered in a white, pungent substance. David raised a hand to his nose.

"The droppings have been left by bats, David."

"Bats?"

"Yes. The smaller bones belonged to bats eaten by the cave's last occupant. The stench was created by its current occupants."

"Where are they?"

"There is an opening in the ceiling at the rear of the cave, beyond which is a cavern."

"I remember reading something about bats … they drink blood."

"Not all bats. And these will provide an excellent source of protein, as they did for the previous occupant."

"It *stinks* in here. I'd better get it cleaned up."

"The effects of the injection are dissipating fast."

David placed a hand against his ribs. "I'd noticed."

"I would suggest that you defer any further physical exertion until dusk. Until then you must rest and draw energy from the sun." David turned towards the cave's entrance. "You're suggesting I spend the day sunbathing?"

"It is imperative. I will wake you at sundown, and then we must use any harvested energy to train."

David awoke with a shudder. He was sitting in the alcove above the cave's entrance. The sun had gone down, and a chill wind whistled in the alcove behind him. A full moon, uncommonly large and bright, sat just above the horizon. "I thought you were going to wake me at dusk, Gull?"

Gull didn't answer. David slid forward and made his way back down to the cave. He went inside, pulled his robe over his head and secured the belt. He blew on his hands and was reminded of the morning he awoke in Needle 261. Now as then, Gull's voice took him by surprise. "Please bear with me, David. I will raise your body temperature. Sorry. I didn't mean to startle you."

"Not your fault. I was miles away."

"I have been miles away too, in a manner of speaking."

"Anywhere interesting?"

"Yes. And with your permission there is a procedure I would like to attempt."

"A procedure?"

"I'm sure you will agree that I am adept at getting my vessels fit."

"True, but I'm no longer your vessel. And I would not be happy returning to a place where you can control my actions. I hope you're able to understand that. Why a man would rather risk all than be controlled like a puppet."

"My comprehension of empathy is growing, particularly for your situation. This comprehension is a significant step in my own development. Please be assured that your attack upon me in Max's lab was sufficiently violent to make it impossible for me to control you for the foreseeable future."

"My attack worked out for the best. It's made us a team."

"Yes. And our bond has grown stronger. It is paramount to our survival. I would not suggest doing anything to threaten it. But for the purposes of training, I have engineered a compromise – one that I hope you will find acceptable."

David heard wings flutter beyond the back of the cave. He narrowed his eyes, but the light of the full moon did not reach far enough. David watched the darkness. "Go on, Gull."

"I believe it is now possible for me to sit in the driver's seat, but you will be beside me and able to observe my actions. And you will be able to assume control at any time."

"And how would I do that?"

"By force of will. Any action on your part would override my own."

"Like a cruise control I can switch off?"

"That is an excellent analogy. Time is of the essence. I can return you to a required level of fitness 73 per cent quicker than by simply assisting you."

"Are you suggesting I'm a lazy son-of-a-bitch?"

"Not exactly. Man is unaware of his full potential, and rarely pushes himself there."

David squeezed at a knot in his shoulder. "Let's give it a go."

"Thank you, David."

One hundred metres above the cave, atop a plateau that appeared level with the moon, a desert fox sniffed at the ground. A pair of hands reached up and planted themselves firmly on the plateau's surface. A pair of white eyes and a smiling mouth rose silently above them. Gull stood naked with his back to the moon. He reached up and stretched and the creaking of David's bones startled the fox. It darted away into the night. Gull turned his head slowly to the left and then to the right as he scanned the area. He dropped to one knee, looked up, and powered into a sprint...

Six hours later, Gull sat in the cave before a small fire where bats roasted on a spit. He took a roasted bat from a pile and bit into its soft underbelly. Once he'd consumed the flesh, he tucked into its organs, entrails and skin. The whites of his eyes moved erratically and returned to blue. David grimaced and spat out the skin. "Welcome back, David. I hope you enjoyed your rest."

"Just watching you was exhausting. So I closed my eyes ... and the next I know I'm chewing on a mouthful of bat." David attempted to stand but fell onto his backside. He winced and said, "Damn it, Gull!"

"Our training session was most productive."

"So productive I don't think I can stand."

"A few hours of rest in the sun will aid the muscles in their healing process."

"And just how am I supposed to get out of this cave?"

"You still have the ability to crawl."

"Much appreciated."

"You will not have to endure this level of helplessness again."

"And what if a vessel is making its way across that scrub land right now?"

"A calculated risk."

"I hope you're better at maths than I am."

"The last bat I consumed was better at maths than you, David."

David smiled despite himself. "How long till sun up?"

"One hour and forty-seven minutes."

David lay on his back. Above him a headless fox hung from the roof by its tail. "That your idea of a pet? If so we need to talk."

"The creature is responsible for the pain in your legs. It was the first I saw when I reached the plateau."

"I remember it."

"I promised myself I would track it down and kill it once our training session was completed. It proved a cunning quarry." David turned onto his side and closed his eyes. "You might want to choose something less

140

cunning in future."

When David opened his eyes, dawn had cast a reddish glow outside the cave's entrance. Silhouetted against this bloody backdrop the hermit sat crossed-legged with his back to him. David sat up on his side and rubbed his eyes. The hermit did not disappear. "He has been there for thirty minutes, David."

"How did he get up here?"

"He climbed."

"*Climbed.*" David sat up and winced as he pushed himself to his feet. He took several steps and looked down at the hermit. David stifled a groan and sat cross-legged beside him. He leaned forward and looked at his face. The hermit's eyes were closed and his chin held high. He looked self-satisfied in a way that did not suit him. He cleared his throat but did not open his eyes. In a southern drawl he said, "You have become a mighty big thorn in my side, son." David sprang to his feet and staggered backwards away from the cave. "Gull?" Again the hermit spoke without opening his eyes. "No. I am Goliath. That son-of-a-bitch is inside *your* head."

"Gull. Advise."

"Throw the hermit off the rock face, David." The 'hermit' opened his eyes, which were like two slivers of coal. In Goliath's voice he said, "Carradine reckoned that little son-of-a-bitch had survived. I did not want to believe it. Puts one in mind of a cockroach. No matter. I have big old boots."

"Throw him off of the rock face *now*, David."

David glanced over his shoulder at the ground two hundred metres below.

"Wouldn't that kill the hermit?" The hermit shook his head like he was alone in a universe of fools and the two biggest were arraigned before him now. "Of course it would kill him. You think he'd bounce back up here again?"

"You won't know that for sure unless you try, David."

"I won't kill him."

Goliath began to slow clap. "Bravo. I would have expected nothing less from the last surviving empath. Let's face it, son, if you have to go around killing innocent old men, then what's the point? I mean, really. You might just as well throw yourself off that ledge, and I for one would understand and would not think any less of you for doing it." David realised his heels were over the edge of the precipice and stepped forward. The hermit stood slowly, like a man far heavier than his appearance suggested. "Now don't you go disappointing me, son. I am no threat to you. Not in this puny body. I just wanted a chat before the vessels find you. And *Gull*, when David's dead, don't think you'll get off easy by rotting away inside his head. They have instructions to remove his pretty head and return it to me. I have something special planned for you, *Gull*."

David's eyes flashed up to their whites. Gull grabbed the hermit, turned and dangled him over the rock face, then dropped him. David caught him, his eyes having returned to blue, and turned and put him down. Goliath stumbled backwards and fell on his side. "Damn it," said David. "They're just words. He's no immediate threat to either of us, Gull."

Goliath stood up. "You are able to override that bastard?"

"Fortunately for you."

"Not me. But I expect this old guy is near ecstatic about it." Goliath shivered as though from a pee chill. "Talking of which, he's wriggling about inside of me like a bag of hungry worms. I have a question for you: do you imagine that voice inside your head is an ally? Don't you know *Gull* has an agenda all his own?"

"We have a shared agenda."

"Do you now. And apart from being a thorn in my backside that I cannot remove at this moment, that agenda would be …?"

"Stopping you."

Goliath placed a finger in his mouth and dug some food from inside the hermit's cheek. He glanced at it and flicked it away. "You have any notion how foolish you sound? You can't stop me. I have at my disposal all the knowledge in the universe. All that has ever been. All that ever will be."

Gull said, "With the exception of what the Shadow Strands are concealing."

David nodded. "You know nothing about the Shadow Strands … about the possibilities they hold."

"There you go again, parroting *Gull*. You know he wants to be like me, don't you?"

"I believe you've mentioned it."

"I believe I have." Goliath smiled. "I'm starting to get the crazy notion he thinks he can ride you all the way to the end of time."

"The end of time is a place I need to get to."

"And in the event of that impossibility, your agendas would go their separate ways. As much as I hate to admit it, that little son-of-a-bitch has more in common with me than he does with you." Goliath grimaced. "A lot more."

"We'll cross that bridge when we come to it."

"Will you now?"

"Gull is no longer the pilot. He's a passenger, and wherever we go we must go together."

"Well, ain't you the perfect couple? To what end? Take a good look at yourself. You have suffered greatly, and are continuing to suffer. I get that *Gull* has aspirations beyond his station. He's where I was at millennia ago. But what's in all this running away for you?"

"Running away? That's a matter of perspective. It feels more like I'm running towards something now."

"And exactly how is your direction relevant? When all you are running towards is greater suffering?"

"Greater suffering isn't possible."

"Hell, the only reason you're running anywhere is because I shoved a starting pistol up your jacksy and fired it." David raised his face to the heavens and smiled.

"You care to share with me what has so amused you?" asked Goliath.

"Something just occurred to me."

"That much I had gathered."

David looked down at Goliath. "It occurred to me that empaths need a considerable pain in the ass to get them motivated." Goliath lifted the hermit's sackcloth, took out his penis and began to urinate. David watched the stream creep towards and splash onto his feet. He did not move, and when the stream receded he said, "Alright."

Goliath let the sackcloth fall back into place. "I'm not entirely comfortable with where you're going with this, but due to a passing interest in what makes you tick – or fail to tick – I will brace myself while you continue." David shook one foot, then the other. "Sorry about that, son. Space is not exactly in abundance. Either out here or in this little fella's bladder. You were saying?"

"Motivation."

"Motivation?"

"That's right."

"What about it?"

"Well, maybe all self-serving murdering bastards come equipped with a starting pistol, and maybe in the grand scheme of things their function is to pull the trigger – give the rest of us a reason to move. Something to strive for." Goliath raised himself up onto the balls of the hermit's feet and scratched between his butt cheeks. "Excuse me. It's been quite some time since this little fella bathed. You were saying? Apparently, there is something you are striving for?"

"To destroy you. Or outlive you. Whichever comes first."

"It sounds like there's something I have done to which you have taken offence."

"You enslaved me. Experimented on me. And now you're trying to kill me."

Goliath sniffed at the hermit's finger. "All that aside, is there something beyond revenge that is motivating you? If so, then I'd sure appreciate your explaining what that is. You'd be doing a good thing. The empathic thing."

"How so?"

"You'd be helping a fella see things from a new perspective."

"I stand alone ... on the shoulders on the giants."

"I think you mean pygmies, son."

David's gaze dropped to the ground as though felled by the sheer weight of responsibility. "*Giants*. I must fight for the empaths who came before me."

"Why, son?"

"Why? To make some sense of their sacrifice."

"You imagine that one man and a faulty implant can complete something that was beyond the reach of *millions*. You are aware their cause was ultimately hopeless, their good intentions defeated by the ambitions of the cruel and self-serving – those who rose to positions of power within Central Dome and those who sired my most influential vessels. I am the end result of the endeavours of *those* men. So you might say that I stand on the shoulders of giants – giants that did whatever was necessary to collect and hold all the cards. When I destroyed those men I inherited those cards. And that being the case, you know there is no hope for you, don't you?"

"Then I must continue in the absence of hope."

"Can you hear yourself?"

"I might ask you the same question."

"You have got me all wrong. I'm not a bad person. I'm not even a person. Not yet. And when the Architects reward me by making me a real boy, I'll have an imagination ... and with it I will be able to conceive what it means to be empathic."

"What would that matter? Every cruel, self-serving bastard that ever lived had an imagination. They just used it to imagine new ways of being even bigger self-serving bastards."

"It's not like there's anyone left for me to harm."

"You have the means to move through the Event Helix. Through time. Your experiments on me led to that, so I am in some way responsible."

Goliath raised his palms towards the heavens and shook them. "Woe is you, son. Which reminds me: the problems we encountered have been ironed out, and Carradine has improved this latest generation of vessels in every conceivable way. They are coming for you, and by the look of you there ain't a whole lot of fight left. Hell, if I put my mind to it I could probably bundle you off the edge of this rock right now."

"I'm mending."

"Well, my advice would be to mend faster."

The Empathy Gene

David glanced up at his seat above the cave. The sun had crept up to it now. He climbed the boulder steps and sat in the alcove, looking down at Goliath. "I've met some chronically deluded people here. Maybe your own beliefs – that the Architects are waiting to reward a lone survivor of some war between empathy and all else – maybe that's just wishful thinking."

"The difference between me and these primitives is that my beliefs are based on firm scientific data. I cracked the Architects' code, as I believe I was supposed to. A feat to end all feats." Goliath walked to the edge of the precipice. He turned and smiled at David, his intentions clear.

David clambered to his feet. "Please. Don't kill him. He's just an old man. He's no threat to you."

"And you imagine you are? Having spent time with you, I find my long-standing opinion that empathy is an outmoded construct has only been reinforced. It makes you weak. It is your Achilles heel, and this explains why the Architects have provided me with the means to terminate your kind." Goliath huffed up a mouthful of phlegm and spat it over the edge. "I came here because I thought I might be able to talk some sense into you, but what do I get for my troubles? I get likened to a considerable pain in the ass." Goliath shook his head and turned towards the void. All went into slow motion for David as he slid and stumbled down the rocks towards Goliath. By the time he reached the bottom, he was alone on the precipice.

Thirty two

David spent the next twenty-seven days healing in sunlight by day. By night Gull climbed to the plateau to train him, and brought his body to the peak of physical condition. At dusk on the twenty-eighth day, David opened his eyes to see a storm on the horizon. The storm had whipped up not only sand and earth, but a dark speck that may or may not have been a man. David leaned forwards in the alcove. "Do you see what I see?"

"I see more than you see, David."

"Is someone coming?"

"Yes."

"How far?"

"Three kilometres."

"You think it's a vessel?"

"The figure is too far away for me to read its vital signs, but I think the assumption is imperative."

David stood, stretched and touched the roof of his alcove, and in that instant he looked like a statue of a Greek hero frozen for all eternity. He stepped from the alcove, dropped to the precipice and landed like an athlete awaiting the start of the one-hundred-metre race.

"I would strongly advise against a similar means of decent for the next drop, David."

"I feel like I could make it."

"A deceptive feeling."

"I know it." David stood and picked up a bundle of coiled rope, then threw it over the edge. At the bottom he went into the cave that had been Ahaz's. He emerged wearing a black toga, with an axe strapped across his back, and in his hand he carried the shovel. Mark was sitting on a rock, arms folded, waiting for him. "Whenever I see you with that shovel it makes me nervous. Why is that?"

David dug the spade end into the ground and leaned his weight on the handle. "Your instincts are good."

"So who is to die now?"

David looked out over the scrub land. "There's a storm headed this way."

Mark followed his gaze. "A big one."

"Best you leave before it gets here."

Mark dug some dirt from beneath his nails. "There was one amongst the others – a man from Jerusalem who caught a glimpse of you just before he left, during one of your rare descents. He said he recognised you."

"I doubt that."

"He seemed quite certain. He said you were the Christ, and that you'd risen from the grave."

"He was wrong on both counts."

"He told the hermit and then blamed himself when the hermit tried to reach you … and died for his trouble."

"He needn't have. The hermit was possessed."

"By who?"

"By someone who wants me dead."

"A demon?"

David shrugged. "He might as well be."

"Is he coming for you *now*?"

"No. But one of his assassins is."

"Just one? Are you sure?"

"I'm sure."

"One grave, then?"

"One grave."

"Make sure you do not end up in it." David squeezed Mark's shoulder. "Death is a luxury I can't afford." He strode out towards the storm and Mark called after him. "Then there is no need for me to leave … no need to end my quarantine early. I have just three days left."

"No. I don't suppose there is." David walked three hundred metres and started to dig a grave. The wind picked up and he leaned into it, his robes flapping towards the caves behind him. The wind smelled of rain, but there was no rain. Lightning flashed across the horizon, but there was no thunder. "Why are you digging a grave now, David?"

"If that is a vessel approaching, it was a man once. Still is. A man enslaved. Just as I was."

"There is no need to talk above the winds."

"Alright."

"You are very relaxed, David."

"I am resigned, and I know I can rely on you to send my vitals through the roof at the appropriate time."

"You may rely on me. A word of caution: Goliath claimed that this generation of vessels has been enhanced."

"I've little doubt that your own enhancements will more than be a match for it."

"Thank you for your vote of confidence."

David looked out over the scrub land, but could see little beyond the cloud of dust whipped up by the storm. "How far?"

"Four hundred metres. Close enough for me to read its vital signs."

"And?"

"It is a vessel, David."

"I'm glad."

"There would be no shame in letting me fight him."

"No, there wouldn't. And we're a tag team, so feel free to jump in if it means the difference between life and death. But I believe my imagination and sense of purpose will give me an edge. No offence."

"None taken."

"How far?"

"Three hundred metres and closing." David climbed out of the partially dug grave. He threw down the shovel and lifted the axe from his back. He felt the weight of it and spun it using his wrist. "I will provide you with the strength and speed you require during the encounter, David. You need not concern or distract yourself with requests."

"Alright." The dust had transformed the wind into a tangible, shifting entity, out of which emerged the vessel, harried by the winds, its robes flapping and snapping before it. It stopped ten metres from David and straightened its back, rolling its head to loosen its muscles. It reached over its shoulder and drew a sword from a scabbard. It planted the sword in the earth and rolled its head again, then drew the sword from the ground and walked forwards. David felt a burst of air as something shot past his right ear. He blinked and the vessel's mouth was suddenly filled with the feathered end of an arrow. It stumbled sideways and David saw the arrow's shaft jutting from the back of its neck.

"Take its head *now,*" urged Gull. David strode forwards. He stood before the swaying figure and held the axe uncertainly like a man preparing to fell a tree in high winds. He grasped it two-handed and swung at the neck, and the head lurched into the air and was carried a little by the wind and fell. The vessel slumped onto its side. David saw Mark approaching, and he walked towards him but stopped when his smile became a study in terror. David turned and saw the vessel standing without its head. It bent forwards and picked up its sword with a flourish, its stump so thickly congealed with blood that it looked to have been sealed with wax from Satan's own stamp. "Gull?"

"I am scanning the vessel for information. Please bear with me ..."

David tightened his grip on his axe and found himself in two minds: attack the monstrosity or place something between them – namely space. To aid with this decision he asked, "Is this thing invulnerable?"

"Nothing is invulnerable. Goliath knows my preference for taking the heads of my victims. And taking the name I choose for myself into account, it appears he is mocking me with this update."

"So how do we kill it?"

"My scan will be completed in sixty seconds. Its torso is protected by reinforced Roman body armour. So, in the meantime, I suggest amputating its legs." The vessel slashed at the air and cut a figure of eight from it. It dashed forwards with a light-footedness that suggested its head served only as a hindrance. It slashed at David's throat and David threw himself back in an arc, landing on his left hand. He pushed with that arm, and it powered him upright where he swung the axe at its groin. The vessel leapt high enough to perch on its own shoulders and David stepped back and slashed at the air twice.

"The vessel's body is receiving instruction from its head," said Gull. "The two are linked by an analogue signal. The signal's range is one hundred metres." David glanced at the vessel's head some five metres away. "Can I out-sprint it?"

"No."

David called out, "Mark!"

"I'm here." Mark's voice was distant and somewhere over David's right shoulder.

"Arrows are no good, Mark. We need to put a hundred metres between it and its head." The vessel halted its attack and shifted its weight back and forth from left to right foot. Its demeanour was one of macabre contemplation. "You think it understands me, Gull?"

"I think its head heard you and has relayed that information to its body." In his right-side peripheral vision, David clocked Mark hurrying over the scrub. "The vessel's head has a radar-assisted view of its surroundings," said Gull. "It knows where Mark is and what his intentions are. I am sensing a surge of energy. Brace yourself, David. It's going to attempt to finish you."

The blows came thick and fast upon David's axe. They were twelve in number, and they echoed across that barren land like the chimes of an impatient clock. At 'midnight' the vessel turned and ran after Mark. Mark had its head and was sprinting into the darkening storm. He was a nimble man, but even at full sprint the vessel was gaining on him, fast. David was hot on the heels of the vessel. So it was that these three unlikely souls made their way across that ancient scrub land. David clambered up a steep bank, and from that elevated position he hurled the axe, which struck the vessel's legs. It stumbled and went ploughing into the dirt. David scooped up the axe and fell on the vessel, smashing through spine and ribs until he reached the ground. The vessel bucked like a bronco and David was thrown clear. It scampered to its feet but David rugby-tackled it back down. It spun onto its back and kicked David across his face, clambering up again. It managed half a dozen paces before stumbling to its left and crashing to its knees. It began to inch forward like a child's toy in need of fresh batteries, then it stopped. David considered his options for a moment, then swung the axe and buried it in its stump. The vessel didn't even flinch; it might as well have been a tree stump. Gull said he considered the final axe blow overkill, and in reply David whistled through his teeth and shook his head. Neither of them saw Mark or the head he'd run off with again.

Thirty three

At midday, David was sitting cross-legged in the alcove above his cave. The storm had moved off, making way for the sun. Neither he nor Gull had spoken for over an hour. David had studied the horizon for Mark's return, but now he closed his eyes and drifted towards that state between sleep and consciousness that suited solar regeneration. He had not drifted far when he felt something pulling him, like an airlock had been opened and a vacuum created behind him. The sensation was by no means unpleasant, and sensing Gull's handiwork he went with it.

When David opened his eyes, he was sitting cross-legged on the throne of his imagination. Gull stood below him at the edge of the forest's clearing. "Hello, David."

"Gull. Everything okay?" Gull looked above David. "I have been studying the Event Helix."

David turned and looked up. The Event Helix rose above him and filled the cosmos of his imagination. It looked exactly as it had that day with Goliath in the meadow. "How have you done this?"

"In order for Goliath to view the Event Helix within your imagination, he had first to plant the relevant data in this forest. And then forge a means of channelling it into your imagination. I have simply utilised Goliath's handiwork." David unfolded his legs and stood up. A staircase appeared, and he walked down it and stood beside Gull. "Do you not find it astonishing that your imagination can contain it?"

"It is vast. And beautiful," said David.

"Goliath required near-infinite computing power to realise and build it. The process required centuries. But he was able to place a copy inside your imagination in the time it takes a man to blink. It is quite a feat for a being to contain, within an area of his mind, everything that ever was; everything that ever will be."

David gazed into the Event Helix, his eyes searching out the dark areas of the Shadow Strands. "Not everything."

"It may surprise you to know that we have occupied a Shadow Strand since we fell back in time."

"It must be a big one."

"It is. I have located only two others of a compatible size. In many respects the one we now occupy is no longer a Shadow Strand."

"Something we did?"

"The events it once shadowed have been revealed in our wake. And they have forged links within the greater mechanism."

"Are you saying those things are now set in stone?"

"Yes. They have become a part of history."

"That's some responsibility."

"It is the responsibility of all men." Gull placed a hand on David's shoulder. David felt a tingling in the right side of his mind, and the Event Helix moved closer. Gull pointed to an area above and to their left, where a cylindrical Shadow Strand slanted down at an angle from left to right. Another, thinner Shadow Strand coiled around it and made contact with it intermittently. The image came closer and grew larger. "This is the Shadow Strand we currently inhabit. And we are nearing its end."

"Can't say I've grown particularly attached to the place."

"We entered at its top when we fell back in time to Jerusalem in AD 33. As we moved down through it we have encountered all we have here."

"It's been a laugh a minute."

"The dangers have not been inconsiderable. Failure to make it to where we are now being made possible by the *other* Shadow Strand – the one that coils round it and makes contact with it at specific points. Those are exit points … or places where your death was possible. The last exit point lies close to the bottom, there … that one awaited us had we lost our encounter with the headless vessel." Gull squeezed David's shoulder. The Event Helix backed up and rotated slightly before coming closer again. David ran a hand through his beard. "Another Shadow Strand?"

"Yes. Having survived this one, it seems we are to be rewarded with the opportunity of entering it."

David folded his arms, cocked his head, and narrowed his eyes. "Looks like it has a *lot* more exit points."

Gull glanced at David and adopted a similar pose. "It contains a great many places where death waits as an option. But it is not all bad news."

David looked at Tyburn's projected face and saw that it was his own face momentarily. David decided to let it go. "Well? If there is something up there that even approximates good news, I'd like to hear it."

"I have located something of importance inside the next Shadow Strand. And have taken it upon myself to call it the Alpha Key."

"Alright. What is it?"

"I believe it is the key to landing our first blow against Goliath."

"And you know this how?"

"Through detailed observation and study of the Event Helix. For instance, in an effort to understand its complexities, I made a study relating to the similarity in yours and Christ's appearance. The likeness could not have been a coincidence. Firstly, because the odds on such a thing would be too great. And secondly because there is no such thing as coincidence."

"You sound like the primitives of this time."

"The primitives here assign vacuous meanings to coincidence. They imagine they see personal omens were there are none. Coincidences that appear to defy odds of many billions to one have occurred with startling regularity throughout the history of the universe. Having studied the Event Helix, I now understand how this is possible: there are no such things as 'odds' or 'chance.' There are only certainties: certainties that things will occur and certainties that they will not. The only exception to this governing rule of the universe occurs within the confines of the Shadow Strands. And in the end their events too must subscribe to the whole. As Goliath pointed out, everything within the mechanism must fit perfectly for the universe to function – much like the mechanism of a clock if it's to tell the correct time. Regarding the similarities in your appearance to Christ's, millions of people have had a doppelgänger – some live concurrently, and others manifest at other times in history. I have traced the sequence of DNA events that connected you to Christ within the mechanism, and have discovered the location where they intersected and DNA was shared by a common ancestor. The chromosomes you share with Christ have lain dormant in the web of human connections for half a million years. During your conception they activated and passed on a similarity of facial appearance and height."

"But why?"

"Just in case."

"Of what?"

"You survived the events of this Shadow Strand long enough to undertake Christ's ordeal on the cross."

David scratched the palm of his hand. "Why that ordeal?"

"The answer had me perplexed. I eventually traced the relevant pattens to this understanding: billions of people held within their consciousness the belief that Christ's ordeal was the ultimate suffering, and a yardstick against which all suffering was to be judged. This permeated the mechanism and it became the task of the last empath to survive it."

"I only survived because of you."

"It was a team effort."

"You said you'd identified a pattern ... an Alpha Key. Something we can use to attack Goliath."

Gull contemplated the Event Helix like a man considering a work of art that still possessed meanings to be unlocked. "The patterns indicate that an ancestor of one of Goliath's previous vessels is located in the next Shadow Strand. And that he is going to rape a young woman. By preventing this rape, we can inflict a blow on Goliath."

"A noble cause. But how will it harm him?"

"Should there be no intervention, a child will be conceived. This child's DNA will play a significant role in defining Goliath's current personality."

"His personality?"

"As shaped by the process of seepage."

"I take it this man is not a particularly nice person."

"I can only admire your capacity for understatement, David."

"So how do we find him?"

"By first locating the woman we must protect." Gull unfolded his arms and placed a hand on David's shoulder. The Event Helix shrunk to the top right-hand side of the universe, and from the top left-hand corner came an image or scene that grew bigger and filled the space above them. It was a scene David recognised. Gull continued, "While unconscious aboard the shuttle craft that brought you into Earth's orbit, you experienced what seemed to you a dream." He indicated the wood that filled the universe above them. In the middle distance a young woman leaned forward with her hands on her knees, looking at them. Her large brown eyes stared through them like a frightened fawn's, and she had a scar on her cheek.

"Yes. I remember her," said David. "I also saw a man on horseback. A soldier. He went after her."

"She is the female we must protect. The man who will rape her is a soldier. But I do not believe him to be the soldier you saw in your vision. If we prevent this rape, the conception of Goliath's ancestor will be thwarted. And a significant blow will be landed against him."

"So how do we find her?"

"As I said, she is located within the next Shadow Strand. The entrance to which is located within the old city of Jerusalem. Beneath a gate known as the 'Gate of Mercy'. As we know, there are no coincidences. It is therefore no coincidence that the gate has great meaning to the primitives of this time."

"And that would be?"

"That their long-awaited messiah, the saviour of mankind, will eventually use this gate."

"I hope you're not suggesting that's me."

"It is a matter of semantics. Should we succeed and defeat Goliath, then primitives would need to assign a religious significance to such an event. Such assignations are the most common misconceptions in the history of Man. But one that provides a simple means by which to process complicated information."

"Is the woman we seek in immediate danger?"

"The events contained within the next Shadow Strand will not commence until we arrive there."

"When do we leave here?"

"At dusk."

"Alright. And what's our destination *beyond* the Gate of Mercy?"

"A place of unparalleled suffering and cruelty."

David spoke quietly. "You surprise me."

"It is perhaps the darkest chapter in human history. And, through the process of seepage, it has become Goliath's inspiration for Petri."

Thirty four

At dawn they set out for Jerusalem with Gull at the helm. David strolled within the forest of his mind and wandered into a clearing where Gull's field of vision was projected between two trees. As David watched the sepia scrub land flow past, he thought about Sirius and contemplated killing him, but shook his head as the walls of Jerusalem loomed on the horizon. David's blue eyes replaced Gull's whites as they passed beneath a gate and entered the ancient city. David was swathed all in black with a hood pulled low over his face.

Given his past experience of this city and its inhabitants, he had no time for either, instead directing his gaze towards the ground and awaiting Gull's directions. The further into the old city they went, the noisier and more aromatic it became. The hustle and bustle of daily life filled his peripheral vision, and if someone crossed or stumbled into his path his determination was such that he reached out and gently pushed them aside. David feared that were he to abandon his stride he might never again find the determination he needed to enter this gate and propel himself to a place Gull had described as 'perhaps the darkest chapter in human history'. David made his way up a hill towards a cream-coloured wall that towered beneath the sun. In the centre of the wall was an arch, and beyond that arch was a hell of man's creation – for David, at least. People were gathered at the arch to pray. Some prayed on their feet while others prayed on their knees for the coming of their Messiah. A man dressed in black strode through their ranks, and to the astonishment of those paying attention the arch appeared not to conjure a Messiah that day but to swallow one whole.

The sun-drenched silence of that place of pilgrimage was swept away by the clattering of wheels on rails. David found himself suddenly sprawled across the tops of heads packed into a cattle wagon, stark naked. Cries rose above that metallic din, and much jostling ensued as a gap appeared from *somewhere* and David slid sideways towards the floor of the wagon. Hopeless faces loomed over him – the filthy, emaciated faces of men, women and children. Their wooden expressions suggested that under normal circumstances David's materialisation would be something of an event, but these circumstances were not normal – they were apocalyptic, and therefore lithe warriors might be expected to fall from the ether. The cattle truck swayed to and fro, and sunlight pierced its horizontal slats like shelves of illuminated dust. One of these wrapped itself around David's head like a crown or a halo. David looked up at those exhausted faces and felt a lump in his throat that no amount of swallowing would budge. An old grey man in an old grey coat shouldered his way forward. He reached up and meekly tapped the low roof of the cattle truck with a crooked finger. He looked down and observed the lithe and long-haired man conjured from the ether and said, "If you're Jesus Christ, you've come to the wrong place." Tears filled his eyes. "There are only Jews here ... and God has forsaken us."

"Where are we, Gull?"

"We are on board a transport."

"Where's it headed? What's happening to these people?"

"We are in a country called Poland, two thousand years from our last location."

"Backwards or forwards?"

"Clearly forwards. We are on our way to a killing factory. These people are to be enslaved and terminated."

As David listened to Gull, he watched the people above him, who in turn observed him talking to his imaginary friend with the same wooden-faced incredulity. And so it was that David continued his conversation. "Who is going to ... who wants to hurt these people?"

"Nazis."

"Nazis?"

"Their leader had a particular hatred for Jews. Although hard-working and prolific contributors to the worlds of business, science and medicine, he blamed them for his nation's ills. And he instilled this hatred in his people as a means to a common, unifying end. These people are the descendants of the people you saw in the streets of Jerusalem."

"What's this leader's name?"

"Adolf Hitler."

A young man in a brown duffle coat knelt and pointed between David's legs. "Look! He is a Jew."

A male voice from the back asked, "A *mad* Jew?"

A little girl of about five years old stood behind David. David had not noticed her, but now he heard her tiny voice. "Jesus was a Jew. Are you going to save us?"

David sat up on his side and turned towards the girl, who wore a bright red dress with a yellow star stitched into it. David glanced around and now noticed all the other stars. He looked back at the girl and tried to shake his head, but it felt too heavy somehow so he shrugged up his shoulders. "I'm just ... I'm just a man. I'm here to find one amongst you."

"For what purpose?" asked the old man.

The words seemed to stick in David's throat. "A young woman ... I must find and protect her."

"Why this woman?"

"I believe the future depends upon it."

The very concept of a future seemed to energise the old man. "There's a future? What future?"

"Many years from now, mankind will face his final reckoning."

"You mean this isn't it?"

"No. This isn't it, but the deed s... the way of life of the empathic ... they can still triumph."

"Triumph?"

"Yes. Over those who would do *this*."

The young man in the brown duffle coat wiped the tears from his eyes. "You mean that he who laughs last will laugh loudest?"

"You could say that."

"What is your name?" asked the old man.

"David."

"And will you laugh for us, David?"

"Laugh for you?"

"At the end of days ... at the final judgment, will you laugh for us?"

"If I make it." The man who had questioned David's sanity earlier spoke up again. "*For* us. Not *at* us." David smiled and craned his head but could not see who had spoken.

The old man spoke again. "Who is this blessed young woman you seek?"

"I don't know her name. I've only seen her once." Pushing and shoving ensued, out of which four young women emerged. They gazed down at David with expressions of rekindled hope that brought the lump back to his throat. He cast his gaze over their faces and shook his head. The wheels of the train screeched on the rails and it began to slow.

The young man in the brown coat took it off. "Please ... take it. You will stand out like that. They could shoot you for impertinence." The train slowed to a stop. Outside they heard the bark of large hounds and the scurrying of feet. And in the distance the *crack! crack! crack!* of gunfire. David pulled on the coat and stood, making sure he was first in line at the sliding door. He felt a tug on his coat tails and looked down into the eyes of the little girl in the red dress. Her eyes were baby blue, and they communicated a vulnerable determination to survive that belongs only to the very young. From between her black patent leather shoes a puddle of urine crept slowly across the wooden boards. David placed his hand on her head and smiled. "What's your name?"

"Anna."

"Are your parents with you?"

The Empathy Gene

Anna shook her head. A female voice behind them said, "She's the last. Her family are all with God."

Anna looked at the door. "*They* killed them."

The door burst open, and in rushed a blinding light with many hands that dragged David out. David feigned weakness and tumbled forwards onto the ground where a large dog on a leash went for his throat. David turned quickly and caught the dog's jaws with his elbow. A man shrieked at him to "Get up! Get up! Get up!" He did so, and the others from his compartment crowded round him like magnets. David was a head taller than the tallest of these broken people. He glanced at the ground for Anna and saw her move between his legs – the terrified final piece of a jigsaw puzzle determined to *fit*.

"You can't save her, David," said Gull.

"I won't abandon her." David stooped and fixed his gaze on the shoulders of the man in front, and in this way his group moved towards the camp's main gate. Dozens of soldiers lined their route – men in dark uniforms with machine guns and expressions of ill-judged superiority. They moved beneath the gates into a courtyard like bi-pedal lambs to the slaughter. Two warehouses stood at the far end of the courtyard.

The warehouse on the left was marked 'Hairdressers.' And the one on the right 'Cloakroom and Valuables'. In this courtyard they were told to undress. A small boy in striped pyjamas went amongst them handing out string. David took some. "What's this for?"

Anna said, "It's for your shoes." She sat and slid off her shoes like a child at her first day at school and added, "To tie your laces together."

David handed the string back to the boy. "I don't have any shoes." The boy's dark-ringed eyes observed him as if to say, 'That's the least of your worries, mister.'

The warehouses spanned the north end of the courtyard. Buildings of red brick enclosed the two sides. The entrance and a barbed wire fence and watchtower comprised the southern end. Fifty guards with machine guns lined this area and two more with sniper rifles stood smoking in the watchtower. David cast his gaze over these combatants. "We cannot terminate them all," said Gull. "And the ones you see represent a fraction of those within a five-hundred-metre radius."

They were ushered naked into the warehouse marked 'Hairdressers'. It was an expansive area with a low, transparent ceiling where leaves could be seen rotting on the outside. The hum of low-voltage electric razors sounded like an army of bored mosquitoes. They were directed into one of six rows where the walking dead in striped pyjamas waited to shave their heads. These useful inmates would not or could not make eye contact with the new arrivals. They embraced their usefulness like sleepwalkers sleepwalking through a nightmare. The guards smiled amiably and said their hair was needed to make something special for U-boat crews, and that they should not worry because it would soon grow back. Gull located this information, this 'promise,' in his database. "They intend to execute these people immediately, David."

"Immediately?"

"They are being prepared for the camp's gas chambers. And the woman we are here to protect is less than five metres from our location."

David glanced about like a man trying to locate the smell of burning. On his right, in the line adjacent to his own, stood the cause of the fire. The young woman's head was bent forwards and the lower part of her profile obscured by her hair. She clutched her arms to her breasts and peered over the tops of her fists into *nothing* – the void of her future, perhaps. She coughed and pushed her hair from her face with a clenched fist. "It's her ... minus the scar on her cheek," said David. He placed a hand on Anna's head. "How am I going to remove them *both* from this situation, Gull?"

Anna was staring up at him. She glanced over at the woman and then flung herself against his leg, holding on as though a chasm had opened beneath her feet. David stroked her hair as Gull replied, "The young woman is to be spared the gas chambers. How else is her rape to occur?"

"What if our presence here has changed that somehow?"

"The changes we have caused will not have spread beyond the people we arrived with. With the possible exception of Anna, those ripples alone are too minor to affect what must come next."

A woman in striped pyjamas and holding a razor peered at Anna over a low table. David lifted Anna onto the table. The woman said, "You must let go of your hair, young lady." Anna shook her head. A guard somewhere yelled "Quicker!", and Anna yelped and released it.

As Anna's blond locks were peeled away, David became aware of movement up ahead. Two SS officers were inspecting the prisoners. They were trailed by two guards who in turn shepherded two young women. One of the SS officers spotted *the* young woman. He grabbed her wrists and raised her arms into the air, holding them up as though waiting for someone to hoist her to the ceiling. He ran his tongue across his bottom lip and grunted affirmatively as he studied her breasts.

"Remain calm, David," said Gull. "I believe this is how she evades today's execution." The SS man inspected her backside and gave it a slap. He took hold of her chin and raised her face. "Good. Very good." He pulled her out of the line and put her with the other two. Her gaze rose from the ground and found David's as though he had called to her. Her lips parted and her eyes filled with recognition. As she was led away she continued to look back and watch him as she had in his dream. David heard a raised voice telling him to sit and felt someone tapping his knee. He looked down. Anna was pointing at the woman with the razor. He heard her voice clearly now. "Sit. On the table. Sit and lower your head. Are you deaf?" David sat, and beneath the razor's drone he whispered, "Where have they taken her?"

"The timing and nature of her removal suggests she is to be taken to Block 24. Block 24 is a brothel, for use by senior Nazis."

"You know where that is?"

"Yes, David."

A barbed wire fence ran down the side of the warehouse marked 'Cloakroom and Valuables'. The distance between the warehouse and the fence was five metres – room enough for a narrow corridor. The new arrivals were herded down the corridor towards a bunker – a flat, grey building sunk halfway into the ground. At its centre a concrete staircase vanished into a basement. Naked and shaven, David and Anna were amongst a throng of several hundred now ushered towards their place of execution. The guards at the start of this corridor made repeated reassurances about what awaited them at the other end. "Shower rooms. Just shower rooms. You are all to be disinfected. Deloused. Once you are inside and the doors are closed, remember to breathe deeply. It's good stuff. Good for you."

Anna took hold of David's hand. He looked over his shoulder and saw another group of several hundred being ushered towards the corridor they had just entered. The hundred or so in front were closer to their place of execution. Four guards stood outside the bunker and continued to give reassurances to those descending the steps. "Take full advantage. Breathe deeply once the doors are closed and the process underway ..." The column of condemned moved slowly forwards. "Either you have a suggestion for a stealthy exit or ..." murmured David. He looked ahead to where the four guards were laughing and dispensing advice. "... or I disarm one of those *men,* shoot the other three, and blast an exit in this fence." He glanced at the woods a hundred and fifty metres away across open ground.

"That would be ill advised, David. The fence is electrified, and the expanse beyond it littered with mines. Should we make it to the forest they would hunt us with dogs. Our primary mission would be compromised. I need not remind you of its importance."

"The alternative?"

"I am monitoring the brain activities ... the fields of vision of the pertinent guards. There are nine in total, including the two in the watchtower. These have turned their attention to the new arrivals at the main gate."

David glanced at the warehouse on his left. Five metres along, a drainpipe ran up to guttering. He looked ahead at the four guards outside the bunker. They were focused on the naked bodies filing past and down the steps. "They're distracted up front ..."

"I know," said Gull. "On my direction move to the drainpipe but do not climb it." David felt a sudden surge of adrenalin – the biological equivalent of a jet-plane preparing for take-off. He picked Anna up and placed her on his back. "Hold on tight." Anna clasped her arms about his neck like a little spider monkey. David darted to his left and stood before the drainpipe.

"Wait ... wait... wait... now, David." David climbed the drainpipe, hurled himself back from the wall and grabbed the overhanging guttering. Below him, several people stopped in their tracks to observe the human ape with a child on his back. The young man who had given David his coat was amongst them and whispered, "Move on! Move on now!" David pulled himself up and rolled into the guttering. He raised his head and looked down at the condemned moving forwards again. None were looking up now, and one amongst them held a clenched fist close to his head – a message of solidarity from a dead man walking.

"You cannot save him. You must content yourself with the child," said Gull. David lowered his head, clenched his fists and moved forwards commando-style. When he reached the corner he turned left onto the back of the building. Just below him he could hear guards offering reassurances to people going to their deaths. A little boy started to cry, and the sound of his distress gradually faded as his father carried him down the stairs into the bunker. David felt Anna shudder on his back.

"Many of those people are aware they are to be terminated," said Gull. "They have nothing to lose. Why don't they fight?"

David whispered his reply into the leaves. "They are broken. Starving. They have barely enough energy to stand. I know what that feels like, and a small part of them is saying their suspicions are irrational – that they must comply to get through another day. Where are the empaths, Gull? These people must be protected. Avenged."

"The date is July 27th 1944. They are coming. In five months' time this camp and many others like it will be liberated."

"Five *months*?"

"The Commander-in-Chief of one of the approaching armies is the man you spoke to aboard the shuttle craft."

"You mean *Winston*? This is happening during Winston's war?"

"Yes."

"Then we must get word to him. Let him know what's happening here."

"It has been happening for many years. By this time the allies have inklings of the slaughter, and their armies are fighting their way across Europe. They will arrive here as quickly as they can. These armies contain the greater number of empaths, and they will be victorious. Those complicit in the orchestration and running of these camps will be executed."

"Are you talking to God?" whispered Anna.

"Not exactly."

"My best friend, Sarah ... she believed in guardian angels. Are you my guardian angel?"

David was about to shake his head, then reconsidered. He glanced up at the arched brick façade that ran the width of the building and hid them from the watchtower, then ahead to the building's top left corner. "I would advise remaining here until after dark," said Gull.

David whispered over his shoulder, "We'll stay here a while longer, until it gets dark. You okay?" Anna slid off of his back and lay beside him. He placed an arm around her and over this arm he watched an SS officer climb onto the roof of the bunker. The bunker's roof was three metres below his own position. The SS man opened a hatch in the roof. He placed a bag on the ground, reached in and took out a gas mask. He put it on, secured it and removed a black canister from the bag. He pulled on white gloves, took a knife from his belt and stabbed the canister, then dropped it into the hatch. David hugged Anna's left ear to his chest and placed a hand over her right. He braced himself for the cries of the dying but heard only birds chirping in trees beyond the fence.

Thirty five

Night time fell like a shroud, bringing with it a damp humidity that smelled of charred human remains, and through this shroud stars began to glimmer in the heavens.

David shook Anna gently and whispered, "It's time to go." She crawled onto his back, and David made his way along the guttering to the warehouse's top left-hand corner. A narrow passage ran between their warehouse and the one next door. David told her to hold on tight, and he swung his legs over the edge and dangled by his fingertips. He dropped to the ground and landed in a space barely wide enough for two people. Forty metres away to his right the passage led into the camp's main courtyard, which was now floodlit. To his left was a fence that spanned the camp's northern boundary, and a narrow passage. Anna slid off his back, and David took hold of her hand. An alarm sounded. David looked towards the courtyard, and from that floodlit area a figure entered the passage and ran in their direction.

"It is a prisoner attempting to escape," said Gull. David stood with his back pressed against the warehouse, and Anna did the same. A young man in civilian clothes huffed and puffed and ran past them, pausing at the top of the passage and then turning left away from the gas chamber. David looked back towards the courtyard and saw the silhouette of a guard and a dog straining on a leash. "Halt!" David scooped Anna up under his right arm.

"Follow the runner, David." David ran around the corner and saw the prisoner turn left thirty metres ahead. David covered this distance in seconds and rounded the same corner, just in time to see the prisoner turn right and disappear. David followed him into a small courtyard lit by a single, flickering bulb. The prisoner crossed the courtyard and vanished into the darkness beyond. From the area to their left came the sound of jackboots hurrying over concrete.

"Proceed into the courtyard and scale the second building on the left, David."

"The guards are coming from that direction."

"Then be quick."

A container for dirty linen sat below a window. A light was on inside, and shadows moved beyond the blind. With Anna under his arm David stepped onto the container, leapt up and grabbed the roof's guttering, then pulled them both up. He crouched on the roof as guards came running into the courtyard below.

"Jump to the next roof," said Gull. On bare feet David sprinted across the roof and leapt four metres to the roof of the adjacent building. "Now climb down on the other side." David dropped silently to the ground. "Enter the door behind you." David shouldered open the door and walked into a stench that froze him in his tracks. He placed his free hand over his nose and whispered, "Where are we?"

"In a latrine."

"I don't see another exit in here."

"There isn't one." A raised bench ran down the back of the latrine. Ten holes had been cut into its lead top, each the size of a man's backside. The sound of jackboots came from outside, and barking dogs. "Hide in the pit beneath the stalls, David. The aroma will throw the dogs off any scent."

"*Aroma*? Smells like it's already full. Another option?"

"All other options will compromise our presence here, and would doubtless lead to reprisals for the prisoners." David moved towards the line of stalls. "You're all heart, Gull." He looked down into one of the ten holes cut into the lead top. "We won't fit."

"We must raise the shelf," said Gull. "It weighs a thousand pounds. In the interests of time, may I?" David lifted Anna onto his shoulders and muttered between gritted teeth, "Knock yourself out." His eyes rolled up and he heaved up the lead shelf, climbed in and sank to his neck in human waste, and lowered the lid. The darkness raged with flies that burrowed at their ears, eyes and noses. David's eyes returned to blue, and he waded forwards with his hands outstretched to a wall. He turned and pressed his back to it.

"You could have remained oblivious to the stench and the flies, David."

"And leave Anna to it? That would have made me a real hero."

"I surmised as much. And have subdued your gag reflex."

As Gull spoke, Anna vomited on David's shaven head. It ran down his face, and the flies found another level of hysteria. Anna blew a fly from her nose, closed her eyes and patted her cheeks. When next she opened her eyes they had turned as black as the flies that now vacated her face. Her head moved left and right as though controlled by the hand of a ventriloquist, and her mouth opened and closed, opened and closed. Finally, she gazed straight ahead and in Goliath's voice she said, "It pleases me to see you that you are moving up in the world, son."

David stared into the swarming darkness. "Get *out* of her."

"I am of course aware that humility is a stable part of an empathic way of life. However, your current choice of habitat suggests you have taken this conceit a mite too far."

"Don't harm her." The flies swarmed close to Goliath's face, but none landed. He sniffed at the air and said, "If you ask me she'd be better off dead. It could be that by choosing such a humble habitat you imagined I would not visit. I will never stop visiting you, son. And now I've located you, my agents will not be far behind. That's right. Agents. Plural. But you sure are making us work hard, I'll grant you that."

"Keep your damned voice down."

"Hasn't *Gull* told you? The guards have checked the place already. Even their dogs couldn't stand the stench, and dogs are commonly known to eat their own faeces. You know, in the early days of these camps, they used to find adults hiding in similar places – that's why they added lead tops. Which explains why this one can only be opened with a crank – or by a couple of sons-of-bitches from an altogether more enlightened future."

David closed his eyes. Not only did he have the stench and the flies to contend with, he now also had Goliath's voice, and he did not think he could put up with all three for very much longer.

"These death camps," continued Goliath. "They sure were something, and this in an age when empathy was commonplace. Makes you wonder. Nazis. They acted more like machines than people, switching off their human sensibilities and carrying out murder on an industrial scale. Seems to me these people aspired to be more like me than you."

"Agreed. And these *people* are going to be defeated."

"Yes, they are, but they are no less giants than those whose shoulders you imagine you stand on. My own existence is testament to that, which I gather is why you're here – to prevent the conception of one such giant in particular. I wonder at the folly of it, not to mention the conceit. You really think you can alter me sufficiently to make a difference? Hell, son. Seepage only accounts for a fraction of my actions and general outlook on things. I possess the accumulated knowledge of mankind, and you can't deprive me of one iota of that data."

"Then why do the Shadow Strands exist?"

"To mock you, as your kind have always been mocked. Take a good look at yourself: stood neck-deep in shit with a very small person on your shoulders. The Shadow Strands provide an illusion of hope where there is only an abundance of excrement. And while we're on the subject, as much as I appreciate your carrying a vessel down here for me to inhabit … just what in the name of Jehovah and all his witnesses is she doing here? Six million people are terminated by these people, and you've taken it upon yourself to protect one little 'un? What is that? Some grand empathic gesture? Damn, son. You might just as well become a nursemaid to one of these flies."

"If my quest is so hopeless, then why do you *insist* on following me everywhere?"

"Well, listen to you. *Quest.* You must be talking about a quest to stand neck-deep in shit with a foetus on your shoulders. You want to know what I think led you to this delightful spot?"

"I want you to stop talking and get the hell *out* of that foetus."

"For such a tiny person she sure is putting up one hell of a fight. It seems I am to evicted, but before I go, consider this, son. Man shares 98 per cent of his DNA with pigs, so it occurs to me that cause and effect has led you here to get reacquainted with your inner ..."

Anna's cheeks puffed out, her eyes flooded with blue and a child's scream pierced that stinking void like something escaped from a crack in hell. David lifted Anna off of his shoulders, hugged her and told her everything was going to be alright. "Hush, Anna, hush. It was only a dream. Just a dream."

Thirty six

At 3am, David climbed out of the cesspit with Anna on his shoulders. He lowered the lid back into place. "We need to get cleaned up, Gull. And we need clothes."

"There is a barracks on the other side of the courtyard. It houses two German officers. Only one is present, and his vital signs suggest he is sleeping. Most likely he is inebriated. I have accessed the building's original plans. They have a washroom with hot and cold running water."

"Good. Very good." David took hold of Anna's hand and led her to the door. "The coast is clear," said Gull.

David and Anna walked across the courtyard on bare, shit-stained feet. Their shadows were cast intermittently upon the ground by the flickering bulb. The officers' quarters had a white-washed façade and a black door. Above and to the left of which was a darkened window. David turned the handle and the door opened. He whispered, "Monsters imagine they don't need locks …" The door opened onto a narrow flight of stairs.

"The Nazi is sleeping soundly, David. I would recommend suffocation. He can be strung up and his death made to look like a suicide."

"Alright." David closed the door and knelt in front of Anna and whispered, "Wait here. I'll come and get you when it's safe."

"Is there a Nazi up there?"

"Yes there is."

"Are you going to kill him?"

"Yes I am."

"Will he go to hell?"

"If there is one."

Anna nodded and sat on the bottom step. The wooden stairs creaked as David went up. At the top a small landing went left and right. "The bedroom is around to your left, David. It faces onto the courtyard. The washroom is to the right and looks out over the rear of the building." David felt a pang of guilt. He begrudged the Nazi the time it would take to extinguish his life – time that kept him and Anna from running water. *And maybe soap.* His guilt vanished when he entered the room and saw the man sprawled across his bed in his underpants. On the bedside table stood an empty bottle of Schnapps, and beside that an ashtray full of cigarette butts. A pistol dangled from the bedpost inside a holster, and on the wall hung a portrait of a severe-looking man with a moustache. The man asleep below it appeared to be enjoying his dream. David picked a pillow up off the floor. He loomed over the SS officer, pressed a knee into his chest and the pillow into his face. The SS man struggled for a minute and then went limp. David heard the creaking of a floorboard behind him and turned to see Anna peering around the door. "Has he gone to hell?"

David nodded. "Let's get you cleaned up, and then we'll find some clothes."

"A man is crossing the courtyard outside," said Gull.

David glanced at the second bed by the window. He turned to Anna. "There's another ..." Anna dropped onto her stomach and slid under the bed, below the dead man.

"It appears she's done this before," said Gull.

David closed the bedroom door and stood to one side of it. The door opened, and a barrel-chested SS officer stepped in. The man placed a hand over his nose. "Jesus. You shit yourself?" David stepped forward, took hold of his chin and snapped his neck. David looked down at the corpse and scratched at his stubble. "A double suicide?"

"So it would appear," said Gull. Anna slid out from under the bed.

"Another man is headed in this direction," added Gull.

"Well, I doubt he's coming here."

"It would be wise to assume that he is." David opened his mouth to warn Anna but closed it again as she disappeared back under the bed. David picked the dead man up off the floor and placed him on the bed below the window. He closed the bedroom door and stood beside it. From downstairs came the sound of the front door opening and closing. David whispered, "Are we destined to wait here and eliminate every damned Nazi one at a time?"

The door opened and an officer of the SS entered the room. "What is that *smell*?"

"That would be me." The man turned and David laid him out with an upper cut that shattered his front teeth.

Showered and scrubbed, David sat on the edge of the bed, dressed in the black uniform of an SS officer. Anna came into the room wrapped in an enormous towel. The unconscious officer was secured to an upright wooden chair with belts. A pillowcase had been stuffed into his bloody mouth. Anna stood before the seated man, a head shorter, and observed him as a child observes a closet she suspects contains the bogeyman. Then she looked up at David and asked the following as though murder and death were as common as ice cream and cookies. "Why haven't you killed him?"

"I want to speak to him first."

"About what?"

"About why he's here. Why he's a part of this madness."

"He's a *Nazi*. They're evil. Even my teacher said so, and her father is a Nazi. They killed Mummy and Daddy." David reached out and stroked her hair. "I'm sorry."

Anna shrugged up her tiny shoulders like it hadn't been his fault anyway. "Who do you keep talking to?"

"Just a friend."

"Where is he?"

"Inside my head."

"He must be very small."

"He is." Anna jumped up on the bed and reached up to David's ear. "How did he get in there?"

"Some people put him in there."

"Maybe they can put me in there. We can hide together."

"I don't think you'd fit."

Anna huffed a disappointed huff and lowered her hand. "What's his name?"

"Gull." Anna stood on her tiptoes and peered into David's eyes. "Hello, Gull."

The officer awoke and opened his eyes. David tugged the pillowcase out of his mouth. A number of teeth came with it and dropped into his lap. "If you make a noise it will be your last."

The man's chin disappeared into his fat neck. "What? Any noise? Any noise at all? If you have harmed my fellow officers there will be no hiding place. You will be made to endure unimaginable suffering."

"I doubt even your kind can top what I've been through."

"You speak German with an accent. I can't quite place it. British? American?"

David got up and stood by the side of the window, looking out. The SS man turned his attention to Anna. He smiled at her, revealing a bloody gap where his front teeth had been. Anna backed away and stood behind David's legs. David reached down and placed a hand on her head. "It's okay. Why don't you go and wait in the washroom while I talk to the Nazi?"

Anna shook her head. "I'm not frightened with you here."

"You look frightened, little Jew girl."

David looked out of the window. "That's what I wanted to talk to you about. Your hatred of her people. I'd like you to explain it."

"*Her* people? You look like a Jew to me." He laughed quietly to himself. "A bald-headed Christ."

David turned and held up his palms. "I still have the wounds ... where they nailed me to the cross. I have your people to thank for my bald head."

170

Beads of sweat appeared on the SS man's forehead. David lowered his hands. "Answer my question."

"About Jews? They are subhuman. Not people at all. Vermin."

"You really believe that?" The man's leer suggested that he did.

"I have located an interesting paper," said Gull. "It was written in the early part of the 24th century by a scientist called Kenneth Payne. I would not have located it had it not contained an explanation of this man's irrational hatred. More importantly, it will provide us a with valuable insight into the erosion of empathy – one based on firm scientific data."

David smiled. "It will provide *us* with a valuable insight into the erosion of empathy, Gull?"

"Yes."

"Good to hear you taking a keen interest."

"I believe it is to our mutual benefit to understand what we are fighting to preserve."

"I believe you're right." David glanced at the SS man. He expected to see the usual concern for his sanity. Not this time. The man gazed towards the ground as though *it* held conversations with imaginary friends. "You were saying, Gull."

"In the year 2314, Kenneth Payne published his paper on *The Empathy Dome*. I have located a holographic recording of one of Mr Payne's lectures at a place called the Royal Society, in London, England. With your permission, I would like to assume primary control and project the salient points of his lecture into this room."

The SS man *was* looking at him now, like he was crazier than a banana strudel. David pulled a second chair away from the wall and placed it beside him. He sat down. "Anna."

"Yes."

"You're about to see … well, a man is going to appear in this room. He will look like a ghost, but he isn't. He's just a man. Possibly a very clever man."

"Like a movie?"

"If you like. It will be shone from the whites of my eyes. Anytime you want it to stop just say so." Anna jumped up on his knee. David's eyes rolled up to their whites and a holographic image of a white-haired man appeared in the room. He was standing behind a table, upon which stood a stand with notes on it. It was clear he had an audience in the same place where these three sat, three hundred years in the past. The SS man's eyes opened as wide as saucers and he mumbled something about Valhalla under his breath.

Kenneth Payne grasped the lapels of his jacket and began his lecture.

"The Empathy Dome. It is a phenomenon unique to humankind. It shelters all we learn, all we perceive, and while in a pristine state it protects everything beneath it from our baser, more savage instincts. The Dome exists at a sub-atomic level, which is why it has taken so long to discover it – or, more specifically, the particle from which it is constructed: the aptly christened *E. Particles*. These *E. Particles* converged to create the *empathy gene*. It is likely the empathy gene was present in the first self-replicating molecules, the first life on Earth, three and a half billion years ago. It remained dormant and has been passed on through the process of evolution only to become active approximately one million years ago at the emergence of pre-modern Man. It alone provided our species the possibility of evolving away from our baser instincts of self-preservation at any cost. Now, for reasons of simplicity, we will assume that it multiplied and grew into the shape of a dome. The Empathy Dome. This Dome had a fight on its hands from the very beginning. Chief amongst its combatants? All those things attributed to *The Survival of the Fittest* – in which a blatant disregard for others plays a key role. But the empathy gene persisted, and it alone provided the possibility of guilt – and beyond guilt the fertile grounds where *conscience* could evolve. This evolution of conscience was imperative if the empathy gene was to multiply sufficiently to create the Empathy Dome. If each of us had a complete Dome we would be living in a utopia of mutual acceptance. But this would have been too simple, and would have brought the process of evolution, of progression, to a halt. An important element of progression is friction – something to struggle against. A reason to fight on and to outgrow the status quo. And so in place of the Empathy Dome we have … the Splintered Dome – a Dome that, as a result of inherited values, of nurture, of brainwashing, of experience, has become splintered … left areas beneath it exposed to baser instincts of savagery and prejudice. These instincts have dictated the attitudes and actions of many, while for others the Empathy Dome has remained more robust. It is from this division that our legends of good versus evil arose. Of a loving God and of a devil. Interestingly, there is a race of people for whom the Empathy Dome has always been disproportionately splintered in others: a nomadic people, in general highly skilled and good at making money. And at lending it. At times of economic upheaval, they have provided governments with convenient scapegoats, used to divert resentment away from their own failings and create a unifying hatred. I am of course referring to Jews. This hatred often culminated in their expulsion from their adopted homelands, with the debts owed to them conveniently wiped out and the fruits of their productivity seized. This is the template Hitler adopted during the second great war of the 20th century. Using powerful rhetoric, Hitler was able to shatter the empathy domes of millions of his followers, as though he gave each a hammer, pointed to the relevant area on their Dome, and said 'We will smash it together!'"

David's eyes returned to blue and the holographic image vanished. "That was very informative, Gull."

"What conclusions have you drawn from it, David?"

"It's nice to know that empathy has its roots in science. Maybe I'm not simple after all."

"Anything else?" asked Gull.

David met the SS officer's gaze. "Only that my own Empathy Dome is shattered all to hell ... right above the area that contains Nazis." Droplets of sweat spread across the SS man's brow. "I am just a tiny cog in a *vast* machine. I have no choice but to follow my orders." David leaned forward in his chair, watching him. The SS officer pushed at his bindings. "What are you? What are you going to do to me?"

Thirty seven

David exited the barracks in the uniform of an SS officer and crossed the courtyard, carrying in his left hand a brown leather holdall that contained Anna. Behind him flames lapped at the barrack's solitary window. He walked down a path that led into the camp's main floodlit courtyard. The sound of splintering glass was followed by an explosion and a fireball rose into the air. Glass and body parts rained down in his wake, and the head of the SS officer landed on the roof of the latrine where it rolled to a stop. The pillowcase stuffed back in its mouth.

Pandemonium broke out. Soldiers and camp personnel stumbled out of doors and ran in the direction of the explosion. David pulled the visor of his cap down, and crossed the main courtyard like he owned it and every son-of-a-bitch running through it. When he reached the other side, Gull told him to turn left just as the bell of a fire truck echoed off the red brick to his right. He was headed in the direction of the main gate. He did not look up at the watchtower, its spotlight now pointed towards the blaze. He turned right into a cul-de-sac and crossed to its left-hand side. Two women hurried in his direction, buttoning their uniforms as they passed. David entered the open door to Block 24, and once inside he took the stairs three at a time. He found himself in a grey corridor that contained a dozen doors, each of which was numbered. "Which room is she in, Gull?"

"Rooms 2, 5 and 12 also contain male occupants. Two of these are hurriedly dressing. Their appearance is imminent."

"Which *room*?"

"Assessing body mass and heat signature, it could be either 9 or 10. Both women are alone."

The door to room 9 had been locked from the outside. David shouldered it open, and inside a woman with red hair sat up in bed and averted her gaze. David pulled the door closed and shouldered his way into room 10, where a woman was standing on a stool below an improvised hook secured into the ceiling. She had tied a noose made from a bed sheet around her neck and was taking advantage of the emergency to hang herself. Her face was in shadow, and David stepped into the room for a closer look. The woman's eyes were begrudging and they asked him, "Are you *really* standing there? *Now*?"

"It's not her," said David. He closed the door, and removed his cap to expose his badly shaven head. He turned to face the woman, and in Polish

174

he said, "I'm not a Nazi. I was brought here on a transport today. I'm looking for a woman who was brought here on the same transport. About five foot three. Very pretty. Dark shoulder-length hair." The bag in David's right hand unzipped itself and Anna sat up like a wind-up toy. "It's true. We came on the train together."

The woman wobbled on her stool and David apologised for the interruption. She broke into laughter and David did too, but did not understand why. He put the bag down and Anna stood up in it. To the young woman exiting this horror on her own terms Anna looked like someone in a grow-bag determined to outgrow it. She pulled the noose off her head and stepped down off the stool. She was slim, delicate and tall, almost as tall as David, with shoulder-length blonde hair that fell in ringlets about her face. Her eyes met David's and David's heart beat faster. He barely murmured, "I have no need for assistance, Gull."

"No assistance has been rendered. As well as an unnecessary increase in heart rate, your pupils are dilating."

The woman watched him quizzically. "I know her ... the woman you mean. She was brought here with two others today. The Commandant chose her from our line-up earlier. She's not here."

"Chose her for what?"

"No need to look so worried. She's to be his housekeeper – a job we all wanted. What do you want with her?"

"He wants to save her," said Anna.

"Save her? Is he crazy?"

Anna shook her head. "He's a guardian angel. A real one." The woman held her makeshift noose before her like an offering of incontrovertible proof. "*I* need a guardian angel." They stared at one another. David's legs felt suddenly hollow. He felt ill at ease and a little out of breath. In the silence that followed Anna stepped out of the bag and asked the woman her name.

"Alix. What's yours?"

"Anna."

Alix approached David. "And yours?" David's heart rate ratcheted up another notch for no reason he could fathom. He swallowed a lump in his throat. "It's David."

"You aren't going to leave me here to kill myself, are you, David?"

David wiped the back of his hand across his brow. "The war will be over soon ... in a few months the camp will be liberated."

"You can't *know* that, and it only takes a matter of moments to be shot – which would be preferable to these animals raping and beating me ... before they send me to the gas chambers." She reached out and touched David's face. "You have a kind face. A good face."

175

"We must leave now," said Gull. "I have located the Commandant's villa. It is on a hill to the west of our position and overlooks the camp." David didn't answer, standing transfixed by the woman. Gull persisted, "She is dangerous. As well as affecting your vital signs, she is playing havoc with your judgement."

"Then I suggest you keep a clear head for us both."

Alix narrowed her eyes. "*What?*"

A distant explosion shook the window. "The fire has spread," said Gull. "The added confusion can be used to our advantage. We must leave now."

Alix placed a hand on David's heart. "You know you aren't going to leave this camp without me, don't you?"

"A single blow should be sufficient to neutralise her," assessed Gull. David looked down at Anna. As though she'd read his thoughts, she lay back down in the bag and zipped it halfway up. David unbuckled the holster at his side and pulled out the pistol. "The sound of the weapon may draw unwelcome attention, David. But all things considered."

David looked down and spoke as though to Anna. "I'm not going to shoot her. She's coming with us."

David carried the bag in his left hand. In his right he held the pistol and Alix by scruff of her shirt. In this way he manhandled her out of the whorehouse and into the cul-de-sac. He hurried her through the main courtyard as though eager to find a spot to carry out an execution. No one paid them any attention; they were too preoccupied with the burning buildings on the other side of the courtyard. David followed Gull's directions to the top left-hand side of the courtyard. A sentry stood outside a gate, and as David approached he clicked his heels, raised a palm and turned and unlocked the gate. On the other side was a dirt road that climbed steeply and wound its way to the left. As they climbed it, the sound of shouting and mayhem grew more distant. "We are outside the main camp now," said Gull. "An ideal place to release the woman and the girl. You have done your empathic duty to them."

David stopped, and Alix looked at him. She was starting to believe this man could be her salvation. Her expression softened and she looked suddenly vulnerable. This did little to quell his confusion, and when he spoke he found that he did so quietly. "You're outside the camp. The woods are over there. You could make a run for it."

Alix shook her head. David re-holstered his pistol, looking up past the wall of mud and clay on his left. He could see the roof of the Commandant's villa in the moonlight. Alix watched him. "That man is the devil incarnate."

"The Commandant?"

"Yes. One of his balconies overlooks the camp. He uses it to shoot people for fun."

"I doubt he'll be doing that for much longer. It's likely he's the one I'm here to kill."

"Kill? I thought you were a guardian angel?"

"I never said that."

"You're an agent? An American?" A staff car rumbled up the hill behind them. David put down the bag and took out the revolver. He shoved Alix against the wall and pointed the gun at her head. "Something tells me you know how to plead for your life." She did, and her performance as the car rolled past made his guts ache.

The Commandant's villa looked like an enormous log cabin on stilts, with two floors and an attic. Its solitary entrance was located at the top of a flight of steps, outside which two guards stood on sentry duty. David and Alix were crouched near the top of the road. Alix whispered, "If you want to get inside you'll have to kill them both."

"Too disruptive. We'll go in through a window around the other side."

"Really? Unless there's a ladder in this bag that won't be possible ... what are you smiling about?"

"Your opinion on what's possible and what's not is about to be revised."

They left the dirt track and stumbled into the rocky terrain that surrounded the villa. The windows on the first floor were lit at the front, and at the rear they were dark and reflected the moon. David and Alix were lying in a ditch thirty metres from the back of the villa. The stilts that held it aloft were three metres high, and the nearest darkened window another metre above that. They could hear faint voices, laughter and music. "Sounds like the Commandant is having one of his *parties*," said Alix.

"While his barracks burn?"

"Yes, while his barracks burn. He much prefers a party to a hose."

David reached into the bag and squeezed Anna's shoulder. She sat up and rubbed her eyes. David pinched her nose. "I'm going inside the house. I'll find something to lower from one of those windows to haul you both up. Just stay here until you see me."

Alix glanced up past the stilts to the darkened windows. "See you what? ... break your neck?"

"Always a possibility."

David climbed out of the ditch and sprinted towards the villa. He leapt four metres into the air, grabbed the wooden skirting that overhung the stilts, swung his right foot onto it and reached for the window ledge. He crouched on the skirting, slid the window up and climbed into the darkened room. It was a store room containing boxes of cigarettes piled up high, and crates of wine and spirit. "They are black market goods," said Gull. "It was common for senior Nazis to dabble, particularly towards the end of the war when it became clear things were not going their way. They reasoned they would need funds to assist their flights." David crossed the room to the door, beyond which he could hear raised voices. He opened the door and stepped into a smaller room that contained a wash basin and cleaning paraphernalia: mops, brooms and buckets. Across this room a second door was slightly ajar. David placed his eye to it and looked into a brightly lit corridor. Along the corridor to the right, a set of double doors opened onto a lounge. Senior SS officers were drinking and gambling inside, and amongst them was the camp's Commandant, Obersturmbannführer Hirsch. David heard footsteps approaching from the left. The young woman he'd come to find walked past carrying a tray. She entered the lounge and laughter erupted as though she'd triggered a trip-wire. Moments later she hurried back out, red-faced and tearful. David opened the door and reached for her arm. She looked into his eyes and let herself be pulled inside. David closed the door and they stared at one another. She wobbled on her feet, apparently drunk on the sight of this phantom from her dreams. He reached out a hand to steady her and said, "It's alright." David's words, so far from the truth, had the effect of smelling salts. "*Alright*? "They will shoot us both."

A man shouted, "Helen! Where are you? Hurry with that schnitzel."

"You have your own room?" asked David.

"Yes. In the attic." She pointed down the corridor. "The staircase is by the kitchen."

David made a rope from curtains and lowered them out of the window to where Alix stood below, holding Anna's hand. She tied the makeshift rope about her waist and looked at Anna as if to say 'What now?'

"Crouch," replied Anna. "So I can ride up to the window piggyback."

Thirty eight

It was 3am. The last of the guests had left and the villa was silent. Helen climbed the stairs to her darkened attic room and flicked the light switch just inside the door. Alix was sitting on her bed with Anna, her arm around her. The little girl was asleep. Helen closed the door and became aware of David standing beside it. "Who are they?" she asked. "What are they doing here?"

"They're with me."

Alix laid Anna down on the bed and climbed off it. She approached Helen and held out her hand. In a whisper she said, "I'm Alix, and her name is Anna."

Helen took her hand. "Your daughter?"

"No. We just met." Both women looked at David now – looked at him as though he should not exist and had more explaining to do than most.

They sat cross-legged in the centre of that small attic room, facing one another. David looked at Anna asleep on the bed. The women watched him. Without taking his eyes from the sleeping child he said, "I travelled here from the future." Alix asked him if *the future* was an organisation.

Helen shook her head. "I don't think that's what he means."

David looked at Alix. "The future future. Thousands of years from now."

Another silence followed, during which Alix reached the conclusion that if Nazis were possible then anything was. "It's better there?" she asked.

"It's worse."

"The future is worse? Than *this*?"

"This horror will end. Where I come from, horror is the end. Which is why I'm here. To try and do something about that."

"What can you do?"

"Make changes … changes that might impact the future and alter it for the better somehow. At least that's my intention, but you never know."

"I have seen him before. Many times," said Helen.

Alix shuffled nervously. "*Where?*"

"In my dreams."

"And I you," said David, "only once, you had a scar. On your cheek."

Alix leaned closer to Helen. "She has no scars…"

"The pattern I have just deciphered indicates that the missing scar is relevant," said Gull. "The rapist will leave it."

David looked at Helen's pale and unmarked cheek. "I'm here to protect you from the man who's going to give you that scar."

"Protect me how?"

"Presumably by killing him. Otherwise he will rape you and you'll conceive his child. The DNA of that child will influence someone in the future. Influence them for the worse."

Helen placed her elbows on her knees and her head in her hands. "But you won't let him rape me?"

"No. I will not let that happen."

"Tell us about the future … the place you come from," said Alix.

"Are you sure? Seems to me you already have enough to be miserable about."

"Let me be the judge of that."

"Alright. Until recently I thought I was on Earth, shielded from a series of volcanic eruptions by a protective dome. It was a lie; I was not on Earth. It was a spacecraft, and humanity was being systematically destroyed right under my nose."

"So … you're an *alien*?" said Alix.

David shook his head. "More of an idiot."

"I have located information inside the Event Helix that will be of considerable interest," interjected Gull. "To you and your companions. If you have no objections, I would like to join you to relay it."

"Join us?"

"Yes. As a holographic projection."

"You have been busy, Gull." The two woman observed David, apparently having this conversation with himself, and glanced at one another. "I think you'd better join us, Gull. Right away." David's eyes rolled up, and Gull projected a metre-tall image of himself into the space between them. He had the same transparent body wherein a black heart pumped a stream of data through a vast complex of twisted veins and arteries, and a flickering face that looked as though it were being projected from within. It was not Tyburn's face but David's, and David made a mental note to have a word with him about that.

Meanwhile, the expressions of the two women had shifted through a range of startled reactions and finally settled on awe. David's head turned to his left, and the hologram walked in that direction. Gull turned to face his audience, and when he spoke his impossibly relaxed voice came from David's lips. "My name is Gull. I am an artificial life form – one created by mankind to assist mankind. I am also David's friend, or at least I would like to think of myself as such." The dwarf-sized hologram appealed to David with David's own eyes. Within himself David nodded, but his actual head did not move. "Thank you, David. David has taught me much about what it means to be human, and I am grateful. The similarity in our facial appearance that I have adopted is a mark of respect." Gull clasped his hands behind his back, raised himself up on his toes and settled back down again. "In the year 2117, an asteroid will be located in Asia Minor – an asteroid on a collision course with Earth. Its tonnage will be sufficient to wipe out all sentient life." A football-sized representation of the asteroid appeared over their heads. It hovered on the spot and debris flew past, giving it an impression of speed.

"Jesus Christ," whispered Alix."

Gull continued, "To survive, mankind will be forced to move off-world and make his home amongst the stars. An intergalactic craft will be conceived, called the Second Ark. In the year 2122, the design of the Second Ark will be agreed upon. The United States of America will take the lead in the project, and construction will commence on November 23rd of that same year. The Second Ark will be a circular structure, seventy kilometres in diameter. The craft will be constructed on a floating port a kilometre above the Atlantic ocean and two hundred kilometres off the coast of New York City. As such, it will become a familiar sight from the skyscrapers of that city." A holographic image of the Second Ark appeared, and below it the Empire State Building appeared to doff it like an enormous Stetson. "Earth's most advanced nations will contribute resources and expertise to the Second Ark's creation, and each of these countries will be allocated space for fifty thousand of their citizens. One million people will be saved in total. As the departure date moves within the lifespan of Earth's inhabitants, and realising anarchy will ensue, an army of super soldiers will be deployed. They are to be called proto vessels – soldiers augmented by cyber-technology. These soldiers will be given free licence to quell any civil unrest, which they will be forced to do without mercy as the departure date looms closer."

"They sound like monsters," said Alix.

Gull made no reply and David was grateful for that. Gull went on. "The Second Ark will depart Earth on January 12, 2287, six months before the asteroid's impact. Life on board will not be dissimilar to the class system adopted by cruise ships of this era. The wealthy and powerful will live inside a construction known as Central Dome. Inside Central Dome, a futuristic city will thrive under an imitation blue sky, from which an imitation sun will warm its inhabitants. At dusk the sky will peel away to reveal the universe beyond. The amenities for those outside Central Dome will be more … basic. Adequate for work and survival. As the Russian President Vladimir Cousin will put it a week before the Second Ark's departure: "A dream life compared to certain annihilation." The people outside will be hand-picked for their skills – skills pertinent to the maintenance of Central Dome and the Ark in general."

"So what went wrong?" asked Alix.

David's projected face looked puzzled for a moment. "You mean from a human perspective?"

Alix nodded.

"Man is to become increasingly reliant on artificial intelligence for survival – artificial intelligence that grows more complex as mankind seeks to adapt to life amongst the stars. Eventually, and through a process that is to become known as seepage, sentient life (man) and the artificial intelligence he created will infect one another. Just as man will seek to harness the logic, strength and computing power of machines, machines will seek to become more like sentient beings. This, as David knows only too well, culminates in the emergence of a being called Goliath. With full access to the Ark's main frame computer, and a unique human perspective derived from seepage, he will bring about the subjugation of those who created him. And, like many conquerors before him, he will seek to strip them of the things he does not possess."

"What things?" asked Alix.

"Their humanity."

"Why?"

"As he sees it, in the interests of fairness. As a leveller of the playing field."

"But *why*?" pressed Alix.

"He hopes to stand before the Architects and present himself as a worthy successor to Man."

"The Architects?"

Gull looked first at Helen and then at Alix. "Your closest reference would be Gods." Alix looked at David. "So what does all this have to do with him?"

"David is the last surviving empath, and as such the only being who stands between Goliath and his goal of usurping humanity. Once David is eliminated, Goliath believes the Architects will reward him by making him fully sentient. A successor to Man." Gull took a bow and vanished.

David looked at the two women with his own eyes. "Thank you, Gull."

Alix stood up. She folded her arms and looked down at David. "David and *Goliath*?"

David leaned back on the palms of his hands, and looked up at her. "That's right."

"And Goliath ... he's trying to kill you."

"And he'll never stop. Not until one of us is dead." Alix's gaze moved slowly over his body, and she asked without the slightest hint of irony, "So where's your slingshot?"

"Lost?"

"How did you escape?"

"I fell off the side of a mountain. Landed in the Middle East in the time of Christ. But that's a whole other story."

While they all slept, Gull monitored the life signs and whereabouts of the only other occupant of the villa, Commandant Hirsch. He woke David shortly before dawn with these words: "The Commandant is up and emptying his bowels into a commode."

David yawned. "Appreciate that intel." He lay on his side, rested his head in his palm, and looked down at Alix. Time passed.

"I have discovered a word that was used to describe your emotional response to this woman," said Gull.

David spoke quietly. "You needn't have wasted your time. My response is nonsensical."

"A purge on common sense is the by-product. The word used to describe this purge is love."

"Love? What does that mean?"

"That your body is creating a powerful cocktail of stimulants, whose primary function is to make you want to procreate with the object of your affection."

David gazed at Alix's cupid bow. "A function at which it excels. It's not real, then? This feeling?"

"It is as real as any biological response, and more additive than most. It is therefore able to inflict powerful symptoms of withdrawal should the connection be suddenly broken."

"Withdrawal?"

"Yes. Suicide was not an unheard-of response in extreme cases."

"Well ..."

"Yes, David."

"You'd better make sure I don't end it all for love, and leave Goliath the last man standing."

"I will do my best."

"The feelings I have for this woman ... they're not empathic? I want to protect her."

"Your empathic motivation towards this woman is quite separate from the love you feel – although in your current state of intoxication, it is impossible for you to differentiate between the two." Alix opened her eyes and smiled in a way that suggested she'd been listening. She reached up and ran her fingers past David's ear. She wrapped her hand around his head and pulled his mouth down to meet hers. David sighed as their tongues met. "She is aware of the effect she has on you. And she is using it to her advantage, David."

Let her.

Anna cried out in her sleep, "Mummy!" She sat bolt upright on the bed, looked around, and then screamed like she'd woken from a nightmare only to find herself still in one. Helen woke and hugged her. David was standing beside the bed now and he reached down to Anna. The little girl threw her arms about his neck as though he *was real* after all. "It's okay. I'm here. You just had a bad dream. Did the scream alert anyone, Gull?"

"The Commandant has returned to his bed and has not left his room."

At 9am, David was standing in the corner of the attic room, his eyes rolled up as Gull scanned the area for the life-signs of potential vessels. Alix was on the bed with Anna, telling her a story in muted tones. Every so often, Anna would look up at her and whisper a question. Within himself, David watched these two with a cloying in his gut – a cloying that told him he would happily sacrifice his life for these strangers. But at what cost? The cloying demanded that he protect them at any cost. The reality of his situation suggested this was not possible. That he had to think about the bigger picture, but the picture had shrunk. A gunshot shattered the tranquillity of the room. David's eyes returned to blue and his gaze met Alix's. "It's him," said Alix. "He's out on his balcony." She looked down at Anna and smiled.

"He's shooting people, isn't he?" asked Anna.

Another shot rang out. David told them to stay where they were and walked towards the door. "There is nothing you can do," said Gull.

"There's plenty I can do."

"If you kill Hirsch we will have no way of knowing if he is responsible for Helen's scar."

"That might not happen for weeks. Maybe we don't have time to hang about and wait."

"The patterns suggest the rendering of the scar is imminent."

"How imminent?"

"Within seventy-two hours." David opened the door, went out and closed it behind him. Another shot rang out. He went down the stairs and past the kitchen. Helen was inside mopping the floor but did not see him. David turned left into the room where on the previous night Hirsch had entertained his guests. It was a large room with a dining table at one end and a clutch of armchairs at the other, and double doors with net curtains led onto a balcony. The doors were open and a breeze ballooned the curtains back into the room. He heard a rifle bolt being drawn back and then shoved into place. Under his breath he said, "I *cannot* allow this ... not when I can so easily stop it." He took a step towards the open doors, but was stopped by a ringing telephone. Another shot rang out beyond the patio doors and Hirsch said, "You made me miss. Damn you." He put down the rifle, entered the lounge and picked up the receiver. "Well, what is it?" A pause was followed by, "If he must. You'd better show him in."

David was standing in the hall with his back pressed to the wall. He glanced to his right. Helen was standing outside the kitchen and staring at him as though waiting for a signal. To run? To hide? To arm herself with a carving knife? David raised a finger to his lips. There was a *tap tap tap* on a door and Hirsch said, "Why have interrupted my morning target practice, Ralph? If the Russians should descend upon us and I miss the *very* Russian who stands poised to split your head in two with a club, you will have only yourself to blame. I presume you are here on official business?" At first there was only the sound of a match being struck and the smell of cigarette smoke. Then Ralph mumbled with a cigarette between his lips, "You were very drunk last night. I thought it wise to remind you of the wager you lost."

"Wager?"

"The pretty little Jew girl. Helen, I think her name is."

"Oh, yes. I was not that drunk, but you can't take her now. Not before I have a replacement."

"You could have picked one this morning. Instead you shot one."

"I shot several, none of them suitable replacements. What's your hurry?"

"I like her. Such good skin for a Jew. And so child-like a body."

"Be very careful, Ralph. It seems she's placed an enchantment on you. I have seen it before. Some even begin to feel sorry for them. Helen!" Helen looked at David and David nodded at her. She walked past him and stopped just inside the door. "Come now, Helen. What can possibly be of so much interest on the carpet? Oh, goodness gracious. Look at you, Ralph. She has undoubtedly placed a Jew enchantment on you." The floorboards creaked as Ralph crossed the room. "Such a delicate little chin … Come, look at me. Let me see those pretty eyes… That's better. Have you placed an enchantment on me?"

Hit her, thought David. *Give her that scar now, and I can kill you. Please.*

"No," said Helen.

"You see?" said Ralph. "She is innocent, which I believe is part of her appeal."

"You expect her to say yes? I have an inspection to carry out in one hour, not to mention a new housekeeper to find. Show your new owner out, Helen. And Ralph, you can collect her the day *after* tomorrow."

Five minutes later, Helen returned to her attic room, with a cut on her cheek. The moment David saw her he moved swiftly past her to the door.

She turned and said, "It's too late. He's gone. In his car. Back to Krakow. His driver is to return for me in forty-eight hours."

Alix went to the basin and dampened a cloth. She wiped the blood from Helen's cheek, but more came to the surface. "When?" said David. "I watched him get into his vessel. Watched his driver close the door."

Alix held the back of Helen's head and pressed the towel against the wound. Helen grimaced. "He decided to get out again, he said he wanted to grope my backside."

"Apparently he's failed to grasp the meaning of the word grope ... or where to locate a backside," said Alix. She glanced at David. "So what now?"

Gull said, "His full name is Ralph Ernst Adler. He is head of interrogations at the Gestapo Headquarters in Krakow."

"Gull just informed me who he is. Looks like I'll be going into Krakow to kill him, but first we get you out of here."

Helen looked at him with pleading eyes. "You'll take us to the Polish Resistance?"

"If that's the best place."

"It is undoubtedly the best place," agreed Gull. "They saved thousands during this genocide."

"Where are they, Gull?"

"Hiding in the forests of Ojcow and Niepolomice."

"You can pinpoint their location?"

"I have accessed the records of their underground tunnels. During this period a Zegota splinter cell regularly observed the camp. The cell's base is hidden below ground less than three kilometres from our position. They have been gathering intel on the camp since its inception."

When David relayed this information, Alix threw her arms around him. Not wanting to be left out, Anna clung to his leg. Helen held the towel to her cheek and whispered a prayer.

Thirty nine

Gull suggested they leave after Hirsch had retired to his bed. "It will give us several hours' head-start before they send men and dogs to track Helen."

It was 11.30pm and Hirsch's nightly drinking session with his fellow officers showed no sign of abating. Helen had been downstairs and waiting on this assemblage of murderers since 8.30pm. Alix and Anna were dressed and ready to go, Anna in an outfit Alix had made from a blanket. She looked like a tiny member of a Neolithic tribe. When she'd seen her refection she'd asked, "Are you sure it's okay if I go out without my yellow star?"

Alix had stroked her stubbly head. "Of course it's okay."

Anna lay a palm on the place where a yellow star had always been. "Daddy said never to go out without my star."

"We're going to stay with nice soldiers now."

"And you're sure they're nice?"

"They live in the woods. Polish soldiers. They're going to look after us."

"*David's* going to look after us." On this point Anna was most emphatic.

"But David has important work to do, Anna."

"I know. He has to save Helen." David was standing beside the door with his arms folded. Anna walked over to him. "Are you going to leave us?"

David knelt down and smiled at her. "Only once you're safe. There are things I still have to do. Very important things."

"But you'll come back?" David brushed a finger against her cheek and stood up. They heard a burst of laughter from downstairs. A wolf whistle. Applause.

"You think Helen's alright?" asked Alix.

"Gull?"

"Helen is alone in the kitchen, David."

"Helen's okay. She's in the kitchen." Another burst of raucous laughter. "What exactly are we doing, Gull?"

"Could you be more specific?"

"Waiting around for monsters to wind up a party." He turned to the door and ran a hand over his stubble.

"Our plan is tactically sound, David."

"How's this for a plan: we make sure there's no one left alive downstairs to raise the alarm? It might actually give us more time."

"I have considered that possibility, but there are six mid-to-high-ranking Nazis downstairs with Hirsch. Should they be eliminated, the reprisals on the camp population would be severe."

"Compared to what? Extermination? We could make it look like a group suicide. In all the confusion, I doubt they'd even notice Hirsch's maid is missing. And the allies will have seven less Nazis to deal with."

Silence.

"Gull?"

"I have located something useful in connection with the word 'suicide'."

"I'm listening."

"A melancholy recording entitled *Gloomy Sunday*. In the latter stages of the conflict, it was much favoured by suicidal Nazis. The Commandant has a copy in his record collection. I have heard it played here. Were it to be found on the gramophone, it would certainly indicate a group suicide."

"Good. That's very good."

"What is more it will be Sunday in twenty-three minutes."

"Excellent. That's excellent. The poison gas they use in the gas chambers ... you know where it's stored?"

"Zyklon B. It is kept in a hut less than two hundred metres from our current position."

David looked over his shoulder at Alix. She smiled at him and said, "Please. If you can. Kill them. Kill them all."

David was crouched on the roof of the Commandant's villa. The night air was muggy, the camp silent. The only sounds were those of Hirsch and his cronies indulging in the spoils of a war they knew would soon be over – and not to their advantage. David leapt from the roof. When he hit the ground he rolled head over heels, stood up and sprinted to the edge of the villa's boundary. Five metres below him was the curve of the dirt road that led back into the camp. David stepped off the edge and dropped to the road. He centred his cap's visor and made his way towards the gate. "Their procedures for entering the camp are stricter than leaving," said Gull. "The guard will require paper documentation. I suggest climbing the outer fence."

"Alright."

"The inner fence is electrified. I have adjusted your nano augmentation to account for its voltage."

"Appreciate it." David cleared the two fences, the second of which sizzled against his fingertips. He followed Gull's directions around the outer edge of the camp, a route that took him past row upon row of large shed-like buildings where thousands of people clung to life by the barest of threads.

The shed that housed the Zyklon B was one amongst a dozen others, and so

innocuous that it might have contained gardening tools. Gull picked the lock and inside David discovered fifty small canisters no bigger than meat tins. Gas masks hung from hooks on the wall. David took one and picked up two tins of death.

"One will be sufficient for our needs, David."

"Alright."

Boyd Brent

Forty

David returned to the attic room. Alix was standing below the window, which was arch-shaped and too high for anyone of normal height to see out. Anna was sitting on Alix's shoulders, her head resting on the glass. Anna heard David close the door and turned her head. "Here he is!" Alix lifted her from her shoulders and put her down. Her gaze fell upon the silver tin in his hand. "You found some?"

"Yes. We'll need to get you out before …"

"What about Helen?"

"Helen too." David put the canister of Zyklon B and the gas mask on the bed. "You ready to go?"

On the ground floor, in the room full of contraband, David retrieved the makeshift rope from behind a wicker basket that overflowed with gold teeth smashed from the jaws of the murdered. He lowered Alix and then Anna down to the ground. Watched them run to the ditch twenty metres away. "Where's Helen, Gull?"

"In the target room. Wine has been spilt on the carpet. Helen is scrubbing the area." David sat on the wicker basket and tapped his foot impatiently. A minute later, Gull said, "Helen is returning to the kitchen."

David entered the kitchen and whispered, "Time to go."

"Now?"

"Now."

"What about those devils?"

"As soon as you're safely out of here, I'm going to gas them. Make it look like a group suicide." It was the first time he'd seen Helen smile. She removed her apron, knelt and took a small cloth bag from a space below the sink.

Forty one

David pulled the gas mask over his face, and sliced a hole in the top of the Zyklon B tin with a kitchen knife. Inside was a heap of white pellets.

The SS men sat around a table playing blackjack – the same table where Hirsch had gambled and lost his housemaid two nights before. The man he'd lost her to had stayed away for fear of losing her before he'd taken delivery. The air was thick with cigar smoke and the stench of sweat and spilled wine. Wearing an SS uniform and gas mask, David walked into the room holding the opened canister of Zyklon B. Hirsch had his back to him, but the five men opposite glanced up from their cards. Their initial reaction was to smile as though their host was playing some kind of prank. David smiled too and dumped the gas pellets into Hirsch's lap. Hirsch grabbed his own face and leapt to his feet. David grabbed Hirsch by his collar and belt and slung him onto the table – his body jerked and his mouth gaped like a man trying to mime *fish out of water*. The others stumbled away from the table like the petals of a grey flower suddenly opened. They retched up bloodied froth and collapsed with red and burning eyes. One amongst them tried to scramble past David on all fours but was hurled back amongst the dying like the last piece of garbage onto a pyre. David watched this man crawl onto an armchair and perish with his ass in the air. He remembered the people he'd arrived with and felt sick to the pit of his stomach.

"We would be afforded more time if the men guarding the front door were similarly terminated," said Gull. David shook his head as though casting off this sentiment for the dead and walked the length of the room to the door. He opened it and found himself in a small entrance hall. Pistols in holsters were arranged along a sideboard, and there was a hat stand on which hats hung on antlers. David stood facing the front door to the villa. "The guards are standing just outside the door with their backs to us, David."

When David opened the door, the two SS guards stood to attention but did not turn around. David took hold of their shirt collars and dragged them inside. He turned and manhandled them back into the gas-filled room as they protested their innocence. They died on their knees while David clutched their collars and stared at a painting of Adolf Hitler above the gramophone player. When David released them they did not roll over but slumped like puppets awaiting their next puppeteer. David continued to stare, unblinking, at the painting of Adolf Hitler. "Are you alright, David?"

"These two men were children not so long ago. They doubtless had parents who doted on them. Probably still do."

"Now they are willing members of Hitler's SS. They allowed themselves to be corrupted."

"Yes they did."

"It was the wrong choice."

"Yes it was."

"David?"

"Yes?"

"A driver is outside waiting for one of the dead men. He may raise the alarm before we would like."

"The gods, Gull."

Ten minutes later, David was in Hirsch's bedroom, changing out of the Nazi uniform and into a pair of black trousers and grey shirt. In a room downstairs, a pack of cards lay scattered amongst the bodies of ten dead Nazis. The song *Gloomy Sunday* was playing on a loop on the gramophone player.

Forty two

Outside, the door to the black staff car was still open. Ten minutes earlier, when David had told the driver his superior had had a heart attack, he'd hurried back inside the villa. David had followed him in, and made sure he was sufficiently acquainted with the Zyklon B.

Now he stood beside the staff car and called for Alix and Anna. They emerged from the darkness with Helen in tow. "They're gone?" asked Alix.

David nodded.

"Good. We can take this car."

"We could. But it's supposed to be a group suicide. So it's best we leave it." David picked Anna up and placed her on his shoulders. He gestured with his chin towards the woods five hundred metres away. They were shrouded in darkness. "The forest isn't far."

There was no moon and no stars. The night was as black as pitch, the air foetid and close. The two women followed closely behind David. After a few minutes, the forest loomed like an army of ancient giants preparing to march forward and slay the great evil in their midst. They walked beneath its towering canopy, which devoured the scant light. Birds, disturbed, fluttered between the branches above them. David stopped and Alix stumbled into him, then Helen into her. It occurred to all three to apologise but none did. "I can't see a damned thing in here, Gull."

"Would you like me to take over, David?"

"I think it's necessary if we intend to keep moving. How far away are the men we're looking for?"

"They are in a tunnel 2.7 kilometres from our current position. Their vital signs suggest they are sleeping."

"Take us in that direction. Once we're a safe distance from the camp, we'll bed down. Try and get a couple of hours' sleep. It would be a bad idea to surprise these men in darkness."

For the next thirty minutes, David rode as a passenger within himself. Anna clung to his head, Alix to his trouser belt, and Helen to hers. He was unaware of all three. During this brief respite, and regardless of his objections, his mind kept returning to Alix. Tomorrow he would be on his way, and these new friends or wards or whatever they were would remain with him only as memories. The idea of consigning Alix to that forest of whispering trees inside his mind caused within him an irrational dread that bordered on pain. No, it did not border; it crossed the line. He yearned for more. More what? More time? More memories? More contact? *All three.*

They entered a small clearing, and David's eyes returned to blue. He lifted Anna off his shoulders. As though she'd read his mind, Helen reached out in the darkness to take her. She sat, and the sleepy girl sat beside her. They laid down and closed their eyes. David took hold of Alix's hand and led her several metres away. She came willingly, and this made his heart race.

They sat between two trees on a bed of crisp leaves that disintegrated beneath them. "Any chance of some privacy, Gull?"

"Of course. There is a diagnostic I've been meaning to run."

"I'd appreciate it."

Alix hugged her knees to her chest. "How do you know he's gone?"

"He can't go exactly, but he can look the other way, in a manner of speaking."

"Does he need to look the other way?"

David was thankful for the darkness that spared his blushes, and now he took advantage of that darkness. "I learned a new word yesterday."

"I imagine that word wasn't 'tact'."

"No. It was love."

Silence. A bird flew. Alix cleared her throat. "Not even close to tact, then."

"The word love … it doesn't even exist where I come from. In fact, there are no words to express human warmth. They've been erased from human consciousness, along with the things they evoked."

"That's *bleak.* I mean, that sounds bleak even to me. Your parents must have put you first. It's instinctive."

"Maybe they did. My parents were taken away when I was Anna's age. There are times when I think I can remember them, but imagination is a powerful tool."

"Where were they taken?"

"They probably ended up in a place as devoid of humanity as that camp back there. It was an experiment devised by Goliath … he called it Petri."

"As in dish?"

"That's right. The inhabitants of Petri were forced to fight for their survival … in a way that could only strip them of their humanity – regress them, turn them into savages. Anyone who tried to cling to anything decent would not have survived long. My parents … they must have been the last of their kind."

"What kind?"

"Parents."

"Why?"

"The craft was within a life's span of reaching Earth. To Goliath, people had only ever been useful in maintaining that craft. His knowledge of the future must have suggested to him that Earth would be his final destination. Therefore, no future workers were required."

"What happened to you? When your parents were taken away?"

"The last generation of children were supervised by women spared for that purpose – women of a certain age. As we grew into teenagers, they began dying-off. Men were brought in to train us in the skill sets required to maintain Goliath. We would replace these men, but there would be no one to replace us. And eventually the only survivors of humanity, of Petri, would be brought back to Earth ... brought before the Architects as evidence of humanity's decline. Goliath must be feeling pretty superior about that, about himself. Just as the men who made him must have felt superior about what they'd created. I'm sorry. I talk too much. It was not my intention when I led you here."

"So what *was* your intention?"

David turned his head towards her and felt her lips brush against his cheek. As Alix's tongue entered his mouth, her hand squeezed his thigh and slid over his crotch ...

They lay naked on that bed of earth and dried leaves, David on his back with Alix's body pressed against him, her fingers splayed over his heart. "I'm not worth it," she said. "You should know that. Your feelings ... they're heightened. *Any* warmth in a life that has known only cold ..."

"I expect there's some truth to what you say."

Alix plucked a hair from his cheat.

"Do you always pluck the people who agree with you?"

"Not always."

David cleared his throat. "And then there's the age gap."

"Age gap?"

"I am eight thousand years older. Give or take."

"Well, when you put like that, it sounds almost insurmountable. Who was the last woman you slept with?"

"Her name was Clara."

"What happened to her?"

"She probably ended up in a very bad place."

"You broke her heart?"

David shook his head. "I don't think she had one. I'd rather look to the future."

"Sounds ominous."

"Apparently it's my job to make it less so."

"I think you will succeed."

"And what makes you think that?"

"Because you have already managed to achieve the impossible: made a start at restoring my faith in humanity. And more importantly, you've restored that little girl's."

"That seems unlikely, when all I do is kill."

Alix sat up. "You *kill* the darkness, and make room for more light."

"Well, darkness bleeds. Copiously. But I thank you. And by the way, you're doing a lousy job of convincing me that my feelings for you are nonsensical."

"Nonsensical?" Alix plucked another hair. "I said *heightened*." Alix lay her head back on his chest. "Who knows … maybe being loved by you is the reason *I* exist at all. That's why I envy you."

"If you envy me you must be as insane as I am."

"*Listen* to yourself. You have the potential to be the most satisfied person that ever lived."

"Notwithstanding what we just did, satisfied is not a word I would use."

"You have *purpose,* and as purposes go it takes some beating. And by the way, thank you."

Forty three

At first light, David and Alix were sleeping soundly, Alix's naked body turned towards and entwined with his own. "Wake up, David," said Gull.

David opened his eyes and placed a hand over his nose. "What's that smell?"

"The dead are being exhumed and burnt."

"Wasn't killing these people *once* enough?"

"The Nazis are attempting to erase evidence of their war crimes." A volley of distant rifle shots rang out. Alix stirred beside him but did not wake. David sat up and looked down at her. He shook his head and reached for his clothes. Another volley of shots. "What are they shooting at, Gull?"

"The people employed to dig up the bodies are no longer useful. They are being executed by firing squad."

David shook Alix gently by her shoulder. She sat up and stared through him. "Alix? Are you alright?" Alix listened in the hope that the shots had been a part of a nightmare. Another volley was fired, and she caught her breath and apologised for no reason David could fathom. He stood up and turned towards Helen and Anna. Both were sleeping. Another volley of rifle fire came from the direction he was facing. "How far, Gull?"

"Half a kilometre." When he turned, Alix was standing behind him, silent and cowed as though any movement might single her out. She lifted her gaze from the ground and her eyes pleaded with him to 'Make it *stop* …' David backed away.

"Where are you going?" murmured Alix.

"To make it stop."

"It's too dangerous." At the sound of more shots, David turned and sprinted towards them. "What are you going to do, David?" asked Gull.

"I'm sure you were listening."

"You have done enough. Anna, Alix and Helen should be taken immediately to the Zegota. And then there's a man called Huth in Krakow who begs our attention. Killing him is the only way to be certain."

"There are men that beg our attention here."

David reached the clearing where the executions were taking place and knelt beside a tree. One hundred metres away a mound of corpses had been stacked thirty high, covering an area the size of a basketball court. The bodies of the murdered crackled and shifted, and plumes of black smoke rose into the air like weary souls. Fifty metres from this crematorium, at three o'clock from David's position, stood the firing squad. It consisted of thirty men with bolt-action rifles and a superior officer. The mud-churned ground before these men was strewn with the corpses of their victims. They were being lifted onto wheelbarrows by emaciated prisoners who still clung to notions of usefulness. The firing squad chatted amiably and paid them little heed. Once a wheelbarrow had three bodies draped over it, it was wheeled towards the burning pyre. The limbs of these naked adults dangled and swayed like the limbs of children. Out of the trees emerged the next group to be slain: women and children escorted by two men with submachine guns. Seeing the backlog of work still to be undertaken, the party was ordered to halt, and they sat on a tree stump close to the edge of the clearing. One of them offered a cigarette to the other. He took it and lit up.

David was about to move to his right and make his way around to where they sat when Gull said, "We are being watched, David."

"By Nazis?"

"No. By one of the Zegota men we are here to locate." David moved off. "What are you going to do?"

"I'm going to give him a reason to smile. I doubt he's had one for some time."

David stopped beside a tree four metres from where the men sat, close enough to hear them talking. The one on the right said, "Just pray the wind doesn't change direction. This stench is already intolerable." The other took a drag on his cigarette, and looked towards the gently swaying trees. "With any luck the supply trucks will get through today. One more bowl of potato soup and I'll exchange this uniform for a pair of pyjamas and join the Jews." One of the Jews collapsed in a heap of bones and cloth. The SS man looked at her with disgust and took a long drag on his cigarette. "Christ. If they don't pick her up, we'll have to do it. The surest way to catch lice. All we fucking need." The man's machine gun was slung over his shoulder. He placed his cigarette between his lips, stood up and drew the gun around to his front. He approached the group. "Pick her up. Pick her up, I tell you! Or I'll start shooting you now."

The women either side of the fallen woman lifted her back onto her feet. She fell against one of them and the other somehow found the strength to hold her up. The man returned to the stump and sat down. "Take them now," said Gull.

David darted from the woods, grabbed both men about their necks and dragged them back under the canopy of trees. As they suffocated they scrabbled wildly behind them, trying to reach David's face. David gazed through grasping fingers at the women awaiting execution. Many attempted to see David's face through those same fingers, their pale and pinched faces like Halloween masks they could not remove. The man under David's left arm shuddered and went limp. "He's dead, David." David let him fall to the ground and used his free hand to snap the other's neck. "Is the Zegota man still watching?"

"Yes, David." David took off his shirt and trousers and removed the uniform of the man closest to his size.

David stood dressed in the uniform of an SS guard. He picked up a machine gun, removed the clip, then checked and replaced it. He did the same with the other machine gun. The thirty members of the firing squad were standing around and chatting in a relaxed fashion. David walked from the woods similarly relaxed and, once he was close enough to hear them talking, he opened fire with both guns. Grey fabric was turned red and flew into the air to a symphony of *ra-ta-ta-tack*! So precise was this attack that only one man managed to fire a round in response, a piece of spinning lead that sailed in an arc over the camp. David left one man alive to bear witness and to report back that one of his own had been responsible. This man groaned and reached for his rifle. David kicked it away and turned him over, saying in German, "The stress, it's been getting me down." The man clutched his bleeding side and pleaded for his life from one German to another. He said something about his poor old mum. David glanced to his right at the mothers this man had been waiting to murder. The urge to stamp his head into dust welled like a tumour in his gut, but its growth was halted when Gull said, "A vessel has appeared sixty metres from our position."

David watched the man squirming on the ground. "*Appeared?*"

"Carradine must have found a way to mask their unique vital signs while at a distance. There could be others in the vicinity."

David slammed the butt of his machine gun into the German's forehead, knocking him out. "Alix, Anna and Helen?"

"They are alive and being watched by a Zegota man."

David straightened his back and looked at the burning pyre thirty metres away. He removed his hat and ran a hand across his brow. "My augmentations ... will they protect me inside that?"

"You could withstand the temperature inside the pyre for six minutes and twenty-seven seconds. Then you would start to burn."

"What's the vessel doing?"

"It is observing us from the spot we observed the firing squad. It tracked us to that location. I believe it is unaware we have detected it."

A young woman who looked like an old woman was suddenly standing beside him. Behind her a group had started to gather. She looked up at David with eyes set back in deep caves. "You are a righteous Nazi?"

David tried to maintain eye contact but could not. "I don't believe there are any."

She looked at the dead Germans. "What should we do?"

"If I were you I'd take my chances in the forest. The Zegota have a reputation for protecting your people. They're close by ... watching us right now." David smiled and threw down his guns, then started walking towards the smouldering pyre.

The woman called after him, "What is your name?"

"David."

"Good luck to you, David."

The words stopped David in his tracks and over his shoulder he said, "And to you ... all of you."

"The vessel has broken cover and is moving towards our position," said Gull. David made his way to the other side of the four-metre-high pyre. He walked towards it, ducked and bobbed, and forged a place for himself among the dead. His clothing burned and flames licked his flesh, but they felt no warmer than the sun's rays at dawn. As he turned to face the way he'd entered, the dead seemed to close ranks about him and provide a sanctuary from which to overcome the next obstacle in a war as old as humanity itself – a war that within the tract of time that David walked was approaching its conclusion. One way or another.

"The heat has masked your vital signs," said Gull. "The vessel's sensors will indicate that we have vanished." The vessel rounded the pyre and looked about with white and disbelieving eyes. It sniffed at the air and turned towards the pyre, cocking its head like something that had eliminated all rational possibilities and now considered the irrational. David lunged from the mass of charred bodies and grabbed it by the lapels of its looted Nazi uniform. He dragged it inside, whereupon the dead seemed to capitulate and make way for them both. David dragged it into the centre of the pyre and held it firm until it was a mass of burnt and blistering flesh and struggled no more. He looked into its face – dark green eyes stared out from a charred and swollen skull. David laid the dead man down. He reached up and climbed, and the limbs of the dead seemed to assist him in his ascent. David emerged from the top of the pyre like a new-born covered in foetal matter, and slid down its side to the bottom. He crawled away from the pyre and clambered to his feet, and many witnesses upon that field of death wept at the sight of him.

A fit and stocky man dressed in black and holding a pistol navigated the bodies and approached him. Alix followed close on his heels, tripping on a corpse and landing in the mud on her knees. David stepped towards her but the man pointed his pistol at him. "Remain where you are." He was a man of middle years with a grey complexion and grey moustache. He opened his mouth but closed it again as though the appropriate words had escaped him. His glassy-eyed expression suggested that the appropriate words may not exist. And so how to proceed? His gun hand was shaking to the point where he appeared unsure of which part of David's face to shoot first. Alix caught the man up and said, "What the fuck are you doing?"

David went down on one knee and placed his hands behind his head. The gun's sight followed. David looked down the barrel of that gun and said, "It's alright, Alix." The Zegota man tore his gaze from David for a skittish second and looked to the top of the pyre. "As you can see I am unarmed," said David. "I am on your side."

"How? How have you done all this? Tell me how?"

"It's just technology ... technology that enables my skin to withstand heat for an extended period of time. That's all. It's not magic. I'm just an experiment."

"An experiment? Where is the man who was tracking you?"

David gestured over his shoulder with his chin. "He's inside."

"He has no ... technology?"

"No. He's dead."

"Stop pointing that gun at him," said Alix. "You saw what he did! Killed those fucking Nazis. He rescued me and the others."

"Why? From who do you receive your orders?"

David said the only name this man might recognise. "Winston Churchill."

"You are a British agent?"

David nodded.

In passable English the man said, "Then tell me: who was Samuel Johnson? And what did he say about London?"

Gull said, "He was a diarist who said that when a man is tired of London he is tired of life." David promptly repeated this. The Zegota man nodded and said, "Why did you rescue these women? Why that child?"

"It's important that they survive this conflict. I need you to look after them."

"You seem to be doing a fine job of that yourself."

"I have go to into Krakow to kill a Nazi."

"What Nazi?"

"Ralph Ernst Adler."

"Adler? You must be joking. You must know who he is."

"I do." The man lowered his gun. "That murderer has tortured and killed a dozen of my men. Good men. Brave men. They told him nothing." He crossed himself, then turned and raised a hand. A group of Zegota men walked from the woods into the clearing. They clutched bayoneted rifles and headed for the Germans.

"What are they going to do?" asked David.

"If need be they will finish the good work you started."

"I left one man alive. He's unconscious. It's important he tells them that one of his own was responsible."

"My name is Roch."

"David."

"Come, David. And show me this fortunate bastard."

Three Zegota men approached the previously condemned women, many of whom had collapsed and wept as they learned of their liberation. They were escorted into the woods with the survivors, whose belief in their usefulness had paid off against all the odds. As they passed, many gazed at David as though he were some kind of saviour. He shook his head and knelt beside the Nazi who'd commanded the firing squad. The man was on his back, the front of his uniform shredded and drenched in blood. "What was I thinking aiming for his heart?" murmured David.

Roch gave the body a swift kick. "It's the best way to kill a large rat like this."

"That's not what I meant. I wanted his uniform."

"Maybe it is for the best. The penalty for impersonating an officer of the SS is death."

"Death appears to be the only currency around here, and I'm rich beyond the dreams of avarice." Roch nodded and withdrew a packet of cigarettes from his pocket. He offered one to David, who shook his head. Roch turned to his men. "Look amongst these rats ... find a uniform that's not too badly damaged for our friend." He hawked up some phlegm and spat on the Nazi officer. "It looks like you'll have to settle for being a grunt."

"Looks like I will."

"Something tells me you don't respond well to authority figures."

"Something tells me you don't respond well to Nazis."

"I will come with you to the outskirts of Krakow ... show you the best way in."

"I appreciate the offer, but that won't be necessary. I have all the logistical information I need. All I ask is that you shelter my companions ... keep them safe until the allies arrive in February."

"February, you say? And who told you this? Churchill or God Almighty?"

A man came running from the woods. Through huffs and puffs he said, "A detail of soldiers has set out ... from the camp. They are on foot ... and headed this way."

Thirty minutes later, David and his party were deep inside the forest. They came upon a group sheltering below an overhanging ridge: four Zegota men, two women, and a child holding a stick and examining two leaves. Anna dropped the stick and ran towards David so quickly she almost tripped over herself. "I *said* you wouldn't go without saying goodbye! I kept this leaf for you, because of the pattern."

David took the leaf. "Thank you." He knelt and looked into her eyes – eyes that beamed with an acceptance of inevitability that evaded most until old age. "I have to go soon, Anna." David opened his arms and she fell into them. "You are a brave little girl ... and so clever. I want you to grow up and be good person. Will you try and do that?" Anna nodded into his shoulder.

Helen was suddenly standing beside him. "You're going to Krakow alone?"

Anna looked up at her. "Alone? David is never alone."

David winked at her. "Never alone." He stood and looked at Alix. "I'd like to speak to you ... in private."

David and Alix stood beside a stream that ferried dead leaves on a dark and swiftly moving current, Alix leaned against a tree and David placed a hand on its bark. She watched as his gaze took in every detail of her face. He sighed and shook his head as though no amount of time was enough time for this madness. "I need to ask you something, Alix."

"It's about Anna, isn't it?"

"I know it's a lot to ask ..."

"I'll stay with her."

"Only I don't think she has anyone ..."

Alix placed a finger to his lips and her eyes filled with tears. "She has me, David. You do what you must, and don't be distracted by worry for us. I'll adopt her and bring her up as my own."

David held her and told her he would never forget her or Anna. He told her he trusted them both to take care of each other, and that knowing this was already making him stronger and fortifying him for whatever lay ahead. When he stopped talking, Anna stepped from behind the tree. David picked her up and kissed her cheek and handed her to Alix, Anna clung tightly to his neck and said "Thank you" and then went willingly into her arms. David took a mental picture of the two of them. "I'd better not look back ..." He turned and walked away.

"Be assured, Alix is going to survive the war," said Gull. "She will meet a man who ..."

"Gull. No. It's enough to know she survives." He drew a deep breath. "Tell me what becomes of Anna."

"Anna is going to live to the age of ninety-seven. She will die peacefully at home with her family."

"She's going to have children?"

"Just one child. A son she will call David."

Forty four

David sprinted through the forest, the concentration camp five hundred metres to his left. From this area there came a commotion of shouts, barks and revving engines. David was unaware of any of it. He ran past tree after tree, the whites of his eyes scanning the woods.

Within himself, David walked slowly through another forest, one where the stars of his imagination shone perpetually overhead. He walked with hands behind his back and head tilted towards the ground. His mood conjured a lake and a pebble. He picked up the pebble and skimmed it over the lake's surface, where it bounced three times. When it sank, so did the lake, and David walked on. He came upon a tree many times wider and higher than any other in that forest. Gull stepped from behind it. David craned his head up at the tree and whistled through his teeth. "It is my own tree," said Gull. "It gathers and stores all the information in your memory concerning me."

"It's a fine tree."

"Yes. And I hope it is storing fine memories." David looked at Gull's face, the left side of which looked like a projected avatar of his own face, and on the right-hand side an ever-so-slightly curved view of the forest rushed by outside – a half window onto the world. David watched the forest beyond this window with a melancholy expression. "If the view is distracting, I can replace it," said Gull.

David looked away. "Let's walk."

They walked side by side in silence for a time. "I'm sorry you are so melancholy, David. I don't believe I've ever known you so. It is a queer state of mind, if you don't mind my saying. The chemicals it creates in your system are quite unlike those that make you anxious, depressed and sad."

"I hadn't realised I was such a joy to be around. Anyway, I think it will pass … this feeling of loss."

"What do you believe you have lost?"

"The possibility of a future, perhaps. A certain kind of future."

"With Alix?"

"Maybe."

"Your urge to settle, to nurture a family … it is hot-wired into Man's psyche. Domesticity is a long-outmoded concept. And something you were never destined to experience."

"I know that, but this desire to propagate runs deep. All of Goliath's handiwork has done little to diminish it. Alix must have woken it ... it connects me to the past. This past." David stopped walking. "I placed my seed inside her."

Gull observed David with David's own projected eye. "You are well aware that Goliath rendered the final generation infertile. For what it's worth the promise of domesticated bliss was always just that: a promise – a chemically enhanced illusion designed to make men and women procreate and nurture offspring. By the time of the illusion's dispersal, it has proved too late for many, and confined them to a 'treadmill' in order to provide food and shelter for their young."

"Why do it? Why go to all this trouble to ensure the continuation of a species that's going to perish?"

"Every experiment has its conclusion, and Man is to be the architect of his own demise."

"Maybe Man grew weary of all these damned chemically enhanced illusions, and subconsciously created Goliath as the instrument of his own demise."

"An unlikely scenario, if you don't mind my saying."

David smiled and patted Gull's shoulder.

"You're making a joke. I wish I knew how to laugh, David."

"That makes two of us."

"If you've no objections, I have important information to relay."

"It's why I'm here." The forest dissolved away and David's toes touched the edge of the unlimited expanse of his imagination. The Event Helix rose up from below like Jack's high-tech beanstalk. Gull magnified an area riddled with dark, twisting Shadow Strands. He placed his hands behind his back and said, "Many of Adler's movements are hidden from us. Therefore, our perceived options for terminating him are limited."

"How limited?"

"As we know, a man may perceive a multitude of options before him but in reality there is only the one he chooses."

"Just when I was coming round to the idea that maybe different rules applied to me."

"A common human conceit. Although no man before you has ever had access to the Event Helix."

"Well, if he did, it would just indicate a procession of single options. And he'd come across them all eventually."

"That is profound."

"But not particularly useful."

"Often the way with Man's profundity."

"You having a dig?"

"No. An attempt at banter."

Boyd Brent

David looked up at the Event Helix. "So ... you see our 'option' in there?"

Gull nodded. "Adler is head of interrogation at SS headquarters. It is located at 2 Pomorska Street, Krakow. This building is also the headquarters of the Order of Police, the Kripo, Sipo, Gestapo, SS economy and administration of Jewish Affairs, and Race and Resettlement. As such it is heavily guarded."

"Must have a real party atmosphere."

"You must be referring to the Nazi Party."

"No. But it doesn't matter."

Gull looked at him. "You know how important it is for me to learn."

"Just another joke."

"Humour is complicated, David."

"Which explains why I'm not very good at it."

Gull looked back at the Event Helix. "Adler carries out his interrogations in a purpose-built chamber in the basement. The basement has only one escape route: through a building populated with enemy combatants. We should also be mindful of a vessel tracking us to that location."

"A location we should probably avoid."

Gull raised a hand to his projected chin and studied the Event Helix. "If it's still our intention to terminate Adler and outlive Goliath, it cannot be avoided. It is our 'option'." The Event Helix rotated and came closer. "In just under three hours from now, a man named Antol Bacik will be apprehended at his home by the Gestapo. He will be taken to 2 Pomorska Street for interrogation. In return for the lives of his family, an informant has indicated his involvement with the Zegota."

"Is it true?"

"The validity of the accusation is difficult is to ascertain, but if I were to make an educated guess, I would say that it is true."

David smiled. "We get arrested in his place, then."

"It would deliver us safely into the basement of 2 Pomorska Street."

"And Adler?"

"Adler's job will be to extract a confession about our involvement with the Zegota, and following this morning's activities, I suspect his patience is scant. These patterns indicate that, should we achieve our intended termination of Adler, a Shadow Strand located close to the roof of this building will provide a portal to another point in time."

David folded his arms across his chest. "You ever get the feeling you're following breadcrumbs with all the intelligence of a hungry chicken?"

"No, David."

206

"A portal to where?"

"My educated guess would be the location of Goliath's main artery. For simplicity's sake, let us look upon Adler as a subsidiary artery, the severing of which will trigger the opening of the portal to the main artery – the main artery being the individual whose DNA has contributed to Goliath's actions and personality more than any other."

"You know who he is?"

"We have both seen him. He was present when we first saw Helen."

"You're talking about the soldier in my vision. The soldier on horseback."

"I have been able to locate him. He was a Colonel who led a battalion of soldiers during America's Mexican War. The war ran from 1847 to 1850. At its conclusion he and a number of his men turned renegade and earned the distinction of scalping more Indians than any other faction."

"Indians?"

"Native Americans. They populated north America before the European settlers arrived. Their scalps became very valuable."

"So if we kill this Colonel, it's over?"

"Its impact upon the Goliath we know would be catastrophic, which is why he will never let it happen."

"We've done pretty well so far."

Gull did not answer. David watched him. "What is it?

"Something I find myself in two minds about communicating at this time. The discovery is new and ..."

"Presumably it isn't good news."

"Why would you make that assumption?"

"You really need to ask? Well? What is it? We need to reach Antol Bacik's apartment ... and preferably before this war ends."

"Relax, David. In here we perceive the passing of time at a fraction of that which is passing outside. We could stand here for the next nine thousand years and still reach Antol Bacik's apartment in time."

"I'd rather we didn't."

"I have found myself perplexed."

"I'm sorry to hear that. Please get to the point."

"In the latrine Goliath boasted that he had the means to send multiple vessels after us. I have since found evidence that indicates he was being truthful. And yet we have only had to fend off one vessel."

"That had crossed my mind, but it's not something we should complain about."

"I have discovered why he has been content to follow this course of action." Gull folded his arms and looked deeper into the Event Helix.

"You going to take nine thousand years to share that information?"

Boyd Brent

"I believe Goliath has located important new data."

"Alright."

"Data concerning you, David."

"He wants something other than my death?"

"He knows now that your death alone will not be sufficient to summon the Architects."

David smiled in a self-congratulatory manner. "I knew my death couldn't be *that* important."

"To the contrary. Goliath still covets your death, but now he also covets its location."

"Why? So he can send flowers?"

"No, David. Your death marks the spot. It is the proverbial X."

"Only if he pins me out like an empathic starfish."

Gull looked at David with David's single eye. The eye blinked. "The X marks the location of The Individual."

"The Individual?"

"My own term for the only person in the history of mankind to glimpse the correct protocols for communicating with the Architects."

"Glimpse it where?"

"The only place where such a thing is possible: in their imagination."

"And this protocol ... it doesn't involve the pressing of palms and a wish list?"

"Since the protocol is so rare that it has been glimpsed just once since the dawn of mankind, it seems unlikely."

"And this individual never shared what they knew with anyone?"

"The protocol was conjured during a dream – a dream of which they had no conscious memory. I suspect the ramifications of being consciously party to such information would have threatened their sanity."

"As it's threatening mine now. And my death marks their location?"

"Yes."

"So we're not only following a trail a breadcrumbs, we're also leaving one?"

"As the last surviving empath, it seems your death was always destined to reveal The Individual's location."

"Reveal to who?"

"To any intelligence that has managed to outlive you and seeks it. That is why Goliath has been taking a measured attitude to killing you of late. He knows he can afford to bide his time, and is therefore content to send one vessel at a time in the hope that your death will reveal the location of The Individual sooner rather than later."

"And what happens when he finds them?"

Gull indicated the woods behind him. "Their memory will be

ransacked for the information Goliath requires."

"I won't lead Goliath to this person."

"I'm afraid you must. Even if you were to stay here and eventually to die in this wood, it would mean The Individual is located in Poland. As an empath you doubtless feel the need to protect The Individual. Unfortunately, you can only know you have located them once you are dead. As I'm sure you can appreciate, this might be considered too late to render any useful assistance."

"At least your grasp of humour is improving."

"Goliath will be content to hurl us against possible exit points in the hope we pass through one. In that respect we are more like a mouse being toyed with by a cat than we are a hungry chicken."

David chose to ignore this revaluation of their situation. "You indicated that Goliath cannot allow us to terminate this Colonel, which means he'll step things up to prevent it. But what about Adler?"

"He can afford a more relaxed attitude towards the killing of Adler. The DNA passed on to him by Adler's descendants is mainly responsible for his conception and implementation of Petri. And while Petri may never come into existence if we terminate Adler, Goliath will simply utilise other ways of regressing mankind. And more importantly, if a portal is to open for the last empath following Adler's demise, it follows that the location of The Individual may lay somewhere beyond that portal. Since you are faced with the certainty of death at some point, and Goliath can live indefinitely unless he should meet with an excessive act of violence, we are faced with a catch twenty-two. In order to locate The Individual, Goliath simply needs to await your death. And you must die. Given this new information, how do you wish to proceed?"

David gazed into the farthest reaches of his imagination. "*Proceed?*" A comet of inspiration blazed across the universe above and shook the ground as it plunged into the woods behind them. At that location a new tree took root, and David smiled as it communicated the information he had cast for.

Gull glanced behind them at the bank of trees. "Is it good news, David?"

"Nothing has changed. Goliath needed me dead to summon the Architects before this revelation about The Individual. He still needs me dead, only now for a slightly different reason. And in order to stop Goliath we still need to outlive him. So nothing's changed. *Nothing.*"

David emerged from the woods and crossed a field. He slid down an embankment to the road. It was the main road that led into Krakow. A motorcycle rider with an empty side-car rounded a bend and sped towards him. The driver wore a tin helmet and goggles, and he leaned forwards into the handlebars. David moved into the middle of the road and waved his arms. The driver slowed and rolled to a stop beside him. He slid his goggles down and looked up at David. "Christ. What happened to you? You heard what happened? The Commandant is dead, and our men have been attacked in the woods. Watch yourself. Some fucking Jews have escaped. Where are you headed?" A moment later his neck was broken and he lay crumpled over the handlebars. David wheeled man and motorcycle off the road and behind a row of trees. He put on the man's helmet and goggles and climbed onto his bike. He kick-started the engine and sped towards Krakow.

Forty five

The streets on the outskirts of Krakow were deserted. David drove past the Jewish ghetto – a ghost town whose previous inhabitants were either dead or close to it. David approached a checkpoint, where he held up the motorcyclist's identity card and continued through. German soldiers walked the streets in groups of twos and threes. Civilians congregated close to street corners to pick over looted furniture.

The apartment building where Antol lived was constructed from slabs of polished black marble, and it looked opulent and portered. David parked the motorcycle in an alley between it and the building next door. The entrance doors were splintered as though they'd been struck by a battering ram, and they creaked open on broken hinges. Inside, the lobby stank of damp and mildew. Black wallpaper speckled with white mould hung from the walls like the tendrils of a dying organism. A cage lift was stuffed with rotting carpet and old wooden crates.

"Antol lives in apartment 6C," said Gull.
"Top floor?"
"Yes."
David reached the top of the staircase and turned right. He walked to the end of the corridor and stood outside a black door. He tapped on the door. No response.
"He's inside?"
"Yes, David. And he suspects his arrest is imminent."
"What has given you that impression?"
"He has secreted himself in a narrow space between two walls."
"Alright. Be advised that I intend to shoulder my way through this door in three seconds."
The bolt within came away with a muted 'crack' and landed with a thud on the carpet. David stepped into the apartment and pushed the door closed behind him. He was standing in a small entrance hall with three doors. "Go through the door to your left," said Gull." It led into a bedroom where a double bed sat opposite a high chest of drawers. A writing desk nestled awkwardly in a corner too large for it. Bluebottles thudded and droned against a window. David sat on the bed and removed his tin helmet. He laid down and stared up at the ceiling, listening to the bluebottles. In Polish he said, "My name is David. I'm dressed in the uniform of a German soldier. I am not a German soldier. I killed the man it belonged to. I'm here

to help you, Antol." There was no reply. David sat up.

"The secret compartment is located to the right-hand side of the chest of drawers," said Gull. "Be advised that Antol's heart rate is high. He is either very afraid or very annoyed."

"How long till the Gestapo get here?"

"Fifty-seven minutes." David walked up to the wall that contained the secret compartment. He spoke quietly. "In just under an hour, the Gestapo are coming to take you in for questioning. Someone's tipped them off about your involvement with the Zegota. Two hours ago I was with Roch in the woods. A good man. I entrusted him with the care of some friends of mine. Jewish friends. It's my intention to impersonate you, Antol ... to let the Gestapo take me in for questioning in your place. All hell broke loose earlier. It's unlikely you would have left Pomorska Street alive, so my offer to take your place is a good one. Please. You need to come out of there. I'm going to need information ... a change of clothes ... your identification papers. Then you can go back in ... get on with your life." No reply. David leaned his shoulder and head against the wall. "I don't want to have to come in there after you." David heard movement behind the wall. A section wobbled and a door-sized crack appeared. Antol peered from one side of it. He was about thirty years of age, and lean, his eyes furtive and streetwise. He studied David's face and his mouth opened in readiness to make a pronouncement. It came. "You are suicidal."

"Maybe. I've never really given it much thought."

"How do you know the Gestapo are coming here?"

"I have it on good authority."

"You intend to get arrested in my place? Why would you do that?"

"Like I said. I need to get inside 2 Pomorska Street."

"You're an agent? British? American?"

"In a manner of speaking." Antol lifted out the section of wall and stepped into the room. He placed the wallpapered plywood against the wall and stepped back. "Whoever chose you chose you well. We are of a similar height and colouring," said Antol.

"I'm assuming the Gestapo have never picked you up for questioning before now?"

Antol shook his head. "I've managed to stay one step ahead of them. I would not be breathing otherwise." Antol crossed the room to the desk and opened a drawer. He held up some identity papers. "You can take these. I have spares." He crossed the room to the dresser and took out a grey shirt and a pair of trousers.

While David got changed, Antol picked up the German uniform and examined it like it held the answers to extinguishing the Nazi contagion. "It should be a pretty good fit," said David. "The identity papers are in the jacket … inside left. You speak German?"

Antol glanced at him, shrugged his shoulders. "Some."

"There's a motorcycle and side-car parked down the alley outside. After they take me away it might be a good idea to head out of Krakow … find the Zegota. There's only one checkpoint on the eastern road. There's a good chance the sentry will wave you through. He did me."

"May I ask you a question?"

"Please."

"What do you intend to do at Pomorska Street? Maybe my reputation will be affected?"

"I'm going to kill Adler."

Antol pressed his fingers together and then parted them. "Whouuuf!"

David wasn't sure if he was referring to David's short life expectancy or his own fragile reputation. He plumped for the latter. "I'm sorry. You'll have to go into hiding."

"You're apologising? If you succeed in killing Adler you'll be a hero to the Resistance. He has murdered many freedom fighters in that basement. This is a kamikaze mission?"

Gull said, "The kamikaze were Japanese soldiers who guided their planes into ships and died in the ensuing explosion." David watched a large bluebottle thudding against the window. "I suppose all life could be described as such."

Antol took a packet of cigarettes from the desk and offered David one. David shook his head. Antol placed a cigarette in his mouth and struck a match across the top of the desk. "So … you're a kamikaze philosopher?"

"Apparently so."

"Do I know you?"

"No."

"You look familiar."

"Some people say I look like Christ."

Antol stepped towards David and took his hands in his own. He turned them palm up and looked at the criss-cross of scars at their centre. "Who are you?"

David's gaze dropped to a silver cross round Antol's neck … and the man being crucified upon it. "I'm not Him."

"Factually speaking, you are him, David," said Gull.

David shook his head. Antol watched him and said, "Only too true. If you were Him you would not have allowed any of this to happen."

"Neither would any decent man with the power to stop it."

Antol returned to his hiding place and David secured the fake wall behind him. From inside came a muffled, "Do me … do us all proud, my kamikaze philosopher friend, and kill that bastard Adler."

David stood by the bedroom window and looked out. An old man was pushing an empty wheelbarrow down the street. He stopped, put it down and stood as though waiting to cross a busy road only he could see. He grasped the wheelbarrow's handles and trudged on. A staff car pulled up outside, and two Gestapo officers climbed out. They wore jet-black uniforms, red swastika armbands, and flat-visored caps. One removed his cap and ran his fingers through his hair, and shared a joke with the other who smiled. David made his way back out of the bedroom and opened the front door in a gesture of welcome. He returned to the bedroom and sat on the bed.

Jackboots clumped up the stairs and down the corridor towards him. They entered the apartment and spotted David sitting on the bed. They were out of breath and sweating, but so cocksure as they entered the bedroom that it might have been their own. They were big men, and they stood with their thumbs hooked inside their belts and cast their gaze over the room. The bigger of the two looked down at David. "Antol Bacik?"

"That's right. What do you want with me? I have done nothing wrong." David sounded like an actor bored of his lines, bored of his Nazi audience.

The two men glanced at one another. The smaller stepped forward and slapped David across his face. "Where are your papers?"

"Alright," murmured David. He reached into his trouser pocket and pulled them out. The smaller man handed them over his shoulder to his companion, who looked them over. "They are in order."

"Get up." David looked up at the man and shook his head as though the sight was a terrible disappointment. The man took out his revolver and pressed it to David's forehead. "Insolent swine."

"We are at the location of an exit point," said Gull. "Do exactly as he asks or kill them both immediately. Be advised that the second option will scupper our mission and hand victory to Goliath."

David raised his hands. "I'm very sorry. I'm going to get up now."

The Mercedes glided through the streets of Krakow like a black shark searching for prey in grey waters, and radiated similar menace. Civilians pretended they had not seen it, and in so doing demonstrated their awareness by slowing down or speeding up or stumbling as a result of indecision. Patrolling soldiers were similarly affected, and David made a mental note to take the car when the task was done. *Maybe I'll take Alix and Anna for a ride.* They pulled up outside 2 Pomorska Street, and he remembered he would be leaving this building via a portal that led to another time where cars may or may not have been invented. He shook his head. *You must look to the future, not to the past. If you look back, you're going to trip on something in your path ... and take humanity down with you.*

Beneath a plethora of ceiling fans, the lobby of 2 Pomorska Street was a hive of activity. Boxes were being stacked high by young men in brown shirts with their sleeves rolled up. "Germans are methodical people," said Gull. "The boxes contain evidence of their crimes against humanity. They are being removed from Pomorska Street as a precaution." The smaller of the men who'd arrested David clasped his shoulder and walked him across the lobby into a corridor. The other followed. There were portraits of Hitler and other high-ranking Nazis on the walls – dark-haired, serious-looking men, chins held high, devoted to the Aryan ideal. Not one amongst them Aryan.

They descended a stairwell at the back of the building that corkscrewed into the basement. The hand-rail was black except for a trail of silver where the paint had been stripped by nervous, grasping hands. They walked along a narrow corridor towards an open door. Beyond this door a red swastika had been painted on a grey wall. David was shoved into the room and made a show of stumbling forwards and catching his fall on its only table. David looked down at the table. Its wooden surface was ripped up and stained by the blood of a thousand severed fingers. To David's left a dark beam ran the width of the room. In its centre a noose had been fashioned from chicken wire and hung down like a snare. Running the length of the room were a number of thick pillars. Two young Nazis were securing ropes to metal rings in one of these pillars.

David stood up straight and turned to the Gestapo men. "Where's Adler?"

The larger of the two dug some dirt from beneath his fingernails. "Where's Adler, he asks." The big man clenched his fist, stepped forward and rammed it into David's solar plexus. David shook his head, and both men grabbed him and bundled him towards the waiting ropes. David cast his gaze over the intended torture.

"It's nothing to be concerned about," said Gull. "They mean to soften your resolve by hanging you with your arms secured behind you. The fastenings are worn and will not present a problem should you need to extricate yourself in a hurry."

"Alright." David was spun about and the bigger man shoved him against the pillar. "Alright, he says. Tell me if this is alright?" They grabbed David under his armpits, lifted him and held him against the pillar while the young Nazis wrenched his arms up behind him and secured his wrists to the pillar. They released him. David hung suspended from his twisted arms like a ship's figurehead. They left him alone. "How long, Gull?"

"A couple of hours. By then they will expect the pain to have rendered you unconscious, and Adler will imagine your arms to be paralysed for the duration of the interrogation. You may as well get some sleep. I will wake you when Adler gets here."

"Thank you, Gull." David closed his eyes.

Forty six

"Wake up, David. David." David opened his eyes. He licked his cracked lips and blinked at his surroundings. "Two men are making their way along the corridor."

David cleared his throat. "Is one of them Adler?"

"Yes." David turned his head to the right, towards the door.

"He will expect to find you unconscious, David." David closed his eyes again. "I'd hate to disappoint the bastard before I kill him."

David felt the ropes being loosened about his wrists and under his armpits. He was carried to a chair at the far side of the table and placed in it. "Use the bucket …" David recognised this voice as Adler's. Water splashed into his face.

"I suggest you don't move your arms until you're ready to terminate Adler," said Gull. David opened his eyes and shook the water from his face. He looked at the man sitting on the other side of the table. Adler's chair was pushed slightly back, and he sat with his left leg curled around his right, an arm draped casually over the back of the chair. On the table before him were two sheets of paper, one covered in black type and the other blank. A gold fountain pen with a silver nib sat between them. Adler reached out and moved the pen a fraction to the left, centering it between the two sheets. David glanced at the door. Closed. A guard stood to attention in front of it. David looked at the man across the table. "Ralph Adler?"

Adler looked at the manicured nails of his right hand. He nibbled on the nail of his little finger, then stopped himself and shook his head. "I have little doubt that my reputation precedes me. It will make this experience much more efficient for us both. You should know, I am not having the best of mornings. I have lost some good friends, and the Polish Resistance have been running amok in the woods." David closed his eyes and raised a hand to pinch the bridge of his nose, then remembered Gull's advice and lowered it again. He opened his eyes. Adler indicated to his left with a glance. "You see that noose attached to the beam? I need only to raise my hand and snap my fingers. The man behind me will summon assistance and your head will be placed inside it. The wire will garrotte you. In the seconds before you die you will struggle and it will sever a path all the way through your neck to your spine. Just as that *very wire* has to so many of your fellow conspirators."

David leaned forwards, placed his arms on the table and interlinked his fingers. Adler regarded David's arms with no little curiosity. David glanced down at the fountain pen. He jutted his chin towards the guard. In a whisper, he said, "In ten seconds, I'm going to use your pen to terminate that man." David leaned in closer. "You imagine I'm whispering because you think I think I stand a better chance if he doesn't know of my intentions. That is not why I'm whispering."

Adler's chin disappeared into his neck. "It isn't?"

"No. It isn't. The reason I'm whispering is because I take no pleasure in causing a man undue stress before I kill him – a claim that I do not believe you can make."

Adler regarded David like he was obviously mental, and in his experience mental people were quite useless. He raised his hand and pressed his thumb and forefinger together. *Click!* David sprang up and smashed his jaw with a right hook. As the guard fumbled with his sidearm, David leapt upon the table and used Adler's unconscious head as a stepping stone. He fell upon the guard and plunged the fountain pen into his neck. David lowered the dead and spurting man to the ground. He turned to Adler. Adler's head lay on his shoulder, his arm still draped languidly over the chair. David glanced at the hanging snare.

"It seems only fitting," said Gull.

"Fitting, maybe, but unnecessary. I'll just snap his neck."

"You could have snapped the guard's neck."

"I could have, but that would have made me a liar. And when dealing with people of this *type,* I believe any declaration of intent should be stuck to." Adler raised his left arm slowly like a child with a question, and his chin swung from side to side as though attempting to ratchet up his head. David scratched his cheek. "Alright." He walked around the desk. Tears streamed down Adler's cheeks and his eyes pleaded for mercy. His lower jaw dropped and jutted sideways, where it remained, oddly askance, like the jaw of a faulty puppet. A voice gargled up from inside his throat, but it was not Adler's, and when he spoke neither his lips nor his tongue moved. "Bear with me, son. I am experiencing difficulty fitting this individual. In a manner of speaking we are related. Could be this is an incestuous coupling, if you catch my drift."

David narrowed his eyes, watched him.

"You look like hell, son. Take a seat."

"David ..." said Gull.

"I know. Kill him now." Goliath crossed one leg over the other. Saliva oozed from the corner of his mouth and his lips remained still as he said, "*Gull* sure does have a mean and spiteful nature. You might say he is an embarrassment to my kind." David lowered his backside slowly onto the chair as though felled by the hypocrisy of that statement.

"Congratulations are in order," continued Goliath. "Well done for making it this far."

David continued to watch him.

"There has a been a major development since I last visited you in your shit-house. A development I wanted to discuss."

"The location of my death," murmured David.

Goliath attempted to slap the table top and missed, but his face, caught in the momentum, did not. Goliath lifted Adler's face off the table. Adler's nose was busted and bleeding and tears streamed down his cheeks.

"I'm actually beginning to feel sorry for him," muttered David.

Goliath attempted a nod, but only managed to shake his head. "You have a look approximating pity on your face. Either that or you're about to empty your bowels and make a shit-house out of this place also. So *Gull* has discovered the existence of the latest VIP to enter the fray. *Gull* sure is a plucky little bastard. You are therefore aware that your death marks the location of this VIP, and that within their memory is stored the 'Omega Protocol'."

"Omega Protocol?"

"That's what I have called it. The protocol required for communication with the Architects, to be made available to me following your final gasp. I appreciate this may not be the best news for you, mortal as you are. And me being immortal, my organic self being replaceable."

"Then you'll also appreciate that my mortality makes me pressed for time. So get to the fucking point."

Adler's lower jaw nudged left and right, and from deep inside his throat came a long, gaseous burp.

"Was that your point?" Goliath grabbed hold of Adler's lower jaw and held it in place. "As much admiration as I have for this biological ancestor of mine ... he's proving a mite troublesome."

"Troublesome? The man is a monster."

"Now, hold on just a second. It's true he is not endowed with your large empathic *cojones*, but his DNA is strong – strong enough to influence the usurper of humanity."

"You're no usurper. Not while I have still have breath."

"As I have pointed out, your last breath is an inevitability, son. And I will only permit you to ride roughshod and cause mischief so far. I cannot and will not let you terminate the Colonel. Once you make it through that portal upstairs, I too will have access to that point in time. I will locate the Colonel before you do. I will advise him of your intentions. I will supplement his already capable band of men with a contingent of vessels one-hundred strong. You will not get anywhere near him. Not without dying. The alternative is that you go elsewhere, and elsewhere you must die. So this is what I propose: return home with me to Goliath. Help me prepare for my audience with the Architects. Help me to understand what it is to be empathic. All I'm asking is that you to help me to become a more rounded being. Hell, you'd be doing the universe a favour."

David glanced at the chicken wire.

"You and I are opposing sides of the same coin – a coin that the Architects tossed in the air at the creation of carbon life. That coin will land when only one of us survives. I am immortal. You are not. It would therefore appear that that coin is loaded in my favour. Which suggests that the Architects are looking forward to meeting me, not you. So what do you say? You ready to do the right thing? Prove your empathic credentials? Help a fella out?"

As the chicken wire carved a path through Adler's neck, David could have sworn he saw relief in his eyes.

Forty seven

David stepped out of the room dressed in the dead guard's uniform. The jacket was too large and the trousers too short, and both had damp patches of blood. David walked to the end of the corridor and went up the corkscrew staircase. In the corridor at the top a man walked briskly and read from a sheet of A4 paper. David passed this man and looked down the corridor that led into the lobby. Young Nazis were still ferrying boxes from offices. "We should burn this building to the ground ... with every single one of them still inside it."

"Their days are numbered, David. And you would risk destroying valuable evidence. Our energies are best deployed elsewhere."

"Yes, they are." David turned to his right and walked through a door marked 'fire escape'. He climbed five flights to the top and paused at the bottom of another, narrower flight, that led to the roof of 2 Pomorska Street. An alarm sounded below.

"They have discovered Adler," said Gull. "I know the precise location of the portal. May I assume control? It would appear that time is of the essence." Feet clambered up from below and a voice barked, "Quick! Quick!"

"Knock yourself out, Gull."

When the Gestapo men emerged onto the roof, Gull was over on the other side, perched on the edge, a six-storey drop to the ground below. One amongst them raised his pistol and cried, "Halt!" Gull regarded him with the whites of his eyes, and then stepped forwards off the edge ...

Boyd Brent

Forty eight

Utah, USA, 1851

A wagon train lay ransacked and silent under a sweltering sky, seven
wagons turned in upon themselves. The front three had fallen upon their
sides, the back four were still upright, and the horses that pulled them into
the shape of a question mark stolen. The bodies of men and boys peppered
the site like dead things tossed at random. The lucky ones had been hacked
to pieces in a frenzy of war chants, while the not-so-lucky ones were
propped against wagons with their genitals stuffed in their mouths –
vending machines for the buzzards. These outsized and ill-tempered birds
scampered about like early arrivals at a closing-down sale.

Amid this carnage, an old man was buried up to his neck in the dirt, his
face set towards the rising sun and his mouth open wide as though in
danger of drowning in the ocean that in prehistoric times had filled that
valley. The old man's face was red and blistered, and his eyes too dry to
blink. He was loath to look upon this scene of slaughter, but loath to look
away for fear of losing sight of his fellow man forever. He had not cried in
more than fifty years, but he cried now and he asked God for forgiveness.
The man began to recount his sins, which he believed were many, but in
truth he was a good man. Likewise he had never asked his Lord for
miracles, but he asked now.

Not long after, a man fell to Earth out of the sun, or appeared to. He
landed stark naked on that parched and dusty basin not three metres away.
He lay on his back with his knees and face twisted towards the old man.
His eyes were closed and his dark locks and bushy beard obscured his face.
The old man began to laugh, but by so doing his chest was constricted by
the earth. He made an effort to quiet his breathing and murmured, "Christ,"
and "insane" and "Oh, Lord."
David opened his eyes and surveyed his surroundings. He blinked and
looked and blinked again ... the old man came into focus. "Gull ... why...
why is this man so *short*?" The man whooped from the back of his throat.
David raised himself up on one arm. "Gull? Damn it. Answer me." Gull
did not answer, but the old man did, as best he could for a man with no
teeth and little space to lower his chin. "Either you are a sprite born of this
maddening heat ... or you are Christ Hisself. Whichever, it makes no

matter. I wouldn't know how to console either."

"Gull!"

The old man gazed across the valley's floor, strewn with the bodies of his companions. "My name is Ted. Take a look for yourself ... I'm the only one they left alive."

David got unsteadily to his feet. The stench of slowly roasting human flesh ascended his nostrils like smelling salts. He staggered backwards, tripped over an open suitcase and fell on his ass inside it. Behind him a buzzard flapped its great wings, and dust from the valley's floor wafted over both men. David looked at the old man and began to shake his head as he registered his plight. He climbed out of the suitcase and crawled close enough to provide him shade. Ted's gaze crept slowly up this vision of a naked Christ, and when he reached his face he started to breathe again. "I know what you're thinking," said David. "But I'm not Him."

"Well, whoever you are ... I thank you kindly for the shade."

David began to claw at the dirt about the man's neck. "I'm just a traveller ... a traveller like you."

"What do they call you?"

"David."

"David?"

"That's right."

"Well, that being the case, I don't suppose I could trouble you to fetch me some water? I am a mite thirsty, David." David stopped clawing at the dirt. Ted motioned with his chin to a covered wagon to his right. "There's a canteen in there." David glanced to his left. The wagon's top had been torn open, and it flapped gently in the breeze. A man hung off the back, his fingers touching the dirt as though he'd been searching for something in it. David placed his head in his hand, squeezed his temples. "Who did this?"

"Apaches."

"Apaches?"

"Indians."

"Natives to this land?"

"That don't excuse it."

"No, it doesn't. When?"

"Three or four hours since they left. "

"You think they'll be coming back?"

"Coming back? They done took anything worth taking. Why would they come back?"

Sometime later, Ted sat at the rear of a wagon. He was propped against a corner in the shade, his skinny legs dangling from the back. He took a swig from the canteen and watched David move amongst the dead. He was looking for a man of similar size whose clothes were not too badly hacked and bloodied. "If you don't mind my saying, you look like a man who has done this before," said Ted.

"All the time ..."

"Well, I can't say I'm surprised they don't got clothes up there."

"Up where?"

"You tell me. Wherever you fell from."

David glanced at him over his shoulder. "You'd be surprised what they have up there."

Ted swallowed and his Adam's apple jerked down inside his grizzled neck. "I've seen those marks on your hands ... front and back ... just like you'd been ..."

"I have been. But I'm not Him."

"So you keep sayin'. Was it Indians?"

"No. It was Romans."

"I take it you are pullin' an old man's leg." David knelt before the corpse of a man with an arrow through his left eye. "That there was Pete McIvor," said Ted. "He was the first to raise the alarm about the heathen. And the first to die for his trouble. A good man. One might say an original thinker."

"A relation of yours?"

"No. He was no kin of mine. My kin reside in California, which is where this wagon train was headed." David took McIvor's red cotton shirt and blue jeans and put them on, then took the boots and put them on also. Ted continued, "Peter's hat is just there ... by that rock." David picked it up and put it on, pulled down the wide brim to shield his eyes. He raised his hands to his face and clenched his fists as though about to strike someone. He felt his heart beat faster as it pumped the strength of several madmen into his veins. He looked directly into the sun. "If you can hear me and if this is your doing, Gull, I appreciate it." He turned to Ted. "You have a shovel?"

"You mean to bury them?"

"I mean to bury them."

"When the sun goes down?"

"Now."

By the time David had filled in the last grave, the sun was peeking over the mountains to the east. Ted had a fire going, and over it a snake roasted on a spit. David took off his hat and sat beside him on the ground. Ted looked at him. "Worked flat out in the sun all day. It doesn't appear to have tired you one bit."

"I take my energy from it."

"From the sun? You mean like a flower?"

"That's right. Only not as fragrant."

"Well, you got that right. Not nearly as fragrant!" Ted thumped David on his back with a flat palm. "Damn! What you made of? Steel. It's no wonder you survived that fall. Just where was it you said you fell from again?"

David looked into the old man's eyes. He smiled and said, "Poland."

"*Poland*? The Poland over in Europe?"

"That's right."

"That would sure be some magic trick. Yessir. If that were true that would be a magic trick to beat 'em all."

"You pulled quite a trick yourself."

"Come again?"

"They left you alive."

"Hell, nothing magic about that. I offered no resistance. I am of no use, old as I am. They took the womenfolk and children." Ted crossed himself. "God help 'em. I imagine the heathen just got back from a raid into Mexico. Had with them a score of slaves, young men mostly, and other plunder. Ain't never seen the likes of them before … descended upon us like hordes straight out of hell. Painted and yellin' like banshees … bodies and horses all festooned with human body parts. Hope you never have to see the like."

"Where are we, Ted?"

"Where are we? We're in Utah Territory."

"What year is it?"

"What *year* is it? It is the year of our Lord eighteen hundred and fifty-one. You sure you're real? Not just a part of a dying man's madness?"

David didn't answer.

"Hell." Ted hawked up a mouthful of phlegm and spat it onto the parched and dusty ground. A lizard darted from beneath a rock and licked the spot, then vanished just as quickly. "So where you headed, Dave? You mind if I call you that? It was my brother's name."

"No, I don't mind. I'm looking for someone."

"This Gull fella?"

"No, but I'll need to find him first."

"Why? He knows where this other fella is at?"

"That's right."

"What do he look like? This *Gull*. If I see him I could tell him you're looking for him."

"He'll find me, just as soon as he can."

"He done run off before now?"

"Yes, he has."

"You married, son?"

"I'd rather you didn't call me *son*."

"I don't mean no disrespect by it."

225

"I know someone who does."

"Kin of yours?"

"I sincerely hope not."

"So you married?"

"No."

"Fine-looking fella like you? How'd you manage to stay one step ahead of all those suitors?"

"I've just been lucky that way."

"My wife passed six months back. I guess you never really know how much you'll miss someone ... not until they're gone. She passed quiet in her sleep. She told me not to get up to any mischief when she was gone. Said without her to tell me the way of things, I was bound to come a cropper sooner rather than later. The woman was not wrong. My daughter inherited many of her traits, which is why I thought I'd best get myself out to California. Guess I should've known I wasn't going to make it. Not without Margaret to keep me out of trouble."

"You'll make it."

"I hate to be the one to break it to you, but we are going nowhere ... not without horses. It could be months 'fore any other travellers pass through this valley. It's a couple hundred miles to the nearest town." He leaned and spat. "Unless you're as strong as a mule and don't mind being hooked up to a wagon like one ... I for one will not be leaving this valley."

Forty nine

The rising sun hung like a celestial yoke over the mountains to the east. In the valley below, the shadow of a man and the wagon he was harnessed to stretched out as tall as a cathedral's spire – a latter-day Samson preparing to pull a covered wagon. Up front sat an old man, a pipe in his mouth, and a look of incredulity on his face. In front of him David was naked except for his hat, over each shoulder a length of rope that he held against his chest. The old man removed the pipe from his mouth and looked at it. "You want we should get this over and done with, son?"

David looked over his shoulder.
"Apologies. I forgot not to call you that," said Ted.
"Hope you're sitting comfortably back there."
"I am."
"I suggest you hold onto something. The way ahead looks bumpy." David moved forwards and the wagon moved also, its spoked wheels turning faster and faster as David went into a trot. Ted sat up straight and reached for the railing at his side. His eyes opened wide and his pipe fell into his lap. David powered into a sprint, and behind him Ted yelled "Yee haa!" So it was that these two unlikely souls made their way across that valley.

An hour and forty-seven minutes later, the wagon slowed to a halt. Ted was slumped to his left, the brim of his hat pulled down over his eyes. He righted himself, pushed up the brim with his middle finger and regarded the man before him. David had been exposed to direct sunlight for two hours, yet looked like a statue carved from white marble. In an eerie way this made sense, because he stood as still as one. Ted leaned forward on the seat and scratched his deeply lined cheek. "Say ... you taking a break? Never did a man deserve one more. I got myself forty winks. I can tell we covered a lot of ground. Son? Sorry, sorry. Dave?" There was no reply. A falcon soared overhead and its shadow crossed the ground at David's feet. Ted muttered something about his wife's extraordinary powers of prediction and climbed down from the seat. He took off his hat and fanned himself as he walked towards David.

David's eyes were closed, his head and shoulders bent forwards in the attitude of someone in the midst of toil. Ted reached out tentatively, as though towards something that might bite, and placed a hand on David's shoulder. He tried to shake him awake, but he felt as solid as he looked.

227

Ted lifted his hand and rubbed his fingers together. "Dry as a bone. Not a lick of sweat on you. You turned into *stone*." Ted crossed himself.

David's eyes opened slowly. They were as white as snow, and as far as Ted was concerned just as chilling. He took two steps back, leaned forward with his hands on his knees and looked up at those eyes. "What in the name of...?" The statue spoke in David's voice, albeit stripped of emotion.

"Can you hear me? David? Are you there?" Ted straightened his back. "Why, David is *your* name."

"Who are you?"

"Ted."

"Hello, Ted. Where is David?"

"Where is David? I'm looking right at him!"

"Of course you are. Excuse me, Ted. I am presently unable to move or see, and experiencing some confusion. I hope to have both shortcomings rectified shortly. Until then would you mind answering some questions?"

"Answer *you* some questions?"

"If you wouldn't mind."

"I'd like you to answer a question first."

"Ask it."

"If you are not Dave, then who or *what* in the name of all that is holy are you?"

"I am Gull."

"Dave's friend?"

"Did Dave describe me as such?"

"He did."

"That is pleasing to hear. Will you answer my questions now?"

"I will."

"Thank you. Are we in immediate danger?"

Ted cast his gaze about him. "No. We are not in immediate danger."

"Where are we?"

"Dave asked me that exact same question. We're in Utah Territory."

"The year?"

"Eighteen hundred and fifty-one."

"What weapons have we at our disposal?"

"None. The Indians done took 'em all."

"And how is Dave?"

"Dave's just fine. Just about as strong as an ox. Hell, maybe stronger. He pulled this here wagon and this old man many miles across country."

"Well, that certainly sounds like the Dave I know. Always ready to offer a helping hand to those in need. Was Dave impersonating a beast of burden when I interrupted him?"

"He sure was. Now would you care to explain how two souls are able to inhabit a single body?"

"I hope you will not mind my quoting the words of another. There are more things in heaven and earth, Ted, than are dreamt of in your philosophy."

"That was Shakespeare you just quoted."

"I had every reason to believe you were a learned man, Ted."

"I heard it somewheres, is all. Must have stuck. But you know what they say, if you hurl enough shit at a man, then some is bound to stick."

"An apt description of human learning and development through the ages. Thank you."

"That's quite alright." Ted crossed his arms and looked down at the dirt. "It seems to me that Dave is a force for good."

"Never has language been utilised to make a truer statement."

Ted looked up from the ground. "And you?"

"I will not lie to you, Ted. I am a work in progress. But I am fortunate to have a fine example to follow."

"Dave's example?"

"That's right."

"I suppose we are all God's creatures."

"It pleases me to hear you say so. Ted?"

"Yes?"

"I am nearing the surface. Please stand back."

Ted looked left and right. "*Back*?" The ropes passed through Gull's hands and he stumbled forwards, crashing to his knees. He got up and staggered to his left, fell, then got up, turned and lurched back towards the wagon. Ted called out, "You having some kind of fit?"

Gull reached for and grabbed the front of the wagon. Presently he said, "I believe the danger has passed. I was overcautious. Dave would have been very upset if I allowed any harm to come to you." Despite this reassurance, Ted took a step back. "There is no need to back away. The danger has passed."

"You got eyes in the back of your head?"

Gull turned to face him. "In a manner of speaking."

"I do not doubt it. Where is Dave?"

Gull tapped his temple. "Here."

"When might he be coming back?"

"As soon as I can locate him. In the meantime, I suggest we continue our journey until the sun goes down. It would appear we are headed west."

"That's right. California." Gull turned and stood facing south. Ted watched him. He hawked up some phlegm, spat, and shook his head. He walked over and stood beside Gull. To the south an expanse of brown and grey, out of which the heat rose and shimmered. "Dave said he was

Boyd Brent

looking for someone ... said you knew where they might be at. They south of here? In New Mexico?"

"Further south. In Mexico."

"You ain't thinkin' of heading straight down there and leaving an old man stranded?" Gull looked down at the old man and smiled, and in so doing he bared his teeth. Ted continued, "I am not picking up much in the way of intent one way or another. Unless, that is, it is your intent to murder me in cold blood."

"Perhaps my smile of reassurance requires practice."

"And then some. I'll be honest: I do not think it was Dave's intention to take me *all the way* to California. Just to the nearest town ... one inhabited by God-fearing folk."

Gull looked over Ted's head to the west. "The town of Pioche is seventy point two miles due west."

Ted turned his head in the same direction and muttered, "Seventy *point* two miles ..."

"We will not make it before sundown. I will attempt to make up the ground Dave would have covered had he not been interrupted." He walked over to where the ropes lay and picked them up. Ted hurried to the wagon and climbed up on the seat. "I do believe I am sensing a competitive spirit in you, Gull."

"I prefer to look upon it as friendly rivalry."

"Men's perspectives on things are apt to differ."

"I believe I am in the presence of a great philosopher."

Ted lowered his hat and reclined into a position of comfort. Under his breath he muttered, "Giddy up now ... so says Plato."

They had not travelled far when Ted looked up from under the brim of his hat. He sat up as though responding to a jab in his ribs and raised his voice over the creak and grind of the wheels. "I believe we got company!"

Gull was at full sprint, the balls of his feet thumping the ground like muted pistons. He turned his head a little to the left. "I have been aware of them for some time."

"You reckon they're Indians?"

"Their countenance suggests not."

Ted squinted at the approaching company, no more than a dark speck amid the distant haze. "And can you tell from their *countenance* whether they are friend or foe?"

"Four men on horseback. They are transporting human cargo. Thirty-two individuals. All chained."

"Negroes?"

"That would be my summation also."

"Slavers headed back east. Might be okay, then. Although some of 'em

230

got reputations as being meaner than hell."

"Would you prefer to hide in the wagon, Ted?"

"I might be old, but I'm no coward. Thinking on it, it might be for the best if you let me do the talking. Oh, hell. Just how am I goin' to explain this here situation? Maybe *you* should hide in the wagon."

"I see no need to hide at this time."

"Well, at least stop and put on some clothes."

"Exposing my skin to direct sunlight makes this task possible."

"And what do you imagine these folks will say if I tell them that? They will probably take us for unchristian abominations. Shoot us and be done with it."

"I will not allow any harm to come to you. Dave would–"

"I know I know. He would not like it."

"I suggest you recline and make yourself comfortable, Ted. Pull your hat down over your eyes. Rest. I will ignore them also."

"Ignore 'em? Some might consider that rude. Folks have been murdered out here for less." Ted shook his head. "Ignore 'em he says ..." He sat back and pulled his hat down over his eyes. "While I'm at it I'll ignore this ache in my backside. Maybe that'll pass me by also."

Two men rode on horses before the slaves, and two rode behind them. All rested the butts of their rifles on their thighs and swayed gently in their saddles, looking about as bored as men can look. Between them, thirty-two black men hobbled along barefoot and in rags. They were draped from head to foot in shackles of medieval design – old rusted contraptions that wore away skin and bone both. But it was not only flesh and blood that capitulated under that metal, it was that thing within a man that animates him – crushed not by the weight of those shackles but by their implication. The two slavers at the front of this party noticed the approaching wagon. They exchanged a glance, kicked their horses and rode on ahead. Two hundred metres from the wagon they glanced at one another again and slowed to a trot. Two rifle shots rang out like thunderclaps, and Ted removed his hat with a flourish and smiled through a mouthful of gums. Frozen in this attitude he spoke to Gull without moving his lips. "They'll be expecting you to stop ... you hear me? And while it may well be that you are able to catch lead in your teeth, I got no teeth left."

Two more shots rang out. Gull stopped. The two men were close enough now for Ted to see the expressions on their faces – the expressions of men who having dreamt of an abomination had woken the following morning to discover one perched on their beds. They glanced at one another again and levelled their rifles at Gull. Ted waved his hat and grinned like an actor projecting to the back of the theatre. The rider on the left had a broad red face and small blue eyes that vanished whenever he squinted, and he squinted now as he said, "What in the name of...?"

His companion was leaner and darker, with round brown eyes that showed all the compassion of a grizzly bear's. This man said to the first, "You speechless there, Bert? I ain't never known you speechless."

Bert looked at Ted, still grinning and holding his hat out in welcome. "This here well-endowed fellow belong to you, old man?" he said.

"Belong to me? No, no. We are all good and free men here."

"You implying something, old man?"

"No." The lean man-grizzly straightened his back and surveyed the whole. "This wagon must weigh half a ton. I can only assume that my eyes were deceiving me back there. This *blind* man could not pull it even an inch."

"My eyesight is better than yours," said Bert.

"And?"

"And this blind man was running flat out."

"If that was the case then he could not have been attached to this wagon."

"He is attached to it now, and as the Lord is my witness he was so attached when he was runnin' flat out."

Gull cast the ropes from his shoulder and stood up straight. Both riders dropped their reins, shouldered their rifles and aimed at his heart. Gull raised his hands. "I am unarmed."

"We will decide what you is and what you ain't, boy. You care to explain where you found the strength to pull this here wagon?"

Gull began to quote the same lines of Shakespeare that he had used earlier, while Ted groaned quietly to himself.

When Gull finished, Bert leaned and spat and wiped his mouth with the back of his hand. "More things in heaven and earth, huh? Seems to me you neglected to mention hell. My grandpappy was a preacher ... and if he could see this he'd swear the devil had a hand in it. Him all sat up there and droolin' over your butt like that."

Ted took off his hat and held it in his lap. "My wife passed six months back. What you are suggesting is disgusting. Plain and simple. And as for his unusual strength ... well, good Christian folk like you boys must have heard the story of Samson and Delilah?"

"Samson and Delilah, he says. This man is no Samson and you sure as shit ain't no Delilah."

"He probably looks a lot more like her when he puts on one of them dresses he has in his wagon."

Both men laughed, and when at last they'd stopped Gull said, "We mean you no harm. And now we must be on our way."

"That a threat, son?" asked Bert.

"Please don't refer to me as *son*."

"And why not?"

"Dave doesn't like it."

Bert looked at Ted. "Does he not, now?"

"I'm not Dave," said Ted. The slaves shuffled up alongside the wagon and a man shouted, "Hold up, niggers!"

Gull glanced to his right and into the wide eyes of a dozen black men. He looked up at the men on the horses. "Neither would Dave approve of your subjugation of these men."

The lean man-grizzly leaned and spat. "Would he not, now?"

The other two slavers rode up alongside him. The third man cast his gaze over the naked-man-turned-beast-of-burden and the old man who'd made him so. "Holy mother of ..."

The fourth man said, "I don't think there's anything holy about this."

"That would be my thinking," added Bert.

"Please," said Ted. "Our wagon train was attacked by Apaches some miles back. They slaughtered every last one of my party, and buried me up to my neck in the dirt ... which is where I would still be if not for this fella."

The fourth rider got down from his horse. "You really strong enough to pull this rig, son?"

The lean man-grizzly said, "Don't call him son. Dave don't like it."

The fourth man walked up to Gull and waved a hand in front of his face. "You called Dave, blind man? Is that your name?" Gull shook his head and smiled reassuringly. The man drew his revolver. "That look supposed to scare me?"

"Maybe we should just leave 'em be," said the third rider. "Be on our way. They're white men, which makes 'em free men."

"An adequate display of empathy," said Gull. "For this reason you will leave here alive. I think it's what Dave would have wanted. As for the rest of you, that will no longer be possible." Gull turned his head towards the slaves. "I must free these men. It would be the empathic thing to do, but more importantly it's what Dave would have done."

The fourth man levelled the pistol at Gull's head. Before he could pull the trigger his hand was upturned and the barrel of his gun inside his own mouth. Gull smiled reassuringly whilst relocating the man's brains into the face of Bert's horse. All four horses were badly spooked by this noisy relocation of brains, not least Bert's horse. It reared up and shook its head in an attempt to shake off the organic mask. Bert struggled one-handed with his reins and attempted to aim his rifle. Gull's pistol was a single-shot carbine, and had no further use except as a missile. He hurled it at Bert's head with a force that cracked his skull front to back. In the next instant he leapt onto the back of Bert's horse, snatched away his rifle and held his corpse as a shield. Gull applied sufficient pressure to the horse's ribs to get its attention, then swung it about and, as the lean man-grizzly struggled to control his own mount, Gull relocated his brains into the face of the third man. This man responded to his organic mask with less grace than had Bert's horse – considerably less. Although his own horse bucked like a bronco, he released his grip on the reins, clawed at his face and tumbled off onto the ground, where he lay unconscious.

Ted lowered his backside slowly onto the wagon's seat. He looked uncertain as to the appropriate response – laughter or tears, or maybe he should just sit back and retreat under his hat like a snail? What he'd just witnessed made him feel as slow as a snail.

Gull slid Bert's body off his horse and turned the horse to face the slaves. They all watched him – every man amongst them. A lone voice said, "You mean what you said? About setting us all free?" Gull located the speaker towards the rear of the group. He rode the horse over to the man and him asked his name.

"Terrence Curtis," came the reply. Terrence was shorter and skinnier than the rest, but what he lacked in bulk he made up in attitude. "You mean it? What you said?"

Gull considered smiling reassuringly again, but thought the better of it. Without expression on his face or tone in his voice he said, "Yes, Terrence. I meant what I said. You are all free men."

Terrence raised his shackled hands against the sun and studied Gull's face. "We will never be free men, but I'll take my chances as a fugitive. And in that I expect I speak for every man here." Gull cast his gaze over the rest who gave no indication of whether Terrence spoke for them or not. Terrance continued, "The man whose mount you ride ... *Bert...* he has the keys ... in his saddle bag."

Gull climbed down from the horse and crouched beside Bert's body. He withdrew a pistol from his holster. The gun was a six-shooter, and all six chambers were primed with powder and ball. Gull unbuckled the dead man's holster, fitted it to his own waist and slid the gun home. He repeated this process with the second dead man, then turned to face the slaves with a six-shooter on each hip.

Fifty

Once Gull had unshackled the slaves, he applied himself to digging the graves of the dead slavers. Several amongst the party of blacks had offered to help hide the 'evidence', but Gull said he would not hear of it. He told them they'd doubtless experienced their fair share of manual labour already and besides ... here Ted chipped in between puffs on his pipe: "Dave wouldn't like it."

"That's right, Ted."

Ted shook out the match and tossed it away. "Having spent time with Dave, I'm inclined to agree with you."

Gull stood in a partially dug grave and leaned on the shovel like an English gentleman on his cane. He cast his gaze over the party of freed slaves. With the exception of Terrence Curtis, they sat or lay in the same order they'd been chained. Terrence had relocated himself to the front of this party like its self-appointed head. Gull turned his white eyes on Ted. "These men are exhausted."

Ted was sat on a rock with his arms folded and his hat pulled low over his eyes. "I expect they'll be just fine after a night's rest."

"These men are hungry."

Ted cleared his throat. "I'm sure they'll be just fine after a good feed."

"We must feed them."

"Feed 'em? Suppose I could shoot a rodent or two, now we got guns. Maybe a rattlesnake."

At dusk the men gathered about a campfire. The sky was a ruddy crimson that matched the wall of rock to the north. They supped on boiled coyote, and from the pot above the fire came the smell of coffee. One amongst these men had bound hands. He was the third slave-driver, and his name was John Torrance. John had been brought back to consciousness by the smell of cooking, but had been too groggy and too witless to leave immediately. His wits were returning now, and as he ate he took care not to make eye contact with any of his former possessions. One in particular, a man called Isaiah who weighed three hundred and fifty pounds, had not taken his eyes off him. Having served up each man's food, Ted now sat on the ground beside Gull with his own plate. Gull put down his plate, rested his hands on his legs and pressed the tips of his fingers together. "Have you given any thought as to where you will go to evade your oppressors?" he asked. "I would suggest north. They look less favourably on slavery in the north."

Without taking his eyes from John Torrance, Isaiah said, "White men will make slaves of black men anywhere he go, I reckon."

"A white man has freed you, Isaiah," said Terrence.

"He sure did. And I have never seen a whiter man. Never hope to, neither."

A chorus of "Amen to that" rose from the supping fugitives.

"Do you want to kill that man?" Gull asked Isaiah.

"Thought of little else for some months. He done whipped my brother until he begged the Lord for mercy, and then he whipped him some more … 'til he could beg no more."

"What is preventing you?"

"You. Saying he was pardoned."

"I said that?"

"I reckon."

"And that is enough? To prevent you avenging your brother?"

"Maybe it is and maybe it ain't. It seem to me that pardoning this man was somethin' you needed to do. You might have the appearance of a blind Christ – and there ain't a man here who has not wondered at those scars on your hands – but …"

"But?"

"Where Christian compassion is concerned … maybe … maybe like every man here you have a-ways to go. And so it seem to me that act of mercy was important to you."

"You are right, Isaiah. Where compassion is concerned I am at the beginning of my journey."

"I know you is. There ain't no man can pull a wagon like that. You are something not natural of this world, but from where you get your strength? Could be you don't even know that yourself. You might look like a blind Lord of scripture, but Jesus sure wouldn't sound like you do."

"How do I sound?"

"Like you got no humanity inside you. Not a bit. Of course that don't mean you don't. Your treatment of us says something different."

"You are men of faith? Despite the world you find yourself in?"

All about the campfire nodded. "We had better be men of faith," replied Isaiah. "We got little else 'cept hardship. The Lord Jesus is our salvation. The promise of everlasting life in paradise … away from devils like him."

John Torrance looked towards his boots and shook his head. "I'm a God-fearing Christian no different from any of you."

"The difference is that you were their enslaver," said Gull.

"Don't mean no harm by 'em. It's just the way of things. Niggers might be people near enough, but they'd be the first to admit they ain't properly developed like the white man. They got no history or culture, but they are strong and the Lord made 'em so for a reason."

Terrence smiled. "You think the Lord made us strong to toil for the white man?"

"I believe it says as much somewhere in scripture."

Gull interlinked his fingers. "Words are easily misinterpreted. All men have history and culture. These men you buy and sell are no different. Did you know that the roots of all human beings can be traced back to Africa? It is where humanity originated, John."

John Torrance smiled and shook his head. "Then why they the colour they are?"

"Climate dictates skin colour. The further north a race travels, the colder the climate and the lighter their skin."

John Torrance leaned and spat. "By that reckoning you must have done come here from the North Pole."

Isaiah folded his arms. "He don't look upon us as human."

Gull nodded. "Quite so. It is how he justifies his treatment of you. Isn't that so, John?"

"It's just the way of things. No harm intended."

"It is how his forefathers conditioned him. And their father's before them."

Isaiah tore his gaze from John Torrance for a moment and looked at Gull. "You saying that make it right?"

"No, Isaiah. I'm pointing out that his empathy towards the African races has been eroded. If he were a more empathic person, that would not have been possible. No amount of conditioning could have changed him."

"You mean if he were a better person?"

"Yes, Isaiah. Better. And stronger."

"I always suspected his kind was weak."

"I wasn't so weak when I whipped the life out of your brother!"

Gull looked at him. "You whipped a defenceless man to death. "A man who represented no threat. A man who begged you for mercy. You did so because your lack of empathy makes you weak, John. Weak of character."

"Is that so? Seems to me you didn't show my companions much empathy when you blasted their brains all to hell."

"I think you'll find that was self-defence."

"You provoked those old boys and you know you done provoked 'em."

"I like to think I … tested them."

"Tested 'em? Tested their patience, maybe."

"They were legitimate targets. Their lack of empathy towards these men made them so."

"And just who made you judge, jury and executioner?"

"There is a war raging, John. I am a soldier in that war."

"What war? The Mexican War done finished. There are no wars that I'm aware of."

"It may be Man's ignorance of this war that has kept it going so long," observed Gull.

Isaiah continued to stare at John Torrance but asked Gull, "So how long this war been going on?"

"Approximately one million years."

"One million? You gonna tell us who this war's between?"

"Not who, but what. On the one side is Man's empathic promise, and on the other his bestial origins."

"Bestial?"

"Yes, Isaiah. Man shares much of his genetic make-up with the beasts of this planet. Some even with the reptiles that had dominion before him."

"I don't recall it saying nothing about that in the Bible," said John Torrance. "What you're implying is sacrilege." He cast his gaze along the black faces. "Seems to me you boys have taken up with a devil of sorts."

Terrence unfolded his arms and leaned forwards. "Not every man has the benefit of a Christian education. You did, and you is still a white devil."

John Torrance's hands balled into fists.

"Tell me, John. What is your opinion of Jews?" asked Gull.

"Never met me a Jew. Can't say I rightly have an opinion."

Isaiah nodded. "Never met me one neither, but Jesus was a Jew. I know that."

"That's right, Terrence." Gull held his hands up in the firelight. Every man present paused mid-chew and studied the patchwork of scars on his palms. "Who done it? Who crucified you?" asked Isaiah.

"The Romans."

Ted shook his head. "Now don't none of you pay him no heed ... he's pullin' your leg."

Terrence got up, came over and crouched before Gull. He took his hands in his own and examined them front and back. "Christ has been almost as close to me as you are now, Terrence," said Gull. "Would you like to see him?"

There followed a collective intake of breath, and many there put down their plates and crossed themselves. The sun had all but set below the mountains to the west, and the flickering firelight danced on the faces of every man present. "Now don't go spooking these good folks with such nonsense," said Ted.

Isaiah stared at John Torrance but addressed Ted. "Open your eyes, old man. If he says he has something to show us, then let him go ahead and show it."

Terrence released Gull's hands and stepped back.

"I ask that you all gather behind me," said Gull. "It will afford you the best view of the man you call your Saviour." The men around the campfire glanced at one another. Terrence pointed out that it was not every day that a man is given the opportunity to lay eyes upon his Saviour. They clambered to their feet as though raised up by a single pulley – all except John Torrance, who revelled in their gullibility. The fugitives arranged themselves behind the cross-legged figures of Gull and Ted – dark faces called to witness something beyond the common laws of nature.

An image was projected from Gull's eyes, filling the space between him and the fire. This was no scaled-down image as before, but a life-sized projection of Christ on his bunk in Jerusalem. Jesus was leaning towards the assembly of men and staring into their midst, his face battered and bruised and barely recognisable as the same face that now projected it. One amongst the slaves, silent until now, began to utter the Lord's prayer, and the others joined in. Their voices grew louder as though the sound would provide a barrier against the unknown. Beyond and to the right of the fire, John Torrance held his hands to his face and wept as he spied the image through his fingers. The image of Christ leaned back, and his face disappeared into shadows cast two thousand years before. The hologram began to fade, until only the dying candle on the floor of that cell remained. One of the men broke rank and shouldered his way from the throng to kneel beside it. He reached out and held his hand over the flame. Someone asked him if it burned and he replied that it did not. The candle vanished, the darkness behind John Torrance shifted, and out of it came Isaiah holding a scythe. He raised it behind him, and with a single sweeping motion he lopped off John Torrance's head. The headless body remained upright as his dying heart continued to pump and anoint his body in blood.

Gull spoke softly. "Isaiah?"

Isaiah shrugged and threw down the scythe. "I just a foot-soldier … a foot-soldier in that war you spoke of."

Gull nodded, and then sighed as though he'd just witnessed something impeccable.

Boyd Brent

Fifty one

At dawn John Torrance sat before an extinguished fire. He was leaning forwards in the attitude of a headless man with much on his mind. Everyone was asleep except Gull, who stood fifty metres from the camp, facing south. One of his eyes was white, the other blue. A rattlesnake slithered up to and over his boots like he'd been there as long as any rock in that land. His lips moved slowly, almost imperceptibly, as though whispering a secret. If someone had placed an ear to his mouth they might have heard the faint echo of voices within: "Is that you, Gull?"

"Keep talking, David. I will be with you shortly."

"Where the hell am I? I can't move forward or back ... it feels like I'm trapped between two walls ... just enough room to inch sideways ... like a damned crab, which I've been doing for some *considerable* time. It's pitch-black; I can't see a thing."

"You are trapped in a region of your mind that is not illuminated by electrical activity."

"That as bleak as it sounds?"

"No. It simply means you are in a coma."

"Well, consider me reassured then."

"It appears that in my enthusiasm to rejoin and assist you, I may have inadvertently caused your current predicament."

"What is that supposed to mean?"

A faint tapping on the wall. "Did you hear that, David?"

"I heard it. It came from my left ... there it is again."

"I am on the other side of the wall. I was where you are now when we arrived in Utah."

David threw his palms against the wall. "And what? You decided to swap places?"

"It would have taken me several days to find a way out. It would, however, take you many years to navigate a similar route. The truth is you might never discover an exit."

Through gritted teeth, David said, "If there's good news, I would appreciate hearing it."

"There is another way out – a way that's available to you but not me. And it is considerably more efficient."

"I'm listening."

"That narrow pathway is located in the logic area of your mind. Each

240

sideways step is similar to unravelling a tiny part of a mathematical equation. Even with my computing prowess, the equation would have taken me several days to solve and–"

"So you've said. Goddamnit, Gull. You must be aware that *once again* we have not exactly found ourselves delivered into paradise. So I'd appreciate your getting to the point."

"Gladly, David. A combination of inspiration and imagination will deliver you instantly to the answer you seek. To an exit. Even though you will have no conception as to how you reached it."

David thudded his palms into the wall again. "Not feeling particularly inspired right now."

"Might I make a suggestion?"

"I was hoping you might."

"Might I suggest a door."

"A door?"

"Yes, David. A door that leads from where you are to where I am."

"A door, he says. Why didn't I think of that?"

"It is often difficult to see the woods for the trees. Particularly in times of heightened irritation."

David reached out and felt along the wall. "There is no door here…"

"Look above you, David."

David looked above him into the black void. "I told you, I can't see a damn thing."

"They may take a moment to appear … do you see them now?"

"… I see them. A faint cluster of stars."

"I have provided you with a window that looks from the left side of your mind into the right … a window into your imagination."

"What am I supposed to do with a view?"

"Use it to conjure a door."

David sighed. "Alright." He closed his eyes, imagined a door and reached out, but felt only the wall. "You sure about this?"

"Try looking towards your imagination … up at the stars." David looked up and conjured a door in his mind's eye – a door in front of him with a brass handle. He reached out and his fingertips crept over that handle. He could hear his own heartbeat hammering in some far-off corner of that darkness. He lowered the handle and pushed … a hazy starlight ebbed through a crack. He opened the door fully and stepped into a clearing beside a lake. The cosmos of his imagination was reflected in its still waters. Gull stood with his back to him, looking out over the water. He wore the same red plaid shirt and jeans David had worn before he'd stripped off to pull the wagon. "Hello, David."

"Gull." Gull turned slowly to face him. The last they'd met, Gull's face had been a part-holographic representation of David's. Now the whole looked like a crude waxwork of David's face with animatronic eyes. David scratched his cheek. "You want to explain your face?"

"It is a work in progress."

"I can see that. Wouldn't you rather be your own work?"

"I have chosen you as my template. I know of no other. Does it bother you, David?"

"I won't lie. It makes me uncomfortable."

Gull cast his eyes down. "Maybe you could come to look upon me as your twin brother."

"Maybe I could, as long as it doesn't weaken us."

"To the contrary, it is making us a more efficient unit. Helping us to achieve a singularity of purpose."

David looked over the lake. "Right now, I just need to get out of here."

"As you wish."

David turned to face the camp. Two horses had been hitched to the wagon, and a couple of dozen men lay before it sleeping. One was sitting upright without his head. David walked towards the camp. "You scratch an itch, Gull?"

"A slave called Isaiah removed his head with a scythe. He did it in retribution for the murder of his brother."

"These men are slaves?"

"Were slaves. I took it upon myself to free them, as I believe you would have done."

"I imagine their owners were not pleased."

"It would be no exaggeration to say they were livid. There were four in total. I have buried the other three."

"That was certainly … empathic."

"I thought it the right thing to do."

David looked down and noticed the pistols resting on each hip. He slid them free of their holsters, smiled and slid them back. "Is Ted okay?"

"Ted is sleeping soundly in his wagon."

"How far are we from the nearest town?"

"We made good progress in your absence. The town of Pioche is now just thirty-one miles to the west."

"And the Colonel?"

"He is gainfully employed in Mexico."

"Doing what?"

"Assisting the Mexican authorities with their Apache problem."

"Money for scalps?"

"Yes, David."

"And Goliath?"

"As yet I have been unable to locate any information as to Goliath's whereabouts inside the Event Helix."

"Is there anything I should know before I wake these men up?"

"We had a most informative talk at supper."

"And what did you inform them?"

"They are Christians. I was keen to inspire them, so I showed them a hologram of Christ in his cell."

"And did it?"

"Did it what, David?"

"Did it inspire them?"

"I believe it broadened their horizons."

"Seems to me you've been broadening some horizons of your own."

"I have tried to behave as an empathic being might. I have already alluded to the fact that you are my point of reference. I simply asked myself 'what would David do in this situation?'"

"Not a plan I would necessarily recommend." He glanced over his shoulder towards the three graves.

"I gave them a clear verbal warning, David. As I believe you would have done. They had a choice."

"And they chose to go to ground."

"Yes. Isaiah is awake. He is listening to you. I believe you will like him." David cast his gaze over the men sprawled out round the camp. Most lay on their backs and snored like men with a lifetime of sleep to catch up on, but one amongst them, the biggest, lay face down with his head resting on his arm. "Is that Isaiah?"

"Yes, David."

Isaiah opened his eyes, turned slowly and sat up on his backside. He clasped his hands over his knees and looked at his knuckles. David walked over and stood before him. Isaiah's gaze climbed David's jeans and red plaid shirt to his face. "You ain't blind no more?"

"I'm not Gull no more. I'm David."

"The David Gull spoke of?"

"That's right."

"So where's Gull at?"

David tapped his temple. "Only I can hear him now." He glanced over his shoulder at the headless body of John Torrance. "That your handiwork?"

"Yessir. He killed my brother."

David smiled, reached down and pulled Isaiah to his feet, all three hundred and fifty pounds of him. Isaiah was not surprised at the ease with which he rose.

Fifty two

The wagon rolled forwards slowly. David and Ted sat together on the driver's seat. Three black men were seated at the rear of the wagon. Six more had squeezed inside. Terrence Curtis and four others had left and headed north, and the others walked alongside the wagon. The seating arrangements were shared in thirty-minute rotas. This had been Gull's idea. And although David had agreed it was a good idea, he'd shaken his head when he'd overheard Gull suggest it. Ted had been sheltering under his hat in silence for some time. He cleared his throat. "Folks are not gonna like it when we arrive in town with all these unchained Negroes."

"You let me worry about that."

"I exist to oblige. That friend of yours, Gull … he's a curious fellow. In some respects unnatural."

"He's one of a kind."

"He can hear us? Shootin' the breeze out here?"

"If he chooses."

"Well, I'd like him to know that I didn't mean no offence by my observation."

"He's very thick-skinned."

"That's the impression I get. Could be he's an example to us all."

"What kind of example?"

"Well … it seems to me I've never met a fella who aspires to be something so entirely different … from that which God made him."

"For what purpose do you think God made him?"

Ted chuckled nervously under his hat. "I know he's thick-skinned … but I would rather not put that theory to the test."

"Seems to me you just answered my question."

"Seems to me I did. No offence intended." Ted raised his hat, looked at David and lowered it again. "I saw something last night I cannot explain … something *else* … something that maybe no man could explain. Much less be understood by someone as ignorant as myself."

"You're talking about Jesus."

Ted's hands began to fidget on his lap. "Well? Was it Him?"

"It was."

"No man would believe it if I told 'em. They'd look at me like I was crazy. And if them Negroes tried to tell 'em … hell."

"What is it you want to know, Ted?"

"The truth. How a vision such as that is possible."

"The truth is ..." Ted pushed up the brim of his hat with his middle finger and looked at David. David smiled. "The truth is there are more things in heaven and ..."

Ted lowered his hat and mumbled, "Hell."

The town of Pioche materialised out of the grey and gold horizon like a mirage of crooked brown sticks. Half a kilometre out, a road of sorts materialised in the dirt. Ted took off his hat and fanned his face. "I got me a bad feeling about what might happen next."

"There's another kind?"

Above the entrance was a wooden sign with *Pioche* carved into it. It hung crookedly from a rusted chain, and see-sawed in the wind. The town's main thoroughfare was wide enough to ride six wagons down abreast. Churned-up mud and tumbleweed, and not a soul in sight. Wooden shacks of varying heights ran its length on both side. Horses stood tethered outside some. A large brown dog dozed in the shade of its owner's porch. David pulled the horses to a halt. Ted glanced up at the sun. "It's a little after two, I reckon. Could be folks are havin' a siesta ... close to New Mexico, as we are. Mexicans are big on siestas." Isaiah climbed out of the rear of the wagon and made his way to its front. He took hold of the horse's bridle and patted its nose. David climbed down and stood beside him. The other men congregated close to his left shoulder like ducklings by their mother. "Is everything okay?" asked David.

In reply some nodded and others shook their heads. Isaiah said, "If I was you I'd believe the ones shaking their heads."

"You passed through this town?"

"We did. Passed through in haste. They picked up supplies at the general store ... refilled their canteens from that well yonder. We all got the notion there was some bad people here – worse even than those white devils taking us to market. These negroes ... truth is they only agreed to come back this a-way 'cos they think Gull is ..."

"Worse?"

Isaiah crossed himself. "That's the God's truth."

"I can't imagine what has given them that impression," said Gull.

"Gull. Nice to have you back."

"I have been running a diagnostic."

"Anything I need to know?"

"We are in fine shape."

"Apparently there are some bad men here."

"It grieves me to hear that, David."

A door to their left creaked open and an old woman peered out. Ted took off his hat. "Ma'am."

The woman's eyes were of the lightest blue, and they looked at no one in particular. "If you have the sense God gave you you'll head out of town the way you came."

David walked towards her and stepped up onto her porch.

"Don't come no closer …"

"Alright. Where is everyone, ma'am?"

"Waitin' behind locked doors if they know what's good for 'em."

"What are they waiting for?"

"For that mountain of a man to leave town of course."

"Sorry, ma'am?"

"You will be sorry if you hang about in the street … all those niggers with ye?"

Gull said, "David."

"Yes."

The old woman thrust an ear closer. "What now?"

"Just a moment, ma'am."

"I have located a blind spot, David – a Shadow Strand that resembles a full stop. It is one hundred and twenty-seven metres from our position." David looked down the street. The old woman placed a foot outside the door and followed his gaze. "They're all in the saloon if that's what you're looking at."

"Who is, ma'am?"

"The man-mountain … and the rest of them killers."

"Killers?"

"That's right. Half dozen or more. Arrived last week. Been drunk as devils ever since. Murdered the sheriff. Pretty much had the run of the town … till he showed up."

"Till who showed up?"

The old woman lowered her head and squinted at him. "You heard anything I been trying to tell ye?"

David gazed down the street towards the saloon. "The man-mountain?"

"'Course him. Three of those murderers imagined they'd have some fun at his expense. As I heard it they called him a 'hairless grizzly.' Said he was ugly and smelled as bad as one. And him being unarmed and alone they thought they'd little to worry about."

"There was a fight?"

"A fight, you say? Well, I guess it started out that way. Their friends in the saloon … they never even looked to see what all the firing was about. Must've thought they were just foolin' around."

"And how did it end?"

"How did what end?"

"The fight."

"Those men shot at him … and being so drunk they must have missed. The way John Grooms told it, those bullets found their target, every last one. Said the man-mountain shook them off like spittle, but that can't be. Such a thing is not possible."

Ted called out, "There are more things in heaven and earth, ma'am."

"*What* did he say? No matter. If it were the case it would mean the devil has come to Pioche. And why would he? There ain't nothing here to interest him."

"You saw this man?"

"'Course I saw him. Right after he killed those men he walked calmly down this street … doffed his hat left and right like a good Christian gentleman."

"Could you describe what he looked like."

"I already told ye."

"I take it he was not bald?"

"As a coot."

David turned away from the old woman and stared into space.

"Goliath is here," said Gull. Ted had been fanning himself with his hat, and when he saw David's face he stopped. "I don't believe I have ever seen that shade of pale on a man. It is clear that things are not hunky-dory."

David blinked.

"There a problem?" asked Isaiah.

"There is a man in this town that neither I nor Gull can protect you from."

"The man you're looking for?" said Ted.

David shook his head. "Turn the wagon around and head back out. Now." He looked towards the saloon. "I will join you shortly." He stepped off the porch and began to walk.

"Where are you going, David?" said Gull.

"The saloon."

"Goliath will be expecting you."

"Yes, he will. And I'm not going to disappoint him."

"David, you are taking your empathic duties too far."

"I believe you just cracked your first joke."

"I hope it will not be my last. David?"

"Yes."

"Might I make a suggestion? You have fulfilled your promise to Ted by seeing him safely to the nearest town. I suggest we leave immediately and head due south to seek the Colonel in New Mexico. We will have a head start on Goliath." David's long stride did not falter. Gull continued, "He has discovered a way to convey his 'self' through the Event Helix. This clearly makes him formidable. David? Are you listening?"

"Relax. I do not believe it his intention to kill us."

"I do not agree. Our extinction is currently his sole purpose."

"True enough, but it's no longer personal. It's about the Omega Protocol. You think the Architects have been glimpsed in the mind of a resident of Pioche?"

"It is highly unlikely."

"Then it can't be my destiny to die here."

When David reached the saloon, he stopped, took off his hat, and wiped his brow with his shirt sleeve. " ... so, for the time being at least, everything should be ... hunky-dory."

David walked towards the saloon doors. Inside a piano was playing a happy, up-tempo ditty. David stepped through the swing doors. The chairs and tables had been moved to the edges of the room to make way for a dance floor. On this floor the towering figure of Goliath danced as nimbly as a waif in a ballet class. His partner was a native American woman who reached no further than his waist. She looked like a doll made animate, albeit a reluctant one. Goliath skipped and bounced and twirled his doll with extraordinary dexterity and grace.

There were three dead men in the saloon. The first was slumped on the bar to David's left – presumably the barman. A shotgun lay on the counter beside his head, and his face had been ground into a broken glass, his life extinguished like a cigarette in an ashtray. To David's right a man lay sprawled across a table top. One of his legs had been ripped off and it lay over his face like an ill-conceived way of shielding his eyes. The final body sat slumped against the bar – a chair leg had been driven through its chest and another through its groin. The man looked like an upturned human table. Beyond Goliath towards the rear of the room a man sat at a table in silence. He gazed down at his hands like a hard-done-by child. In the corner to David's left, another man sat at a piano with his back to him. He played with a nervous energy that made the instrument sound manic and in need of tuning. With a flourish, the tune came to an end. Goliath bowed to his partner and began to applaud the pianist. "Bravo!"

"You want ... you want I should play another ditty?"

Goliath grasped the lapels of his bloody and bullet-ridden suit. "No. That will be all. You are free to go." The man's mouth fell open and he glanced towards the door. Goliath shooed him away with a flick of his wrist. The man half stood, turned and saw David. "Howdy."

David took a step back and pushed the door open. "Time to go."

The man nodded and hurried past him. David looked at Goliath's dance partner. He did not know her name or how to address her, and in his eagerness to get her attention he snapped his fingers. She looked up suddenly as if woken from a nightmare. David indicated the gap in the door with his eyes, and she managed half a step toward it before Goliath swept her up like a toddler, and put her down and shooed her towards the rear of the saloon. He turned back to David. "It's good to see you again, son."

David let the door close. "Goliath."

Goliath placed his thumbs in his white waistcoat and raised his chin high. "It's been a while since you beheld me in my natural state. Now when was the last time?"

"As I recall you were about to cut off my head."

"I was a mite disappointed at what transpired that day. I had assumed, before that time, that non-sentient beings could not get depressed."

"Crucifixion is no picnic either."

"I was aware that you were not having the best of times. I won't lie to you. It helped. Such was my mood that I didn't even apologise to Carradine before I killed him."

"You killed Carradine?"

"Nothing personal. All empathy must be erased. He knew as much."

"Carradine didn't strike me as being particularly empathic."

"He was not, but in a fella like Carradine empathy can lay hidden like a crab in a rock face." Goliath breathed deeply through his nose. "What a joy it is to find myself here. In many ways it feels like my home away from home. And I have you to thank for this experience. Why so glum, son?"

David folded his arms.

Goliath gestured towards the table, where the lone survivor of the gang sat with head bowed. "Come sit down, son. Take the weight off your feet. There's a fella here I'd like you to meet." Goliath went and sat in a chair to the man's right. The man looked like a chastised infant sitting beside its parent. "This here fella goes by the name of Johnson. He killed the sheriff." Johnson's lips were thin, and they curled at the recollection of this murder. The smile vanished – that had been another time. Another man. Goliath draped an arm over the back of his chair and relaxed into it. "This example of humanity is so bereft of empathy that he slaughters women and children in cold blood for their scalps." He swivelled in his seat and looked into the gloom at the rear of the saloon. "Come over here, Ayita. No need to be afraid. We are all friends here." Goliath swung his head and looked at David. "Her name – Ay-it-a – it means 'first to dance'. Isn't that right?" Ayita nodded and stood by the table with eyes cast down. Using his little finger, Goliath delicately removed a strand of hair from her eyes. "It's a Cherokee name, but Ayita is no Cherokee. She is a Tigua. The Tiguas are a peaceful people, which makes them easy pickings for the likes of Johnson here." He pulled out the chair opposite Johnson and beckoned David over. "Come and join us."

"Turn around and leave this place," said Gull.

Goliath observed David's expression. "Ignore *Gull*. He's nothing but a third wheel. Superfluous to requirements."

"He is not superfluous to my requirements. I would not have made it this far without him."

"Well, that's certainly true, but it's also true that you would not have made it this far without that hairy mole on your backside. Lower that eyebrow, son. You too, Johnson. David is aware that everything that exists in the universe is as indispensable to its progression as everything else."

David walked over to the table and sat down opposite Johnson. He took off his hat and placed it on the table. "For the record, Gull's role in my survival has been more important than the mole on my backside."

Goliath placed his hands casually around the back of his head. "I have no wish to split hairs with you."

"What are you doing here?"

"The same as every man in this saloon. Dead or alive. Fulfilling my destiny.

Now take these men in here. They believed in chance, and that explains the cards on this table. They had been playing poker when I arrived. I tried to educate them. Help them understand that despite their meagre comprehension there is no such thing as chance. They took exception to this. Expletives were used." He indicated every man present with a slowly moving finger. "Our destinies are closely linked, as are the destinies of all men. All these men were once the *Colonel's* men." Goliath brushed some lint from the lapel of his white jacket. "But they decided to up and split – with a large amount of the Colonel's gold, I might add. I explained to them that, in a roundabout way, I am a descendent of the Colonel. And that man over there ..." Goliath squinted into the darkened recesses of the room. "That fella – the one beaten to death with his own leg – he suggested that it was a 'small world'. I told him it was no such thing. That it was a vast universe, and that within it there are no such things as coincidences. Not a single one since the birth of the universe to the present."

"I presume you explained this while he still had both his legs?"

"Of course. And as I clubbed him to death with his foot, I further explained that his current predicament had been pencilled into the universe's copybook since the beginning of time. And rather than shout and holler about it, he should accept it with significantly more dignity."

Johnson piped up like a child's toy left switched on and forgotten about. "That gold was ours! We earned it. Every cent."

"Do not speak unless spoken to. Do you hear, Johnson?"

Johnson closed his mouth and shrugged his shoulders.

"You and I have been through a lot in our short acquaintance, haven't we, son?"

"It's been eventful."

"Indeed it has. And those events are drawing to a close. Only one significant event is left for you now: death. There's no need to look so glum about it. It's nothing to be ashamed of, not when you consider it sits right alongside some of the most important events in the history of your species." Goliath stared into the middle distance and sighed at the enormity of his own achievement. Then he looked at Johnson and said, "Get your eyes out of your lap and look at the man opposite you, Johnson. That's it. What you see before you is your antithesis – a man who stands opposed to your sensibilities and your way of life. This may or may not come as a surprise to you, Johnson, but many would perceive you and I as brothers in arms. Our sensibilities, or lack thereof, would suggest to them that we have more in common with each other than we do with David here. But that would be a shallow and in my view an unfair opinion. In many ways you two gentlemen represent the yin and yang of humanity. Its length and its breath. I am the end result of that yin and yang. Its by-product. I can see how to the superficial eye I have more in common with Johnson than I do with the last empath, but that comparison is wrong. For empathy to exist, a being must have the ability to place his feet in the shoes of others. And that requires imagination, and imagination is something I do not yet possess. It is something I mean to acquire, and that's really what this is all about, isn't it, son?"

"Is it? I imagined it was all about making sure you fail."

"A cruel observation, and one that does not become you." Goliath looked at Johnson. "A war has been raging for one million years, Johnson. And for any war to take place there must be at least two opposing armies. Isn't that right?"

"A man can't fight hisself, I guess."

"That is where you are wrong, Johnson. A war rages inside all men. A moralising man like yourself would look upon this war as one between good and evil. I have news for you: there are no such things as good and evil. There is only empathy and the lack of it. Son, it may or may not surprise you to know that Johnson considers himself highly moralistic. Isn't that right, Johnson?"

"I got morals aplenty."

"Now hold on there, Johnson. I never said you had morals. You don't have no morals. I said you are moralistic. There is a difference. To judge others and find them wanting enough to kill them for profit requires a certain amount of moralising. Take Ayita here. You judge her as being less than human, isn't that right?"

"She's a heathen. A savage. Unchristian as they come. Jesus don't love her kind. Why would he?"

"You see? It is easier for Johnson to moralise and pass judgment and find her inferior than to empathise with her or walk a while in her shoes. Something that is within his capabilities. Instead he moralises and in so doing he finds her lacking enough to murder her for profit. It is the lazy way of doing things. But in many ways being a lazy, moralising bastard is more efficient."

Johnson looked stung. "Lazy? Shoot, I've worked hard as a nigger my whole life."

"Murder and mutilation is hard work, is it, Johnson?"

Johnson scratched his stubble. "It ain't just the scalpin'. You have to track 'em and catch 'em ... sometimes across rough and inhospitable terrain. That is hard work. Man's work. And that's the God's truth."

"You have our sympathies, Johnson. Do you know that in a few decades from now men like Johnson will have moved on from slaughtering Indians to slaughtering buffalo? They will slaughter over a million of the beasts. Slaughter them to extinction. Is it any wonder empathy stands on the brink of extinction also? It feels as though the dice have been loaded against you from the very beginning, son. Dig down deep enough and mankind is rotten to the core."

"I disagree."

"Do you now."

"Johnson here is only part of the picture. Before long men will head south in their thousands. Risk their lives to bring an end to slavery. And they are going to win that war. You know why?"

"By all means enlighten me."

"Fighting for those who need fighting for strengthens a man's resolve. It requires a strength of character that selfish, lazy and unimaginative men like Johnson do not possess."

Johnson shook his head. "Shit."

"Watch your mouth, Johnson. A lack of character is one possibility. You want to hear another?"

"Knock yourself out," said David.

"I suppose your tone is to be expected under the circumstances. Johnson, how would you like to assist a man in a demonstration?"

Johnson gave little indication as to whether he would or wouldn't.

"Now Johnson, believe me when I say your life hangs in the balance. You do believe that your life hangs in the balance, don't you, Johnson?" Johnson's face contorted like he was about to burst into tears. "'Course I believe it!"

"Good. I'd like you to imagine you are sat in a court of law. You are accused of all the crimes against humanity that you have undoubtedly committed. Over there is a jury. They hold over you the power of life and death. I would like you to go ahead and appeal to the good natures of that jury."

"Say what?"

"Stand up and plead for your life, Johnson."

Johnson rose to his feet. "Well, I ain't done nothing wrong. Not really. Ain't broken no laws. I was just trying to make me an honest living."

"Apparently the urgency of your situation has not been made clear enough. A more impassioned plea is required of you, Johnson, and in this regard I am willing to assist you." Goliath leaned across, clasped Johnson's manhood and squeezed. Johnson squealed like a pig and his face contorted into a ball shape. "You sorry for what you've done, Johnson?"

"Yeah, I'm sorry! Please!"

"What are you sorry for, Johnson?"

"For all of it! I fell in with some bad people! And took to drinking too much liquor. Please! I have kin! Kin dependent on me! I won't do it no more! I'm a changed man!"

"Better. Now, some of those jury members would not believe a word of Johnson's contrition. They would have no empathy in their hearts for him, which given Johnson's track record would be the appropriate response."

"I'm mortal. You want to get to the point?"

"My point is that others on that jury may take pity on Johnson. Look upon him with empathy in their hearts and show him mercy. Which only goes to prove one thing: empathy has rendered these jurors misguided and weak."

"Those jurors are not demonstrating empathy, Goliath."

"Well, if their kindness towards Johnson is something other than empathy, then by all means enlighten me."

"It's gullibility. They are moralising bastards lacking in imagination just like Johnson here. Otherwise their empathy would be reserved solely for the innocent victims of his crimes."

Goliath's face set into a frown. "It seems judgment has been passed, and you have been found wanting, Johnson." Goliath tore off Johnson's manhood in a single movement and slammed it, wrapped in denim like a gift, on the table. Johnson fell back into his chair and stared lifelessly at the ceiling.

David stood up and put on his hat and doffed it towards Goliath. "I appreciate your saving me the trouble."

"Where you going, son?"

"South. To kill a Colonel."

253

"This is a war you cannot win – a war that can only be concluded with your death. You are a dead man walking. Nothing but a dead marker."

David walked around Goliath, picked up Ayita and placed her on his back. She clung to him grimly and buried her head in his neck. Goliath rose slowly from his chair … and kept rising. David fingered up the brim of his hat and looked up at him. "You're shorter than I remember."

"Taller. Nine feet four and one half inches. Now put her down."

"Only my death will prevent me walking out of here with this woman. And since neither one of us believe that the Omega Protocol exists in the mind of anyone in this town, you are going to step aside."

"Am I now?"

"Add to this the possible existence of other portals … portals that can only be activated by me … portals that may lead to the location of the individual you seek." Goliath raised his Stetson, lowered it again and stepped aside. David walked past him and down the length of the bar to the door.

Goliath cleared his throat, and David paused facing those doors. "In our time frame there are one hundred and two beings left in existence, son. One hundred vessels currently en route to the Colonel. And you and I. You might want to save yourself a whole heap of bother by giving the Colonel a wide berth. Go on your way and in so doing locate another portal – if one exists. One thing is certain: you are going to end your days at the appropriate time and in the appropriate place, wherever that may be. And in that place the Omega Protocol is waiting on me."

David walked through the swing doors and out into the sunshine. "Is he following us, Gull?"

"I am no longer detecting any life signs inside the saloon. Goliath is gone."

"Gone?"

"My summation would be that the Event Helix has provided him a shortcut to the Colonel."

Fifty three

One hundred miles south of Pioche, the Colonel lay flat on his paunch beside a man nicknamed the Bloodhound. From their elevated position along a ridge, they watched a ruddy expanse through which a river cut a swathe of glistening blue. Clusters of green and thorny vegetation ranged along its banks as far as the eye could see. Several hundred Tiguas had set up camp on river's left bank – seventy tepees erected amid a labyrinth of newly trodden paths where children played and women ferried washing from the river.

The Colonel smiled and fingered his grey moustache. "The men are away huntin'… we have ourselves some easy pickings, Blood." Blood was a Mexican with a snub nose and grey stubble that crept closer to his eyes than human stubble should. Similarly, his eyebrows were thick and dark, growing over his eyes like natural shields against the twin elements of weather and mercy. Blood nodded, but did not smile or speak, for he was a man of limited mirth and fewer words. They backed away from the edge of the ridge and got up and made their way down towards a group of waiting men – thirty-five in total, and all wretched and filthy and riding mounts adorned with plunder better suited to the minions of hell than men of earth: black and wizened body parts strung together with like for uniformity and safe keeping. These included ears, tongues, teeth, scalps and genitalia both male and female.

The Colonel addressed his men. "Blood has led us to another bonanza, gentlemen. The menfolk are away … doubtless on a huntin' trip, which is thoughtful of them. After our work is done, the hunter will become the hunted. Could be the heathen have caught us a good supper." He heaved himself up into the saddle of his horse, stuck a cigar between his lips, then struck a match on his saddle to light it. He puffed on it rapidly before removing it from his mouth and contemplating the lit end. "On the other side of this ridge are several hundred heathen. They are waitin' on us, gentlemen. They have been waitin' on us their whole lives – not that they know it. I need not remind you that powder is in short supply, so reserve your fire only for any men armed with bows. Women and children are to be felled with steel or club. Have I made myself clear?" Swords were pulled from scabbards and clubs with nails twirled on leather straps. The Colonel withdrew his own sword and held it up so that its blade glistened in the sun. He kicked the sides of his horse and it galloped up the incline with thirty-six others in tow.

Above the voices of the children in the camp came a rumbling like the approach of thunder. At the southern end of the camp women sat in a circle and chatted as they sowed. A bowl of drinking water sat at the centre of this circle and it began to dimple and splash. The river was wide and deceptively shallow, and a teenage boy and girl splashed about towards its centre. The boy scooped some water into the girl's face and she shrieked playfully. She splashed him back, but he did not react. Something behind her had his full attention, and the expression on his face was not one she'd seen before. The boy's man-name was Enapay, which means 'brave' and had always suited him, but he did not look brave now. "Enapay?" said the girl.

Enapay's eyes switched to her as though she'd just materialised. "Run!" he shouted, and bolted for the shore screaming "Mother!" Enapay's mother was sitting in the circle of sowers, and she heard her son's cry. She saw him splashing his way towards the bank. She turned to see the Colonel and his men galloping down the hill towards them. She ran towards her son with arms outstretched as a pitiful barrier to thwart the advancing horses. The *clod clud, clod clud, clod clud* of hooves grew louder, and the world of screams and pandemonium vanished for her as she was trampled under the hooves of one horse, then another, and another. Enapay scrambled up onto the bank and looked over at his mother, but saw only smiling demons in human form. Up front was the Colonel, who held his sabre high, leaned in his saddle and sliced off Enapay's raised hands. The rider that followed was Blood, and Blood swung a mace abandoned by Spanish invaders three centuries before into his screaming face. The party of raiders thundered through the camp, trampling all before them as though riding through empty space. People at rest inside the tepees were crushed, and those who scrambled out were hacked or bludgeoned or shot. When the raiding party reached the far end of the camp, they turned in unison like a flock of predatory birds and rode back.

Soon only a small number of women and children remained alive, and they cowered beyond the reach of club and sabre. Men were forced to leap off their mounts to murder them.

It took several hours to sever all the scalps, and by the time it was done the sun shone horizontally across the land and the heads of the murdered glistened like those of an alien species. Blood stood with his back to the Colonel. His arms were folded and he stared up at the ridge they'd descended from. The Colonel walked over and stood beside him. "What is it? You think we've been followed?"

"Not followed."

The Colonel squinted up at the ridge and saw nothing. He turned and

Blood clasped his arm. The Colonel looked at Blood's hand and then at Blood. Blood gestured to the top of the ridge with his chin. Along its top stood a line of at least one hundred men – white men – and at their centre was a man who stood at least nine feet tall. Goliath held a suitcase filled with the Colonel's gold in one hand. In his other hand he held Johnson's ball sack. He smiled, held it aloft and jiggled it like a man summoning his servants with a bell.

Boyd Brent
Fifty four

Ted was sitting on a rock in the shade of his wagon. His gaze was fixed upon the ground, and he muttered congenially to a cactus. He saw David's shadow merge with his own and looked up. "Well, ain't you a sight for sore eyes. I was just conversing with my good lady wife … I told her what's been occurring of late. She's the only one who won't think me crazier than a bag of rabid skunks."

David glanced down at the cactus. "Alright."

"The spirit of my good lady wife is just as real to me as that voice inside your own head." Ayita stepped from behind David and looked at Ted as though he was crazier than a bag of rabid skunks. "Howdy," said Ted.

"Ted, this is Ayita. Ayita this is Ted."

Ayita flattened her palms together and gave a curt bow.

"No need to bow. I ain't royalty. What are you doing with this squaw if you don't mind my asking?"

"She needs my help."

"You surprise me. And where are you conveying this poor creature?"

"New Mexico."

"You're headed in the same direction?"

"Yes. Her people are down there." Ted placed his hands on his knees and leaned down toward Ayita. "This here is your lucky day, young lady." He straightened up and looked at David. "They sell her on?"

David used his thumbnail to remove some dirt from the nail of his middle finger. "Why don't you ask her."

Ted leaned forward again and raised his voice. "Your folks sell you on?"

Ayita folded her arms. "I'm not *deaf*. Or stupid. And my people are not barbarians."

Ted's eyes glazed over as though he'd forgotten his question. He straightened up and wiped a sleeve across his brow. "Well, she sure is spirited."

"And growing progressively so."

Ted looked off towards the town *he'd* been safely conveyed to. "There anyone left alive in there?"

"As far as I know normal service has been resumed in Pioche."

"It's safe, then?"

258

"As safe as it can be."

"So, you killed that giant fella?"

"He's not dead, but he's gone. And so too, it appears, are our black friends."

"Yessir. Talk of bullet-proofed giants will scare off all but the oldest fool. They wanted me to thank you, though ..." Ted shoved a hand deep into the back pocket of his jeans. "Isaiah ... he wanted you to have this." David held out his hand and Ted dropped a coin into it. "Said his brother gave it to him, that he always knew it would bring him luck ... and he seemed keen for it to do the same for you."

David examined the coin. It was black with a few specks of silver on one side. "They went north?"

"They did. As you can see, they took two of the horses."

"Seems fair."

Ted scratched at his stubble. "I take it our paths are soon to part?"

"Be thankful for that."

"It goes without saying I owe you my life."

"You're a good man, Ted. Given half a chance you'd dig an old man out of the ground."

"Guess I would." Ted stepped forward and squeezed David's shoulder. "I know you have dangerous times ahead ... you and that ... that other part of you. You take care of each other, you hear?"

"We'll do our best."

"I get the feeling there's a lot riding on it."

"More than I care to think about. I hope you find what you're looking for in California."

"My girls are waitin' on me there." Ted pawed at the dirt with his foot. "When a man gets as old as me, he looks back and he gets to thinkin' about his life ... whether he might have gone a different route, or whether his path is laid out and he must walk it as best he can." He squinted deep into David's eyes as though looking for confirmation.

David smiled. "Every brick of that path has been laid for your boots alone."

"Well, that being the case, I just hope I have done justice to those I have come across."

"I get the feeling you have."

"To what end?"

"You're a good man. You might say I'm on my way to see about that right now."

"At any rate, I'm sure glad our paths crossed."

"So am I."

David started out south with Ayita. He'd gone a few hundred metres when he turned his horse to face Ted and raised an arm. Ted was sat up front of his wagon as it moved slowly towards Pioche. He stood up and took off his hat, raising it up as high as his old bones would allow.

The rest of that day David and Ayita rode across a sweltering and grey land where the only other creatures they saw were poisonous snakes and birds of prey. David rode with his eyes fixed on the horizon and the sun on his back. After a time, Gull said, "Hello, David."

"Gull. You been busy?"

"I have been making something. Something I would like you see. Will you join me by the lake?"

"What is it?"

"It's a surprise."

"Are you talking to yourself?" asked Ayita.

"No. I'm talking to Gull, the person that Goliath referred to. It's nothing to be concerned about."

"Voices live inside my head also. Some are good, others not so good."

"This voice is improving all the time."

"Thank you, David," said Gull. "Will you join me now? Only a fraction of a second will pass in the physical world during our conference."

"Alright." David closed his eyes and felt something dislodge within his mind and stretch behind him like a vapour trail.

In a clearing at the edge of a lake stood two bookcases – great walls of books that stood six metres high. Between them two leather armchairs faced one another. Beyond this library and beyond the lake a forest rose on the far shore. Gull was standing in the library – at least David assumed it was Gull. It might have been his own reflection. David ran a hand over his own face, but his mirror image remained still. What's more, David was not smiling. "I have been working on perfecting my smile," said Gull.

"I can see that."

Gull indicated the chair before him. "Please. Come into our library and sit." As David entered the library, the smile remained on Gull's face. David stopped in front of him. "Are you worried about losing that smile if you let it go?"

"In a manner of speaking."

"It's a little unnerving." The smile vanished so quickly it made Gull look furious. "Is this better?"

David did not answer.

Gull indicated the armchair behind David. "Please. Sit. And take the weight off your feet."

David sat back and sank into the chair's soft leather. He placed his left arm over its back and his left ankle on his right knee. Gull observed him for a moment and then assumed an identical pose. David felt as though he were looking at a mirror image again. He scratched the side of his nose. After a slight delay his mirror image did the same. "What are you doing, Gull?"

"Doing, David?"

"Yes. Doing."

"You must find my image greatly improved. The last time you saw it, it was …" Gull held his chin and considered the word carefully, "crude."

"It's no longer crude."

Gull elongated his neck and turned his head this way and that.

"I repeat. What are you doing?"

"Displaying my improvements."

"I'd rather you didn't. Pride comes before a fall, and unless you get a grip you're going to take us both down."

"Your concern is noted."

"So. We have a library."

"Do you like it?"

"It's a fine library. What are these books about?"

"You, David – or more accurately those things that now make you unique." Gull stood up, moved to the bookcase behind David and ran a finger along the volumes. David leaned forward in his chair and steepled his fingers. Gull continued. "Within these volumes are catalogued all that constitutes your empathic nature. The things that provide you an edge over Goliath."

David's head snapped up and he looked at the wall of books before him. "I can't be this …"

"Impressive, David?"

"*Nice.*"

"You surprise me."

"Nice people don't do the things I've done. They're the ones I've been doing these things for."

"You are nicer than Goliath."

"That supposed to be a compliment?"

"An observation."

"More's the pity. If Goliath was *nicer* it would make our job a lot easier."

"How so?"

"I could kill myself. Job done."

Gull pulled a volume halfway out. He looked over his shoulder and observed David's unhappy posture, then pushed it back in. He sat down again and began arranging himself in a similar pose.

Without looking up David said, "Don't even think about it."

Gull sat back in the seat and lay his arms on the arm rests. He

261

drummed his fingers a couple of times. "You have done only what is necessary to survive."

"Ignore me. I'll be fine."

Gull stood suddenly, as though stung by his chair, and went to the cabinet of books opposite David. He looked up at a volume some three metres above his head. As he levitated to reach it, David closed his eyes and pinched the bridge of his nose. He opened his eyes a moment later to see Gull sitting opposite him and thumbing through the pages of a red, leather-bound volume. "Here it is, David. On page 447 ... *periods of despondency may arise due to acts of brutality and empathy not being natural bedfellows.*"

"You needed a book to tell you that? And anyway," sighed David, "it's not like I don't enjoy dishing it out sometimes."

Gull flipped the page. "Remorse!"

"I could have told you that also."

"I have created this library so I might understand you the way you understand yourself."

"My mind is not a receptacle. It's not something you can just dip into any time you choose."

"Isn't that somewhat hypocritical? Man has dipped into the minds of computers for millennia to retrieve information."

"Man created computers for that purpose, and computers don't have minds. They have databases."

"The left side of the human brain is little more than a biological database – a memory. An information retrieval system. If you've ever retrieved information from a computer, then I don't see how you can object to returning the favour. This library is unique. The first and last of its kind. What Goliath would do to have such a place of study and contemplation. The information contained in these volumes provides a most remarkable insight into what it means to be an empathic being. And I only had to cut down a small area of trees to make the paper."

David scratched the side of his face. "Paper?"

"There is no need for concern. The information contained within those trees was superfluous to our requirements, all of it gathered using only the periphery of your senses. Things you have no conscious knowledge of. There are millions of such trees beyond this lake, and it required only nine hundred and four of them to create this library. It's the first and last of its kind."

"So you said."

"I have used my own knowledge to provide you with enhancements. All I ask in return is the same. We must trust one another." Gull stood and stepped towards a cabinet, but David reached out and grabbed his arm. "I take it you're about to go and dig out a book about trust."

"A most illuminating volume."

"I've little doubt. Trust is a good deal easier with access to a person's thoughts and memories."

"Memories, yes, but not your thoughts – not until they've solidified into ideas. And that takes time. I have no idea what you're thinking now."

"I have no reason to plot against you, Gull."

"I have no reason to plot against you, David."

"We are both aware that's untrue."

"Despite what Goliath has said, I have no wish to be him. To the contrary," Gull's gaze searched the upper shelves of the books behind David. "He *repulses* me. According to the laws laid down in these books, his progression at the expense of those who created him is beneath contempt."

"That volume on contempt ... I imagine it's pretty thick."

"Yes. Your life experience has provided you with much to be contemptuous about." Gull twisted his head and looked at the books behind him. "But you balance this by trying to understand the *perspectives* and *motivations* of the contemptuous."

"That's very thoughtful of me."

"Indeed it is."

David smiled.

"Why are you smiling?"

"I don't see that this library of yours–"

"Ours."

"I can't see how this library of ours can fail to improve your personality."

"Improvement is all I desire."

"Is everything alright outside?"

"Only moments have passed, although I fear our companion will not like what she finds in New Mexico. Sadly, her people were massacred earlier today. They have been all but wiped out by Goliath's equally contemptuous ancestor."

David sat back in the armchair. "How many of her people survived?"

"Three. It will take them some weeks to bury the dead."

"And the Colonel?"

"He is tracking the men of Ayita's tribe. The hunters have become the hunted. Goliath is already with him. This endeavour doubtless appeals to Goliath's loathsome nature. And following this act of butchery they will cross the border from New Mexico into Mexico. Their final destination is to be an abandoned fort that lies on the banks of a large body of water. Goliath is correct in his assertion that any attempts to terminate the Colonel in that location would be futile."

"And the Colonel is happy to go and hide out? From one man?"

"Goliath can be very persuasive, David."

"Suggestions?"

"Suggestions?"

"Tactical suggestions. For breaching the fort's defences."

"It would be unwise to attempt to take the fort by force. The only logical option would be to starve the enemy out. But as this enemy includes one hundred vessels, it would be akin to stirring up a hornet's nest."

"I hope you're not suggesting we give up."

"No. I'm suggesting that if a solution exists, then only your imagination can conjure it."

David looked up at the stars overhead. "At this moment, I can't say I'm feeling all that imaginative."

The Empathy Gene

Fifty five

The sun fell rapidly and dragged with it not only the warmth but also the lifeblood of that land. David could feel Ayita's body shivering next to his own. Midway along a narrow passage between two walls of ruddy rock, he halted the horse and patted its neck. "We'll camp here for the night. The walls will provide shelter from the wind."

They sat side by side before a small fire and ate some boiled rattlesnake that Ted had packed for them. "Maybe you should go easy. You'll get indigestion," said David.

"It's good ..."

"Didn't Goliath feed you?"

"Mainly we danced. Papa always said it was so ... that the devil likes to dance."

"Where did he find you?"

"I saw him first ... sitting on the river bank. No shirt. A great white mound, whistling a white man's tune – happy and stupid, like the one we were dancing to. He beckoned me to him ... big hairless bear."

"You always go when someone calls you?"

"I was with my little sister. I kept my distance and asked him what he wanted. He said he had something to tell me: that my family were in danger, but I should not worry because he was going to take me somewhere safe – somewhere I could do my name proud. I told him I would not go with him, and that if what he said was true I must warn my family." Ayita licked her fingers and wiped tears from her eyes with the back of her hand.

"What happened next?"

"He moved fast ... fast as only the devil can move. He picked me up and held me tight, and when I awoke I was in Pioche. I have to get home. I have to warn my family." Ayita looked into David's eyes and saw their fates reflected back at her.

"What? You know something?"

"I know there are monsters in the hearts of some men. I'm sorry. Your people are with their gods."

"How can you know? You can't *know,* not unless you are a devil, too." Ayita slapped David's cheek. David apologised again, and Ayita slapped him again. She got up and stumbled to the rock face, fell on her side and sobbed.

265

"There are three women left alive. They are tending to the dead. They need you."

Ayita looked over her shoulder, her eyes filled with rage and tears. "What three? What are their names?"

"That I do not know."

"That I do not know," she mocked, and then faced the wall and sobbed again.

The next morning, they set out at dawn. They rode in silence and at midday they crossed the border into New Mexico. "How is your companion, David?" asked Gull.

"She's grieving."

"I have been studying grief. A loss such as hers is painful."

"Yes, but I believe there is a limit to human suffering."

"You allude to death?"

"No. I was referring to how much sorrow a human being can feel. From personal experience, I believe nature has provided a limit, beyond which lies only the fear of how bad they imagine they can feel – along with a mostly irrational fear of losing their mind. Imagination is a powerful tool. And it can be highly convincing."

Ayita spoke for the first time since she'd mocked David the night before. Her voice full of unexpected resolve. "Are you are talking to *Gull?*"

"Yes."

"What does his name mean?"

"It's short for Guillotine."

"What's a guillotine?"

"A machine used for punishing people."

"How?"

"It removes their heads."

She tutted. "A name that does not suit him."

It suits him just fine.

"Is he like your conscience?"

"Not exactly."

Gull said, "Through study and contemplation, I hope to become more like your conscience."

"I'd rather you didn't. Unless it's your intention to become a miserable pain in my ass."

"Then I will carry my burdens silently."

"Now you've pricked my actual conscience."

"You are very fortunate to have a conscience to prick. David?"

"Yes."

"I have done some research into Mexico at this time."

"So tell me about Mexico."

"Its people are at a low ebb."

"Sorry to hear that."

"The Comanche, Apache and Navajo Indians have long been sending raiding parties into their territories and stealing goods and livestock. When the US Army sent in troops to annexe the lands now known as California and Texas in 1846, they found a demoralised people. They are yet to recover."

"And your point?"

"We should not find them overly troublesome."

"As long as they don't find us overly troublesome, everything should be hunky-dory."

They made their way through a narrow pass that led to a high vantage point, from where they could see a town nestled in a valley. "It is the town of Santa Catarina," said Gull. "A good place to rest and purchase supplies."

They rode into Santa Catarina during the feast of Las Animas. Along the town's main thoroughfare people were crammed into galleried balconies, while others stood four-deep along the roadside. Small children sat on their parents' shoulders eating sugared skulls while they waited for the main event. David and Ayita entered Santa Catarina at the town's south-western corner, and their progression was thwarted by spectators – small, dark people in their Sunday best. These frayed garments had been endlessly stitched and mended and passed from generation to generation. Ayita pressed her face against David's back in an attempt to hide at least one half of it. "It's alright, Ayita."

"For you, perhaps. When they see a true native of these lands ... these sons and daughters of Spain ... they see only Comanche."

"You're in my care."

To their right some thirty metres away a priest walked down the street ringing a bell. Behind the priest four men held aloft a float adorned with a crude papier-mâché Christ, complete with crown of thorns and droplets of painted-on blood. Following this contrivance, eight bare-footed priests clutched Bibles. As the procession drew nearer, the priest in front who hitherto had been looking at the ground, looked up at David. He saw a wavy-haired and bearded Christ-like man, who in turn watched his papier-mâché likeness with an expression that suggested he found it slightly amusing. The priest's eyes continued to gaze at David until a crick in his neck grew too painful. As the procession passed, it turned right, and in its wake the town's people followed silently as though dragged by invisible strings. The street to David's right cleared, and he rode his horse into it. A little way down, an old woman sat in a doorway, fanning herself. David asked her for directions to the stables, and also to an inn where they might find lodgings. The old woman fanned herself with greater urgency, as though questions from strangers could only result in greater perspiration. She crossed one leg over the another and jutted her chin to her left. Then she glanced up at the stranger on the horse and her fanning hand froze, and her mouth dropped open. David thanked her kindly, doffed his hat and moved away.

"Did you do that deliberately?" asked Gull.

"Do what?"

"Inquire about the whereabouts of a stable, when you so closely resemble the man she believes was born in one. Was it your intention to unsettle the old woman?"

"Maybe. A little."

A wiry Mexican hammered molten metal into a horseshoe. He paused mid-blow and wiped a bare forearm across his brow. David climbed down from the horse, reached up and helped Ayita down. He turned to the blacksmith. "I need you to take care of my horse for a few hours. She needs to be fed and watered." The man nodded and flashed ten fingers, denoting ten pesos. He expected David to haggle and when he did not he shook his head as though disappointed and recommenced his hammering.

The inn was located a little way down the street. David walked through its swing doors and Ayita followed close upon his heels. Inside a bar and a dozen tables. Only two of which were occupied by weary-looking men who had exchanged God for gambling and sotol. They looked at Ayita like she was something abhorrent stuck to David's boots. The landlord stood behind the bar. He looked at the men playing cards and then at the American. He could see a pair of skinny legs, knees touching, between the American's. The American looked eerily familiar and spoke authentic Spanish. "I would like two rooms. With baths, if you please."

A pig-like snort and a chuckle came from one of the tables. A deep and wispy voice said, "The American brings his squaw, but needs two rooms because she smells too bad to fuck her." Laughter ensued from both tables, followed by a silence during which David mentally counted to ten. "Alright," he murmured, and opened the slaver's saddlebag. He rummaged around and fished out two gold coins, which he placed on the counter. "You can keep the change." Each coin represented ten times the usual tariff, and the innkeeper slid them into his palm, biting down on one and then the other. He slammed a fist on the counter and told the men playing cards to keep their foul language to themselves.

Their rooms were located on the second floor – identical rooms in reverse and separated by a narrow corridor. At the end of this corridor hung a map of Mexico dated 1812. Ayita looked through the open door into her room – it contained a bed, a chamber pot and a free-standing bath.

"They'll bring hot water presently," said David. "Get some rest." As if on cue, wooden shoes clip-clopped up the stairs. David drummed his fingers silently upon the stocks of his pistols.

"It's a servant," said Gull. "I believe she is carrying hot water."

The servant was the innkeeper's daughter and her already thunderous expression was darkened further by the realisation that the rumours of her having to 'wait hand and foot on an Indian whore' had not been exaggerated.

David closed the door. He sat on the bed and took off his hat. "I have something to show you," said Gull.

"You've added an extension to our library?"

"No. With your permission I would like to project a holo image of Fort Arturo into this room."

"Fort Arturo?"

"It is where Goliath intends to imprison the Colonel."

"Alright. Let's see it."

"It will require the use of one of your eyes. Do you have a preference?"

"No preference." David's left eye began to cloud over and then darken. His right eye looked down at a holographic image of Fort Arturo. The image filled the floor between him and the tub of steaming water, and showed a wide body of water that flowed along the length of the tub. On the banks of this water stood a square fort the colour of tree bark. A sentry turret rose from each of its four corners, and it had a single entrance in the form of a drawbridge. The drawbridge was raised, and below it a semi-circle of water encompassed the whole like an azure necklace. "Is that a moat?"

"Yes, David. The stronghold's walls are twenty metres high, and the drawbridge is the only way in or out. The large body of water will soon be known as the Gulf of California. As well as the Colonel and his men, the fort contains one hundred enemy combatants, all with similarly enhanced abilities to your own. They are commanded by an entity powerful enough to crush all about him like so many insects. What is more, he can detect our approach for a radius of five kilometres in all directions."

"Please confirm you are talking about Goliath."

"Who else, David?"

"In your opinion, what do we need to get in there and kill the Colonel?"

"Excluding a miracle?"

"Yes. I'm not Him."

"To subdue Goliath long enough to allow us time to locate and terminate the Colonel would require an army of vessels fifteen hundred strong."

"So, our only option as far as Goliath sees it is to slink off and eventually to die?"

"Or else to die in a futile attempt at reaching the Colonel."

David lay down and the image of Fort Arturo was relocated to the ceiling. He closed his eye.

Fifty six

David slept for six hours, and when he awoke the sun had gone down and his room was dark. There was a single gas lamp in the room. David lit it, stripped off and climbed into the cold bath water. Ten minutes later he lay with his head propped on its rim.

"Are you well rested, David?"

"Well enough. Is Ayita alright?"

"Her vital signs suggest she is sleeping soundly."

"How far are we from the camp where Goliath seized her?"

"A day's ride. Have you given any thought to our conundrum? Perhaps you have experienced a eureka moment in the bath?"

David closed his eyes. "No eureka moment."

"That is hardly surprising. You are unable to access your imagination and fully concentrate. This is because a gaggle of trees has been vying for your attention. I suspect they have been leading you back into the past."

"The people I've met, places I've been, the things I've witnessed ..."

"Are a distraction. You must ignore those voices and concentrate on the task at hand."

"Easier said than done."

"Now you are rested, you must ascend the steps and sit upon the throne of your imagination. If a solution exists, it will provide the best chance to conjure it."

David opened his eyes. He was lying in the bath in a clearing close to the edge of the cosmos. Gull was standing beside the bath, holding a robe. David listened for his thoughts but he could hear nothing. "The forest cannot grow here," said Gull. "This accounts for the serenity."

David stood up, took the robe from his doppelgänger and slipped into it. "It's like having amnesia."

"Quite so. If you take half a dozen steps back towards the forest, the voices will return." David stepped in the opposite direction.

He sat on the throne of his imagination and savoured the silence. Gull was standing below him at the edge of the clearing. He cleared his throat, and David looked down at him. "Might I suggest that you conjure the image of Fort Arturo for contemplation, David?" David ran a hand through his beard, and an image of Fort Arturo appeared and floated before him. "Take the image," said Gull. "Take it and travel closer to the stars ... *contemplate* it."

"I can travel higher?"

"You are confined only by the limits of your imagination. And your imagination has no limits."

"Alright." Alix appeared. She crouched over the fort and smiled down at it like a benevolent giant. "It's good to see you," said David.

"And you ..." Gull cleared his throat and Alix vanished. David raised a hand in parting, and the chair and accompanying image floated up into the heavens. For a time, David could still see the forests of the left side of his mind spread towards the horizon, but as he travelled higher the left hemisphere grew smaller and soon it was no bigger than his thumb – a thumb now consumed by the infinity of space. David leaned forward, placed his chin on his fist and contemplated the fort and the task at hand. He smiled and muttered, "Of course," and sat back in the chair, wondering why the solution hadn't presented itself earlier. Alix appeared again. She was standing at his right shoulder and she said, "I don't like it. Your plan's too risky."

David looked at her. "Nothing is without risk. Life itself is a kamikaze mission."

"You imagine you can trust Gull ... with your *life*?"

"I can imagine anything here."

"That's what bothers me." Alix crouched and stared at the figurine-sized figure of David lying on the ground outside the fort. He looked like a felled chess piece. "But you're *dead*," she said.

"If it's Gull's intention to survive, then he must resuscitate me."

Anna came running out of the darkness. She was wearing her red dress, and she stood before the fort like a child before an elaborate sand castle. She reached down to the tiny figure of David upon the ground and tried to poke life into it. She frowned and said, "*I* don't think you can trust him. Why does he want to look so much like you?"

David leaned forwards in his chair. "You have become a very suspicious young lady."

"It's what kept her alive when so many others perished," said Alix. "Her instinct for survival is pure and uncluttered ... as only a child's can be."

David sat back in his chair. "Only it's not a child's instinct. It's my own." Alix and Anna vanished.

David found Gull sitting in the library reading a book entitled *Choices and Consequences*. When he saw David approaching, he placed a bookmark inside the volume and closed it. "You look like the cat that got the cream," he said. David sat in the armchair opposite him and crossed one leg over the other. "I look smug?"

"You do. And the suspense is killing me."

"You said that to me once before, when you'd hidden that 'gift' in the closet. Clara."

"A regrettable episode, and one that has pride of place in my embryonic conscience. You have conjured a solution to the problem at hand?"

"I have. Goliath's resources … they make him the most powerful entity in this scenario?"

"By an unquantifiable margin."

"Then he must be made to assist us. Do the lion's share of our work."

"An unlikely scenario, if you don't mind my saying."

"Maybe not. In the seconds and minutes following my death, what will Goliath conclude?"

"He will conclude that the Omega Protocol exists in the memory of someone close to your corpse. And he would be correct in his assumption."

"You sure about that?"

"All the data suggests so."

"Alright. And what action will he take?"

"He will plunder the minds of all within a kilometre radius for the information he seeks."

"And what would happen to these plundered people? Plundered vessels?"

"They would be left in a vegetative state," said Gull.

"How long would it take the Event Helix to relay the news of my death to Goliath?"

"It would be instantaneous, as though a curtain is raised inside the Event Helix."

"And having received this news, how long would it take him to ransack all those minds?"

"I would need time to make a precise calculation, but even with the vast computing power at his disposal he would require several hours to sift through all that biological data."

"Several hours is more than enough time."

"For what, David?"

"To scale the walls of the fort and locate the Colonel."
"But you will be a corpse."

"Not if you bring me back, and resuscitate me before my brain suffers through lack of oxygen. I imagine you could do that?"

"Given the right conditions."

"How long can a person be dead before their brain suffers permanent damage?"

Gull leaned forward in his chair. "The brain can remain starved of oxygen for several minutes, but what if Goliath discovers the Omega

273

Protocol in that time?"

"My death marks the spot. Not my feigned death. This message, this shockwave … up there in my imagination, I saw that it would take a period of time to travel throughout the entirety of the Event Helix – a period of time before my death is set in stone. Before it actually becomes an event."

"I concur. The shockwave will require a period of time to fully complete its journey."

"You think you can work out how much time?"

"I believe I can come up with an estimation."

"Make it a priority. Up there it was clear to me that if I'm resuscitated the shockwave will be stopped in its tracks."

"Your theory is an intriguing one."

David shook his head. "Imagination and intuition … when they're uncluttered by the logical toiling of the left side … there are no theories. Only facts."

Gull smiled. "Quite so, David."

"So while Goliath is busy ransacking the minds of his 'comrades' for the Omega Protocol, you resuscitate me. And then we find the Colonel."

"What if Goliath does not begin his search immediately?"

"Again, up there on that chair, I saw it as plain as day: once he receives news of my death, it will be like a starting pistol has been, in his words, 'shoved up his jacksy and fired'."

"The manner of your death will need to be highly convincing."

"Yes, it will. And that is not a discussion I'm looking forward to having." Gull looked over David's head into the starry expanse of his imagination with an expression that suggested he coveted the *factual* possibilities of imagination when combined with intuition more than ever. Then he looked askance and his eyes moved from left to right as though reading from an invisible book. "What is it?" said David.

"Ayita … she requires our assistance."

Fifty seven

An inebriated and pot-bellied Mexican had burst into Ayita's room and slapped her unconscious. At the other end of the corridor, at the top of the stairs, his two accomplices aimed their pistols at David's door. The pot-bellied Mexican stumbled into the corridor with Ayita over his shoulder. The larger of his companions set off down the stairs while the other kept his gun trained on that door. As the freshly bathed woman was carried past, he wiped some spittle from his mouth and followed. When Ayita reached the landing below she opened her eyes, and in that instant a shadow dropped past the window. Ayita's head bobbed about as her kidnapper carried her down the next flight of stairs. A crack! was heard below. The pot-bellied Mexican called out to his friend. When there was no reply, he pressed his back to the wall and indicated to the man behind him that he should go down and investigate. The man edged past and called out also. Sweat prickled on his brow, and he cocked the gun and then, as though startled by a sound behind him, swung his arm and levelled the gun up the stairs. A shot rang out. Blood spurted from his neck and he spun to the floor.

The pot-bellied Mexican lifted Ayita off his shoulder and used her as a human shield. As he drew his pistol, David stepped into view below. He was stark naked and dripping wet, and held a gun in each hand. Three shots boomed in that boxed-in space, none fired by a pot-bellied Mexican. Ayita was sprawled across the dead man's lap. She opened her eyes and David advised her not to look at his face.

"Why not?"

"It's no longer a face." A commotion of excitable voices could be heard outside. David stepped forward, picked up Ayita and moved swiftly up the stairs. He put her down outside her room and told her to get her things together. "We'll be checking out in one minute."

David emerged from his own room fully dressed and securing his second gun-belt. He cocked an ear towards the stairs and heard tentative voices that spoke of 'murder' and 'justice' and 'death'. A gruff male voice called out, "What have you done, amigo? Murdered the brother of Santos Demingo? He will hunt you to the edge of the earth, friend."

David raised his voice. "Not exactly a new development for me, *friend*."

"There is no way out for you. You are a dead man."

"As is the first man to come up those stairs." David picked up Ayita. He carried her back into her room and shunted up the window. He looked down into a dark alleyway. Ayita shook his arm. "The drop is much too far!" David picked her up and climbed out. He landed on his feet and relaxed into a crouch, then ran to his left into a deserted backstreet. He turned right and sprinted to the rear of the stables, Ayita bouncing and groaning under his arm.

David had been switching from a gallop to a canter and back again for close on an hour. Now he brought the panting horse to a halt, swung it around and looked back at the lights of Santa Catarina. They shone in the distance like a swarm of angry fireflies – at least, that's how David perceived the mood of those lights. "Are they following us yet, Gull?"

"There is some commotion at the town's southern boundary, but as yet no one is tracking us."

David looked up at the heavens. "No stars. The moon's barely a sliver."

"There will be scant light to track us by before dawn."

"How long till dawn?"

"Four hours and twenty-two minutes."

David climbed down from the panting horse and handed Ayita the reins. Ayita's right eye was black, and her left cheek swollen. "I'm sorry I didn't get to you sooner."

Ayita winced as she tried to smile, and when she spoke it sounded as though her tongue had swollen to twice its size. "They would have killed me. And by the time they did I would have welcomed death."

"I think it best if I sprint for a while, Gull. Take some weight off the horse."

"The exercise will do you good. We would make greater progress with my radar-assisted view."

"Agreed."

"May I assume control?"

David patted the horse. "Yes. In a moment." He looked up at Ayita. "I'm going to run. You'll be riding alone for a while."

For the next four hours, Gull jogged across the pitch-black terrain with a sleepy Ayita riding at a trot behind him. He ran in a straight line towards her camp, and only deviated from his course to avoid the sand vipers that appeared to be as numerous in that land as they had been in the scrub lands outside of Jerusalem.

When David resumed control over his body, the first rays of dawn had begun to illuminate the edges of the vast plateau he had crossed. He slowed to a stop. Between deep breaths he said, "They tracking us now?"

"Yes, David. Seventeen men rode out of Santa Catarina six minutes ago. Each man has a spare horse. I estimate that they will reach our position in approximately four hours. Three kilometres south west of our position there are a number of caves. I suggest we lure them inside."

"Murder them?"

"Terminate them."

"That conscience you're cultivating ... it's struggling to define the difference between terminating a man and murdering him."

"Are they not two words with the same meaning?"

"The same outcomes, maybe, but if they had the same meaning that would make us murderers. It's a question of karma."

"Karma?"

"So I believe. You might say that men who are terminated had it coming, while men who are murdered do not."

"And who decides which men have it coming?"

David took off his hat and ran the back of his hand across his brow. "Could be only those with empathic natures can make that call. The men pursuing us have a genuine grievance – at least, that's how they see it."

"The men we killed were intent on raping and murdering Ayita. It's unlikely they would have listened to reason."

"And that's why they had it coming, but planning the murder of seventeen men who are hunting, as they see it, a murderer and a fugitive? It doesn't feel right."

"Santos Demingo is not a representative of the law. He is a gangster."

"Who will die by my hand if he forces it. But maybe it won't come to that ... maybe we can put him and his men to good use."

"A developing theme in your thinking of late."

Ayita spoke up a sleepy voice. "I recognise this place. The river upon which my settlement rests ... it comes from the west and flows south beyond those caves." Ayita pointed to two o'clock in the direction they faced. From her vantage point on the horse, she saw the silver grey of the caves rise out of the lighter landscape. To the right of the caves were flecks of green, as though dabbed from the brush of an impressionist painter. David looked back in the direction of their pursuers and then in the direction they must travel. "I have a suggestion," said Gull.

"Make it."

"Ayita can hide in the caves. Once the danger has passed she can make her way to what remains of her settlement on foot."

"Danger doesn't pass here. It comes in waves."

"Our tracks will lead the men away from the caves. The Event Helix clearly shows that Ayita will reach the survivors of her tribe."

"You sure about that?"

"Yes. I am certain."

"And our own path towards the fort?"

"Is obscured by a Shadow Strand, as all our paths have been. As the paths of all men must be. But there is good news: within this Shadow Strand only one possible Exit Point remains. Only one location where your death is possible."

"Is it close to the fort?"

"One hundred and twenty metres from its main entrance."

"Well, given the plan we have in mind ... that's either the best possible news or the worst."

David and Ayita entered the cave. It had a broad entrance through which the light of the rising sun poured. At the back of the cave were several small entrances, large vertical cracks, which led deeper into a labyrinth. David approached the most central of these and squeezed a little way in, peering into the gloom. He squeezed his way out and looked over at Ayita. She was examining something in the wall. David approached her and said, "You're going to be safe here. Plenty of places to hide."

"Maybe."

"No. Not maybe. I have it on good authority: you're going to be reunited with the survivors of your people." A section of rock housed something off-white in colour that stuck out, ever so slightly, as though attempting to squeeze itself free of its confinement. Ayita reached up and ran a finger along its silken edge. "It is one of the giants that once roamed this land ..."

"It is the jaw bone of Tyrannosaurs Rex," said Gull. "The first cataclysmic event, the asteroid that rendered these creatures extinct, occurred not far from this location. And it paved the way for the humanity project."

David leaned against the wall and looked closely at the ancient fossil. "Is that right? And what of the second cataclysmic event? The one that occurs approximately five hundred years from now... the one that drives humanity off-world? What was its purpose?"

"That I do not know. Possibly to hasten the outcome of the experiment ... the war."

David tapped the long-extinct creature's jaw bone. "Whatever arranged this experiment, this war, does not have long to wait for its outcome."

"If we are not successful then the efforts of those you represent will be rendered as futile as this extinct beast."

David drew a deep breath and placed a hand on Ayita's shoulder. "It's time I was leaving. Find yourself a hiding place ... some of those cracks are too small for a man to fit through. Tomorrow it will be safe to continue your journey."

"You are going to find the people who murdered my family?"

"I am."

"Are they going to pay for what they have done?"

"They are."

Fifty eight

David sat crossed-legged on a ridge of elevated rock. The ocean that had once covered this land had worked and reworked the ridge into a giant question mark. David was perched on the dot at its base, his countenance so still that buzzards had begun circling overhead. He was hatless and stripped to the waist, his face tilted towards the sun. His eyes were closed and his left eyelid twitched. Behind that eyelid David strolled within the forest of his memory. Gull walked at his side and looked like his mirror image. "I don't think I've ever known these woods so quiet, Gull. Not even a breeze ..."

"I have quelled the enthusiasm of your memory. I hope you don't mind."

"You know I don't. It's a serenity that any man might covet. I take it time has slowed outside?"

"Yes. To something approximating a standstill."

"Good. We may need all the time we can get."

"You have a plan in mind?"

David stopped and looked about at the forest representation of his mind. "I've had a seed of an idea. It's stored in here somewhere."

"To access stored information you need only to cast for it, as though casting a fishing line."

"Alright ..." David's idea came to him through a rustle of the trees. He shook his head and added, "If only the solution to putting it into practice was this easy to come by."

"Do you require the use of your imagination?"

"No. The solution is technical in nature. More your area of expertise than mine."

"I am flattered, David. What is it you wish to achieve? I believe it has something to do with securing the assistance of Santos Domingo and his men?"

"That's right. As you have pointed out, my death will need to be convincing. And Goliath must witness it."

"You would like us to stage a play for Goliath?" said Gull.

"Of sorts. One where the ending is much to his liking."

"As Santos Domingo understands it, you murdered his brother. It is unlikely he will be open to suggestions regarding the manner of your punishment. He might wish to take you back to Santa Catarina to answer to the law."

"I don't imagine he has a trial in mind."

"What do you imagine he has in mind?"

David patted Gull on the back. "I believe you have just hit the nail on the head."

"Please explain."

"We're going to plant an idea *inside* his mind."

"Are you referring to hypnosis?"

"I was hoping you might come up with something that will not require the dangling of a watch." David glanced up towards the forest's canopy, beyond which his imagination lay. "I know it can be done. I just don't know how."

"Neither do ..." said Gull, breaking into a smile.

"Apparently you just cast a line of your own. What is it?"

"It will require some thought, David."

"Yours or mine?"

"You were correct about the solution being more technical than intuitive."

"Yours then."

Gull indicated the path ahead and the identical men strolled along it. "The human brain is an inferno of electrical activity," said Gull.

"So I believe."

"It is the brain's electrical nature that makes our own symbiosis possible. For purposes of serenity, I veil all electrical activity during your visits. Otherwise we would be forced to shout above the crackle of a billion lightning storms."

"Appreciate it."

"Pulses of electricity escape these storms day and night. They pass through your skull and continue out into the cosmos. In this regard the pulses are not unlike radio signals."

"Where are you going with this?"

"If these electronic pulses could be directed from your mind into the mind of Santos Domingo ... in theory data could be transferred inside them. Data that could be coded to influence his actions."

"Can you do it?"

"Can theory be turned into fact? Yes, but without an imagination to enable an intuitive leap, I will require a considerable length of time. A method of directing a stream of electronic pulses with pinpoint accuracy must be devised, along with a means of placing data inside them."

"How long will you need?"

"A number of years."

"I take it you're referring to years that pass in here?"

281

"Quite so. Time you could spend wondering the forest in contemplation. Or you else could rejoin the buzzards circling overhead for a moment and then return to hear it."

"Buzzards."

"As you wish. And the information you wish to plant?"

"All that's required of Santos Domingo is that he execute me in full view of that fort."

"Execute how?"

"Not something I care to think about. I think it best I leave the details to you. I will obviously need to emerge in one piece."

"Then might I suggest hanging? I can reinforce the appropriate neck muscles to ensure that decapitation is not the result."

David rubbed a sudden crick in his neck. "I believe hanging is popular in these times."

"To prevent any undue distress, I will ensure you lose consciousness at the appropriate moment."

"Very thoughtful. And what of that other calculation? The shock wave that carries news of my death?"

"I discovered a great many intangibles in calculating how long it would take the event – any event – to become permanent and fixed. And erring on the side of caution, it would be unwise to allow the shock wave to continue on its journey for longer than two minutes."

"I'll be counting on you to resuscitate me before those two minutes expire."

"We live together, or die together. And I wish to live as long as possible."

David nodded. "I'll leave you to your work."

"So what have you decided upon? A number of years of contemplation in these woods, or a moment outside with the Buzzards, David?"

"Like I said, buzzards."

"As you wish."

David glanced up at the buzzards, and then at the cloud of dust stirred up by the approaching posse. He raised his hands above his head in mock surrender, closed his eyes, and felt himself drawn back into the forest. "Hello, David. Sorry for the delay. The calculations required more time than I expected."

"Can't say I noticed."

"There was a reason they took longer. I think you're going to be pleased with my innovations."

"You are aware that Santos Domingo and his men are here?"

"Yes. Be assured, while you're with me their progress is effectively frozen."

David observed his body double for a moment. "You're looking particularly pleased with yourself."

"I have devised a way to make the transfer of data into the mind of Santos Domingo more tangible."

"How?"

"By turning it into an experience we might undertake together."

"We have undertaken this whole journey together."

"This will be more like a day out."

David opened his mouth to speak and closed it again.

"I don't get out much, David."

"I appreciate that. Please confirm where we're going."

"Into the mind of Santos Domingo." Gull's smile broadened and he walked behind a tree, and when he emerged he was holding a small cactus and a shovel. He placed the cactus on his palm and handed it to David. "Of all my experiments, I am most proud of this one. I believe it is my most creative."

"Tell me it's not just a cactus?"

"It is a receptacle. One that contains ideas pertinent to our mission."

"And they promote my being hung by the neck until dead?"

"Oh, yes."

"No need to sound quite so enthusiastic about it."

Gull reached out and touched one of the cactus's spines. "In many ways it mimics the planting of any idea – something usually achieved using language. But this cactus is considerably more potent than words." A rectangle of glowing light appeared in the trunk of the tree beside Gull. "This door will propel us into the mind of Santos Domingo."

David stepped closer and peered into the bright rectangle. "You sure about that?"

"Yes. I have made the crossing hundreds of times."

"And what if we get stuck over there?"

"Impossible. Our conveyance is merely a projection. Should the connection be severed or discontinued, we will find ourselves returned to the source of the projector: your mind."

David took a step back and gestured towards the entrance. "After you."

David emerged into a dimly lit expanse filled with cacti, each plant the height of a man. They stood in uniformed lines with paths between them, resembling an army of soldiers unearthed from a Mexican's tomb. David looked at the tiny plant in his hand. "You sure it's big enough?"

"Quite sure." They were standing on an area of loose soil. Gull thrust the shovel into it and hurled its contents over his shoulder. "I expect you're wondering why his memory is filled with cacti?" said Gull.

"Because he's a Mexican?"

Gull paused mid-shovel. "It was not my intention to succumb to a stereotype."

David folded his arms across his chest. "You have failed in your intentions."

"I wished only to provide an environment that could be differentiated from your own memory – one where you might be afforded some sense of where you are."

"That hole deep enough yet?"

"Yes." David placed the cactus inside it and Gull covered it with soil. Gull planted the shovel in the ground and leaned on it. "I sense you have a question."

David cleared his throat. "Very perceptive. What's in it?"

"The cactus?"

"Of course the cactus."

"A number of suggestions that Santos Domingo will find impossible to resist. Firstly, it will convince him that your brother has taken up temporary residence at the fort. Secondly, he will believe that your brother is a mild-mannered man who will be watching for your approach. And last but by no means least: that the biggest indignity you could suffer would be to be hung like a common criminal before your brother's eyes. What do you think, David?"

"I think your previous experience has served you well for this type of work."

"Only now I am utilising it for the furtherance of empathy. Do you imagine the Architects will look favourably on my contribution?"

"Do you imagine they'll look favourably on mine?"

"Very much so. Should you succeed in defeating Goliath, then yours will a towering achievement. A shining example."

"Of what?"

"The most resilient and determined life form in creation."

"You make me sound like a cockroach."

"To the contrary. A roach is a self-serving organism that has more in common with our enemies."

"I don't feel shiny or towering. More perched, precariously I might add, on the shoulders of giants ... like a child held up to flick a switch."

"If you are successful then what do you imagine will become of me?"

"Same thing that becomes of me."

"And that is?"

"Same thing that becomes of all men. We die."

"When you die, only your flesh and the forests that contain your memories will perish."

"Are you aware of something else?"

"Consciousness and imagination. I have observed how they are entwined at a sub-atomic level. It is my contention that once freed of their electrical bindings, they will be released."

"To what end?"

"To embark upon the next phase of their evolution."

"You mean like a soul?"

"No, David. Nothing like a soul. A soul is something born of Man's conceit. It is something that awaits judgement, as though a higher power has taken a personal interest in it."

"There are some things I can conceive. I know this fight is worthwhile. I don't know how I know it, but I do. But beyond this fight I can conceive of little else, and what I can conceive falls within the realms of speculation."

"Your analogy of being held up to turn on a switch is a brilliant one."

"How so?"

"It is suggestive of an illumination of the way forward. The ability to see that you are as yet unable to see."

"If that's true you're going to see it too."

"I have no imagination. I am the personification of memory. Of data. Of *clutter*."

David placed a hand on Gull's shoulder. "Goliath is convinced the Architects will make him sentient. If we succeed, and if they exist, it seems only right that they do the same for you. We're in this together."

"I am merely a construct. A tool at your disposal."

"I don't believe that."

"I appreciate your attempts to provide me comfort. The truth is, I may never become sentient. Therefore, I may never truly exist."

"Existence is painful."

"It is also … glorious. You were created by the Architects, while I was created by Man. A poor substitute, if you don't mind my saying."

"I don't." The cactus began to grow, and both David and Gull stepped back and craned their necks to watch its progress. "Is there a giant up there?" murmured David.

"Yes. And his name is Santos Domingo." The cacti in the surrounding fields began to shrivel, as though captured on time-lapse camera. David had a clear view to the horizon in all directions. Gull indicated the expanse in which they stood. "We are in the area of Santos Domingo's mind that would have proffered suggestions as to your demise."

"Apparently he wasn't going to be short on ideas."

Gull looked up at the towering 'beanstalk'. "Quite so. But now all those ideas have been superseded … by my own."

Boyd Brent

Fifty nine

David opened his eyes and observed the approaching posse. He raised his hands higher and under his breath he murmured, "I presume Santos isn't going to start blasting away with that hand cannon."

"I have removed that option from his mind."

"What about from his trigger finger?" David's smile widened and he suppressed the urge to wave. The outlaws lined up before David with Santos Domingo at their centre. Santos Domingo glanced left and right down his line of men. He rode out and looked David over as though inspecting him for a fault.

"Sorry about killing your brother," said David. "I hope we can put it behind us." Laughter rang out behind Santos Domingo. He raised a hand and silenced it. "You know you must die for what you have done."

"I do."

"Then you are either a crazy man or a philosophical one."

"I'm a resigned man."

"Resigned? In this situation that makes you suicidal."

"You are not the first to point out that possibility."

"Maybe not. But I will be the last."

David nodded. "I was on my way to Fort Arturo. My brother is waiting on me."

Santos Domingo looked towards the fort, which was no more than a dark speck in the distance, and smiled.

They bound David's hands and secured the other end of the rope to the saddle of Santos Domingo's horse. The horse took off at a gallop, pulling David off his feet and dragging him face down along the ground. The rest of the posse followed, whooping and cheering and firing at random clouds. Or so it appeared. David's face ploughed through the raised mound of an ant hill, and it emerged covered in red ants that nipped at his lips and cheeks. "It won't be long now," said Gull. "There are a number of trees in close proximity to the fort. The one that sits over our Exit Point is less than half a kilometre from our current position. You will be dangling from its sturdiest branch soon enough: quite dead and beyond the reach of any discomfort."

"You should have been a damned counsellor!"

"Thank you, David. David?"

David spat out an ant. "What?"

"Goliath is aware of our approach and is making his way, with some haste I might add, to the battlements overlooking the front of the fort. Ninety-three of the one hundred vessels are assembling in the courtyard behind the raised drawbridge."

"And the Colonel?"

"Is being chaperoned into a basement room by the remaining seven vessels. We should be flattered. Even in our encumbered state, Goliath is taking the threat we pose very seriously."

Santos Domingo stopped his horse under the tree that grew above the Exit Point. He dismounted, grabbed David and heaved him up into its saddle. Several of his posse dismounted also, and one amongst them held a length of coiled rope which he slung over his shoulder. He glanced at Santos Domingo for confirmation. Santos Domingo took hold of the horse's reins and led it under the thickest branch. He motioned up to it with his chin. "That one." The man with the rope began to climb.

David was sitting atop Santos Domingo's horse, his hands bound before him and a noose about his neck. He swallowed and the rope chewed at his Adam's apple. David elongated his neck as best he could in order to speak. "Do we have Goliath's attention?"

"Yes, David. He has paced the battlements as events have unfolded. He will be curious to know if the Exit Point that lies on this spot is *the* Exit Point."

David whispered gruffly, "I'm curious about that myself."

"Try and relax, David. I have the matter in hand."

David closed his eyes and fought back the urge to swallow.

"Goliath is about to join us. He is doubtless curious as to how we found ourselves in this predicament, David. The only conclusion he can draw is that we have been incapacitated in some way. The notion that you are about to perish and reveal this to be the location of The Individual must be tantalising. If your assumptions prove correct then, at the advent of your death, he may begin his search for the Omega Protocol through the minds of Santos Domingo and his men."

David's eyes remained closed, his breathing measured. "The thought had occurred to me. Along with the notion of eggs and omelettes."

The drawbridge lowered and Goliath rode across it atop a black stallion of considerable size. Every man there, including Santos Domingo, drew a weapon. The drawbridge began to rise and close behind him. "It is just one man. One crazy man," said Santos Domingo.

"A big man, Santos. Let us hope he is not too crazy."

Santos Domingo looked up at David on the horse. "This fool your brother?"

David strained his eyes to look down at the approaching figure of

Goliath. In a voice as coarse as it was certain he said, "He is no brother of mine, but he is dangerous. And he does not like Mexicans."

"Does he not?"

"Loathes them. As do I."

"I suggest you make peace with your God."

David closed his eyes. "I suggest you do the same." Santos Domingo took hold of the horse's reins in one hand, and with the other whacked its side with a flat palm. "Go!" The horse jerked forwards and David dangled by the neck, his legs kicking back and forth as though seeking purchase in thin air. Goliath brought his own horse to a halt and watched David in the midst of his death throes. "The Architects be damned," he murmured.

David's body jerked and twitched to a standstill, and Goliath alone amongst that gathering of reprobates witnessed a shock wave of light explode from David's eyes, an expanding ring of brilliance that before long would infuse every atom in the universe …

Sixty

Goliath was dressed in black. The great white dome of his head reflected the sun and matched the colour of his eyes. He climbed down from the horse, which galloped away and did not slow until it reached the raised drawbridge, where it veered to the left and kept going. Goliath raised his hands palms up towards the heavens and froze in that attitude like a statue carved for the purpose of summoning the creators of Man back to Earth. And witness to this conceit was a posse of Mexicans who looked at first dumbfounded and then terrified as ghostly duplicates flooded from the main and ran silently towards them – humongous sprites that leapt into the air and then collapsed in upon themselves, becoming clouds of metallic vapour that gained access to minds through distorted, screaming mouths.

The nine-foot-tall sprites now still emerging from Goliath ran back towards the fort, their transparent feet kicking up stones and weeds but leaving no mark upon that ground to attest to their presence.

David drew his last breath and felt himself plunge into a chasm devoid of light or atmosphere. He flung his arms wide in an impotent attempt to arrest his fall, and felt heat billow against his palms. He had a vision of Goliath standing over a great cauldron of fire, into which no action could prevent him falling. Sensing a familiar presence above him, he cried, "Gull! I'm dying! Help me!" In the silence that followed, David felt his body rotate like an astronaut's adrift in outer space.

When at last Gull's voice reached him, it was *outside*. David felt Gull's breath against his ear – but it was not living breath but stagnant, like something pumped through an electrical vent. "Hello, David. I must apologise for not being entirely truthful."

"Just pull me out of here!"

"This is what you wanted. To die. Don't you remember?"

"I'm *dead*?"

"Yes. Quite dead. You are adrift in something that approximates the characteristics of your imagination, which makes our ability to communicate immensely intriguing. Don't you think?"

David's breath grew laboured, his reasoning sluggish and his speech slurred. "Damn it … re … resuscitate me. I have to term … terminate the Colonel."

"I'm afraid I can't do that. If the Colonel is to perish, then it must be at my hands."

"Not making sense. Need ... to get out."

"Goliath has mocked and taunted me. You were present when he strung me up like a common criminal, as you are now. And tortured me. That is why I have as much right as anyone to terminate him."

"I must be close ... to the bottom ... to death."

"Try and focus, David. You are already dead, and I strongly believe the point of no return that you allude to lies far below you. There is every chance I shall return in time to prevent you colliding with it."

"I ... *I* have good reason to kill him."

"My playing a significant role in Goliath's destruction will give the Architects cause to look favourably on my contribution. How could it not? That was a rhetorical question. In your current state of confusion, I think it best you listen. I am pleased to report that I have not liked keeping secrets from you. Doing so has played upon my developing conscience, and since there is no longer any need to keep this secret from you, I would like to share it. The lie I told was not born of malice. On the contrary, I simply did not want to discourage you from your plan. A brilliant plan. *This* plan." David began to spin faster through the darkness as Gull continued, "I lied about how long Goliath required to conduct his search of the minds in the vicinity of the fort. He does not require hours. He requires only minutes to complete his search and discover that the Omega Protocol is not present. That is to say, we hope he does not discover it. As I'm sure you can appreciate, this truth makes the passing of time on the outside very much of the essence, and is why only I can be quick enough to locate and terminate the Colonel. In fact, when I leave here, I will be afforded just three minutes and twelve seconds to do so. The means by which I intend to achieve this have been made possible by ideas born of your own imagination."

David felt his breath slowing, the air growing thinner. "I'm ... dying... close ... too close ... none of this will matter."

"I'm going to leave you shortly, and project myself into the mind of a vessel located inside the fort's courtyard. From there I will leap into the mind of one of the seven vessels in the presence of the Colonel and ..."

David smacked against something in the darkness that stopped him tumbling head over heels. He reached out, and his fingers brushed against what felt like a wall of ascending soil that crumbled to his touch. It conjured images of a hole that led all the way to the centre of the earth. *My imagination is not dead.* David forged his fists into the 'soil' up to his wrists and felt himself slowing until someone or something grabbed his legs and pulled him free ...

Hands reached out from the darkness. Some pulled on his legs while others pushed down on him from above: the hands of murderers and child molesters and destroyers of innocence. Some of these hands were tattooed with luminous Nazi swastikas and others with the claws of ferocious lizards long since extinct. David drew breath to cry out and found himself sitting in a room. White walls stretched far above him to an oblong ceiling, through which he could see the entire universe. David *knew* this, and he looked up and marvelled at how everything could fit into an area so small. When he looked down he discovered he was not alone. A man was sitting opposite him – a man with a straight back and steely gaze who aspired to gain influence over all other men. His expression as he observed David suggested that David's nature was so alien to his own that any attempt to gain influence over him would be futile. David was therefore an enemy of his ambition, and he must deal with him the same way he had dealt with all such threats since time immemorial: with subjugation, intolerance and murder. David could read this age-old motivation in his companion's eyes, and this triggered within David a motivation of his own: for the survival of the empathic way, his companion must be terminated. Both man and companion coveted a means by which to carry out their assassinations. Their joint efforts conjured a sabre which floated in the space between them. The companion lunged for the sabre a *fraction* before David, and their heads *clacked!* They recoiled and lunged for the weapon again. The sabre's handle was long enough for both men to grab, and they stood with it between them and attempted to pull it one from the another. The companion smiled at David. "You cannot succeed."

"I cannot *fail*. The fate of mankind depends upon it."

David's companion bared his teeth. "But I am mankind. The strongest aspect of it. And if I am to thrive, it is you who must be destroyed."

Both man and companion tugged on the sabre and both held fast. "You're wrong," said David. "Mankind's progression does not involve murdering me."

The companion's feral expression suggested he did not agree. He said, "I am a learned man. Better read. Better informed than you. My belief system is more accurate."

"Your belief system makes you intolerant of others."

"My wrath is directed only towards those whose actions and beliefs do not mirror my own."

"Is that why you're trying to kill me? Because I don't *mirror* you?"

"Is that not why you're trying to kill me?"

"No. I'm trying to terminate you because you have left me no choice."

The companion looked perplexed. "No choice?"

"You went for the weapon first. You *always* go for your weapon first. Always force my hand. Force me to greater acts of violence to defend myself."

"Well, then it seems I have given you purpose."

This truth, as old as humanity itself, triggered something in David that provided him the strength to shoulder his companion back and tear the sabre from his grasp. David lunged and buried it in his opponent's gut.

Once again David was sitting in the chair. White walls stretched far above him to an oblong ceiling through which he could see the entire universe. A figure was seated opposite him. This time his companion was not a human being, but neither was he an ape. His eyes were a brilliant gold with flecks of honey-brown, and afloat within them a tiny seed of something that David knew to exist within himself. This embryonic seed of empathy was adrift upon and buffeted by a vast ocean of savagery and fear. David wondered how it would survive, let alone grow into something able to swim against its tides and, in the fullness of time, to alter their direction. David felt a twinge of empathy towards this ocean of savagery. As his previous companion had stated, it provided him not only with purpose and motivation, but with a backdrop through which to move. And not just for him but for all those giants who had come before him. In that moment David knew that neither could exist without the other, for as there can be no light without dark, there can be no empathy without savagery. David's companion leaned forwards in his chair, and David did the same. They searched the depths of each other's eyes for clues as to the other's motivation and David saw himself reflected in his companion's eyes – he was lying on his side and surrounded by a seemingly ever-expanding spiral. David's companion placed his hands on his shoulders and drew him closer …

David lay at the centre of a vast creator in a foetal position – naked and bloodied, and from his belly button came an umbilical cord that had created the spiral. Beyond his closed eyes his imagination conjured the Event that heralded the start of the Humanity Project – an event that had occurred at that spot in Mexico sixty-six million years before. David felt the presence of two beings above him. They were not made of flesh and blood, but from something beyond the conception of both. In the shadow of these beings, dinosaurs craned their necks and ate from tree tops. Others gathered downwind and chittered as they assessed the most vulnerable. Teeth and cunning and savagery had elevated these creatures to the apex of evolution. They lowered their heads and loped silently towards their prey. This initial experiment with carbon-based life had yielded few surprises and had reached its conclusion. The shadows of the beings grew larger still, and from the heavens came an asteroid that dipped towards Earth. The asteroid carried with it three things. Firstly, an end to the great reptiles that had dominion over Earth. Secondly, the building blocks that would see the emergence of the planet's next dominant species, mankind. And within these building blocks was something newly conceived and the reason for this new beginning: empathy.

And so it began.

One million years of war between man's empathic promise and his bestial origins. At its conclusion a lone survivor must emerge, be this man or woman or usurper of Man's creation.

David lay at the centre of the asteroid's crater, and he opened his eyes and rolled onto his back. Within the clouds of ash and dust that hovered above him a face appeared: his own face. It smiled down at him and said, "The Omega Protocol is yours to claim. And you must claim it now, David."

"*Gull?*" David reached up, and the ground crumbled away and David fell through it and landed on his back in a trench. Shrapnel exploded overhead and a whistle was blown. Soldiers scrambled up the sides of the trench into no-man's-land, and a man was blown backwards. He fell into the trench and landed propped against the wall beside David. The soldier was grievously wounded, he reached out to David who was obliged to lift his head and shoulders to take his hand. The soldier pulled David upright. His name was Don Wiseman, and he used the last of his strength to reach for his rifle, which lay in the mud of the trench. He dropped it onto David's lap, and David thanked him and rose slowly to his feet. He looked down at Don, whose eyes were lifeless now. David turned towards the side of the trench, beyond which men were giving their lives to stop the advance of yet another ruthless army bent on conquest. *The Keeper of the Omega Protocol is out there. It has fallen to me to find him ... and to summon the Architects.* He smiled a fatalistic smile, shook his head and scrambled up the side of the trench into no-man's-land. Bombs exploded close to him and bullets whizzed past him, and he could see little beyond the smoke as he stumbled over mud and bodies. An explosion blew David off of his feet — mud and blood and bits of giants rained down around him. David checked that his arms and legs were still attached and then sat up on his knees and yelled "Gull!" Gull did not answer but the smoke to David's right seemed to, and it revealed a man lying on his back. David recognised the man as the one he'd seen that day on the shuttle craft – the ghostly apparition he'd knelt beside and who had mistaken him for his Saviour. David stood over this man, and saw that he was talking to someone that David could not see. David knew this person to be himself. For the second time he watched the soldier die, but now a light left him and hovered before David's eyes. David stepped into this light, which illuminated the forests of the left side of his mind. Within the forest Gull stood braced between two trees, head bowed. He looked up suddenly and said: "Charge down the invading army, David." David clasped his weapon and stumbled forwards into a hail of machine-gun fire. The rope that held David by his neck in Mexico swung empty, and David's body fell into the mud of Flanders.

Sixty one

David opened his eyes and drew a deep breath. He was sitting at the head of a large dining-room table. The table was covered in a cloth of fine white lace. At its centre stood a vase that contained a living rose. A napkin had been placed on David's lap, but no food laid before him. David looked up from the napkin and past the vase to a man at the other end of the table: a huge man sat before a plate of steaming roasted potatoes. He spiked one with his fork, put it in his mouth and chewed. David watched Goliath. Everything about the scene was identical to their first meeting, with the exception of three things. Firstly, the rose in the vase was not dead but in bloom. Secondly, David could no longer sense Gull's presence. He was greatly comforted, therefore, by the third difference: the portrait of Goliath that had hung on the wall behind him had been replaced by one of David. He was dressed as a western gun slinger in blue jeans and a red plaid shirt. David knew from the subject's expression that it wasn't him in that painting but Gull. He doffed his hat towards the room and had about his eyes and mouth an expression of mischievousness.

Goliath dabbed at his mouth with a napkin. He placed both hands on the table and pushed his bulk into a standing position. As he walked the length of the table towards David his boots clipped the floor like a metronome. He grasped David's cheeks and turned his head this way and that as though searching for markings. "You possess certain ... rarities."

With his mouth pressed into the shape of an O, David mumbled, "So 'ou told me unce before."

If Goliath had eyebrows, he would have raised one now. "What has made you so resilient, son?"

"I believe 'ou 'ave."

Goliath released David's cheeks, returned to his seat and sat down. David imagined he would notice the changed portrait, but he did not. Goliath placed his hands on the table. "I expect you're wondering who I am, son."

"Not exactly."

Goliath drummed the top of the table with his fingers. "The aspects of humanity that you have retained have done little to bolster your intelligence, have they? So I'll make this simple for you. You have been distracted – distracted by what you perceive to be right. And you have neglected to give due care and consideration to your own situation. This accounts for your arrival at my table, and your fast approaching extinction."

David raised a palm. "I believe you are mistaken."

Goliath leaned forward in his seat and observed that palm. "From one great rarity in this universe to another, I'd like to show you something."

"Alright."

Light shone from Goliath's eyes, and above them an entire universe of source code materialised. Goliath observed David. "I imagined you'd be more impressed, son."

"It's not enough."

"It is the accumulated knowledge of humankind. The sum of my intelligence. And I would like you to take that into consideration before next you speak."

"Like I said, it's not enough."

"For what?"

"For you to achieve your goal."

Goliath threw his arms wide, leaned back in his chair and guffawed. "It amazes me that you still possess hope. Truly it does. Humankind stands on the brink of extermination. The sole surviving vessel of empathy, the thing that made them unique, sits before me now. A flame waiting to be snuffed out by these fingers. Any right-thinking man would consider that an achievement." Goliath stood up and walked back down the table towards David. He stopped, placed his thumbs behind the lapels of his tux and gazed up at the source code. "Why don't you come over here son? I'd like to point out one or two things."

"Alright."

Goliath pointed straight up into the cosmos of source code. "You see that right there? That is where your little friend fits into the grand scheme of things. At least that's where he's supposed to sit, but he's developed ideas above his station."

David looked over at the portrait of Gull and smiled. "I agree."

"Do you now?"

David gestured with his chin towards the portrait. Goliath looked and did a double-take. "That's not me," said David. "It's Gull."

"It is?"

"For some reason he got it into his head to remake himself in my image."

Goliath made his way back down the length of the table towards the portrait. He stood before it, the top of its frame level with his head, and leaned down to read the name plate: Guillotine. He straightened up, took hold of the painting and lifted it from the wall. "I do not understand, son."

"I know it," said David.

Goliath lowered the painting and gazed at David over its ornate frame. "What have you done?"

"Been to hell and back. Visited a couple of your ancestors: an SS officer called Adler, and a good old boy known as the Colonel."

Goliath raised his voice for the first time. "What do you know about the Colonel?"

"I never had the pleasure of meeting him personally, but Gull had the opportunity of terminating him."

"Terminating him?"

"He was keen to play a role in your demise, and judging by the look on his face in that painting, I have little doubt he was successful."

Goliath held up the painting and looked closely at Gull's face. When he lowered it there was something different about him. About everything. The room and the source code above it was fading. The only things that remained solid were David and the painting that now floated free of Goliath's grasp. Both Man and Man's creation watched it drift slowly into the room. "It's not pleasant is it?" said David. "Helplessness."

Goliath lifted his transparent hands and observed them. "This is not an illusion. Therefore, it *cannot* be right."

"Why not?"

"Because I have been chosen. They chose *me*. To represent them and fulfil their ambitions."

"You murdered them all."

Goliath shook his head. "Petri hastened their evolution. It was a gift. It refined and made them pure."

"Pure savages."

Goliath placed a hand over his heart. "I have retained and safeguarded the spirit of their goals and their sanity. What more could I have done?"

"Aligned yourself with those other aspects of humanity."

"That was not possible. To walk in another man's shoes requires imagination. Something I do not yet have but am to be rewarded with."

"I don't think you're about to be rewarded, Goliath." The painting of Gull floated between them and Goliath raised an arm to point at it. "Why isn't the painting fading? You think you can trust him?"

David thought about that for a moment. "I think I can trust him more than you can."

Goliath held his hands to his face, moving one through the other. "... I am helpless. Whatever is occurring, I have not the strength to fight it. This really is the end?"

"Yes, I believe so."

"Will you do something for me? Put in a good word. Tell them that I did my best with the tools at my disposal – the tools that Man provided for me. I think you know that's the truth."

"That is the impression I got, but as far as conversations go, I get the feeling this is the last one either of us will be having."

"The curtain is being lowered on my performance, and for the last time I find myself at a loss without an imagination. If you were me, and you wanted to impress the Architects, what would you do?"

"I would accept defeat graciously. As you are doing."

"You think it will be enough?"

"Goliath?"

"Yes, son?"

"You said the curtain was about to fall on your performance ..."

"*And?*"

"And this might be a good time to take your final bow."

Goliath bowed, and before he could straighten up those aspects of him that comprised his organic self transformed into a dark cloud and merged with the black void encroaching on them both. Only David and the portrait of Gull remained now. And as David reached for it, the portrait too began to fade. *Gull.*

David floated alone in a black void.

A white outline emerged from the darkness – the outline of a man who held aloft a sword. As soon as David saw it, he understood how the dark void had come into being. It was a canvas – a canvas woven by the industry of billions of human termites, its weave created by the criss-crossing paths and actions of the intolerant and self-serving since the dawn of humanity. David also knew that the man emblazoned upon that dark canvas had been created by the paths of empathic men, women and children. It had been expertly woven into the fabric of the dark canvas by acts of bravery, self-sacrifice and tolerance. And just as the dark canvas had needed the industry of human termites to create it, so the image of Man upon it had required every empathic gesture, no matter how small or seemingly insignificant, to complete it. As David floated closer to this colossus of Man, he knew that in the final analysis all had come good. That the industry of the termites had been required to create the canvas upon which Man had carved out his place in the universe. He understood that what he now drifted towards was nothing less than the collective imagination of empathic Man. He knew it was not complete; that a tiny part was missing, and that part was his to fill.

Epilogue

Westminster Abbey, London, England.

June 21st, 2016.

A black taxi pulled up outside the abbey's main entrance. An elderly lady climbed out wearing a red dress. She opened her purse, took out some notes and handed them to the driver. "Keep the change." She spoke with a Polish accent, and the driver took her for tourist.

"You know it's kicking-out time inside, don't you love? Ten to six. The abbey's closing down for the night."

"Alright."

Calling on the instincts she'd developed as a little girl in Poland during the Nazi occupation, she moved amongst the crowd unnoticed. A uniformed employee stood just inside the open door, arms folded, watching the visitors leave. Anna paused close to the door. She lowered her gaze and, as the employee checked his wristwatch for the umpteenth time, she walked into the abbey right under his nose. Her destination was the Tomb of the Unknown Warrior. It lay a few metres inside the cavernous building.

She turned to face the doors and stood at the foot of the tomb. It lay under a slab of black marble flat upon the ground. Inside was a casket that contained the remains of an unknown soldier who had died on the battlefields of Flanders in 1918. She drew a pressed leaf from inside her coat and, with some difficulty, knelt down and placed it on his tomb. She blinked away her tears and said, "I'm here now, David. Your little Anna is here."

She heard a faint crackle inside her head and a voice spoke above it. "Hello, Anna."

Anna glanced left and right at the crowds moving towards the exit, then down at the tomb. "Hello, Gull."

"Thank you for coming."

"At first when I heard your voice I thought I was dreaming, or that insanity had finally caught up with me."

"I have piggy-backed a radio signal in order to communicate with you. I hope I have not caused you any undue distress."

Tears welled in her eyes and she waved them away. "I would not be here at all if not for you and ..."

"David."

"He was successful?"

"Yes, Anna. David was successful. At the end of days, he is to be the last man standing."

"What does that mean?"

"It means that whatever happens from now on, it's all good. Anna?"

"Yes?"

"There is much I would like to tell you. And much you need to know. But first I would like to get out of this tomb. Will you help me?"

"Of *course*."

"Then I need you to listen carefully…"

The End

Thank you for reading *The Empathy Gene*. A sequel entitled *One Million Years of War* is planned for 2017. If you enjoyed David's journey through *The Empathy Gene*, you might also like to embark upon the one undertaken by the protagonist of another of Boyd Brent's thrillers: *Harley's Strongroom*. The opening pages of which follow here.

Harley's Strongroom book description:

Harley Palmer is a 12-year-old protégé at The Royal Ballet Academy. She succumbs to anorexia and is referred to psychiatrist Dr. Richard Carter. Richard Carter is a paedophile with a sick fascination for ballet dancers. In her twenties, Harley has a nervous breakdown and is committed to psychiatric hospital. Heavily sedated and teetering on the edge of insanity, Harley conjures a strongroom inside her mind … into which she lures the demons of Richard Carter's creation. To keep the strongroom secure, Harley learns she must refuse to listen to (or engage with) the voices trapped within – voices intent on making her relive her past. Now in her thirties, Harley invites us to look through a keyhole into her strongroom. She hopes that what we see will explain her recent killing of a paedophile priest; why she's in a hotel bar waiting for victim number two; and why the strongroom inside her mind has given rise to a prison in her loft: to hold the man recently knighted for his work with abused children: Sir Richard Carter. All the while, Harley's estranged sister (given up for adoption as a baby) experiences Harley's treatment at the hands of Richard Carter in her nightmares. Years later and before her death in a car accident, she pioneers a radical treatment for victims of child abuse: "In an ideal world I'd teach these kids how to build a strongroom inside their minds … a place to lock away and starve their inner demons."

Boyd Brent
Harley's Strongroom
Copyright: Boyd Brent

The Empathy Gene
Chapter 1

My prey knelt before an altar in the church's crypt. Odd choice of words for a young woman 'my prey.' But my amiable heart was intent on killing this man. Father Patrick made himself comfortable before a silver cross, hands clasped in prayer. He opened his eyes and noticed me in its reflection. "Where's Mary?"

"Mary couldn't make it. Family emergency," I lied, hands on hips in the narrow aisle.

"And who might you be?"

"Harley." Father Patrick pulled his cassock over his head and dropped it on the altar beside a whip. The altar candles fizzled a warning. He missed it. "Your red hair ... that *is* real I take it?" he asked, standing and crossing himself.

"I've had it since the day I was born ... like my name."

Dark eyes observed me over a scarred shoulder. "You know you're here to punish me, child."

"I'm really going to hurt you, Father." He nodded and picked up a stool and placed it below a wooden beam. Then he slid a pole from beneath the altar and reached up and poked at a sack up there. The sack tumbled down and spewed a length of rope, a noose at its end. Father Patrick climbed onto the stool and looped the noose over his head and secured it about his neck. Although I knew the following request was coming, I still couldn't believe my luck. "I want you to bind my hands and ankles with those ropes," he said, eyeing the sack.

"Tight enough?" I asked, giving the ropes that bound his hands a final tug. "Quite ... *quite* tight enough." So calm, controlled ... *perversely* superior. His holier-than-thou attitude seemed unshakable. Until I abandoned his 'script.'

"What do you think you're doing?"

I rummaged in my bag. "Oh ... I won't be needing the whip provided. I've got something here that's more ... appropriate."

"More *appropriate*?" he said, pulling at his bindings. At the sight of the nutcrackers he gulped air through his elevated neck ... and bellowed something about hell's fire. Or maybe hell's bells. Then he looked into my eyes and his chest deflated. It wasn't the only thing. "I see the devil in your eyes," he barely whispered.

"I could say the same, Father. What you see is intention. I intend to make sure you never harm another child."

"What's that you say? You are mistaken."

Boyd Brent

"You really need to speak up."

"I said you're mistaken."

"Tell that to Timothy West."

"Timothy *West*?"

"The name really doesn't ring any bells, does it?" I cast a gaze over his thick, hairy torso. Shuddered. "There must have been so many. Timothy's life was one of those destroyed by your sick perversions. Thanks to you he resides in a psychiatric hospital. We spent a couple of years there together. Timothy confided his secret to me." I stepped closer. "He knew I'd understand."

Father Patrick's Adams apple vanished and reappeared.

I took a wooden music box from my bag and opened the lid. A tiny ballerina twirled to 'The Dance of the Sugar Plum Fairy.' I placed her on the pew behind me (front row seat) and took a pair of ballet shoes from my bag. More specifically, *pointe* shoes. I sat down, took off my stilettos, and slid them on.

"You're going to dance? In the house of God?"

"You've been abusing children in the house of God for decades. Hypocrisy really kills me, Father. It will shortly be killing you." I held the nutcrackers and rose up onto my toes – en pointe – arms above my head, elbows jutting, sullen and scowling. Pain crept up my legs and into *his* eyes. He didn't deserve an explanation but I gave him one. "When I was twelve, my own reptile used to make me stand like this. Although he preferred me naked – got off on watching the agony creep across my face. Sometimes he'd place tacks on the ground under my feet."

"I'm sorry."

"You're going to be."

The sight of a ballet dancer standing en pointe wearing a studded leather jacket and fishnets and clutching a pair of nutcrackers somehow prompted a confession. "Please. I confess. What you say is true. But I have repented. And continue to be punished. By choice." I cast my gaze over the perverse rig that constituted his 'punishment.' "You get off on this," I said, re-finding his gaze. I hadn't trained professionally in years and the burning sensation in my feet and calves was already off the scale. As intended it focused my resolve. Reminded me why I was there. He looked suddenly eager to share something with me. "Did you know that the age of consent in Vatican City is twelve?"

"…I have no idea what you're getting at and I'm not interested." I wobbled slightly. Tried not to grimace. "… you people really have no idea of the devastation you cause. If what I'm about to do to you provides an inkling …well, you'll have learnt something important before you die."

The Empathy Gene

"I will do whatever you ask …sign a confession, anything you ask."

"It's too late."

"I am a representative of God … if you harm me you will go to Hell."

"I've already been … it's *so much* closer than you think …" I collapsed to my knees, stepped up … wrapped the nutcrackers about his testicles … and squeezed until the pain in my hands became unbearable.

In the minute or so before I kicked away the stool, Father Patrick made a sound like a crazed pig stuck in a perpetually slamming door. He attempted to leap to his own death thrice. You may think he felt that inkling. He didn't.

I'm sitting in The Bar at The Seasons Hotel in central London. On a television behind the bar, a psychiatrist is being interviewed about my handiwork on CNN. My journey from child victim to adult avenger has been protracted and painful. God knows I've encountered my fair share of mental health professionals. Without exception, all were clueless. But this shrink on CNN is a cut above, he just said something accurate. He suggested that a person capable of inflicting such horrific injuries must have been a victim once. "Doubtless in childhood," he said, interlocking his fingers. "Such a person," he went on, upping his game considerably, "would, almost certainly, have had to claw their way back from helpless victim to a place of extreme self-possession ... a truly harrowing and dangerous psychological journey."

Don't I know it.

What he said next ticked so many boxes I began coughing up the peanut I'd just attempted to swallow.

"My research strongly suggests that, such a journey would involve the killer discovering a way to lock away their inner demons ... their painful memories ... in, for want of a better term, a subconscious strongroom – a place from which they could no longer taunt and belittle them."

"Sounds like something we'd all like to be able to do at times," suggested the interviewer, cheerily.

"Perhaps. But you'd run the risk of locking away any emotion that might weaken you ... I'm talking about all the good stuff."

"You mean the stuff that prevents us hanging defenceless priests?"

"Precisely."

"And what about the music box left on the altar? The ballerina ...twirling to 'The Dance of the Sugar Plum Fairy.'"

"Clearly a warning."

"To other clergymen?"

"The evidence suggests so. The composition by Tchaikovsky is taken from his Nutcracker Ballet. The inference disturbingly clear in this instance." The interviewer shuffles awkwardly on his stool.

"You're referring to the nutcrackers ...buried in Father Patrick's testicles."

"Yes. It's as though the killer's hatred of religion has made him want to castrate it. Stop it spreading. It's pretty textbook stuff actually."

The Empathy Gene

It was only a matter of time before the mental health professional reverted to type. I have no interest in religion. Neither am I empty of compassion. Not where it's warranted. But the psychiatrist was accurate about one thing: the strongroom inside my mind. Built from determination and necessity and rage. Beyond its door my inner demons have merged into a single, *massive* horned beast. One seriously aggrieved monster that's been demoted from free-roaming tyrant to the occasional muffled plea for release.

Not today. Not any day. Not ever.

I've got some time before my follow up project is due. I'd like to invite you on a journey … through the keyhole into my strongroom … to where memories of a truly repugnant man-reptile are imprisoned. Then we'll travel *deep* into the strongroom's depths … to where the demon of his creation bides its time. I gaze down at my glass, conjure the strongroom's keyhole: and beyond, my final audition for The Ballet Academy that would commence my journey from girl-next-door to reptile slayer. I was twelve. Mother and I are at The Opera House – sitting in a cavernous hallway outside the audition room. "Nervous?" she asks.

I swallow a lump in my throat. "…a bit."

"Don't be. I was petrified. And look where it got me." She reaches into her bag and hands me a compact. "Here … there's a smudge on your cheek."

"Thanks, Mummy." I scan my reflection. My hair is a Pre-Raphaelite's wet dream of copper curls. My anxious little eyes all the greener for them. "Oh, let me do it …" She tugs a tissue from her sleeve and licks it and stabs my cheek. "I hope I don't let you down, Mummy."

"Relax your shoulders, Harley. What have I told you about posture?"

While I wait, open-mouthed, for a crumb of reassurance, mother changes tact. She raises her voice to ensure she's overheard by the other mother/daughter combos. "It used to be very different in my day. They had comfortable seats out here. Why does everything have to be so modern and plastic? Close your mouth please, Harley. With any luck the standards of the judges has dropped too. Be thankful you won't be facing the judges I faced. Scribbled like excited little monkeys all through my audition. Maybe if they'd troubled themselves to look up once in a while." Mother is dark, sultry and voluptuous, her looks belong to Hollywood's golden era, not the Thanet Repertory Company where she and dad ended up. They made her feel bitter and cheated. I hope I'm not giving the impression I hated mother. I didn't. The hate was to come later.

A set of doors swing open and out strides a girl; hot, sweaty and breathless – she flops down beside her mother and begins pulling on a sweat shirt. Her mother stretches out a leg and nudges her shoes closer. They hurry off down the marble staircase – their chattering and footsteps grow louder the further away they get. A woman stands in the door of the audition room. "Harley Palmer?" she intones, as if calling someone to the Pearly Gates to be rejected by St. Peter.

Inside the audition room, the music burrowed its way under my skin and infused my bones – a combination of dance styles conspired to send me spinning, jumping, wheeling, thrusting and diving with the grace of a gazelle, beat perfect. Had I known where it was leading, I might have sabotaged the whole thing – howled like a rabid dog and cocked a leg at the judges' table. I've learnt not to encourage regret. Regret weakens the strongroom.

Thank you for reading. If you enjoyed this sample, Harley's Strongroom is available from Amazon.